About the Authors

Kim Lawrence was encouraged by her husband to write when the unsocial hours of nursing didn't look attractive! He told her she could do anything she set her mind to, so Kim tried her hand at writing. Always a keen Mills & Boon reader, it felt natural for her to write and she can't imagine doing anything else. She is a wife and mother and cook and enjoys taking long walks with her Jack Russell. Ki

Ta can't remember a moment when she wasn't lost in a book, especially a romance which, as a teenager, was much more exciting than mathematics textbooks. Years later Tara's wild imagination and love for the written word revealed what she really wanted to do: write! She lives in Colorado with the most co-operative man on the planet and two daughters. Tara loves to hear from readers and can be reached at tara.pammi@gmail.com or her website tarapammi.com

When Canadian **Dani Collins** found romance novels in high school, she wondered how one trained for such an awesome job. She wrote for over two decades without publishing, but remained inspired by the romance message that if you hang in there you'll find a happy ending. In May of 2012, Mills & Boon bought her manuscript in a two-book deal. She's since published more than forty books with Mills & Boon and is definitely living happily ever after.

Greek Playboys

Greek Playboys: The Ultimate Game

KIM LAWRENCE

TARA PAMMI

DANI COLLINS

MILLS & BOON

First Published in Great Britain 2022
By Mills & Boon, an imprint of HarperCollins*Publishers,* Ltd
1 London Bridge Street, London, SE1 9GF

www.harpercollins.co.uk

HarperCollins*Publishers*
1st Floor, Watermarque Building,
Ringsend Road, Dublin 4, Ireland

GREEK PLAYBOYS: THE ULTIMATE GAME © 2022 Enterprises ULC

The Greek's Ultimate Conquest © 2018 Kim Lawrence
Blackmailed by the Greek's Vows © 2018 Tara Pammi
The Secret Beneath the Veil © 2016 Dani Collins

ISBN: 978-0-263-30461-9

MIX
Paper from
responsible sources
FSC™ C007454

THE GREEK'S ULTIMATE CONQUEST

KIM LAWRENCE

CHAPTER ONE

WHEN HAD HE actually last slept…?

The medication that the medic had administered to him in the field hospital had only taken the edge off his agony and since he'd got on the military air transport to Germany it hadn't even done that, despite the copious amounts of alcohol he'd downed in an attempt to self-medicate.

But now he was finally about to fall sleep, the moment was delayed as a half-burnt log in the open grate disintegrated, sending a star burst of sparks outwards and pulling him back from the brink. He watched through heavy half-closed eyes as the flames flared briefly before fading, leaving dark specks on the sheepskin stretched over the wood floor.

The woman lying across his arm stirred gently before burrowing into his shoulder. He flexed his fingers to relieve the numbness that was creeping into his hand, and with his free hand pushed back a hank of hair tinged silver by the moonlight shining through the open window. He glanced down, the soft light caressing her face revealing the smooth curve of her cheek.

She was, simply, beautiful. It wasn't just the bone structure and the incredible body, but she had something else about her…a *glow*, he decided, smiling at the uncharacteristically sentimental thought as he rubbed a strand of her hair between his fingertips. She was the sort of woman that at any other time in his life he would have gravitated towards. But even though he'd picked her out immediately when she had entered the bar earlier—with a noisy, youthful après-ski group oozing the confidence that came with privilege and intent on having fun and spending money—he had not reacted. Instead shutting out the sound of upper-class voices, he'd turned back to the drink he'd been nursing as he'd sunk once again into his black thoughts.

Then she'd come over to him. Up close she was even more spectacular, and she clearly had the self confidence that went with knowing it as she approached him. A real golden girl complete with golden glow, long gorgeous legs, her lithe body lovingly outlined in tight-fitting ski gear that was suited to her sinuous, athletic body. Her fine-boned face had perfect symmetry, the full lips and the deep blue of her wide-spaced eyes made him think of an angel, a sexy angel with a halo of lint-pale hair that glittered in the reflection of the beaten copper light shade suspended over his table.

'Hello.'

Her voice was low, accentless, and had a slight attractive husk.

A flicker of uncertainty appeared in her eyes when he didn't respond, then after a moment she repeated the greeting, first in French and then Italian.

'English is fine.'

She took the comment as encouragement and slid onto a stool beside him. 'I saw you from…' Without taking her eyes from his face—*they really were the most spectacular eyes*—she nodded towards the group she had arrived with, who seemed to be involved in a noisy shot-down-ing game. The sight of the bunch of spoiled socialites giving the bar staff a hard time twitched his lips into a contemptuous sneer.

'You're missing the fun,' he drawled.

She glanced back at her friends, giving what appeared to be a wince before training eyes that were a shocking shade of blue on him. 'It stopped being fun about two bars ago.' Her soft lips still smiled but a quizzical groove appeared between her brows and her head tilted a little to one side as she continued to stare at him. 'You look…*alone*.'

He gave her a look then, the one that made ninety-nine out of a hundred people back off. The hundredth was generally drunk, although it was obvious this woman wasn't; her blue stare was clear and candid, unnervingly so. Or maybe what unnerved him was the electric charge he could feel in the air between them, a low-level thrum but undeniably present.

'I'm Chloe—'

He cut her off before she could introduce herself fully.

'Sorry, *agape mou*, I'm not good company tonight.' He wanted her to go away, he wanted to be left alone to slide back into the darkness, but when she didn't, he wasn't really sorry.

'Are you Greek?'

'Among other things.'

'So what do I call you?'

Nothing worse than he'd called himself. 'Nik.'

'Just Nik?'

He nodded and after a moment she gave a little shrug of assent. 'Fair enough.'

When her friends had left she had stayed.

This was her room, an apartment in an upmarket chalet—not that they'd made it as far as the bedroom. A trail of their clothing traced their stumbling path from the door to the leather sofa where they lay.

He had always enjoyed the physical, sexual side of his nature but last night… Nik still couldn't quite believe how raw it had been, a true sanity-sapping explosion of need, and for a few moments he had felt free, free of grief, guilt and the oily taint left by the things he had witnessed.

He trailed a hand down her back, letting his fingers rest on the curve of her smooth bottom. As he breathed in her scent he desperately wanted to close his eyes, but for some reason every time he thought about it his glance was drawn across the room to where, he knew, even though the light was too dim to see properly, his phone lay after it had fallen from his pocket.

How did he know it was about to vibrate?

Then it did.

He glanced down to see if the sound had disturbed the sleeping woman and every muscle in his body clenched violently in icy horror and shock, trapping the cry of visceral terror in his throat. He was staring down, not at a warm, beautiful woman, but at the pale, still face of his best friend. The body he held was not warm and breathing but cold and still, the eyes not closed but open and staring up at him, blankly empty!

When he suddenly awoke, gasping, he was not in his bed but beside it on the floor on his knees, shaking like someone in a fever, sweat dripping from his body as he gulped for air. The effort of drawing oxygen into his lungs defined each individual sinew and muscle in his powerful back as he rammed his clenched fists against his rock-hard thighs. The scream that clawed at the edge of his mind remained locked in his raw throat as he struggled to reclaim reality from the lingering wisps of his dreams.

It finally came, and when it did he felt…well, he felt no better or worse than he had on any other of the countless times previously he'd woken out of exactly the same nightmare.

Slowly Nik got to his feet, the normal fluidity of his actions stiff, the athletically honed body so many envied, and even more lusted after, responding sluggishly to commands as he lurched across the room to the bathroom, where he turned on the cold tap of the washbasin full blast and put his head under the stream of cold water.

Fingers curled over the edge of the basin hid the fact he refused to acknowledge, that his hands were shaking, but as he straightened up he was unable to avoid a brief view of his own reflection in the mirror before he turned away, knowing that although the blinding visceral fear was temporarily back in its box, the shadow of it remained in his eyes.

The shower did not entirely banish the shadow either, but it did revive him. He checked the time; four hours' sleep was two hours too little but the idea of returning to bed, probably only to relive the nightmare yet again, held little appeal.

Five minutes later Security buzzed him out of the building, the concierge dipping his head and wishing him a good run when he exited, while privately probably thinking that the guy from the penthouse who regularly took a pre-dawn run was insane. Maybe, Nik reflected grimly as he pulled up the hood of his sweatshirt against the rain, he had a point.

The exercise did the usual trick of clearing his head so by the time, shaved, suited and booted, he skimmed through his emails the night horrors had been banished, or at least unacknowledged. He had other things to focus on, things that were nothing to do with the message on his phone. After noting the caller identity with a grimace, he slid it into his pocket.

He knew without looking at the content that it would be a reminder about the dinner party his sister was hosting that evening, the one he had agreed to attend in a moment of weakness. With Ana it was easier to say yes, because *no* was not a word she understood, neither was single or unattached, at least where her younger brother was concerned.

He slowed as he reached another set of traffic lights that had sprung up overnight, and smothered a sigh as he struggled to push aside the thoughts of his evening entertainment and the inevitable candidate for the position of wife, or at least serious girlfriend material, who would be seated beside him.

He loved his sister, admiring her talent and the fact she juggled a career as a designer with being a single parent. He was ready to admit she had many good traits but unfortunately conceding defeat was not one of them!

Part of his mind on the increasingly heavy traffic he was negotiating, he tried to put the evening ahead out of his mind, but maybe due to his disturbed night the prospect of being polite to one of the perfectly charming women his sister produced on a regular basis to audition for the role of potential mate weighed more heavily on his mind.

He knew that as far as Ana was concerned all his problems would be solved the moment he found a soul mate. He still couldn't decide if she really believed it and though there were occasions when he found her rosy optimism sweet, usually after a bottle of wine, mostly it was intensely irritating.

Hell, if he'd thought love was a cure-all he'd be out looking for it now, but as far as Nik was concerned the search would be in vain. It was a stretch but he was prepared to suspend disbelief and concede that it was possible that there was such a thing as true love, but if this was the case, the way some people were born colour-blind, he was love-blind.

It was a disability he was prepared to bear. At least he was never going to be in the position of having to experience the falling *out* of love process. It would be hard to find two people more civilised, more genuinely nice than his sister and her ex, but he had watched their break-up and eventual divorce and it had been toxic! The worst aspect of the split had been the child stuck in the middle. It didn't really matter how hard you tried to protect them from the worst, and they had tried, a kid had to be affected by it.

Give him plain and simple lust any day of the week, and as for growing old alone, surely it was better by far than growing old next to someone you couldn't stand the sight of!

He was prepared to concede that there were happy marriages around but they were the exception rather than the rule.

The car moved five yards before he came to another halt, and someone farther down the line of stationary cars sounded their horn in frustration. Nik raised his eyes heavenwards, the frown lines in his brow smoothing out as his glance landed on the neon-lit face on the advertising billboard across the road.

The advertising agency had clearly gone old school. There was nothing subtle about the message they were sending, just a straightforward fantasy for men to buy into. Use the brand of male face product clutched to the generous bosom of the woman in the bikini and you too would have similarly scantily clad and gorgeous women throwing themselves at you.

Not this one... His mobile mouth twitched into a sardonic smile; he was probably one of a handful of people who knew that this particular object of male fantasy was in a secret same-sex relationship. Secret, not because Lucy was concerned about any negative impact on her career, but because of a deal the couple had struck with her partner Clare's soon to be ex-husband. The guy wouldn't contest the divorce if the women waited to go public with their relationship until after he had landed the contract worth multi millions he was in the middle of negotiating with a firm who had built their brand on family values and a squeaky-clean image.

Maybe, Nik mused, if the guy had spent as much time on his marriage as he did on nurturing business deals he might still be married...? After all, if you believed everything you read, maintaining a good relationship took time, energy and hard work. Well, he definitely didn't have the time. As for energy, he was quite prepared to be energetic, but not if the sex seemed like hard work... No, marriage really was not for him.

He was jolted from his reverie by another blast on a horn, from behind him this time. It had a knock-on effect...not *quite* a eureka moment but pretty damn close and, like all good ideas, it was perfectly simple. Actually he couldn't quite figure out why it had not previously occurred to him to counter his sister's relentless matchmaking by turning up with a date of his own choosing and acting like a man in love.

He smiled up at the inspiration for the idea looking down at him...was Lucy Cavendish in town? And if she was, he wondered if the idea would appeal to her sense of humour; failing that he'd appeal to her conscience. After all, she did owe him one as he was the person who'd introduced her to Clare.

The caterers were carrying boxes through the open front door when Chloe arrived. Tatiana had asked her to be early but maybe this was *too* early?

'Go through to the office. Mum's in there.'

Chloe did a double take and realised that one of the caterers holding a box was Eugenie, Tatiana's teenage daughter.

The girl saw her expression and nodded. 'Yeah, I know…not a good look, but Mum insisted I work at least half the holiday to reduce the danger of me being a rich spoilt brat who thinks money grows on trees. You look great!' she added, her eyes widening as she took in the full effect of the sleeveless silk jumpsuit Chloe wore. 'Of course, you have to have legs that go on for ever to get away with it.'

Chloe laughed as the girl whisked away.

The door of the study was open and after a brief tap Chloe went inside. The room was empty except for the dog that was curled up on top of a designer silk jacket that had been flung over a chair. Even crushed and underneath a Labrador the distinctive style of the design made the label it bore unnecessary. *Tatiana* had become famous for her use of bold, brilliant colours and simple wearable designs.

The animal opened one eye and Chloe went over, drawn by a silent canine command. As she stroked his soft ears she looked curiously at the drawings set up on the massive draftsman table that took centre stage in the room.

'Oh, don't look at those. I was having a bad day,' Tatiana exclaimed, walking into the room. In one of her own designs, the petite brunette projected an air of effortless elegance. 'Down, Ulysses!' She gave a little sigh when the dog responded by wagging his tail and staying put. 'Nik says a dog needs to know who's master, but that's the trouble—you already do, don't you, you bad boy?' she crooned.

Chloe gave a smile that she hoped hid the fact that her first thought whenever she heard the name of Tatiana's younger brother was, *Oh, God, not brother Nik again!*

Nothing Tatiana said about her brother challenged Chloe's growing conviction that the man thought he was an expert on everything—and was not shy about sharing his expert opinion.

But then, being reticent and self-effacing were probably not the most obvious characteristics for someone who was the head of a Greek shipping line, and though Chloe knew that Nik Latsis had only stepped into his father's shoes relatively recently, it sounded to her as though they fitted him very well indeed!

Tatiana didn't seem to question or resent the fact that her younger brother had inherited the company simply because he was male, so why should Chloe?

Maybe because she wasn't Greek.

And there was no doubt the Latsis family considered themselves Greek even though they had been London based for thirty years. They were part of a large, well-heeled Greek community that had settled in the British capital. Rich or nouveau riche, they all had the rich part in common, that and being Greek, which seemed to be enough to make them a very tight-knit community where everyone knew everyone and traditions were important.

As she gave the dog one last pat she caught sight of her

reflection in the mirror that made the generously sized room appear even larger, and made a conscious effort to iron out the frown lines that the thought of Tatiana's invisible brother had etched in her forehead.

The invisible part was no accident. It was eighteen months since his father's stroke had brought forward the younger brother's ascension to the 'throne' of Latsis Shipping and he had kept a very low profile, something you couldn't do unless you had loyal family and friends, limitless resources and, she supposed, an inside working knowledge of how the media worked that being an ex-journalist would bring.

The point being, Chloe, she told herself sternly, *is that he is invisible. You've never met the guy, and yet here you are making all these judgements on the basis of a few comments and gut instinct.* Something that she'd have been the very first to condemn in anyone else.

'You're being a hypocrite, Chloe.'

The softly voiced self-condemnation caused Tatiana, whose eyes had drifted with a distracted expression to the fabrics pinned on one of the boards, to look up. She directed an enquiring look at Chloe, who shook her head.

'Those colours are beautiful,' Chloe said, nodding to the fabrics, and lifted a finger to touch one piece of silk that was a shade or two deeper than the blue wide-legged jumpsuit she was wearing.

'It would suit you, but I'm not sure…' Tatiana stopped and shook her head. 'Sorry, I just struggle to switch off sometimes.'

She smiled ruefully as she moved to kiss Chloe warmly on her cheek.

'The trials of being artistic,' Chloe teased.

'I don't know about that, but I do know that I am a bit of a workaholic…the work-life, home-life balance always did elude me.' A wistful expression crossed her face. 'Maybe that's why I got divorced…' She shook her dark sleek head slightly and smiled. 'But never mind about that tonight…just look at you!'

Hands resting lightly on Chloe's slim upper arms, she pushed the taller woman back a little. The sombreness of earlier drifted across her face when her glance stilled momentarily on Chloe's legs covered in loose folds of sky-blue silk, but it was gone by the time her eyes reached Chloe's face.

'You look stunning, as usual. I'm not saying it's all about a pretty face, but it definitely helps when you're trying to get men to open their wallets for a good cause… and before you ask you have my permission to put the hard sell on everyone here tonight.'

'People are usually very kind,' Chloe said.

'Especially when they are being guilted into it by the sister of a future queen. But why not use your connections? That's what I always say, and, while I might not have the right sort, your sister certainly does.' She sketched a curtsy and Chloe laughed. Her sister might be a princess and one day destined to be the Queen of Vela Main, but Chloe could not imagine anyone less *royal*. Both sisters had been brought up to believe that what a person did was more important than their title.

'I'll do my very best for the charity,' Tatiana continued in earnest now. 'In my book, I owe you.' She walked across to the mantel where the marble surface was covered with framed photos. She selected one and held it up in invitation for Chloe to see it. 'For what you did for Mel,' she finished, looking fondly at the photo she held.

Chloe shook her head, uncomfortable with the praise. As far as Chloe was concerned, the young Greek girl was her inspiration. 'I didn't do anything.' She took the frame that Tatiana offered and looked at the photo it held. It was a snap taken the previous month in a pavement café on a girls' trip to Barcelona. 'She's a brave girl.'

Chloe had known Tatiana by sight and reputation before the other woman had boosted Chloe's career by mentioning her blog in an interview she'd given covering London fashion week, two years ago now, Chloe realised, though it seemed more like a lifetime. Back then the interview was pretty much responsible for her blog becoming a profitable overnight success.

Chloe had contacted Tatiana to thank her for the plug and they had exchanged the odd email but they had never met in person.

That had happened in a very different context a year ago, after the designer's god-daughter was moved into the room next to Chloe's own in the specialist burns unit. Chloe had already been in there for three months; she'd known every crack in the ceiling and had been living vicariously through the love lives of the young nurses designated to her care.

Though the burns Chloe herself had received in a road traffic accident had been severe and painful and the healing process long, her own scars were easy to hide from view under her clothes. But the young woman in the next room had not been able to hide the damage done to her face by the fire caused by a gas explosion. Then, as if life hadn't already thrown enough rubbish at her, the day after she had arrived at the burns unit her boyfriend had dumped her, at which point Mel had turned her face to the wall and announced she didn't want to live.

As she'd listened through the partition wall Chloe's heart had ached for the other girl. Their first conversation later that night shouted through the wall had been a one-sided affair, but it had been the first of many.

'You got her through it, Chloe,' Tatiana choked. 'I'll never forget that day I arrived and heard her laugh—you did that.'

'Mel helped me as much as I did her. Did you see the information sheet she put together for me on make-up techniques?' she asked, placing the photo back on the shelf. In doing so she accidentally nudged the one next to it and straightened it, admiring the frame; it was an antique one, the ebony wood delicately carved and rather beautiful.

Chloe was admiring the craftsmanship, running her fingers across the smooth indentations, when her glance drifted across the photo it held. Her mouth tugged into a smile; with a white-knuckle ride in the background, a younger Eugenie smiled back at her, complete with braces, from under the peak of a baseball cap with the logo of an adventure park emblazoned on it.

The jeans-clad man crouched down beside her in the shot was wearing the same cap, and he was… Chloe's smile vanished like smoke as brutal stinging reality hit her like a slap across the face. Pale as paper now, she stared at the male in the picture, wearing jeans, a tee shirt, and a teasing, carefree expression on his handsome face, a face that bore no signs of a tortured soul. There were no shadows that she felt the need to banish; he was just a regular guy…well, only if the *regular* guy in question was more handsome than any man had a right to be with a body that an Olympic swimmer might dream of possessing.

She stood like a statue staring at the photo she held in a hand that quickly developed a visible tremor—the tremor penetrating past the skin level and moving deep inside her.

By sheer force of will she released the breath she was

holding in her lungs, but not the avalanche of questions whirring in dizzying succession through her brain. She felt as though a dozen people were inside her shouting so loudly she couldn't make out the individual questions.

Obviously it couldn't be him but, equally obviously, it was! The man in the photos was the same man who she had spent a never-to-be-forgotten night of lust with. If all learning experiences were as brutal as that one had been, it would not be worth getting out of bed in the morning—happily they weren't and she had moved on.

But that didn't mean she'd forgotten any of it. Forgotten the feelings of emotional hurt and humiliation that had made her physically sick the next morning when she'd realised he'd slipped away during the night. And the worst part was, she had no one to blame but herself. Because she had been the one who had followed her instincts when she'd approached him in that bar, telling herself that what she was doing was somehow meant to be… If they had been handing out awards for naivety and general stupidity that night, she would have walked away with an armful of prizes!

She'd wondered if his name really was Nik. It seemed utterly incredible to her now that she'd ever thought it part of the romantic fantasy element of their night together that she hadn't even known his full name! Time had stripped away the romantic gloss and revealed it for what it truly was—a cheap and tacky one-night stand, even if the sex had been utterly incredible.

Keeping her voice carefully casual, she half turned to Tatiana, as yet unable to tear her eyes from the snapshot. 'How old was Eugenie in this one?'

Tatiana came across and looked at the photo of her daughter and she gave a nostalgic sigh. 'Oh, that was taken on her tenth birthday, although just five minutes afterwards she was throwing up. Nik let her eat a bag of doughnuts then took her on some white-knuckle ride.'

Chloe's own knuckles were bone white where her hand was pressed to her chest. Her poor heart was vibrating against her ribcage, her insides were quivering as she told herself sternly to get a grip, not to mention a sense of proportion. It was only a photo after all, and he was old history.

Note to self, she castigated herself, *the next time you decide to make love, don't do it with a complete stranger! No, Chloe, let's be grown up and honest here—it wasn't making love, it was having sex.*

It hadn't been until she'd accepted that particular fact and realised that what they had shared that night had had absolutely nothing to do with a spiritual connection but everything to do with blind lust that she had been able to move on.

Move on—really? So why was she shaking?

She put the photo down carefully and smoothed her hands down over the fabric of her jumpsuit. She would not let that man do this to her again; she was not that silly naive girl any longer.

It had been a painful learning experience, but once her pride had stopped stinging and she had stopped feeling basically stupid she'd understood that while empty sex with anonymous strangers could obviously be physically satisfying, it probably wasn't for her. She wasn't exactly holding out for the love of her life, but she did think maybe a bit of mutual respect might be nice.

'So that's your brother Nik,' she said flatly. Sometimes it seemed as if fate had a very warped sense of humour.

Her eyes skimmed the mantel. The same man, she recognised now, was in several of the photos. It wasn't just the time difference that made him look younger, it was the absence of the cynicism and dangerous darkness she had sensed in him that night they'd had sex. What had happened to the man in these photos to turn him into the one she'd met only a few years later?

She dug her teeth into her plump lower lip as she squared her shoulders. Nik Latsis, *her* Nik—it was *so* weird to finally be able to put a full name to the man who had introduced her to sex and the fact it really was the only thing that some men were interested in. Well, his name was actually pretty irrelevant and she couldn't care less what had happened to turn him into such a cold bastard.

Not that she wasn't totally prepared to take her fair share of the blame. After all, 'naive closet romantic meets utter bastard'—it was never going to end well, was it? But she was not that person any more.

'I forgot, you haven't met Nik…have you?' Tatiana asked.

The truth or a lie?

Chloe settled for somewhere in the middle. 'He does look a little familiar…'

It's the clothes that threw me.

She brought her lashes down in a concealing sooty curtain and fanned her hot cheeks with a hand, causing the bangles she wore around her wrist to jingle. 'I think summer might finally have arrived,' she commented, ignoring the house's perfect air-conditioning system.

'You might have seen him on the television, perhaps?'

'Television?' A puzzled frown drew Chloe's brows together above her small straight nose. 'I don't think so…' Then it clicked; Tatiana wasn't talking about the present day but her brother's previous life. 'Oh, when you said he was a journalist I thought you meant he was in print…'

His sister nodded. 'He started out in print journalism

but Nik was a war correspondent, and he was on the telly quite a lot actually. He won awards.' Tatiana's pride in her brother's achievements was as obvious as her distress as she enlarged. 'He spent the last two years of his journalistic career embedded with the military, in the worst war zones you can imagine. Nik has always been the sort of person who doesn't do half measures.'

He had certainly been no half-measure lover or, for that matter, halfway callous!

'On his last assignment his cameraman, his best friend, was shot.'

Chloe blanched in shock. 'Did he…?'

Tatiana nodded. 'He died in Nik's arms, but the worst part—at least for the families—was that for three days we knew that there had been a fatality. There were about ten journalists, all from different media outlets pinned down, but we didn't know their identities or who had died.'

Chloe gave an empathetic murmur of sympathy and touched her friend's hand as the older woman closed her eyes and shuddered. 'We all loved Charlie, he had just got engaged…but at the same time we were all so incredibly relieved that it wasn't Nik. It made everyone feel so guilty.'

'Survivor's guilt,' Chloe said, thinking of her sister who, after the accident from which she had escaped unscathed while Chloe had not, had been helped by a therapist. Well, Nik Latsis could afford the best help money could buy.

'You've probably seen him, although professionally he used Mum's maiden name, because he didn't want to be accused of using the family name. Does Kyriakis ring a bell…? Nik Kyriakis?'

Chloe shook her head. 'I've never watched much TV.

There was a rule when we were growing up, half an hour's television a day, and then when I could decide for myself I suppose it had become a habit I never really broke. Even now I listen to the radio rather than switch on the box. It must have been hard for your brother going back to work after what had happened…?'

She had gone back to the spot where the accident had happened—had it been therapeutic? Only in the sense that she had proved to herself that she could do it?

That had been how she had privately charted her recovery: the things she was able to do, the things she could move past—looking at her scars, showing them to her family, getting into a car, driving a car…going back to the winding mountain road where the accident had happened.

'He didn't go back. A day after he returned, our dad had his stroke and couldn't run the company any more; the plan had always been for Nik to step up when the time came.' She stopped, an expression of consternation crossing her face. 'Nik doesn't ever talk about what happened to Charlie, so don't mention it tonight, will you?' she finished anxiously.

If he wanted to bottle things up in a stupid manly way, that was fine by her; she definitely wouldn't be getting him to unburden himself to her. In fact, the idea of seeing him, let alone passing the time of day with him, made the panic gathered like a tight icy ball in her stomach expand uncomfortably.

Ironically there had been a time when she would have paid good money to confront her runaway lover, but that time was long gone; she had no intention of having any sort of conversation with Nik Latsis.

He was history, a mistake, but not one she was going to beat herself up over any more, and one she really didn't want to come face to face with, but, if she absolutely had to, she was going to do it with pride and dignity.

Well, that was the plan anyway.

'I won't,' she promised as the voice in her head reminded her once again that her plans often had a habit of going wrong…

CHAPTER TWO

'YOU'RE LATE.' TATIANA kissed her brother's lean cheek, grimacing a little as the sprinkling of designer stubble grazed her smooth cheek before one eyebrow rose. She struggled to hide her surprise as she shifted her gaze from her impeccably turned-out brother to the woman who stood with one hand possessively on his dark-suited arm.

'You know Lucy Cavendish?' Placing a hand across her shoulders, he drew the model, her famous dazzling smile firmly in place, close into his side. The redhead tilted her head. Unusually for a woman, in her heels she topped his shoulder.

'I did Tatiana's last catwalk show in Paris. What a lovely home you have.' Lucy's expertly made-up green eyes moved admiringly around the entrance hall with its chandeliers and dramatic staircase.

Tatiana inclined her dark head and delivered an air kiss. 'Thank you. You're looking well, Lucy...' Tatiana looked up at her brother. 'You growing a beard, Nik?'

'With your views on facial hair, Ana, would I dare?'

'Oh, I just *lurve* the moody, broody look.' Lucy's eyes sparkled with teasing amusement as she stroked his cheek, letting her red fingernails slide familiarly over the stubble.

Nik removed the hand firmly from his cheek where it

had lingered and whispered so only she could hear him, 'Don't overdo it, angel.'

As they moved across the hall the sound of voices and laughter drifted out through the open double doors of the drawing room.

'Anyone I know here?' Lucy asked.

'Just a small gathering of friends.'

Letting Lucy go ahead of them, Nik fell into step beside his sister. 'Hope you didn't mind me bringing Lucy.'

'Why should I mind?'

'I thought you might have had me paired off with some good breeding stock…?'

'I don't—' Tatiana stopped and gave a shake of her head, admitting ruefully, 'I suppose I do, but I just want you to be happy and…like you used to be…before…'

Impelled by an inconvenient spasm of guilt, Nik stepped in to hug his sister as suddenly the charade with Lucy seemed less of a good idea. 'I am happy.'

'I like Lucy. Are you two together?'

Nik's glance slid away. She looked so hopeful that, although this had been the idea, he felt reluctant to raise her hopes, knowing full well they were false ones. 'Early days,' he prevaricated slickly.

'I just hope Lucy won't be bored silly,' Tatiana fretted, glancing towards the model who was walking through the double doors. 'It so happens that there is a woman here who might interest you—'

'Just when I thought I might have misjudged you,' he began sardonically.

'Not in that way!' Tatiana cut back. 'She's a good friend of mine.'

'And you wouldn't wish me on a friend?'

She slung him an irritated look. 'I just want you to set a good example when you meet her, and give a *really* generous donation to the charity—set a good example for the others.'

'Another of your worthy causes, Ana?'

'This is important to me, Nik.'

'Fine, I'll be generous.'

Chloe glanced at the clock…maybe he was a no show? Annoyed with herself for caring one way or the other, she turned her back on the doorway and focused her attention fully on the man beside her, a middle-aged Greek man who ran a property development company and seemed genuinely interested in the charity.

'I admire your enthusiasm but, and I don't want to be negative, aren't you being a little overambitious? Have you costed it up properly? The premises alone would—'

'Yes suitable premises, especially here in London, will be difficult.'

'Which is where I come in?'

Her smile glimmered. 'Your specialist knowledge and advice would be much appreciated.'

'And my money?' he added shrewdly.

Chloe's dimples appeared. 'I know that Tatiana has already spoken to you about…sorry, I really can't do this.'

The recipient of her half-empty glass of champagne looked startled and then amused as Chloe popped the finger food she had been holding into her mouth, swallowed, then smiled. 'That's better!' she said as she held out her hand for her glass.

Tipping his head, her companion replaced the crystal wine cup in it.

'Mostly I can multitask,' she told him cheerfully. 'I can do food or drink but not both at the same time. You wouldn't believe how many outfits I've emptied glasses of wine down, which makes it sound as though I always wander round with a glass of pinot in my hand, which I don't.' She delivered another smile. 'I can assure you that your donation will be in sober and sensible hands.'

The older man gave an appreciative chuckle at her tactics. 'Nice try, but I don't recall saying yes.'

Chloe conceded his point with a nod. 'But you didn't say no either and I'm an optimist.'

This time the man's chuckle was loud enough to divert some of the attention currently being given to the model who was making her entrance. 'So let me get this right, you'd like me to let you have the lease on several buildings for a fraction of what they are worth, and what do I get?'

'A warm glow knowing you've done the right thing? Or, failing that, the sort of publicity that money can't buy? The sort of publicity that comes from having your company represent the caring face of capitalism,' Chloe said, thinking wryly that she was getting quite good at this.

The man gave her an approving look tinged for the first time with respect. 'I think we should schedule a meeting, Lady—'

'Call me Chloe,' she cut in quickly.

He tipped his head in acknowledgment of her request. 'Right, Chloe, how about…?'

As the man's eyes moved over her head and his voice trailed away Chloe turned to see what had snatched his attention. The answer was immediately obvious in the shape of a glamorous redhead in a glittering gown more suited to a red carpet event than a dinner party.

Immediately tolerant of her companion's distraction, she turned to study the new arrival with some curiosity. In her experience people you had only previously seen beautifully lit on the screen or airbrushed in magazines rarely lived up to expectations, but Lucy Cavendish did and then some.

She looked beyond her hostess and the model to see if Lucy had come with someone. The woman's past boyfriends had included not one but two Hollywood A-listers, a Russian oligarch and the heir to a banking fortune, so Chloe was expecting a handsome face or serious money, someone who might be interested in donating to a good cause, perhaps?

She got neither…or rather actually what she got was both!

What she also got when she saw that Lucy's date was Nik was a jolt similar to the occasion her hairdryer had given her an electric shock, times a hundred. A home-made and dangerously uncontrolled defibrillation that felt as if a hammer had landed on her chest and made her limbs feel weak.

But this was fine; she could totally deal with it…

Not dealing with it, Chloe!

Ignoring the mocking voice in her head, she took a deep breath, straightened her slender square shoulders, cleared her throat and readjusted the chunky necklace of raw amethyst slices that hid the pulse pounding at the base of her throat.

Breathe…she told herself, so she did, and for good measure she focused on the positive.

The worst was over and, as *worsts* went, seeing the man you'd made the mistake of sleeping with without knowing his full name was, on the scale of things, pretty low-key. A couple of minutes and her nervous system would catch up with the message and by tomorrow she'd be laughing—all right, maybe *smiling* about it.

But that was tomorrow; being realistic today, as in the

next sixty seconds, she was aiming for a less ambitious goal. Her legs stopping shaking would be a good start.

She stifled a stab of impatience; her nervous system was getting this situation way out of proportion. After all, what was the worst that could happen?

And what was the worst anyway: him remembering her or him not?

Her mobile lips quirked into a smile as she considered the alternatives. An awkward reunion or a hit to her ego?

Did it really matter?

The fact that she could even ask herself the question was a sign of how much she'd changed in a little over a year. There had been a time when, despite the outward confidence she projected, what people thought about her had mattered, and she wanted the right people to like her...she wanted to fit in.

The journey to where she was today had not been easy, but everything had changed. Well, maybe not *everything*, she conceded, watching the new arrival above the rim of the glass she raised to her lips. Still, even at a distance, he had the ability to make the muscles deep in her pelvis quiver...so it was lucky she could consider this phenomenon in an objective way, wasn't it?

She might not be able to achieve total physical indifference to the male magnetism he oozed, but she was more than a bundle of hormones...despite the fact that he was, she thought, studying him through the protective sweep of her lashes, just as incredible-looking as she remembered.

They said you always remembered your first and it turned out they were right. The self-mocking glint in her wide-spaced sky-blue eyes faded and a tiny pucker appeared between her darkly defined feathery brows as she realised how intact her memory of him was, not just the way he looked, or moved, but the texture of his skin… the smell of his… She took a shaky breath and straightened her shoulders, slamming the door on that particular memory. *It was just a lapse of judgement, ancient history, Chloe,* she told herself. *Do not revisit.*

'What a stunning woman!'

Chloe started slightly at her companion's comment and tore her eyes from the tall figure whose dominant presence had made her forget about the woman he'd brought with him, although they made a pretty magnificent couple. 'Yes, she is.' Stunning was probably an understatement.

'But I'd say she's high maintenance, and I can't see her climbing Kilimanjaro.

The comment startled a laugh from Chloe. 'It sounds to me like you measure all women by some pretty high standards.'

He smiled and nodded. 'My wife is an extraordinary woman.'

Chloe stood and listened as the man launched into what was clearly his favourite subject. An emotional lump settled in her throat as he talked about his wife. What would it feel like to be the centre of a man's universe? she wondered wistfully.

Nik walked past his sister and moved to where Lucy stood.

'Maybe this isn't such a good idea,' he muttered.

'I was the one who told you that,' the model reminded him. 'But you've been my beard on more than one occasion, darling, so I kind of owe you. Do you realise how much money is in this room tonight?'

His eyes moved over the heads of the fellow guests assembled; most were members of the Greek expat community, and all of them would have considered not having a private yacht as being poverty-stricken. 'That figures. Ana is raising money for one of her causes again.'

'So you're not in danger of meeting Ms Right here. Does that mean you're dumping me already, darling?'

'Funny… God, I need a drink.'

He placed a guiding hand under Lucy's elbow, and she immediately exclaimed mockingly, 'Ooh, darling, I do so love it when you're masterful. Ah!'

She staggered a little as Nik suddenly released her arm without warning.

It was an automatic response to a soft peal of laughter that made Nik turn his head. Although it hadn't been loud, there was something attractively infectious about the sound that tugged his lips into a smile.

As his eyes surfed across the heads of the other guests to the source of the sound, his smile snuffed out as recognition crashed through his nervous system like a tsunami, and for several seconds his mind went a total blank, the effect of sheer shock colliding with serendipity.

He took a deep breath and decided he'd call it something more mundane—*convenient*. Or he would once he got his rampant, raging libido under control. It took another few deep breaths to think beyond the heat that had streaked down his body and settled painfully in his groin.

His cognitive powers were clearly working on the reserve battery. He had no idea how long he stood there paralyzed, it could have been a second or an hour, before, like a man waking from a trance, he finally shook his head.

The air trapped in his lungs hissed out as in a single urgent sweep his dark, penetrating stare took in every single detail of her. The soft shiny blonde hair falling from a slight widow's peak down her back and cut shorter at the sides to frame a vivid beautiful face, the sinuous curves of her lush body outlined by the flowing lines of blue silk.

She was stunning.

He'd sometimes wondered, generally around two a.m., if he exorcised the woman, would he finally exorcise the nightmare? The two seemed so intrinsically linked, maybe they were interdependent? It had been an intellectual exercise he'd never really taken seriously as he hadn't expected their paths to cross again.

Well, it was no longer intellectual, and neither was the roar in his blood, and he knew that not to explore the theory now that he had the opportunity would be insane!

Chloe knew Nik was standing there even before Spiros's glance moved past her, alerted by the fine invisible downy hairs on her body rising in reaction to his invisible presence.

She emptied her glass carefully, wiped her expression of anything that could be interpreted as a desire to dig a big hole and jump in it and mentally circled the wagons against attack.

If she refused to be defined by the scars she wore, she was definitely not going to be defined by a past mistake, even if he was six foot three and sinfully gorgeous!

Her defensive stance wasn't against anything he might say or do, as there was a very strong possibility that he wouldn't even remember the night they had spent together, but against her own indiscriminate hormones, which still, it seemed, responded independently of her intellect to his rampant animal magnetism.

Oh, for God's sake, Chloe, you need to get a life!

While she was silently chastising herself Nik had moved level with her. 'Spiros.'

His voice had the same rough velvet, almost tactile quality she remembered...but this time she was only shivering because she was standing in a draft, she told herself stubbornly.

They were actually standing level, side by side as he stretched out a hand to the older man, but Chloe didn't turn her head. She didn't need to, because she could already feel the sheer physical power of his tall, muscled frame.

'No Petra tonight?'

'No, she's resting up. She sprained an ankle during training.'

Nik made a sympathetic noise in his throat. 'For *another* marathon?'

The older man gave a rueful nod. 'I think it's addictive.'

'You not going to join her?'

'I know my limitations.' Chloe, who felt as though her *casual* social expression could do with some work but needed all her focus to control her too rapid breathing, took encouragement from the fact that Spiros didn't seem to notice anything amiss as he touched her arm and looked at Nik. She was still working her way up to it. 'Do you know Chloe?'

She held her breath.

'Of course; we go way back,' Nik said smoothly.

'Royal connections—you kept that quiet, Nik.'

No longer able to delay the moment, Chloe turned her head, her features arranged in a smile that was intended to project polite indifference, although she had a horrible feeling that a touch of the hunted animal had crept in!

Her first hope had been that he wouldn't remember her; the second was that up close he would have some flaw she had forgotten, but again her fairy godmother had not granted her wish.

So Plan B it was, then: be polite, be distant, be… Oh, God, on an intellectual level the dark, predatory, raw animal magnetism stuff did nothing for her, only it seemed the message hadn't filtered through to the non-intellectual parts of her that were only listening to the hormonal clamour—but then it was pretty loud.

His male beauty, and beauty was no exaggeration, hit her at a purely visceral level. She had never experienced anything like it before—well, just the once.

His high knife-sharp cheekbones, strong aquiline nose, and angular jaw even dusted with stubble gave his face a patrician cast, though this was offset by the overtly sensual outline of his mobile mouth, twisted at that moment into a faintly cynical smile. The same emotion was reflected in his eyes, his quite simply spectacular eyes; deep set and heavy lidded, and fringed with dense, straight, spiky lashes, they were a stunning dark chocolate brown.

Pinned by those dark eyes, she experienced a 'rabbit in the headlight' moment and froze.

'How are you… *Chloe*?' He seemed to roll the word over his tongue as though he were tasting it.

As *he'd tasted her*… Chloe pushed the thought away but not before her body's core temperature had raised a few uncomfortable degrees. She lifted a hand to her neck to feel the dull vibration of her heavy pulse, and she fingered the uncut gemstones that felt cold compared to her skin.

From somewhere she manufactured a smile but the effort made her cheek muscles ache while she silently struggled to keep the door locked against forbidden memories. It wasn't about wanting to forget him, she thought, but more not wanting to remember and be reminded of the things she strongly suspected she might never experience again.

And maybe that was a good thing, she rationalised. Yes, head-banging, uninhibited sex was good—it was pretty excellent—but so was waking up with someone who actually cared for you, or for that matter was physically still there in the morning.

Refusing to acknowledge the sense of loss that still lay like a heavy weight in her chest, she reminded herself that she was looking, or she would be when the time came, for more in a man than his knowledge of the female anatomy... Hell, clumsy with feeling was infinitely preferable to the refined torture of a skilled touch with no emotion behind it.

'How long has it been?' he asked coolly.

'I'm not sure,' she lied, thinking, *Eighteen months, eight days and thirty-one minutes...not that I'm counting.*

She stiffened when without warning he bent his head and brushed her mouth lightly with his. His lips were warm, reminding her of when they had been even warmer, when he had tasted of her... The muscles low on her pelvis cramped as she stood as still as a statue, fighting with all her might the shameful urge to lean in and kiss him back.

The gasp she locked in her throat ached as she breathed in the warm male scent of him through flared nostrils.

It wasn't until he lifted his head that she realised she was holding his sleeve, though she had no memory of grabbing it. Disturbing, but there was no point reading too much into it, she decided as she let it casually fall away, ignoring the tingling sensation in her fingertips.

Nik smiled. The quiver he'd felt run through her body as he'd kissed her reminded him of just how receptive she'd been that night…how *giving* she'd been. And he'd taken… He countered the irrational slug of guilt with a reminder that she was the one who had taken the initiative that night, she'd made all the running and she hadn't acted like a woman who would take no for an answer.

His smile, the glimmer of dark danger glittering deep in his eyes, elicited an involuntary spasm of excitement in her belly that made Chloe feel ashamed.

'You look well.' She looked incredible, though up close there was less of the outdoorsy golden glow he remembered. Her skin was creamy, the faint touch of colour in her cheeks highlighting the smooth contours, the freckles along her cheekbones paler too, but she was, if anything, even more delicious than he remembered.

'Thank you, and how are you—sorry, Nik, wasn't it?'

The composed words aimed somewhere close to his left ear were prim, but the message shining in her deep cobalt-blue eyes as they glittered up at him was neither prim nor polite.

They said quite clearly, *Go to hell!*

Her reaction threw him off his stride, in the same way he realised he'd have been thrown if he'd reread a favourite book and found a main character had suddenly been given a different personality.

Except the woman in his dreams had never had a personality beyond being warm, giving, passionate and available when he had needed her, and he had not been curious about what lay beyond those qualities.

Realising that there *was* a beyond came with a sense of shock as Nik struggled to consider her negative reaction to him dispassionately, but got sidetracked by his own reaction to her.

The problem being there was very little room left for dispassion after the explosive blast of primal desire that obliterated everything else when he looked at her. It was like walking…no, *running* full pelt into a ten-foot wall of lust.

The time it took his stupefied brain to push past this fresh blast of raw hunger was only moments but it felt longer, and the mere fact that he *had* to make the effort deepened the frown lines in Nik's broad forehead.

In his previous life, he had cultivated dispassion until it required no effort, and it was second nature. He'd seen men and women in his old line of work who hadn't managed to do that, and the personal toll it had taken on them had not been good to see. You needed to be able to keep an emotional distance.

He had witnessed acts of bravery and self-sacrifice that were humbling, but for every one of those inspiring acts there were a hundred acts and images of suffering and inhumanity. You carried those nightmare images around with you and they ate you from the inside.

The sheer absurdity of comparing a war zone to a dinner party where people were toting glasses of wine instead of automatic weapons almost dredged up a smile. *Almost.*

CHAPTER THREE

'I'm—'

'With Lucy Cavendish…' Chloe paused, head tilted in challenge, to let the reminder sink in and had the satisfaction of seeing an expression of shock chase across his handsome face.

'Lucy…hell, I forgot about her!' A quick glance located the model, who was deep in conversation with another guest. Nik dragged a hand across his hair-roughened jaw in annoyance; he must have left her standing there looking like… He gritted out a curse. 'I'm never going to hear the end of this.'

The wrathful, choking gasp of sheer disbelief that escaped Chloe's lips drew his attention back to her face.

If there had been even the *faintest* suggestion of guilt in his reaction, she thought it would have gone some way to redeeming him…actually, no, it wouldn't!

Wanting to make excuses for him made her even angrier—as if there could be any excuse for a man who arrived with one woman and then came on to another with all the subtlety of a sledgehammer!

It made her wonder whose bed he had walked straight into after being in hers.

There had been a time when the thought would have hurt…now it simply made her stomach quiver queasily.

'It's so inconsiderate of a woman to expect you to re-member that you came with her.' She produced a saccha-rine-sweet sympathetic smile, waiting until he frowned slightly in response to her comment before slinging out sarcastically, 'I suppose she even expects you to be there when she wakes up in the morning.'

The words hung there, every syllable oozing with ex-actly the sort of subtext Chloe had wanted to avoid. She sounded just like what she hated most: a victim.

Someone to pity.

Her narrow-eyed glare dared him to show it, but, al-though her comment had surprised a flicker of reaction, it was something else she saw move at the backs of his eyes. Fine, she could deal with something else, actually *anything* else, but *pity*.

'You were asleep.' This was the reason he avoided one-night stands; there was the potential for the stranger you went to bed with assuming that one night of sex con-nected you in some deep and meaningful way.

'I'm not talking about me.' She lifted her feathery brows in an attitude of mild surprise that he should think otherwise, then, willing herself not to blush, she pro-nounced bluntly, 'We had sex but we were not in a re-lationship. Although it would have been useful if you had woken me as I had somewhere I needed to be.' She wrinkled her brow, giving the impression she was try-ing to recall the sequence of events—events that couldn't have been more indelibly imprinted on her had someone branded them into her soul. 'I'm pretty sure I was late.' In her head she clutched the invisible award to her chest as a voice pronounced, *And the award for most convinc-ing liar goes to... Chloe Summerville!*

The dream had once more become a nightmare be-fore he'd ever reached the moment where he'd made the choice to leave her sleeping, not that waking her had ever really been an option. Good manners versus getting to his dying father's bedside after receiving the call about his stroke had been a no brainer.

And yes, he'd been relieved not to have to speak to her again.

Relieved to avoid the potential morning-after awkwardness and recriminations. It hadn't been his first one-night stand, but those other encounters had all been with fellow journalists, and there had been some mutual respect on a professional level between him and the smart, independent women who had shared his bunk. There had been no need to explain the desire he had felt to escape the sights and sounds of war for a few hours and let passion drown it all out. The connections had been brief, pleasurable, but nothing deeper remained.

He wouldn't have cared if any of them had forgotten his name, or implied that the memory they'd walked away with after sleeping with him was that they'd had somewhere else to be but had overslept! His ego took a few startled seconds to recover from the blow while recognising the irrationality of his reaction. Chloe Summerville's cool attitude was *exactly* what he looked for in women he gravitated towards. Women who had a male approach to sex; women who did not expect or even welcome sentiment in their liaisons, but enjoyed sex in an uncluttered and simple way.

'Sorry, I had someplace I needed to be too…but unlike you I wasn't too late.'

His father's prognosis had been grim. The doctors had been all for calling time and letting nature take its inevitable and cruel course, but his mother had insisted they try a third lot of clot-busting drugs. When Nik had walked into the room, his father had been sitting up with nothing but a slight hesitation in his speech to show he'd even had a stroke and people had been talking about miracles.

'Well, it's…nice to see you again, lovely to catch up…' Chloe said absently, adopting the tone you used when you bumped into someone whose name you kept forgetting. 'But if you'll excuse me, tonight is about work and I need to circulate.' Giving her best impression of a woman with her priorities firmly sorted, she flashed him a generic smile and turned back towards where Spiros stood talking to a small group of guests.

Even if he'd taken everything else out of the equation the dismissal would have awoken his interest, if only for the fact that it was new territory for Nik. Women did not usually walk away from him. His curiosity overcame his irritation… So, all right, it was something a lot stronger than irritation, but he didn't need to waste energy trying to identify it as it morphed seamlessly into the much easier to deal with lust and his eyes became riveted on her long, sinuous curves and the gentle sway of her hips.

If sleeping with her again was the way to finally lay his nightmares to rest, great. If not, the trying was going to be fun. Not trying at all had stopped being a possibility the second he'd set eyes on her.

The frustration raging through his veins made it hard for him to formulate a plan of action, as there had been no plan required in his dreams. On a conservative estimate he'd been making love to Chloe every other night for the past year…except this wasn't a dream, it—*she*— was the real deal! And Chloe Summerville was *more* in every way than the woman he remembered. A halfwit could have worked that out in thirty seconds.

And Nik was accounted to be quite intelligent.

She had been pulled into a group several feet away

from where he stood alone, and he watched like a hawk as she lowered her lashes over a smile in response to something Spiros had said. In profile he could see the little quiver of the fine muscles in her throat and along the delicate line of her jaw, and he wondered why he found it so fascinating.

Was he finally losing his mind?

Chloe's legs were still shaking but, as there was no longer any imminent possibility they would give out beneath her, she let go of the image of herself lying on the floor and people staring down at her. Sad, they'd say, she used to be able to stand on her own two feet... She suddenly realised a moment too late to avoid awkwardness that the extended silence was one she was meant to fill. Chloe gave an apologetic smile.

'Sorry. I wasn't following; I was just trying to remember if I put an aspirin in my bag.' She delved into the limited depths of her bag, her hair falling in a concealing curtain around her face.

Still she couldn't quite escape the conversation replaying in her head... When he had asked her how long it had been since they'd met, she'd had a nasty shock. Up to that point she hadn't known that she knew the answer even to the day and hour, but she clearly did... God, but it was terminally depressing.

What, she asked herself, had she ever seen in him?

Beyond of course the face, the body, the high-voltage charge of raw, scalp-tingling sensuality he had oozed... Beyond that, nothing at all!

Other than the dark brooding aura tinged with danger and a touch of vulnerability.

Well, he wasn't vulnerable now and she was no longer the romantic little fool she had been, but, considering her reaction to Nik just now, it was lucky that she had decided celibacy was the way to go… Not for ever—just short term. Who knew what the future held?

But one of the advantages of celibacy was that she could stand here now and look at this incredibly…really incredibly sexy man, and remember, in a way that sort of felt as if it had happened to someone else, how it had felt to have his warm, no, *hot* flesh slide over hers and it wasn't a problem.

God, you are such a liar, Chloe Summerville.

In fact, if she had truly believed she was cut out for celibacy long term, it would have simplified life in general, she concluded, studiedly ignoring the scornful voice in her head.

'You have a headache?' a woman whose name Chloe couldn't recall, despite being normally good about that sort of thing, asked.

'It's not that bad.'

Then Nik touched her arm. She knew it was him without even looking at his long fingers brown against her skin, and suddenly it was *extremely* bad. The thump, thump in her temples was keeping time with her heartbeat as Chloe felt a primitive thrill run along her nerve endings. Deeply ashamed, she waited for the fluttering inside her to subside and, under cover of looking in her bag again, calmed her breathing.

'Lost something?' he asked.

'Just an aspirin; I'm getting a headache.' *And I'm looking at it.* But she wasn't. She looked everywhere but at the tall dynamic figure towering over her, which was not something that happened often when you were five feet ten.

Eyes she had control over, but not her thoughts that drifted back to the moment she had first seen him, as if she were stuck in some sort of mind-destroying time loop. The last thing she had anticipated when they had crowded into the almost empty bar was that she would leave with a total stranger. She'd never been a person who was led by her hormones and, while she'd had any number of male friends, she'd not had a lover.

She had dated, obviously, but things had usually ended in an *it's me not you* sort of way. And she had started to think it was—that she was simply one of those women who weren't highly sexed.

Until that night.

Whatever had been lying dormant within her had surfaced with a vengeance!

'Oh, Chloe, have you met Olivia?' Spiros asked, oblivious to any atmosphere, drawing a striking middle-aged woman into the group.

Chloe shook her head, welcoming the opportunity to turn her back on the biggest mistake of her life to this point.

'Olivia, this is the young woman I was telling you about. Olivia was very interested when I told her about your project; her husband, who isn't here tonight, is a plastic surgeon.'

Chloe beamed. 'That's why you look familiar!' she exclaimed. 'I've seen the photo of you that your husband has on his desk at work.'

Listening to her, Nik twisted his lips in a cynical smile. The plastic surgeon must be very good at his job because you really couldn't tell Chloe had had any work done at all. Whatever it had been, he decided, watching her expressive face as she chatted with animation to the older woman, it hadn't been Botox.

Though now he thought about it there were changes, though not those he associated with surgical intervention. Some of the youthful softness he remembered in her face had gone, had become more *refined*, revealing a breathtaking bone structure. As he continued to study her the therapeutic benefits having sex with her might bring to him slid to the back of his mind, leaving having sex with her as soon as possible just because he wanted to very much in the forefront.

'So sorry,' he interjected.

This time with the touch of his cool hand on her wrist Chloe couldn't stop herself turning towards him; the intention was defensive, the result was not!

He was standing very close to her and she stiffened, her chest lifting as she took a deep breath and held it while, inside her ribcage, her heart rate climbed like that of an athlete waiting for the starter's pistol.

Fighting the impulse to cover her mouth with her hand as his eyes drifted to her lips and stayed there, she waited until he had stepped back far enough for her to escape the heat from his body to release the air trapped in her lungs, but unfortunately his aura of sexuality had a wider radius.

'You don't mind if I steal Chloe, do you?' he asked, taking her elbow. To an observer his attitude as much as his body language was suggestive of a long and intimate relationship with her.

The suggestion might have drawn a smile from her if her facial muscles were not locked in what she sincerely hoped was an expression of indifference. What they had shared had been little more than a collision! Granted, an extremely *intimate* collision... As a series of freeze-frame images flashed through her head they had an almost out-of-body quality to them.

She had fallen asleep in his arms, and as she'd drifted off she'd found herself thinking that she had never felt more comfortable with anyone in her life.

Comfortable was something she didn't feel right now as he half dragged her across the room; if she could, she would happily have crawled out of her skin. But pulling away would have made her look even more conspicuous.

He came to a halt in one of the deep window embrasures where the half-drawn curtains gave it an element of privacy that Chloe could have done without.

She immediately pulled away, retreating as far as physically possible. He countered her action by raising one sardonic brow.

Chloe embraced the anger that prickled through her with something approaching relief, while simultaneously ignoring the worrying excitement that popped like champagne bubbles in her bloodstream, making her feel light-headed, which probably made the little head toss with attitude she gave a mistake, but she did it anyway.

'What the hell do you think you are you doing?' she muttered under her breath.

The silky fair hair that streamed down her slender back settled into attractive waves around her face. As he watched the process he suddenly remembered it had taken a long time to gather it all up in his hand and each time his fingers had brushed her skin she had shivered.

Good question, Nik. What the hell was he doing?

He said the first thing that came into his head. 'So you're a royal of where?'

'Do you mind? I was having an important conversation back there!'

He shrugged his magnificent shoulders. 'So have a conversation with me.' *So I can look at you.* 'And if by important you mean you were about to get a donation for whatever charity it is… I'll double it,' he said casually.

She expelled a hissing sigh. 'Am I meant to be impressed by your altruism, seeing as you don't even know what the money is for?'

'Does it matter?'

She gritted her teeth and fought the impulse to slap him—anything that would break through his armour of sheer selfishness.

'Clearly not to you!' she countered contemptuously.

'You still haven't told me…'

'Told you what?'

'Royal how?'

She gave a growling sound of aggravation through her clenched teeth. 'My family,' she said finally in a bored, reading-the-telephone-directory voice, 'lives on East Vela; it's an island.' Most people didn't have a clue where it was, though most had watched the recent royal wedding on the television.

Nik proved a little more informed.

'The Vela that has just been reunified.'

She nodded.

'So where do you fit in?'

Chloe used her stock reply. 'I'm the sister who hasn't married the future King.'

'Lucky you.'

It was not the usual stock response and Chloe bristled defensively at the slightest suggestion of criticism of her brother-in-law. 'Lucky me? Most people envy my sister!'

'Do you?' The speed with which she had jumped to the man's defence made him wonder if there wasn't a personal element to her reaction, and the possibility tugged his lips into a cynical sneer.

The sheer unexpectedness of his response made Chloe blink and shake her head. 'What sort of question is that?'

He ignored the spiky question and reverted to his original comment. 'I meant lucky because a queen with any kind of history has to be a nightmare for the PR people-lovers with kiss-and-tell stories coming out of the wood-work,' he explained, pointing out the obvious.

She was tempted, but only for a moment, to retort that her *only* lover was more concerned about keeping a low profile than she was, so that was problem solved. But what would he say if he knew that? The question circling in her head jolted her back to her usual common-sense mode.

Unable to adopt a sufficiently *shallow socialite* tone while she was looking at the outline of his disturbingly sensual mouth, Chloe switched her focus to his hard, stubble-covered jaw. 'Yeah, it really was a lucky escape for me,' she began, and then stopped, her eyes darkening as the memories of feeling cheap and used, still fresh and raw, surfaced once again. Why was she pretending to be someone she wasn't? She didn't care what he thought of her and her chin lifted a notch in defiance. 'Oh, why don't you just call me an easy lay and have done with it?'

His half-closed eyes lifted from the heaving contours of her breasts and collided with her blue shimmering glare. She pulled in a deep breath and, lower lip caught between her white teeth, took a moment to control the quiver in her voice before she drove home her point.

'Just because you treated me with zero respect, Nik, do not assume that I don't respect myself!'

She was lecturing him! Nik was too astonished to immediately react to her accusation and too ashamed to admit anywhere but in the privacy of his own thoughts that he probably deserved it.

'And for the record this is the twenty-first century; no-body expects a prince to marry a virgin bride these days!'

'Again, that's lucky or the European royalty would be a doomed species...' As he spoke the gaps between his words extended as he almost lost track of what he was saying. Her currently outraged attitude meshed with the images and little snatches of memory from that night in his head, flickering faster and faster until he could hear his own thoughts from back then—*so deliciously tight*, so *excitingly shocked*… As if everything *was* new to her, shockingly new! Had she been a virgin?

'We are a doomed species anyway, I suspect,' she was saying. 'They call it evolution, but I suppose royals are a bit like dinosaurs. In the future there will be entire floors of museums displaying our fossilised remains in glass cases.'

'Evolution is preferable to revolution… How didn't I treat you with respect?' he suddenly shot at her, trying to catch her by surprise so she would answer him truthfully.

She said nothing.

'So you *did* have a problem with me walking out on you?'

Her eyelids half lowered. 'It was a first for me, I admit.'

A first? A first of what, exactly? The idea that she could have been a virgin, considering the way she'd approached him that night, was totally crazy, and even if it were true, did he actually want to know? Didn't he have enough guilt in his life without adding any more? The problem was that now the idea was out there, swimming around in his brain, he had to voice it, even if he did end up looking like a fool.

'The first time you'd woken up with the pillow beside you empty, or the first time for you full stop?'

She felt a trickle of sweat trace a sticky path down her back and decided to deliberately misunderstand him. 'First one-night stand? You really haven't read any of the surveys in the magazines, have you? Everyone's doing it.'

'The thing about those surveys is that people lie.'

His intent stare made her feel as though he were look-ing directly into her head and she could feel the blush she was willing away materialise until she felt as though every inch of her skin were on fire.

'And I'm not talking about one-night stands,' he added flatly.

Pushed into a corner, she reacted with cool-eyed hau-teur. 'I really don't think there's any need for a post-mor-tem…but if you're asking what I think you're asking, I don't think I owe you any explanation.'

'So you *were* a virgin.'

'Weren't we all once…even you?' Hard as it was to imagine. 'How old were…?' Her eyes flew wide. 'Oh, God, I said that out loud, didn't I?'

'I was sixteen and she was…older.' The glamorous, bored stepmother of one of his friends at boarding school, and he'd been very willing to be seduced. 'But even at sixteen I would not have thought it the greatest idea in the world to pick up a total stranger in a bar and have sex with them.'

'It wasn't exactly planned!'

'Look, I'm fine with youthful rebellion. I've been there and done that, but I sure as hell don't much like being the unwitting partner of it.'

Chloe felt her embarrassment slip away, incredulous anger rushing in to fill the vacuum; his hypocrisy was staggering. 'So now you're the victim and *I* should apolo-gise? Not that there is a victim, I mean… I just saw you that night and…' She met his eyes and looked away. 'Oh, for heaven's sake, it's not as though you were fighting me off with a stick, is it?'

A laugh was wrenched from Nik's throat before he closed his eyes and wondered how a man could feel like a defiler of innocence and incredibly turned on at the same time.

'I guess I crushed a few of your romantic illusions,' he said heavily.

She sucked in a deep breath. 'Well, it had to happen sometime so relax; after the therapy I'm totally fine.' She stopped suddenly, remembering that she was talking to someone who might really have needed therapy for something more than making a poor choice. She'd slept with the wrong man; he'd seen his friend die in his arms. 'Not that there is anything funny about therapy…in fact, it's a very useful tool,' she told him earnestly.

A nerve began to slowly clench and unclench in Nik's jaw, and it had a mesmeric effect on Chloe.

'What has my sister been saying to you about me?'

Chloe began to shake her head, thinking his sister's opinion of him proved that love really *was* blind… *Lust*, however, was a completely different proposition… She tilted her chin and refused to acknowledge the shameful ache of arousal she felt just looking at him, but in her own defence this man took the term eye candy to a whole new level! 'Absolutely nothing…except of course that you are an expert on just about everything. To be totally honest with you, I'd got sick and tired of hearing the sound of your name.'

All the time she had been ripping up at him he'd stood there looking at her in that disturbing way. When she finally stopped talking he placed a finger against her lips just to make sure he was not interrupted. 'You are really, truly *perfect*! Hell, I so want to take you to bed right now.'

The raw driven declaration, barely more than a husky whisper, made her catch her breath, the air between them shimmering with suppressed sexual tension. She could only stand there, her eyes wide as he moved his finger down her cheek, the light touch, barely there, making her shiver with delicious sensation.

Her eyes had half closed in drugged pleasure when from somewhere a sliver of sanity shattered the sensual haze.

What the hell are you doing, Chloe?

'Does that line really work for you?' She was pretty sure it did, and she'd have been yet another of the women who'd fallen for it if it hadn't been for that one word... *perfect*! He still saw her as the woman with the perfect body he remembered from eighteen months ago.

The ugly reality would surely have him running for the hills.

'It isn't a line.' His heavy-lidded eyes moved in a slow approving sweep from the top of her glossy head to her feet in kitten-heeled slingbacks. 'You look fantastic.'

'Yes, I know.' But *looks*, she reminded herself, were cruelly deceptive. Even if she had been tempted to accept the offer he was making, she knew that it wasn't about her; it was only the perfect body that he wanted.

The body that no longer existed.

Loss was something she didn't normally allow herself to feel but it slammed through her now.

'I'd forgotten how direct you were. It's really refreshing,' he said.

The memory of how direct she'd been brought a flush to her face. If she ever regained the sort of confidence she'd once had, then it wouldn't be with a man like Nik Latsis. It would be with a man who could see beyond her scars, and who would want her for the woman she really was.

'Ah, well, I'm so glad to have refreshed you, and speaking of which, if you'll excuse me, I'm going to refresh my glass. I'm not interested—is that direct enough for you?'

'I'd be devastated if I believed you,' he returned with a level look.

'Believe me, you are the *last* man in the world I would be interested in!' Interested, no, she was *fascinated*...but equally she recognised it was an unhealthy 'moth to the flame' sort of fascination. One that would only lead to her being burnt up, and not in a good way.

'Never mind, Nik. If I was interested you'd be the first man to know...or maybe the second,' Lucy Cavendish corrected. 'My dentist has the loveliest eyes.' Her smile deepened as she looked at Chloe. 'So have you.'

Chloe's face burned with embarrassed heat.

Just how long had the model been standing there listening to them? And yet she didn't seem even a jot put out by what she'd heard... Maybe because she had heard it all before? Chloe speculated. Maybe she was fine with sharing her man? Or even...? *None of my business,* she told herself, swiftly closing down this lurid avenue of speculation.

'Dinner is served and I'm starving,' Lucy drawled, then, turning to Chloe, she added, 'I loved your blog, by the way. If you want to know any of the dirty details on this one, I'm the girl to come to.' She gave her a conspiratorial wink before leading Nik away.

CHAPTER FOUR

DAZED AND BEWILDERED, Chloe experienced a quite irrational sense of abandonment as she watched the couple walk away arm in arm. She hung back as the guests made their way through the double doors, which had been flung open revealing a long table covered in white linen and groaning with antique crystal and fine china. The last to enter the room, Chloe saw that Eugenie was directing guests to their places. As she watched Nik bent down and kissed his niece's cheek.

'I'm working, Uncle Nik,' she remonstrated, kissing him back despite her protest.

Chloe watched him throw a quizzical glance at his sister. 'Child labour, Ana?'

'Laying the foundations for a healthy work ethic, you mean,' Tatiana shot back.

'You were right the first time.' Eugenie raised her voice as her uncle moved away. 'No, you're down that way, Uncle Nik,' the girl called, pointing in the opposite direction from where her uncle was heading.

'No, kiddo, I think I'm sitting here.' Nik picked up one of the place cards and held it up to show her his name.

His niece frowned, pulling a slim tablet from her pocket. 'But I thought…'

Her mother leaned in and closed the tablet. 'It's fine,

love,' she said drily, picking up a card from the floor and, glancing at the name on it, placing it at a gap on another table.

Her brother reacted to the pointed look she sent him with an unrealistic innocent expression.

Watching the interplay, Chloe had a sinking feeling, and so she was unsurprised when the teenager smiled at her and directed her towards where Nik was holding out a chair next to his place.

Chloe's eyes brushed his and her stomach vanished completely!

The prospect of spending the entire meal next to him made her feel nauseous. *Oh, get over yourself, Chloe,* she told herself sternly. *What's the worst that can happen—you get indigestion?*

'Now, isn't this nice?' The innocence was gone and instead there was a feral gleam of challenge in his steady stare as he stood behind the chair waiting for her to take her seat. 'So cosy,' he murmured, pushing in the chair neatly behind her legs before taking his own seat.

Cosy? Huh. Chloe decided, nodding to the woman seated to her right, that was the last word she would use where Nik Latsis was concerned, so she didn't voice any of the half-dozen sarcastic responses that trembled on her tongue. The best way to cope with this situation was simply not to rise to the bait; instead, she would rise above it.

'Thank you,' she murmured, rather pleased with her aloof little nod, a nice combination of condescension and coldness. Yes, she decided, the high ground was *definitely* the route to take in this situation. Right but not very easy when even without looking at him she could feel the male arrogance he was radiating.

He set his elbows on the table and looked at her. 'You're dying to ask me, so go ahead.'

She squared her shoulders, and took a long swallow of the very good wine, looking at the plate that had been put in front of her; it smelt fantastic but she had virtually no appetite. 'Sorry, I don't know what you mean.'

'I'll put you out of your misery, then. You're right, Lucy and I are not a couple, just, as they say, good friends.'

'Well, that's a relief. I wouldn't have been able to sleep tonight if you hadn't explained that to me.'

Far from annoying him, her sarcastic riposte drew a broad grin. 'Ana often invites potential mates to her cosy little dinners.'

'This dinner isn't little or cosy or, as it happens, all about you.'

A smile quivered across his lips. 'Ouch!'

'You could always try dating agencies, which would be a bit more scientific than relying on your sister to set you up,' she suggested.

'I've always thought a sense of humour is overrated, especially when I'm the joke. Ana wants to see me settled down; she thinks that marriage is the magic bullet that will solve all my problems. She means well but it can get…tiresome. But you don't want to know all that; the point is… Lucy isn't my girlfriend.'

'Why are you telling me this?'

'Because I want you to say yes when I ask you to come home with me tonight.'

Having delivered this conversational dynamite in the same manner a normal person would discuss the weather, he calmly turned to the man on his right and inserted himself into the conversation concerning the most recent banking scandal.

Chloe couldn't hear what they saying, because she couldn't hear anything much beyond the static buzz inside her own head. Of course, she was going to say no to him.

She rested her hand on her thigh, running her fingers lightly across the raised damaged skin under the fine blue silk. The outline of the ugly ridges beneath her fingertips had an instant mind-clearing effect, and the doubts fluttering around in her head vanished. A man who hadn't bothered hanging around to say goodbye the morning after they'd had mind-blowing sex wasn't interested in her emotional journey; he only wanted perfect.

'I used to be a fan of your blog…is there any chance of you resurrecting it?'

Chloe snapped clear of her reverie before it reached self-pitying territory and smiled at the woman sitting across from her who'd just asked her a question. 'Well, never say never, but at the moment I can't see it happening.'

The woman looked disappointed. 'You were very successful and you had so many followers, but I suppose you've got your hands full at the moment.'

Nik had disengaged from the conversation he was involved in and took an indulgent time out to study Chloe, watching as the fine muscles along her firm jawline quivered beneath the smooth creamy skin. Her long fingers tightened around the stem of her wine glass, and he noted the absence of rings.

'So what is this blog I keep hearing about?' Nik asked curiously.

He had just announced his intention of inviting her to spend the night in his bed and now he was making small-talk! Did he compartmentalise his life as neatly as he did his conversations? she wondered, envying him the ability.

'It was a fashion blog. I started out just writing about things that caught my attention, fashion tips, current style trends, that sort of thing, and it took off after your sister—' she glanced towards Tatiana '—gave me a plug.'

'Was?'

She nodded and directed her gaze to the wine swirling around in her glass. The crystal caught the light of the chandelier that hung over the table, sending little sparks of colour through the flute. 'I've moved on to other things.'

Dreams were not reality, they were an exaggerated, distorted form of it, and Nik had assumed his memory had been guilty of making some editorial cuts, smoothing out the flaws and adding a rosy tinge to the reality of the woman who had shared her body with him. *Sharing* hardly seemed an adequate description for the lack of barriers that had existed between them—but actually sitting beside her now, he realised that the reality was even better than his memory. And she'd been a virgin— her cagey reaction had virtually confirmed his stab in the dark—but it still didn't seem possible.

'I suppose a lot of people would get bored quickly if they didn't have to worry about paying the rent, *Lady* Chloe.'

His efforts to needle her into a response were rewarded when she slung him an angry glare and drained her glass in one gulp.

It was not the first time that someone had added the title and her background together and come up with the totally inaccurate conclusion that she was a lady of leisure who didn't have to work for a living.

They weren't to know that, although her family had the aristocratic family tree and the castle that came with it, they didn't have any money, which accounted for the holes in the roof, the ancient plumbing and the fact she and her sister had always been expected to work for their living. Of course, it didn't make them poor by most people's standards but the man sitting there judging her was not *most* people.

Even at this table, where conservative estimates of all the guests' wealth were eye watering, he was probably worth more than them all combined.

Her indignation fizzed hot under the surface as she fixed him with a smile of dazzling insincerity and batted her lashes like the social butterfly he seemed to think she was.

'Oh, and how I envy the *little* people with their *simple* lives... I've even heard that some people don't bathe in ass's milk or have anyone to put toothpaste on their brushes for them.'

'Did I say something to annoy you?' His glance slid from her blazing eyes to her tightened lips and his body stirred involuntarily as he remembered kissing them, tasting her... The need to do so again as soon as possible made his body do more than stir.

She shuddered out a breath and their gazes connected. Chloe was aware that she was breathing too fast as she fought to escape the message that seemed to vibrate with a palpable force in the air between them.

'You breathing annoys me!' *Too much honesty, Chloe,* she thought, aware she had lost her moral high ground the moment the childish admission left her lips, but at least she was no longer thinking about kissing him, which was good. Taking a deep breath, she glanced around to see if anyone had heard her comment. Greatly relieved when it seemed they hadn't, she directed a straight look at him. 'Look, Tatiana is a friend and I don't want to be rude to her brother.' *Or go to bed with him.*

'Or alienate a potential donor?'

Chloe realised guiltily that the sobering reminder was

necessary. She *was* in danger of forgetting that tonight was about getting the charity off the ground. Tatiana had done her bit, inviting people with deep pockets who were sympathetic to Chloe's aims, but the rest was up to her.

It was a crowded market; there were so many good causes around Chloe knew that she needed to make a positive impression on these people if she was going to make a difference.

'True, and all donations are gratefully received.'

'You already have Ana on board, so how long have you two known one another?'

'She took an interest in my fashion blog, but we'd never met. We actually met in person only a year ago, a few months after the—' She stopped abruptly, her lashes lowering in a protective sweep.

'After what?' Against his better judgement, her sudden impersonation of a clam made him curious, and, even though he knew on one level that this should be an exercise in exorcising his demons, he found he really wanted to know what made her tick.

'After I got bored with it,' she countered, deliberately not analysing her reluctance to discuss the accident with him. She applied herself to her starter, trying to simulate an interest in her food, which she couldn't even taste.

Nik, who continued to ignore his own food, propped an elbow on the table and studied her. 'So what do you do now, besides selling raffle tickets?'

'I'm working to raise the profile of the charity.'

For *working*, Nik translated, she had probably arranged a charity fashion show or a masked ball, which was fine, but hardly enough to stimulate someone of her obvious intelligence. His dark brows flattened as he recognised but struggled to explain a sense of disappointment.

It wasn't as though he had any expectations of her, and God knew she wouldn't be the only titled socialite who didn't hold down a real job. Maybe it was just that he was surrounded by strong, driven women. His mother was a partner in a law firm, who had raised brows when she had continued to work after she was married, and his sister juggled a successful career with motherhood. Ana might be in the fashion industry, but he knew that his sister would have been appalled if her daughter had thought being decorative was more important than getting an education, which made this friendship with Chloe all the more puzzling. He really couldn't see what the two women had in common.

'I don't have my wallet with me, but I do have my chequebook and I am a dutiful brother,' Nik said.

Before Chloe could react to the patronising undertone that brought a sparkle of annoyance to her eyes, across the table an elderly silver-haired Greek businessman began to laugh.

'I wouldn't be so quick to give her a blank cheque, my boy. If that young lady gets you in a headlock, she's relentless.'

Nik elevated a dark brow. 'I thought that was just a rumour.'

'She's cost me more than my wife.'

'Which one, Joseph?'

The question caused a ripple of laughter around the table.

'It's all in a good cause,' Tatiana said, patting his hand. The soft murmur of agreement that followed her words left Nik feeling excluded, as he seemed to be the only one who didn't have a clue what the old man was talking about.

'And what *cause* would that be?'

The rest of the table had returned to their own conversations and Nik's curiosity was the only thing left to distract himself from the ache in his groin. Messing with the seating arrangements had seemed like a good idea at the time, but he really hadn't factored in the painful strength of the hard throb of need, which was becoming increasingly impossible to think past.

Insane... When had a woman made him feel like this? He looked at her mouth, remembering how it had tasted, and wondered. Last night about three a.m. she had vanished from his dreams like mist, as she always did. What if he woke up with her in his arms for real? Would she and the nightmares be gone for ever?

Chloe shifted in her seat before looking up from her contemplation of her empty glass. Strands of blonde hair fell across her cheek and she brushed them away, puzzling at her own reluctance to discuss the subject so passionate to her heart. It struck her as ironic considering she'd spent the evening selling the cause, and in all honesty she felt she was pretty good at it.

'Helping burns victims. Originally the idea was to raise money for specialised equipment for the NHS that under normal circumstances they can't afford.'

It was the last thing he had expected to hear. 'And now?'

'Oh, we'll still do all those things, but, in conjunction with that goal, we are also aiming to set up centres where there is access to physical therapy like physiotherapy, rehabilitation and so forth, alongside psychotherapy and counselling, plus the practical stuff like learning how to apply make-up to cover scarring and job retraining. In essence it will be a one-stop shop where people can access what they need or just come in for a cup of coffee and a chat.'

He watched her face change as she spoke and the animation was not something that could be faked. She was truly passionate about this charity. 'That is a very ambitious scheme for someone so young.'

She lifted her chin. 'I really don't see how my age has anything to do with it, and I was always brought up to aim high.'

'So you're saying positive thinking works miracles?'

'I'm not after miracles. Everything we are aiming for is achievable and I have the facts and figures to prove it. As for positive thinking…well, that is helpful, but there comes a point when action is needed. This isn't some sort of game to me.'

'I can see that.' His admission came with some reluctance. He didn't want to admire her; he wanted to bed her. *Liking* was not a prerequisite for compatibility in the bedroom. In fact, it was a complication.

'So why this particular cause?' he asked.

'I met someone in hospital…'

'You were ill?' He visualised an image of her lying in a hospital bed and didn't dare analyse the emotion that tightened in his gut.

She dodged his interrogative stare and looked down at her fingers, watching as they tightened around the stem of the wine glass she held. She had recovered her composure by the time she responded, explaining in a quiet measured voice wiped clean of any emotion, 'I parted company with a motorbike.' The shaky laugh was less planned. 'Or so they tell me.'

The how and why remained a blank to this day. In fact the only thing she remembered that might not have been a dream was climbing on the bike calling to her sister to follow her, and then nothing until the smell of burning and sirens. If it hadn't been for her brother-in-law she wouldn't even remember that.

She wouldn't be here at all.

Some people needed their drug of choice to be happy, but she was alive and that was all the buzz she needed. The knowledge that life was so fragile had made her determined to do something with her life that would leave something tangible behind.

'I hope the driver didn't get off scot-free.' The corners of his mouth pulled down in disapproval as he imagined her slim arms around some leather-clad idiot, her lithe body pressing into him.

'I wasn't riding pillion.' It occurred to her that her pride was misplaced; after all, how well had the going-solo scenario been serving her so far?

The problem with being so independent was that when you messed up there was no one else to share the blame with.

'So you like to be in charge?'

'In charge? If by that you mean do I like to make my own decisions, then, yes, I do,' she told him calmly. 'It's never been my fantasy to be dominated by a male chauvinist.' *Just a bit too much protesting there, Chloe!*

'You're a risk taker, then?'

Holding his gaze and reacting to the challenge glittering in the ebony depths was about the most dangerous thing she had done in a long time. 'I'm not the one who made a living dodging bullets.'

He stiffened, and their eyes connected once more. The shadows in his gaze belonged to a man who had seen far too much trauma for one lifetime. A moment later his expression shuttered and the change was so abrupt that Chloe was momentarily disorientated.

'It's a phase I grew out of.'

It was the bleakness in his voice that made her realise she hadn't imagined it. For a few seconds she was back in the bar, turning without really knowing why and seeing him sitting there, the most handsome man she had ever seen or actually imagined. In the confusing mesh of emotions—attraction colliding with empathy—she'd felt the pain he was unconsciously emanating.

Dragging her thoughts back to the present, she extinguished the ache of empathy with a large dose of objectivity. *You don't need another cause,* she warned herself, *and you definitely don't need this man.*

'So was anyone else hurt in the accident?'

'Several people, including my brother-in-law, though he wasn't then…my brother-in-law, that is. Apparently there had been an oil spill earlier on a blind bend and… it just happened. There was no one to blame but me and fate.'

He tipped his chair back to look at her, though it was hard to read his expression thanks to the thickness of his long lashes. 'So you believe in fate?'

She shrugged. 'I believe you make choices and have to live with the consequences.'

'Well, you don't seem to have suffered too many long-lasting consequences.'

He really had no idea. She struggled not to touch her leg again, and instead let her eyelids lower, shading her expression with her own long, curling lashes. 'I was very lucky,' she agreed quietly.

'So what else do you believe in?' He believed in very little and he found himself almost envying her her idealism, but equally he was disturbed by the idea that it might have been some form of this idealism that had first led her to his bed, or him to hers… Had she seen him as some sort of romantic hero or had it meant nothing to her beyond a rite of passage?

He wasn't actually sure which possibility disturbed him more.

'I believe in the resilience of human spirit, I believe that you should never take anything for granted and I believe…' She gave a sudden self-conscious laugh, her eyes sliding from his. 'I believe that I'm in danger of boring you.'

It came as a shock to realise that they had reached the coffee stage.

'I'd prefer to be dead!'

The horrified exclamation by one of the female guests coincided with a lull in the conversation.

'So what is it you prefer death to, my dear?' The man to her right voiced the question on everyone's mind.

'Being a size fourteen!' She gave a theatrical shudder. 'Can you imagine?'

Chloe sat there and imagined what this woman would say if she saw the scars on her thigh. She knew full well that her reaction would not be unique.

'She's an eating disorder waiting to happen and the sad thing is she has a daughter who she'll probably pass on her neuroses to.'

Anger struck through Chloe; while she might have agreed with the sentiment Nik had privately voiced in her ear, she doubted he had ever dated a woman who carried any extra weight.

'So I suppose appearances don't matter to you,' she charged bluntly. 'You'd date someone who wasn't perfect, would you? You honestly wouldn't care if your wife gained a hundred pounds or suddenly went bald.'

His brows lifted at the heat of her accusation. 'That

sounds rather personal. Were you an ugly duckling before you became a swan? A fat child with acne…or is that a wig you're wearing…?'

She reared back as he went to touch her hair.

'You switched the place cards, didn't you? So you could sit next to me and drive me around the bend.'

'You didn't answer my question.'

'You didn't answer mine.'

He tipped his head in acknowledgment. 'I have some skills,' he admitted modestly. As he spoke he held out his hand and turned it over, extending his long brown fingers. Then with a flick of his wrist he produced one of the place cards from the sleeve of his opposite hand. 'Distraction and sleight of hand. I have other skills.'

She compressed her lips and made a point of not asking him what they were.

'Have you thought about what I said about you coming home with me tonight?'

She choked gently on her mouthful of wine before giving him a direct look. 'I assumed you were joking.' She was quite pleased with the compromise; it was a way of saying no without injuring his male ego.

Unfortunately, he didn't appear to appreciate the favour she was doing him. 'Then I'll have to think of a way of showing you that I'm not.'

Her nerve ends tingling in response to the throaty purr of his challenge, she gave a little gasp and knocked over a glass as she bolted to her feet. Aware that people were looking at her, she calmly folded her napkin and dabbed at the damp spot on the snowy cloth. 'Send me the dry-cleaning bill,' she joked.

People responded to her quip with smiles and barely looked at her as she walked around the table to where Tatiana sat.

'I promised to ring the palace to check on…'

Tatiana's sympathy was instant. 'Of course. Use my office if you want some privacy, then join us for coffee in the drawing room.'

CHAPTER FIVE

SHE LISTENED TO her sister, who spoke at some length on the joys—*not*—of morning sickness. It wasn't until she hung up that Chloe identified the odd achey tightness in her chest as envy, but she refused to acknowledge it. Her sister deserved her happiness; it just made her aware of the things she didn't have and maybe never would.

Catching the self-pitying direction her thoughts were taking, she got to her feet, but halfway to the drawing room she chickened out and slipped into the bathroom, where she spent a great deal of time admiring the decor.

Sometimes discretion was *definitely* the better part of valour. Hoping no one had sent out a search party for her, she waited there long enough to be sure that her arrival would coincide with people leaving. Hopefully she could slip away unnoticed without any further confrontations with Nik.

She had just stepped out into the hallway when she heard Lucy's voice and ducked back into the bathroom. It was instinctive and she felt foolish the moment she locked the door. It wasn't Lucy she was hiding from, but that didn't matter; it was the fact she was hiding at all that filled her with self-disgust.

With a sigh she turned, dumped her bag on the vanity

unit and, palms flat on the marble surface, she looked at herself in the mirror.

Her face illuminated by the spotlights above looked pale and her eyes were too bright. She leaned in and touched the fine skin under her eye; the make-up helped but did not quite conceal the blueish half-moon, which was the result of a week of disturbed nights that had preceded her decision not to continue with further surgery.

The decision had felt liberating, she'd felt completely in control and yet what had it taken to throw that equilibrium into chaos? One single encounter with Nik Latsis. She made a sound of disgust in her throat and turned her back on the mirror.

She sighed. She hadn't felt in control tonight, she'd felt… She shook her head, unable…unwilling to examine her emotions as she turned, taking care not to look in the mirror, and twisted the cold tap onto full.

She stood there with her wrists under the running water, waiting for her heart rate to slow, wanting to reject outright the idea that she was attracted to Nik Latsis. The lie would have been easy, easier than admitting a man like him would never want someone less than perfect, but she couldn't.

It was a fact.

She turned off the tap, lifted her chin and looked at herself in the mirror.

'It is what it is, Chloe.'

She made her way back downstairs, where the hallway was empty but the door stood open. There was no sign of Tatiana, so she decided to call for a cab before saying goodbye to her hostess.

She had started to punch in the number when a voice at her elbow made her jump.

'Have you been hiding?' Nik asked.

'What?'

He was wearing a long tailored dark overcoat that hung open, his hair glistened wet and the same moisture glistened on his face. He had brought the smell of outdoors and rain into the room.

Chloe struggled to hide her dismay and the illicit excitement that made her stomach muscles quiver. 'You haven't gone yet.'

'Ever the gentleman, I have been escorting the ladies to their cars.' He held up a large umbrella.

Chloe clenched her fingers over her phone, ignoring the little ribbons of warm electricity making her aware of the tingling nerve endings in her skin. 'I'm just ringing for a taxi.'

He watched as she began to punch in a number, noticing that her face had a fresh scrubbed look as though she'd taken off her make-up. She still looked good, very good, but she looked more vulnerable…delicate, even. He felt an emotion swell in his chest but refused to acknowledge it as tenderness.

'You don't need a taxi.'

The harshness in his voice drew her glance upwards. 'Thanks, but no, thanks,' she said firmly, ashamed of the moments of self-pity she had indulged in.

'You're still here!' Tatiana's relieved voice rang out before Nik could respond.

Chloe was glad of the interruption but puzzled by the older woman's sense of urgency. 'I was just ringing for a taxi before I came to say goodbye, but did I forget something?' She nodded to Lucy who had appeared behind her host; the redhead was wearing a denim jacket over the slinky red dress and carrying off the contrast in considerable style.

Tatiana shook her head. 'Spiros just rang to warn anyone left not to try taking…well, just about any road, I think. The peaceful protests apparently turned out not to be so peaceful, and the police have closed down half the streets. Spiros is stuck, and he saw a car alight too. I really think it would be better if you all stay here for the night. There are reports of the disturbances spreading and even looting.'

'I'm walking home, so it's no problem,' Lucy said.

Tatiana looked alarmed.

Lucy put her hands on the older woman's shoulders. 'Relax, I'm not going to my home, I'm booked into the new boutique hotel around the corner. It's only a hundred yards, so I think I'll be safe.' She air-kissed Tatiana and thanked her, landed a kiss on Nik's cheek and waved to Chloe. 'Interesting night.'

Chloe didn't even try and translate this cryptic utterance.

'And I'm going Chloe's way so that's her problem solved,' Nik announced in a tone that brooked no argument.

Not from where she was standing!

'How do you know which way is my way? That is,' she continued, lowering the levels of antagonism in her voice, 'I wouldn't dream of bothering you.'

'Nonsense!' Tatiana sent her brother a warning glare. 'He's fine with it, aren't you, Nik?'

Chloe clenched her teeth as, with a totally unconvincing display of meekness that made him look even more like a wolf, he tipped his dark head.

'Absolutely.' Slower than Tatiana to jump back squealing when he shook the umbrella, sending a spray of cold water droplets that hit everything in the immediate area, Chloe was the only one close enough to hear his not at all meek-sounding addition. 'My way is whichever way you're going.'

She brushed her ear where the sensitive flesh still tingled from the touch of his warm breath and glared at him, while he continued to look smugly satisfied with himself.

'Well, that's sorted, then,' Tatiana said, looking relieved. 'You will text me when you get home safely?'

Chloe promised.

She gave a sigh and rubbed the tip of her nose with her finger. The truth was, there was a part of her, a clearly twisted part of her, that had…*enjoyed* their flirtation. No, that was the wrong word. It hadn't been flirtation; that was far too gentle. Combat probably better described the heart-thumping, skin-tingling adrenaline charge of their exchanges tonight.

She had felt what…? *Like a woman.* Her eyes flew wide with shock as the recognition of her too-long-suppressed sexuality crashed through her.

'Are you all right?' Nik asked.

'I'm fine!' she lied.

She read criticism in his eyes as they swept her face. 'You look like you're in pain.'

'The only pain around here…' at the last second she managed to apply the brake to her runaway tongue and lowered her eyes, muttering '…is a slight headache.'

Actually pain was pretty accurate for what she felt, as though the circulation were returning to a limb deprived of blood. It hurt and so did this—the part of her that had been in hibernation since the accident had finally woken up and it was tingling!

She wasn't ready yet; she wanted that part to go back to sleep. It was such awful bad timing! At this point an affair of any kind, let alone the sort of superficial no-strings fling Nik Latsis had in mind for them, was the last thing she needed.

She lifted her chin, defiance sparking in her eyes, as she thought, *I deserve more than that! I deserve better than Nik Latsis!*

Even if she had been in the market for a man, which she wasn't, he would not have made the shortlist. If she had needed reminding, and she didn't, how shallow he was, tonight would have driven the point home to her.

Yes, she was attracted to him, it was actually too exhausting to try and pretend otherwise, but in her defence he had more sexual charisma in a single hair follicle than most men had in their entire bodies. Although *attraction* hardly came close to describing the visceral reaction he evoked just looking at him… *Then don't look!* she told herself.

She needed to stop over-analysing everything. Nothing was going to happen between them because it couldn't. She brushed her leg with her hand, not that the numbed scar tissue registered the touch. She found herself wishing fiercely for a moment that the numbness went even deeper, that she could anaesthetise the emotions that tonight had reawoken in her.

She squared her shoulders. If he had been the Nik who had vulnerabilities, and not this insensitive, slick predator, she might have been in trouble, but he wasn't, so she was completely safe.

As safe as being circled by a tiger, she thought, injecting as much grateful insincerity into her smile as she could.

'I hope it's not too far out of your way, Nik.'

It was Tatiana who replied. 'Don't be silly, Chloe…'

'Looks like that's settled, then.' Nik walked ahead and left Chloe to walk beside his sister. When they reached the open front door she realised with a stab of shame that she didn't have a clue what the other woman had just been saying to her.

This had to stop, she told herself. Nik Latsis was the past, not a mistake because the last few months had taught her that thinking about mistakes meant you couldn't move forward. She had moved forward and she would continue to do so.

'It's stopped raining.' Nik, who had walked outside ahead of the women, lowered the umbrella he had raised and held up his hands to the sky. He grinned, twirled the umbrella and stamped in a puddle.

Fighting the urge to run out and join him, Chloe was conscious of an ache in her chest. She snatched a quick breath, knowing that the image would stay with her, but not knowing why…or at least not asking herself why.

'You're welcome to stay over if you like.'

Her friend was looking concerned as she reiterated her offer; if Tatiana had picked up on her distress, Chloe just hoped she hadn't picked up on the cause! She was tempted, she really was, but accepting the offer would mean she was afraid to be alone with Nik. And she wasn't, because nothing was going to happen between them. Chloe gathered herself and turned with a smile that felt stiff and forced, although she was unwilling to admit that even to herself.

'Thanks, but no, it would be good to get home.' She raised her voice a little to make sure that Nik could hear what she was saying and get the message. 'I'd like to sleep in my own bed.' The way her mind was working overtime she doubted there would be much sleep for her tonight.

After a pause, Tatiana nodded and kissed her cheek. 'Take care…and drive carefully, Nik,' she called after her brother, who lifted an arm and waved.

* * *

Chloe trudged on head down, Nik beside her, not touching her but close, close enough for her to be aware of the tension that stopped him dead in his tracks at the sound of distant sirens.

He stood there, head sharply angled, his lean, tense stance making her think of a wolf sensing danger, nostrils flared, scenting it in the air.

The sound retreated and he shook his head as though clearing it before glancing down at her. 'I'm parked over here.'

It took Chloe a moment to recover from the expression she had glimpsed on his face before she fell into step beside him.

'Are you all right?' she asked softly. Haunted; he had looked haunted.

He glanced down at her, the sounds of war, the explosions, the disembodied screams and the discordant staccato peal of shells still sounding in his head. 'The silences in between the shelling were the worst. Somehow they tapped into a man's primitive fears...the calm before the storm.' He stopped and the street light above them showed the shock reflected on his face...as if he'd only just realised he'd spoken his thoughts out loud.

Then it was gone, as quickly as it had appeared.

Another time his car, a low, gleaming monster, would have drawn a sarcastic remark from Chloe about macho power statements, but all she did was slide into the passenger seat when he opened the door.

She ached for his pain but she knew she couldn't let him into her life...every instinct of self-preservation told her this. The memory of that morning waking alone, when she'd waited for him, imagining the reasons for his absence—he'd stepped out for coffee, he'd gone to find a red rose—made her cringe, but even worse was when the penny had finally dropped and she had acted like someone heartbroken.

The memory she filed away as water under the bridge. Mistakes were fine—it was repeating them that was unforgivable! He was a fragment of her history and, after all, you were never supposed to forget your first lover. Well, only time would tell and she was an optimist.

'I need to stop off at the office first…there are some contracts I must sign tonight,' he said.

Any delay, any reason to prolong the time she spent in this enclosed space with him filled her with dismay, although it was mitigated with a relief that he was sounding normal again. If he was acting she was glad…she simply couldn't deal with his trauma and her own reaction to it. A vulnerable Nik was a very dangerous Nik to her peace of mind!

'At this time of night?' Her voice sounded calm but her agitation revealed itself in the smooth stroking motion of her hands as she moved them up and down over her silk-covered thighs.

'I think they'll let me in,' he said, thinking about how her legs had wrapped tight around him as he'd thrust inside her.

'Of course,' she said, feeling stupid…then something more uncomfortable than stupid when she realised his eyes were following the mechanical motion of her hands. She stopped and folded her arms defensively across her chest.

He cast a glance across her face and was distracted for a moment because she was chewing her plump lower lip and all he had to do was bend in a little closer to taste it for himself.

'Look, Nik, tonight I think I might have… If I seemed

like I wanted you to…' She swallowed and stopped; if she really hadn't wanted Nik to flirt with her, why hadn't she just told him straight out about the scars that remained after the operations, the puckered, discoloured patches of flesh on her right thigh? It would have been amusing to see how fast he retreated.

Except it wouldn't have been *amusing*.

She told herself that people's attitudes to her scars were their problem, not hers, and most of the time she believed it, but there was a world of difference between theory and fact, not to mention a world of humiliation, and she wasn't ready for that yet.

'You were saying…?' he prompted, wondering if she knew how expressive her face was. The drift of emotions across it was almost like watching a silent film.

'I think it's a very bad idea to try and relive something that happened in the past. Much better to remember it as it was.'

'So am I a happy memory or a bad one?'

'A bit of both,' she admitted, thinking that she had reached the stars with him and discovered the depths of despair. She buckled her belt, reminding herself that self-pity was for people who did not have a life and she did. She was not going to waste her time thinking about what she'd lost; she was going to celebrate what she had.

Nik watched her, the knot of frustration in his belly tightening the muscles along his jaw. He enjoyed a challenge as much as the next man but this was different… He swore under his breath as he started the engine.

'So how long have you lived in London?' he asked in an attempt at a normal conversation.

'I went to college, but I wasn't very academic…'

'You dropped out?'

'More like I was invited to leave, which was fine because I had begun to make money with the blog, which seemed so amazing at the time. I've always been lucky.'

'And accident prone,' he commented.

'People died in that accident so I was still lucky,' she retorted.

'I'm guessing you are a glass-half-full kind of person.'

'I really hope so…' She turned her head to look at the glass-fronted building he had pulled up in front of.

'I won't be long.' He leaned across and snatched the phone she was nursing on her knee.

A moment later he tossed it back to her. 'My number's in it, and if you see or hear anything, call me,' he directed sternly.

It took her a few moments to realise what he meant. Some of her antagonism faded, but she remained sceptical that his caution was warranted.

'I think Spiros might have been exaggerating the danger.' Other than the initial couple of distant sirens, which was not exactly unusual, they had encountered nothing that suggested widespread rioting.

'You might be right.' He gave a concessionary nod and slid out, closing the door behind him with a decisive click.

Chloe leaned back in her seat, relaxing enough for her shoulder blades to actually make contact with the leather, and she watched him walk away, his hands thrust deep in his pockets, up the shallow steps to the building. He paused for a moment and she heard the decisive click of the car doors locking.

'I don't believe it!'

There was no one to hear her exclamation, and her angry bang on the window went unnoticed. Then there was nobody but the uniformed security guard, who'd come out when Nik went in, who just stood there ignoring her, his eyes constantly scanning the areas to left and right.

When Nik reappeared exactly three minutes fifteen seconds later, the two men shook hands and exchanged a few words before the man walked back into the building and Nik got into the car.

Chloe stared stonily ahead as he flung some files onto the back seat. 'You locked me in.'

'I didn't want any looters stealing my car.'

She compressed her lips. 'That man ignored me—'

'That man is an ex-marine. He knew what you were doing.'

'Oh. Do you have a lot of ex-marines working for you?'

'The transition is not always kind to men who have given their lives to protect us. Dave, back there, flung himself on a landmine and saved three others in his squad, but he lost a leg below the knee.'

Their eyes connected and in his dark gaze she saw something she didn't want to acknowledge. In seconds the heat banked inside her burst into life, starting low in her pelvis and spreading out until her entire body was suffused by the same blazing fire. The instant conflagration scared her witless... It was a warning, she told herself, a warning that said if she had an ounce of self-respect she'd get the hell out of that car right now.

Panic hit her hard. 'Stop the car.' She used the anger when he ignored her to drag herself free of the last of the dangerous languor that lingered in her brain. 'I said, stop the car,' she said calmly.

He took his eyes off the road to briefly glance at her face and she could hear the irritation in his voice. 'Don't be stupid.'

The only stupid thing she had done so far was getting

into this car with him and Chloe had every intention of keeping it that way.

'You're acting as though we have unfinished business, but that's not the case. Look, I spent the night with you, end of story. It is not something I have any wish to repeat.'

'So you want to pretend it didn't happen at all.'

The suggestion, his tone, his attitude they all struck a jarring note inside her, so she counted to ten and fought to dampen the resentment she knew she had no right to be feeling.

'I'm not pretending it didn't happen; I'm admitting it shouldn't have.'

'I—'

'Get down!'

It was the tone as much as the terse instruction that made her stomach clench. 'What's wrong?'

'Just do it. There's a blanket there, cover yourself with it and duck down.' The odd instruction was delivered in a light, calm tone, but when she leaned forward and saw what he had already seen, she didn't feel very calm at all.

Ahead of them the road was filled with crowds of people. Some had banners and some carried dustbin lids, which they were banging.

He wound down the window and the suggestion of noise became a loud, discordant din.

'They sound mad.' Fear fluttered in her belly.

'They are a mob.' And it was the nature of the beast, anger and unpredictability, the pack-animal mentality, that could make the whole group do things that as individuals they would never dream of doing.

'I don't like this,' she said, once again gnawing at her plump lower lip, a nervous habit she'd never managed to break.

'I would be more concerned if you did. Duck down and pull the cover over your head.'

If he had faced this situation alone he would not have broken a sweat, not because he was brave or fearless, but because he had been in far worse situations, and as far as he could see the only thing he stood to lose was a car.

But he wasn't alone, and knowing that Chloe's safety was his responsibility changed everything. He had talked his way out of much worse situations, but with Chloe here he wasn't prepared to take even a calculated risk.

'No, I'm not hiding and leaving you exposed,' she stated, but her fists were clenched tightly.

'Why does beautiful so often go with stupid?' He sighed.

Her wrathful gaze met his in the mirror and he smiled. If she was angry, at least she wasn't afraid. 'Relax, *agape mou*, I will not let anything hurt you.'

She believed him, although it seemed that she ought to be more concerned about her mental well-being than her physical! She caught his arm and he paused, his eyes going from her fingers curled into the fabric, to her face. 'You're not going to do anything stupid, are you?'

'Could you be more specific?' he asked.

'I don't know...like fight them.'

He let out a loud throaty laugh. 'Me against fifty, sixty people? I don't much like those odds, but I'm sorry if I disappoint you in the hero stakes.'

'I promise you I never thought you were a hero.'

One corner of his mouth lifted in a lopsided grin and there was something about him...a combustible quality that made her think it would have been a brave person who bet against him, even if the odds were stacked against him.

'But I do think you're capable of doing something stupid.'

'Like they say, a good general chooses his field of battle. I am not good or a general but the concept holds true.'

'Are you going to drive on through them?' she asked nervously.

Nik had been going to reverse, but a glance in the rear-view mirror made it clear this was a now-or-never choice. The street on one side—he adjusted the mirror and silently corrected himself—on both sides of the road were full of people streaming towards the main artery road. It was hard to be accurate but he suspected that their options would close in seconds, not minutes.

'Hold on, this might be a little bumpy.'

She connected with his eyes and made a shocking discovery. 'You are enjoying this, aren't—?' She let out a shriek and closed her eyes as the car went into sudden reverse, travelling at what felt like the speed of light. It continued backwards even when it hit obstacles, objects in the road flung down by rioters.

The banner-waving maniacs followed initially, but they quickly fell away and by the time the car reached the gaggle of police cars the protestors were nowhere in sight.

'Wait here.'

She narrowed her eyes, tilted her stubborn little chin and thought, *Oh, yes that is* really *going to happen!* Who did he think he was, issuing orders to her? She opened her door and got out.

Two uniformed officers were already moving towards the car, and Nik walked towards them, looking calm and confident.

By the time she was within hearing distance, the police were complimenting Nik and shaking his hand.

'Thank you, sir. If all witnesses could be so clinically precise it would make our job a lot easier.'

'More resources,' the younger one said, 'would too.'

In response to a look he received from his colleague, he added a defensive, 'It's no secret that we're over-stretched.' Then he stopped as he saw Chloe coming towards them, his eyes widening.

Before he could speak to her, Nik moved, cutting off her approach. With a firm hand on her elbow, he turned back to the men. 'We won't get in your way, officers, and thank you. Come on, Chloe.'

She was hustled back to the car with equal ruthless efficiency. 'You didn't let me say a word to them! What did you think I was going to do?' she demanded as Nik folded his long length in beside her.

'Distract them from their job,' he replied succinctly.

'So what happens now?' she huffed.

'Now I take you home. The police have given me a route that should be clear and, before you ask, the Tube stations are closed, so don't even think of asking me to stop the car again.'

The rest of the journey was completed without incident and in total silence.

She waited until he had neatly reversed the car into a parking space clearly marked reserved outside her building before releasing her seat belt.

'I should thank you.'

'But you won't.'

'That's not what I...' A sound of irritation rattled in her throat. He drove her insane! 'All right, I *do* thank you.'

'It was my pleasure.'

He moved to open his door and she shook her head. 'No, don't get out; I'm fine.'

'I will see you to the door.'

'I'm not going to be ravished or kidnapped between here and there,' she said, nodding to the Georgian building behind them. Once it had housed one family; now it was split into twenty one-bedroom apartments, a bit down at heel, or, in estate-agent speak, ripe for improvement. Chloe had no cash to improve hers as she had poured all the money her blog had made into buying the place.

'Looking like that, I would not be so confident.'

'You mean I would be asking for it?' she countered crankily.

His exasperation increased. 'I mean that you are a very beautiful woman, this is a fact, and it is also a fact that a man who forces himself on a woman is no real man.' His nostrils flared in distaste. 'And a man who excuses the actions of such a person is no less of an inadequate loser.'

He got out and walked around to her side of the car, standing there silently as she got out.

She tilted her head to look at his shuttered face. 'I've offended you.'

He arched an eloquent brow.

'Sorry.'

He bowed slightly from the waist. 'Accepted.' A glimmer appeared in his eyes. 'Friends again?'

Chloe looked at the hand extended to her as if it were a viper. It was news to her that they ever had been friends, but he had got her home so she reached out.

He took her hand but not to shake it. Without his seeming to exert any overt pressure, she found herself colliding with his body.

His dark face lowered to hers. 'It's all about sleight of hand and distraction,' he whispered before his mouth came crashing down on hers.

The kiss was hard, hot and hungry as he plundered her mouth with ruthless efficiency. For a split second, shock held her immobile, then as his dark head began to lift something snapped inside her. Chloe felt it, even heard it, as she dragged his dark head back down to hers, parting her lips to invite a deepening of the slow, sensual exploration.

It was an invitation that he accepted, driving his tongue deep into the warm recesses of her mouth.

She was distantly conscious of the throaty, mewling little sounds but didn't make the connection between them and herself. Her hands curled into his jacket to stop herself falling as tongues of flame scorched along her nerve endings, and she felt a deep shudder ripple through the hard, lean body pressed close to her.

'Oh, God!'

Her shaken gasp seemed to break the spell.

The thud that Chloe heard when she fell back to earth seemed almost as real as the searing humiliation she felt as, still shaking, she looked up at him, to see that he was perfectly fine. Standing there as though nothing had happened, she thought, her indignation going supernova... then cooling slightly as she noticed the streaks of colour along his cheekbones and the fact he was breathing pretty hard.

At least he had put enough distance between them to make the basic stuff like breathing a whole lot easier. She tilted her head but it was impossible to make out his expression. Even with her eyes narrowed, his face was just a dark blur, which was probably a blessing of sorts because he no doubt looked as smug as a man who had just had his point proved could look.

She took a deep breath. 'I am not sure what that was meant to achieve.'

'Achieve?'

She ignored the interruption and didn't even register the odd strain in his voice.

'I already knew that you were a good kisser.' He was a good everything, that was the problem.

'So the problem is…?'

Arms crossed over her chest, she rubbed her upper arms with both hands. 'I enjoyed the night I spent with you, but I happen not to be quite as casual about sex as you are. That's not a criticism,' she hastened to assure him. 'I mean, as far as I'm concerned, each to his own.'

'So now you have developed a puritanical streak?'

She slung him a look of simmering dislike. 'Last time you looked…hurt…lost…' *And what's your excuse this time, Chloe?* 'I don't know, but—'

'You are saying you had pity sex with me.'

'No.'

'So are you looking for a deep and meaningful relationship?'

The sneering tone of his voice set her teeth on edge and tightened her expression into a glare, though she fought to keep the edge of antagonism from her voice. 'I'm not actually looking for any sort of a relationship just now, but when I am… I'd like to find a man who will accept me for who I am inside, and not care about the way I look.'

He gave a hard, incredulous laugh. 'Well, if that's the kind of man you're looking for, I'd start looking for a couple of nice cats instead, if I were you. What's so wrong with being beautiful? It's not exactly a curse; women spend their lives and fortunes trying to look like you and they never will. How is noticing you're beautiful an insult to you?'

She stuck out her small determined chin. 'I'm a hell

of a lot more than that, not that you're ever going to know, and, believe you me, that's your loss!' she flared, secreting the security card she'd extracted from her bag in her palm.

She widened her eyes and looked into the middle distance. 'Oh, my!'

As soon as he turned his head to see what she was staring at, Chloe ran to the door. Her security card swiped first time and she stepped into the foyer, slamming it shut a split second before he reached it.

She pressed the button on the intercom. 'It's all about sleight of hand and distraction.'

A reluctant smile fought its way to his lips. 'I thought you never hid.'

She might not know about distraction, but she understood about odds. Her father owned the leg of a racehorse and she knew the odds were good that if Nik kissed her again and she got another taste of that raw power, if she felt the impression of his erection grinding into her belly, instinct would take over and reason would fly out of the window.

And everything would be hot and marvellous until he got an up-close-and-personal look at the part of her that once had been perfect and now wasn't. Did she want to carry the memory of his look of disgust or embarrassment as he pulled away from her? That was a no brainer.

'I'm not hiding from you. I'm walking away. There's a difference.' The moment she turned away from him the tears she had been holding back began to fall, and, running up the stairs, she swiped at them irritably.

Just sex was really not worth it!

CHAPTER SIX

IT WAS NOON when Chloe got back to her flat, but the first thing she did was strip off, push her clothes in the linen basket and step in the shower. The act of washing was purely symbolic; she knew the scent of hospital was in her mind, because the only thing the doctor's consulting room on the top floor of the rather beautiful Georgian building it occupied had smelt of was his expensive aftershave.

Hair still damp, she tightened the belt of her robe around her waist and flung herself down on the sofa, keying in her sister's number on her phone…but it went straight to voicemail.

With a sigh she dropped the phone in her robe pocket and padded barefoot over to the kitchen. Of course, if her sister had known about the hospital appointment she would have been waiting for the call—no, she would have come with her—but she didn't know. Chloe deliberately hadn't told anyone about it, *especially* her family.

They had been through enough during the long months after the accident—not that her choice not to tell them was entirely selfless. She knew that they, or at least her parents, would struggle to understand her decision not to have further cosmetic surgery. Down the line who knew how she'd feel about it? While it certainly was an option, right now she'd had enough of hospitals and she felt that to go through all that again was unbearable, especially as there were no guarantees regarding exactly how much improvement there would be, as the doctor would not give any promises.

She had taken a sip of her scalding coffee when her phone rang, and she lifted it to her ear and said hello.

It was not her sister who replied and, stifling a surge of disappointment, she said, 'Can you just hold on a second?' and reached out to shut the door of the fridge, which was buzzing to remind her she'd not closed it. 'Hi, Tatiana.'

'S… Sorry, is this a bad time?'

Chloe's reaction was immediate; elbows on the counter, she leaned forward, concern furrowing her brow. 'No, it's fine…is anything wrong?' When they had spoken earlier today, Tatiana had sounded relaxed and happy, issuing an invitation that Chloe had refused, which had been to join her on the family estate on the Greek island of Spetses. But now, only a few hours later, she was obviously close to tears.

'I told you, didn't I, that I agreed to Eugenie spending the first week of the holiday with her friend Pippa in Hampshire…?'

'Yes…has something gone wrong?' Chloe asked.

Tatiana gave an unamused laugh. 'You could say that. Pippa's parents in their wisdom decided that two fifteen-year-old girls were mature enough to be left alone in the house while they went away for the night.'

'Oh, dear!'

'Oh, yes, definitely *oh, dear*. The girls decided to have an impromptu party with supposedly just a few friends but, to cut a long story short, it was gatecrashed by lots of other kids, the place was wrecked and the neighbours called the police! Eugenie has been cautioned by the police and she is waiting at the local police station to be picked up. Pippa's parents have decided she is a bad influence—can you believe it? The problem is, my grandmother has a really high temperature, so I can't leave her, and my brother's not picking up his phone and no one seems to know where he is.'

'What can I do?'

A sob of relief echoed down the line. 'Could you pick her up for me and take her to the airport?'

'Of course.'

'The Gulfstream jet was in Frankfurt; I have no idea what my parents are doing there. Anyhow, I made some excuse up to say I needed the plane, but I really don't want them to know about this. It should be there by the time you arrive.'

'Don't worry, I'll drop her off safely.'

'Drop her off? Oh, no, Chloe, I need you to travel with her to Spetses, and sit on her if necessary! I'm not risking her pulling another stunt.'

It was only the rising hysteria in her friend's voice that stopped Chloe pointing out that there seemed little possibility of her daughter coming to any harm on a private flight to a Greek island. 'Fine, I'll sit on her.'

'I knew I could rely on you. Thank you so much, Chloe. I'll never be able to repay you.'

Actually, Chloe realised as she picked up her car keys, it was Tatiana who was doing her a favour. Left to her own devices she'd have spent the evening brooding over her decision and planning how she broke the news to her parents. Instead, she had plenty to distract her.

A cloudburst proved to be one of the distractions she hadn't figured on.

Chloe was drenched to the skin as she sat in the police

station studying a poster on the wall that proclaimed in large letters *Don't be a victim,* a sentiment she agreed with wholeheartedly, when Eugenie appeared walking alongside a fresh-faced policewoman who barely seemed older than the teen.

The girl's face dropped when she saw Chloe.

'I thought Uncle Nik was coming to get me.'

'Your mum couldn't contact him.' Chloe struggled not to sound judgemental about that as her imagination kicked in, supplying a slide show of selfish reasons for Nik being off the grid, all revolving around beautiful women and bed.

Well, you declined his offer to spend the night with him, Chloe reminded herself. *Did you expect him to go back home and weep into his beer, or did you expect him to pursue you?*

He clearly hadn't done either, which reinforced the obvious: it had been an opportunist offer, made in the heat of the moment, and when she'd refused he had chalked it up to experience and moved on.

A circumstance she told herself she was relieved about.

'Uncle Nik would understand…*he* wouldn't lecture me,' the girl said, her defiant expression suggesting that Chloe couldn't even begin to do so.

In contrast to the girl's dramatic pronouncement Chloe kept her voice light and friendly. 'I'm not here to lecture you,' she returned, thinking, *Thank God, it's not my job.* 'Just get you to your mum.'

The girl pouted and tossed her head. 'Well, you took your time.'

Chloe smiled and counted to ten. 'Yes, I thought I'd take the scenic route as it's such a lovely day for a drive.' She gestured to the window, where the rain was falling from a leaden summer sky. 'And obviously I had nothing better to do.' Without waiting for the girl's response, she turned to the policewoman. 'Thank you very much for looking after her.' She glanced at Eugenie. 'Ready...?'

The girl nodded. Minus the truculent attitude, she looked so miserable and very young standing there shifting her weight from one spiky heel to the other that it was all Chloe could do not to hug her.

Instead she slipped off her jacket and draped it over the girl's bare shoulders. 'It's a bit chilly out there.'

Eugenie turned her head to look up at Chloe. 'Is she really mad? Mum, I mean?' she muttered.

'I'm afraid I'm just the chauffeur.' Chloe hesitated, choosing her words with care. 'I've zero experience of being a parent, but I have been a daughter and when my parents were angry with me it was usually because they were worried about me.'

'There was no reason for her to be worried.'

'If you say so.'

'You don't believe me, do you?'

'I'm parked just over there.'

'Uncle Nik would believe me—he'd understand.'

Well, bully for Uncle Nik, Chloe thought, keeping her lips sealed over her resentment. Uncle Nik, who would no doubt have beautiful babies, and was, as far as she knew, somewhere right now trying to make one.

She frowned, rubbing her upper arms through the silk of her already drenched blouse, and pushed the accompanying image away. Wherever he was too busy to pick up his phone, it was bound to be some place nice and warm while she was drenched to the skin and walking on eggshells with a teenager who made her feel about ninety!

Just as she was on the point of deciding that parenthood was clearly a mug's game, her sulky charge stopped. Impatient, Chloe turned back.

'Thank you for coming for me,' Eugenie said in a small quivery voice.

'You are very welcome.'

Chloe fished her keys from her pocket and opened the passenger door of her own utilitarian hatchback. 'Sorry you're slumming it today.'

'*That* is your car?' The girl's astonishment was almost comical, as was her horror. Chloe strongly suspected that the idea of being seen in anything so uncool worried her more than the idea of parental ire or a jail cell.

'So what does it do, thirty with the wind behind it?'

'If we're lucky.' *Speed* had not been a priority when she had first got behind the wheel of a car after the accident, but safety had. Not that she expected the girl, or anyone else for that matter, to understand that this car represented a personal triumph for Chloe.

She could have rationalised it and it would have been easier than admitting her fears. Far easier to pretend that she was doing her eco bit for the planet by using public transport, asking how convenient actually was it to have a car in the City?

Instead she had admitted she had a problem, and her family had been proud when she had conquered her fears, but the truth was her honesty had certain limitations. She'd never told them that her hands still got clammy when she slid into the driver's seat and her heart rate took a few minutes before it settled into a normal rhythm.

Time, she hoped, would eventually finish the healing process.

'I thought you were meant to be royal or something...'

'Or something,' Chloe admitted with a laugh. 'You can always duck down if you see anyone you know—'

The sound of a car that was neither safe nor slow made them both turn as a limousine complete with blacked-out windows drew up behind them.

The girl's pale face lit up. 'It's Uncle Nik.'

Chloe already knew that. As he got out of the car her minor palpitations suddenly became critical.

'He'll understand.' The relief in the girl's face faded away to uncertainty as she realised what Chloe already had. The man striding towards them was furious.

His face set in hard lines, his dark brows drawn into a straight line above his hawkish nose, he stopped a couple of feet away from them. He was breathing hard and looked like a well-dressed version of a dark avenging angel as the wind caught the hem of his long coat, making it billow out behind him.

'What the hell did you think you were doing?'

As the teenager shrank into her side Chloe wondered if Nik knew he had gone from hero to villain in just one short sentence.

Nik's narrowed eyes followed the protective hand Chloe slid around the girl's shoulders, and his jaw tensed as he flashed her an arctic glare.

'Thank you for your…*help*.' The word emerged reluctantly through his clenched lips. 'I'm assuming that Tatiana contacted you?'

Her chin lifted in challenge. He had managed to make the statement sound like an accusation. *No, I just happened to be passing.*

It took an effort but she managed to keep her lip buttoned on the snarky retort that hovered on the tip of her tongue, and she dipped her head in acknowledgment, reflecting that surely *one* of them had to act like an adult in front of Eugenie.

'Well, I'm here now.'

As if that could have slipped anyone's notice! So this was Nik in business mode; impressed hardly covered her reaction. His designer-cut business suit didn't disguise the hardness of the body it covered, but it did emphasise the effortless power he exuded.

Nik dragged his eyes away from the outline of the lacy bra covering Chloe's breasts, clearly outlined beneath the drenched silk, just in time to see her roll her eyes at him. He wondered why, of all the people she could have turned to for help, his sister had chosen this woman, who was nobody's idea of a responsible adult. Hell, she didn't even have the basic sense to leave the house with a coat in a storm!

'Get in the car,' he ordered his niece.

'I'm not going anywhere with you!' was the response.

If his scowl was any indicator, he only saw the surly expression on Eugenie's face, and not the fact that her defiance only went about a cell deep despite the dramatic pronouncements. Clearly it wasn't his incredible insight into female behaviour that got him the girls, Chloe thought sourly.

'I hate you!'

Chloe sighed. It was a long shot, but she felt obliged to at least make an attempt to smooth things over.

'Look, clearly you're both feeling pretty intense...'

Two pairs of antagonistic eyes zoomed in on her face.

She cleared her throat and attempted a smile. As far as feelings went, her own were pretty much all over the place and had been from the moment she'd identified the person getting out of the car and her heart had started fibrillating madly. It had not even begun to calm down when he'd stalked towards them looking deliciously sexy, hard and... She gave her head a tiny shake. This wasn't about her, or her hormones; it was about Eugenie and Tatiana.

'Maybe now...' she continued, channelling sweet reason and calm while wondering if it was all right secretly wanting to do the wrong thing just so long as you actually resisted the weakness.

'Now what?' he bit out.

She dragged away her eyes, which were showing a disastrous tendency to drift up and down his long, lean, loose-limbed frame without her permission, and cleared her throat. What she needed right now was cool thinking, logic and maybe a bit of inspiration. What she didn't need or, for that matter, want was this animal attraction, insane sexual chemistry or a vivid imagination supplying her with memories of how he'd looked naked.

'Now is not the right time to—'

The teen shrugged off the arm across her shoulders and, with hands on her hips, took a defiant step towards her uncle. 'It wasn't my fault.'

Chloe sighed and wondered why she had even bothered to try. If she had any sense, which she did, she would get in her car, drive off and let these two slug it out, but then she reminded herself that Tatiana was her friend, and she had promised her she'd look after Eugenie.

Nik felt his grip on his temper slipping, but he breathed through the moment.

It had not been a good morning. He'd had a breakfast meeting with a guy the normally reliable firm of headhunters had sent, and in the space of thirty minutes the candidate had broken every unwritten rule in the book: drunk too much, confided personal problems, bad-mouthed colleagues and talked politics. Then Nik had returned to the office and found all the messages on his machine his stand-in secretary had not seen fit to respond to.

But compared to his present situation, faced with a

niece who appeared to loathe him while challenging his authority, and the woman who hadn't been out of his head for more than three consecutive seconds ever since they'd parted company nearly forty-eight hours ago, he was extremely frustrated and close to snapping point!

He'd spent the last two days considering the best way to seduce Chloe Summerville. Seduction had never had much to do with the kind of recreational sex he enjoyed; usually it wasn't about anything but slaking a hunger and for a short space of time blocking out everything else. Mutual attraction was certainly involved, but comparing it with what had sparked into life between himself and Chloe would have been like comparing a light shower with a monsoon!

And the attraction between them was mutual, he knew that without question, which made her rejection of him all the more teeth-grindingly frustrating.

He didn't make the mistake of reading anything deep and meaningful into their attraction; it was more to do with the timing and circumstances of their first meeting than anything else. Those circumstances had just intensified the chemistry that existed between them, that was all—a chemistry that would inevitably fade.

If when it did, so did his nightmares, that was only an added bonus. Getting her into bed was definitely going to happen; it was just a matter of when. His instincts could not be that far out, surely?

'Get in the car,' he repeated to his niece, digging into reserves of tolerance that had already been seriously depleted.

Chloe took a deep breath and came to a decision. Stepping forward, she put herself between the angry male and his niece. 'Actually, I promised Tatiana that I would deliver her personally, so, Eugenie, get in my car.' The slam of the car door told her that the girl had obeyed. Chloe felt a stab of relief; she would have looked pretty silly if Eugenie had ignored her.

Nik growled. He wasn't used to having his decisions challenged or his instructions ignored and suddenly the emotions that ran rampant through him had nothing to do with their natural chemistry and everything to do with the fact that Chloe was a pain in his backside! He made to move past her but Chloe mirrored his move.

She held up her hands, her expression determined.

'You think my niece needs protection from me?' he demanded incredulously, his voice pitched to a low, private rumble.

Not half as much as I do, Chloe thought, despising the part of her that couldn't help but notice how incredibly good he looked clean-shaven. 'Don't be absurd!' she snapped, fighting the urge to follow his lead and respond in kind. Instead she modified her tone. 'Of course I don't! It's just that in a situation like this—'

'And how many times have you been in a situation like this, *Lady* Chloe?'

'You might be surprised,' she retorted, but as the antagonistic glitter faded from his eyes she admitted, 'Fair enough, I've never been arrested, but I think you're the last person in the world to be throwing my life of imagined privilege in my face.'

'You're encouraging Eugenie to think this is a joke.'

She flung him a pitying look; for an intelligent man he was being pretty dense. 'She doesn't think it's a joke. She was scared stiff. I just think you're making a big thing out of this when—'

'My niece has been arrested. I call that a big thing!'

'She was only cautioned, and according to the sergeant I spoke to—'

A hiss of impatience left his clamped lips and she changed tactics.

'Look, Tatiana wants to keep this low-key, so you could force Eugenie to travel with you, but what would be the point? I mean, do you even know what you're letting yourself in for? Teenage girls tend to have a taste for melodrama and, I can assure you, she'd make the journey hell for you.'

'Is there a problem here?'

Chloe turned to see the policewoman from earlier standing looking at them. Well, actually she was looking at Nik and her mouth was ajar.

Chloe cleared her throat and gave the girl time to recover, as she had some sympathy for her dilemma.

'You know what it's like—you wait for a bus and two come along at once. This is Eugenie's uncle and we were just discussing it.' She turned to Nik. 'So is it OK if Eugenie comes with me?'

He didn't miss a beat. 'Absolutely and we can catch up on the way. Fred, my driver, can follow us.'

Her air of complacence vanished in an eye blink. 'You want me to give you a lift to the airport?' she squeaked, forgetting to avoid his eyes. They were shining with malicious amusement as if he knew perfectly well that the very thought of being confined inside her car with him for an hour was already making her break out in a cold sweat.

She closed her eyes and breathed out through her nose as she subdued her panic; he'd called her bluff and now she'd have to live with it. An hour was only sixty minutes, she reminded herself, yet somehow the maths wasn't particularly soothing so she decided not to work out the seconds as she watched him speak to the driver of the car.

* * *

Maybe it was wishful thinking but lately she liked to think that she was not quite as tense behind the wheel, but either way this journey was going to put her back months.

Nik was not a relaxed passenger; she could feel the tension rolling off him. Maybe he didn't like women drivers…or perhaps it was just her… He certainly couldn't be comfortable as he had to draw his long legs right up in order to squeeze himself into the space.

Served him right, she decided uncharitably as she stared doggedly ahead, ignoring him and the subtle spicy notes in the male fragrance he used.

The expression on her face when Nik had invited himself had seemed worth it at the time…but the decision had come back to bite him. The physical discomforts aside, and there were several—he had intermittent cramp in his left leg, and was losing the feeling in his foot, and the torture didn't look like being over any time soon, if ever—she drove at a maddeningly slow speed that he found at odds with her personality.

He suspected that if he mentioned it she'd go even slower just to annoy him, but when a caravan overtook them he lost the battle with exasperation. 'You drive like an old woman.'

'Sexism and ageism in one sentence…wow, impressive.'

'You haven't even got out of second gear yet.'

'Enjoy the scenery. Is he going to follow me the entire way?' She glared into the rear-view mirror that reflected the limo that was following close behind.

'That's the idea.'

'Is your driver ex-army too?'

The question startled a surprised look from him. 'What makes you say that?'

She shrugged. 'He has that look, you know, tough, hard...the catch-a-bullet-in-his-teeth type.'

Nik grinned, thinking Fred might quite like the description. 'He's a veteran.'

'You do employ a lot of ex-servicemen.'

'I'm not being charitable...'

He said it as if being considered charitable was an insult.

'I simply employ people I can rely on.'

And where he'd lived and worked, she supposed, you had to trust and rely on the people around you. 'Do you miss it...?' She bit her lip. 'Sorry, I didn't mean to remind you of...anything...'

'So Ana has been talking.'

'She mentioned what you used to do and—'

'Relax, you haven't reminded me. Losing a friend is not something you ever forget.' *Or forgive,* he thought as once again the familiar sense of guilt settled its suffocating weight over him.

She glanced in the rear-view mirror again. Eugenie had her eyes closed, and even over the engine the muffled bass boom coming from the music she was playing through her earphones was audible. 'Of course not... sorry.' She winced—the response to what he'd said seemed painfully inadequate and she pressed a hand briefly to the base of her throat where a blue-veined pulse was pounding in the hollow.

The action drew his eyes to the vulnerable spot, and the arrow-piercing thrust of raw desire caught him off guard and fed into the resentful anger he was feeling. 'If Ana has recruited you to her cause, please don't bother—'

'What cause?' She felt the suspicious brush of his dark hostile eyes over her bewildered face.

'It doesn't matter,' he said after a moment. 'My sister

is overprotective and a great believer in *talking* about everything.'

Comprehension dawned. 'Oh, she wants you to talk through your…experiences with…someone.' And for a proud man, a man used to being in control all the time, that would be anathema. She wished Tatiana good luck with that endeavour, but she didn't envy her the task of persuading her macho brother it was not a sign of weakness to talk about his feelings.

Nik's lips twisted into a cynical smile. 'How delicately put,' he mocked. 'But I don't want to forget.'

'Therapy isn't about forgetting. It's about living with the memories.'

'What would you know about it?' he jeered.

'We plan to use the services of therapists in our centre; it's an intrinsic part of the recovery process.'

'An *intrinsic* part of *my* recovery process is a glass of whisky and a night of f—'

'*Nik!*' Pretty sure what he'd been going to say and equally sure he wouldn't want to risk his niece hearing him say it, she jerked her head towards the back of the car, her eyes wide in warning.

Dark strips of colour stood out darkly against the uniform gold tones of his olive skin, emphasising the slashing angle of his high cheekbones.

In the back Eugenie began humming off-key to her music, her eyes still closed. The sound broke the awkward silence that had settled in the front of the car. 'She'll probably be deaf before she's twenty. I don't know why Ana allows her to use those things,' Nik muttered.

'Maybe you won't sound quite so disapproving when you're the parent of a teenager.' Her smile faded. The idea of Nik with children of any age was quite a depressing thought.

'Ana's a great parent,' he agreed.

Chloe was surprised to hear an unusual tone of humility in his voice, and she was even more surprised when he added, 'So is Ian.'

'I've never met him.'

'He's a nice guy, and they made a great couple. If they couldn't make it work I really don't know why anyone tries.'

'Love, maybe?'

His laugh was hard and cynical...leaving little doubt in her mind about his opinion of love.

For some reason the sound brought back a memory of another laugh, soft instead of harsh, a laugh she'd heard when her tongue had been moving across the hard pebble of his nipple, his fingers tangled in her hair, his body hot as he'd collapsed onto the bed, pulling her on top of him.

Then a minute, an hour, a lifetime later—time had stopped having much meaning—that laugh had come again as he'd rolled her onto her back, pinned her hands above her head with one hand and slid the other between her legs...

'You should be careful—you almost hit forty miles an hour then.'

His voice jolted her free of the images playing in her head and she drew her bottom lip over her upper one to blot the beads of moisture there. She felt the heat that suffused her body travel up her neck, threatening her with the mother of all blushes, so she dealt with it by choosing to pretend it was happening to someone else and it was this anonymous person who was feeling the shameful ache between her legs, not her.

'I'm trying to concentrate,' she snapped, glancing guiltily in the rear-view mirror, relieved when she saw that Eugenie was busy texting on her phone.

He looked at her fingers, which were locked, knuckles bone white, on the wheel. 'Do have you points on your licence or something?'

'Or something,' she said in a flat little voice.

He glanced in the mirror. 'She's texting again.'

'You don't know many teenagers, do you?'

'It's a day for new experiences, it seems. Is there a reason you drive this old thing?'

'Reliability.' A very underrated commodity.

'I have a reliable lawnmower but I don't go to work on it.'

'You could always get out and thumb a lift with your friend Fred.'

'That's a difficult choice. He has terrible taste in country and western music…anything involving heartbreak and tragic lives and he's happy. But if I stay with you, I might never walk again.' He grunted as he attempted to stretch out one leg in the confined space, while beside him she released her death grip on the steering wheel long enough to push a strand of hair behind her ear. Though her hair was almost dry now, the scent of her shampoo still permeated the enclosed space.

Seeing the action out of the corner of her eye, Chloe permitted herself a smirk, which she suddenly doused, feeling ashamed. Maybe she should have allowed him to take Eugenie; after all, he was her uncle.

Had she done the right thing?

The obvious thing would have been to check with Tatiana, but the thought vanished as a sharp pain made her wince and she moved her head to try and ease it. Reluctant to take her eyes off the road, especially as they had just passed a road sign that announced they were approaching a series of tight bends, she twisted her head sharply in the hope that the action would free the earring that had got tangled in her hair, but instead it just tugged harder, bringing tears to her eyes.

'Let me help…'

'I'm fine!' she snapped, unable to keep the note of panic from her voice, but then his long fingers brushed her neck and she flinched, desire clenching like a fist low in her belly.

It was crazy, she knew that, but recognising this fact did not lessen the physical impact, although she didn't have to embrace it!

'These things are lethal,' he said, lifting the weight of her hair to lessen the tug of the earring on her earlobe.

One element of her discomfort eased, Chloe stared straight ahead. Having her earlobe torn or her hair wrenched from her scalp would have been a hell of a lot more comfortable than feeling the warm waft of his breath on her cheek.

'They're one-offs, hand forged, the silversmith is a friend…' She spoke quickly, trying to distract herself.

She remembered reading somewhere that the ear had a lot of nerve endings, and all of hers were definitely screaming right now.

His brows drew together in a dark line of disapproval. 'Your earlobe is bleeding; you must have one hell of a high pain tolerance.'

An image floated into her head of her in hospital, repeatedly pressing the pain-relief button that for weeks had never left her hand. 'Not really.' Actually, not at all, she corrected silently, thinking of the lovely floating feeling after she'd pressed that button. The pain had still been there in the background, but she had been able to float above it.

She felt rather than saw him looking at her.

'I fainted when I had them pierced, although that might have been the...ouch, be careful!'

'Sorry. Hold on, I've almost finished...'

Almost was not soon enough. It seemed to take for ever for him to unwind the silver spiral. Her relief was so intense when he gave a grunt of triumph and leaned back in his seat that she would have punched the air in triumph had she not had such a tight hold of the steering wheel. Instead, she contented herself with heaving a huge sigh.

'Cool!' Eugenie, her earphones now dangling around her neck, leaned forward and snatched the silver spiral that dangled in her uncle's fingers. 'Where did you get them from? I'd love a pair.'

'A friend of mine makes them.'

The girl moved forward asking eagerly, 'Boyfriend?'

Aware that beside her Nik was now sitting with his head bent, fingers pressed to the bridge of his nose, she shook her head. 'Her name is Layla.' She slid Nik a sideways glance and lost the fight against her concern. 'Do you have a headache? There should be some painkillers in the glove box and a bottle of water—'

'I'm fine.' He let his hand fall from his face and exhaled slowly. The headaches hit without warning, but he never took medication. Perhaps he deserved the pain, not that it ever left him feeling cleansed of his sins.

'Uncle Nik is never ill. He's bulletproof *literally*,' she enthused with awe. 'He never got a scratch when he was working in war zones,' she chattered on, lifting the earring to her own ear and craning her neck to admire the effect in the rear-view mirror. 'Mum says the only thing he's got is survivor's guilt...' She stopped abruptly as her uncle caught her eye. 'Well she might have said something like that but I don't quite recall.'

Chloe couldn't see Nik's face but she could feel the raw tension vibrating off him.

In the back seat Chloe gave a sigh. 'How much longer? It's not mine,' she added when the audible sound of a vibrating phone suddenly echoed through the car.

Nik swore. His phone had fallen in the gap between the seats and, eyes still closed, he reached out a long arm for it.

Chloe gave a grunt as an elbow landed in her ribs.

'Sorry,' he muttered and, delving further, he gave a grunt of triumph as he managed to get his fingers around it.

'Your mother,' he said to Eugenie after reading the text message, before switching his attention to Chloe. 'Telling me not to bother, not to worry, that she arranged for someone else to pick you up… I contacted her when I started out but she must have sent this straight away. Looks like you're calling the shots here.'

Embarrassed, Chloe shook her head. 'You're Eugenie's uncle.'

'My sister must really trust you, but it might take me a while to work my way back into her good graces.'

'She'll understand.'

He huffed out a laugh. 'Why should she?'

'It's what family do. Where were you anyway? Not that I have any right to ask, I know…'

'My secretary has the flu and her stand-in hadn't charged my phone.' Louise always did it for him. 'And when I said I didn't want to be disturbed I made the mistake of assuming she would know that didn't include family emergencies. She let all Ana's calls go to the messaging service and when I tried to ring her back there was no signal. Then when I asked her why she hadn't put the calls through she just burst into tears.'

'Poor woman, she was probably scared of you.'

He gave a snort of disbelief. 'Then she'll be much happier working elsewhere.'

Chloe was shocked. 'You didn't sack her!'

'My father would have, whereas I'm a much more tolerant employer and, employment laws being what they are, I just shipped her back to the department she came from.'

'You're afraid to let anyone see you have a heart,' she charged and, expecting to see him discomfited by her discovery, she turned her head to look at him, but found a very different expression on his face.

She looked away quickly, but not before the need she had seen shining in his eyes had awoken the same feeling in her belly.

He shot a quick furtive glance in the back before announcing very quietly, 'I have a heart and I am very anxious to prove it to you.'

'It's not your heart you're offering me.'

'All parts of my anatomy are on offer.'

She shivered and stared ahead. 'I'm not discussing this with you now.'

'Later, then.'

A hissing sound of frustration escaped her clenched teeth.

'Chloe…'

Chloe started guiltily at the sound of the curious voice from the back seat. 'Do you live in a castle?'

'My sister does, but where my mum and dad live is more properly termed a fortified home.'

'Normal people do not live in castles.'

'Normal people do not have a rota for the shower because there's never enough hot water to go around! Trust me, we are not at all glamorous—in fact, we're just a little bit last century. I was at college before I ordered my first takeaway pizza.'

'God!' Eugenie breathed.

'Take the next exit,' Nik said suddenly as they approached the roundabout. 'You just went past it,' he said with an air of resignation.

'Roundabouts are made for going around.' On this note of logic she did so for the third time.

CHAPTER SEVEN

THEIR PROGRESS THROUGH the private airport was swift. Once they were on the plane one of the male attendants drew Nik apart as Chloe and Eugenie were seated.

Their conversation in rapid Greek lasted a few moments.

'I'm travelling up front,' he said to Chloe as he moved past her.

'Can I come too?' Eugenie cried in the act of unclipping her belt.

'You're grounded, or I'm assuming you will be, so no…behaving badly doesn't get rewarded, kiddo.' He flicked her nose affectionately with his finger and walked on, vanishing through the cockpit door.

'I'm going to get my pilot's licence as soon as I'm old enough. Uncle Nik got his when he was seventeen.'

Did that mean he was flying the plane now? Chloe wondered, tensing a little as the plane started taxiing; she was fine with flying but the take-off and landing always tied her stomach in knots.

Once they were in the air, Chloe accepted the offer of tea but refused anything to eat. Eugenie, who seemed to have recovered from her brush with the law, tucked into some hot beef sandwiches.

She finished and sighed in pleasure. Chloe pointed

to her chin and the teen wiped away the spot of relish there.

'So how long does it take to get to Spetses airport?'

The girl looked surprised by the question. 'Oh, there isn't an airport on the island. We land at the small private airport just on the mainland opposite and then we'll fly over on the helicopter.'

Questioning her decision not to simply hand Eugenie over to her uncle when she'd had the chance, Chloe took a sip of her tea. The return flight might not be as simple to organise as she had imagined.

On the helicopter trip over from the mainland Chloe sat next to Eugenie, who went into tour-guide mode the minute they took off. By the time they landed Chloe felt pretty well informed about the island of Spetses and its aristocratic heritage; she could have written a paper about the colourful mansions, the history of blockade running, its significance in the Napoleonic wars, and its long association with the master sailors.

While Chloe was being educated, Nik sat next to the pilot in the cockpit. The two men obviously knew one another pretty well and, with his sleeves rolled up and his dark hair tousled, Nik looked relaxed and very different from the man she remembered from that night in the bar.

Or for that matter from any time since.

It would be very easy, she mused, to let her defences down with this Nik. Just as well she was only here to chaperone Eugenie.

She turned her head at the sound of a phone ringing, struggling to make itself heard against the noise of the helicopter.

'It's Mum, for you,' Eugenie said, holding her own phone out for Chloe.

Chloe pressed the phone close against her ear, raising her voice above the background noise. 'Hello.'

'How can I ever thank you, Chloe?'

'No thanks required. I'm glad I could help.'

'How is she?'

'Fine.' She gave the worried-looking teenager a thumbs-up signal. 'I know a great deal about Spetses now. Did you know that Spetsiots were heroes of the War of Independence?' Chloe was pleased to hear the older woman laugh, then listened to her friend launch into another fulsome apology for imposing on her. 'Eugenie was no problem,' she said honestly, adding when Tatiana made sceptical noises, 'It was good practice for when I have my own children...' She lifted the phone away and waited for the static crackle to subside before shouting, 'I said it was good practice for when I have my own children!'

It was only when she realised the signal had cut out and she lowered the phone that she realised Nik was standing right beside her, so there was zero chance he'd not heard every word she'd said. But if she'd had any doubts his first comment dispelled them.

'Thinking of starting any time soon?'

Working on the assumption that if she ignored her blush he might not notice, she managed a small laugh. 'My body clock is not ticking too loudly just yet.'

'Just wanted to say, another five minutes and we'll be landing.' He turned away and moved back to the cockpit.

Once he'd gone, Chloe closed her eyes and pushed her fist against her mouth to stifle her loud groan. The other hand was pressed to her chest, where her heart was performing all sorts of life-threatening gymnastics.

It was ridiculous...bewildering and humiliating. Why did she react this way to him? What was it about him that seemed to tap into something inside her...a *need*...

a *hunger*…? An image of the answering hunger she had glimpsed in his eyes flashed into her head and her heart gave a heavy traitorous thud then started cantering crazily again.

She was complaining a hell of a lot, Chloe reflected, but if she really didn't want Nik chasing her, throwing temptation in her way, why hadn't she done something about it?

She could.

And she knew it. There was a fail-safe way, a one-hundred-per-cent-guaranteed method to make him back off at her disposal… It wasn't as if she'd even have to show him; just using the words would have the desired effect. She could casually throw into the conversation that she had some ugly scars and always would have.

In Nik's head she was perfect. She inhaled and lifted her chin, a little smile playing across her mouth. She had been perfect and she had taken it for granted. Strange how you didn't appreciate something until it was gone.

The smile vanished and along with it the enduring sadness; she'd been lucky and she knew it. She no longer wallowed in self-pity or asked herself why it had to happen to her.

She contented herself with imagining that one day there would be a man in her life; of course, he might not make her think of passionate, all-consuming sex the moment she saw him but there were other, more important things in a relationship…deeper things that lasted the test of time.

It would be nice to have both, but she was a realist and she knew few people were that lucky.

They had disembarked the helicopter when Nik joined them, his tall, broad-shouldered figure drawing glances

from the handful of fellow travellers that hovered nearby.
Watching his approach through the shield of her lashes,
Chloe had to admit it was not surprising he drew every
eye; he might be the most irritating man on the planet
with an ego to match, but he was also the most supremely
elegant and by far the sexiest.

'If you don't mind I'll hang around for a bit and hand
Eugenie over to her mum personally,' she said.

There was a slight time delay before he responded and
the enigmatic smile that briefly tugged at the corners of
his mouth troubled her, but as she'd been geared up for
an argument his non-reaction was a bit of an anticlimax.

'The car should be waiting; it's this way.' His gesture
invited Chloe to step ahead of him.

The waiting car was another long, shiny monster, and
as they approached the driver jumped out, a Greek version of Fred.

Nik called out to him in Greek, the man called something back in response and walked around to the passenger door, but before he had a chance to open it an
open-topped Jeep driven at speed drew up behind it.
Chloe stepped back from the cloud of dust it threw up,
but before it had even settled Tatiana, wearing a cotton
shirt over a tee shirt and shorts, her shiny bell of dark
hair pulled back off her make-up-free face in a severe
ponytail, jumped out.

Chloe felt the teenager beside her tense and heard
her sharp intake of breath, before she stuck out her chin
and quavered out defiantly, 'Before you say anything—'

'How could you?' her mother ground out.

'I...' Without warning the youngster's belligerence
vanished and she started to sob heartbrokenly. A second
later she was in her mother's arms being told everything
would be all right. Chin resting on her daughter's head,

a shiny-eyed Tatiana shot a look of gratitude in Chloe's direction.

'We are so, so grateful to you, Chloe.'

'It's fine. I'm glad I could help.'

The image of Chloe sniffing into a tissue at the scene in front of her while she blinked hard made something tighten in Nik's chest, but he ignored it and drawled out sarcastically, 'Are you going to cry too?'

'I am not crying!' Chloe snapped back, blowing her nose hard.

'Do you mind travelling back with Nik?' Tatiana asked, glancing at her brother for the first time. 'I could do with talking one to one with this one.' She kissed the top of her daughter's head. 'Alone.'

Chloe minded very much. In fact, the idea of sharing the back seat of the limo with Nik filled her with horror, but she hid her feelings behind a smile and shook her head.

'Actually I don't mind waiting here to catch a lift straight back to the mainland.'

Tatiana looked blank and then shocked. 'You don't think we'd let you go straight back, do you? Heavens, you're here as our guest for as long as you like.'

'I couldn't possibly stay.' Chloe tried to sound firm, but all she sounded was tired as she lifted a hand to her ticcing eyelid.

'Perhaps Chloe has other places to be.' And other people she'd rather be with, he thought sourly, and the silent addition caused the line between his dark brows to deepen.

'You can't fly straight back,' Tatiana argued.

'Not unless she sprouts wings,' Nik inserted drily. 'Marco is refuelling the jet and then heading straight off to Düsseldorf.'

He slid effortlessly into Greek as he added something to Tatiana, who nodded in agreement.

'Well, that settles it, then, you'll stay with us…at least for tonight…to let me say thank you…?'

'But your grandmother is unwell…' Chloe began searching desperately for a legitimate reason to refuse their hospitality, or at least a reason that wasn't, *I really can't be around your brother because I don't want to be reminded of something I want but can't have, and shouldn't even want to begin with!*

It sounded convoluted even in her own head, but then so was her relationship with Nik. Except she didn't have a relationship with Nik. She closed one eye as the eyelid tic started up again.

'She's a lot better.'

'Yaya is a tough old bird,' Nik said gruffly, the warmth in his voice when he spoke of his grandmother unmistakeable.

And I'm sure there are some serial killers who love their grannies too, Chloe reminded herself as she fought hard against any lowering of the levels of antagonism that she felt were essential to maintain. Bad enough that she lusted after him, liking him as well would be too, *too* much to take.

'Well, that's settled, you'll follow us,' Tatiana announced.

Chloe, who was pretty sure that she hadn't agreed to anything, not that that seemed to bother anyone in the Latsis family, opened her mouth to protest but Tatiana was telling Eugenie to throw her bag in the back. 'Or, better still, Nik can take the scenic route and show Chloe…oh, no!' Her eyes slid past her brother and her enthusiasm morphed into dismay. 'Get in the car,' she said sharply to her daughter, then, after adding something urgent-sounding in Greek to Nik, she climbed in beside the girl and slipped back into English, saying hastily, 'Sorry, Nik, but I don't want Eugenie to get caught up in this.'

Nik, who had turned to follow the direction his sister was looking, nodded. 'You get going. Chloe, get in the car.'

Tatiana was already starting up the engine and Chloe couldn't help turning round to see what had caused her friend to rush off.

There was a woman approaching them, about fifty feet or so away now, who was by turns running then walking, or rather stumbling, towards them, her uncoordinated gait suggesting she'd been drinking.

Chloe didn't have a clue what was happening, but she was the only one, it seemed. Even the driver, who had murmured something in Greek to Nik and got back behind the wheel after receiving a nod in response, seemed to be in the know, but she did recognise an order when she heard one. She told herself she wouldn't have obeyed him on principle, even if she hadn't been eaten up with curiosity to discover what was going on!

'I said—' Nik began, still not looking at her, but Chloe could feel the tension coming off him in waves. His taut profile looked grey and grim, and the muscles along his clenched jawline were set like iron.

'I heard you, which isn't the same as obeying you,' she said calmly.

He turned his dark head then, flashing her a look of seething impatience, and ground out, 'I really don't have time for this now.'

The woman was close enough now for Chloe to see that she was correct in surmising that the woman was drunk; she could smell the alcohol from yards away. So, it seemed, could Nik, who set his shoulders and turned back with an air of forced resignation as he waited until she was within hearing distance.

'Hello, Helena.'

The woman was probably pretty when she remembered to comb her hair and her eyes weren't lost in black-smudged circles of mascara that had been washed by tears running in dark rivers down her face.

The sound coming from her was half sob, half breathless pant as she walked straight past Chloe, her attention totally focused on Nik, her eyes burning with hatred.

Nik didn't move an inch as the woman staggered up to him, glaring.

'I wake up every morning wishing you were dead!' she slurred. 'I wish I was dead!'

The mixture of venom and despair in her voice sent an ice-cold chill down Chloe's spine but Nik just stood there. What made it all the more bizarre was that he didn't look angry, he looked…sad, compassionate and, most telling of all, guilty.

Chloe's imagination went into overdrive. What had he done to this woman?

'I'm so sorry,' he said finally.

The woman's face screwed up and an anguished high-pitched shriek left her open mouth as she pulled back her arm and aimed a closed-fisted blow that made contact with Nik's cheek.

Chloe gasped in alarm, her hand going to her own cheek, but he just stood there and continued to do so as the woman started to pound his chest with her flailing fists, shrieking hysterically the whole time.

As the frenzied attack showed no sign of abating, although God knew where the woman got the strength from, the shock that had held Chloe immobile abated.

'No!' She wasn't even aware that she'd voiced her pro-test or had moved forward until Nik looked at her and moved his head in a negative motion.

It was the total absence of anger in his austere, strong-boned face that hit her, that and the profound sadness. It added a deep ache of empathy to the already present confusion and horror—too many layers of emotion for Chloe to comprehend.

His headshake coincided with the woman running out of steam and she finally slumped her head against Nik's chest, weeping in a way that hurt to listen to.

After a moment Nik lifted a tentative hand to her head, smoothing the tangles of hair down in a gentle stroking motion.

'I'll take her.'

Her focus totally on the tableau before her, Chloe hadn't heard the approach of a man wearing a harassed expression. 'Come on, honey, that's it. I didn't know where you'd got to.' The woman lifted her head slightly at the sound of his voice.

'The bastard should be dead!'

For all the reaction Nik showed to this venomous dec-laration he might as well have been, the skin drawn tight across the prominent bones on his face giving them the appearance of stone.

The stranger took the weeping woman, who reminded Chloe of a puppet whose strings had been severed, and pulled her against him, wrapping a supportive arm around her ribs as he half dragged, half lifted her away from Nik. 'Sorry, you know she doesn't mean it; she doesn't know what she's saying.' The woman continued to weep uncontrollably as she slumped up against him.

The stranger looked from the woman he held to Nik with an expression that brought a lump to Chloe's throat. 'It's not always this bad, but it's particularly hard today…'

Nik nodded, his face still granite.

'She's been drinking all morning. I thought maybe being here with family would help.' He stopped and shook his head. 'Bad idea. I stopped for gas and she must have seen you… I had no idea that you'd be here.'

'Neither did I. It was an unexpected visit. Is there anything I can do…?'

The woman's head lifted at that. 'Haven't you done enough already?' she slurred, before pressing her face back into the man's shoulder as he turned and began to walk away down the road.

Nik watched for a few moments before he looked at Chloe. Some of the rigidity had gone from his tense posture, but not the lines of tension bracketing his mouth or the shadow in his eyes. 'Have you seen enough now?'

She flinched, but didn't react to the unspoken accusation, which was both harsh and unjust, that she had taken some voyeuristic pleasure at the scene she had witnessed.

'Are you all right?' she asked, wincing inside at the crassness of her words, and she wasn't surprised when he just flashed her a look.

The muscles along his taut jaw tensed as he turned away. He didn't want or deserve Chloe's sympathy.

Are you *all right*? she'd asked. Well, he was certainly more all right than the man who would have been thirty-five today if he'd lived. An image floated in his head, of Charlie grinning as he delivered the punchline of one of his terrible jokes, Charlie looking guilty when he explained this would be the last time they worked together because he was letting his lovely Helena finally make an honest man of him.

Nik remembered feeling pleased that he'd managed to

guilt Charlie into one last assignment, though he hadn't succeeded in planting a seed of doubt in his friend's mind when he'd predicted that Charlie wouldn't be able to live without the adrenaline buzz.

You know when it's time to quit, Charlie had said.

CHAPTER EIGHT

CHLOE WAS LEFT standing there when without a word Nik got into the front seat of the car beside the driver. She blew out a breath and for once in her life wished someone would tell her what to do or at least what to think.

A reel of the terrible scene still played in her head. She had only witnessed it and she felt shaken and physically sick; she couldn't begin to imagine what Nik was feeling and she had the distinct impression he wouldn't be telling her any time soon.

She gave her head a tiny shake and slid into the back seat. In the front Nik was speaking to the driver, issuing instructions, she assumed, but she didn't know for sure because it was literally all Greek to her.

Apart from that, they drove in absolute stony silence. A couple of times Chloe cleared her throat to ask how long it would take to reach their destination or for that matter where they were heading but chickened out at the last moment. So silence reigned until about maybe ten minutes into the journey when Nik suddenly spoke in Greek once again.

The driver responded in the same language and pulled onto the side of the road. The car had barely stopped when Nik flung himself out, and, leaving the door open, he strode off into the scrub at the side of the deserted road up an incline, immediately disappearing from view as he went down the other side.

So what did she do now?

Did she sit here and wait, or did she follow him…? She caught the eyes of the driver in the rear-view mirror, and his expression was sympathetic but he just shrugged.

'I think I'll stretch my legs,' she said, not sure he understood her or if he'd try and prevent her from leaving the car.

He didn't.

Grateful her shoes only had moderate heels, she stumbled her way across the steep slope of the rough ground, waking up tiny little things in the undergrowth as she picked out a path between the rocks, following roughly—she hoped—the route she had seen Nik take. The linen trousers she wore were of a loose style that ended mid-calf, protecting most of her legs from the razor-sharp ends of the long tough grass that poked through the rocks. But her calves already ached; the incline was steeper than it looked.

She had lost track of time today but the sun overhead was still high in the sky that was a uniform blue. It was very hot and she became uncomfortably aware of rivulets of sweat trickling down her back. Pausing to rest, she turned her head to make sure that she had not lost sight of the car.

Getting lost really would add the finishing touch to this day. Nik had seemed to vanish from view after only moments, so either he was astonishingly fit or she had somehow gone off course and attacked the slope at a wider angle.

Probably both, she decided, pausing again, this time just below the top of the incline. She ran her tongue over her lips; they felt dry and she was thirsty. Without the crunch of her footsteps, she could make out a distant whooshing sound above the softer constant buzzing of the bees that smothered the sweet-smelling wild thyme that filled the air with a deep sweet fragrance.

She closed her eyes and inhaled.

What are you doing? she asked herself wearily. *So you find him—what then? Does he strike you as a man who needs a shoulder to cry on?* Like a wounded animal, he'd gone away to lick his wounds; he clearly wanted privacy and she was going to crash it. It had seemed like a good idea at the time—but *why* exactly?

She puffed out a gusty sigh. This was starting to feel like a very bad idea, but, torn between turning back and pushing on, she hesitated only momentarily before tackling the last few feet of slope.

As she crowned the hill her efforts were rewarded by a view that made her catch her breath. In contrast to the steep slope she had just climbed, the other side was a very gentle incline, the vegetation spare where it grew out of the sandy ground, but she barely noticed as her eyes went to the horseshoe curve of a bay ringed by rocks. Alternating stripes of pebbles and silvery sand ran down to the water. Beyond the gentle waves that frothed white as they broke on the beach, the blue of the sea deepened, interspersed with iridescent swirling areas of deep green and dark turquoise before it met the sky.

The view was so unexpected and so soul-soothingly beautiful that for a long moment all she did was stare, but the moment of spiritual peace shattered into a million shards as her eyes reached the figure standing at the farthest point of the beach before the rocks rose up out of the water.

Nik stood, his tall, remote figure a dark silhouette against the backdrop of bright blue. The strength of the empathetic sympathy that swelled in her chest took her by surprise, and, without pausing to examine it or the need to be with him right now, she began to jog towards him, the downward journey on the smooth, gentle slope far less taxing than the climb up it.

Once she reached the sand she slowed until finally pausing to remove her shoes. Swinging them from the fingers of one hand, she continued slowing as she picked her way across the bands of smooth stones that were sandwiched between the wider bands of powdery sand.

The closer she got to the water, the more she felt the breeze, warm but very welcome as it lifted the damp strands of hair from her neck. She stopped a few feet away from Nik, suddenly unsure what to do next, which seemed to suggest she'd ever known. The thought that she actually knew what she was doing or had any sort of plan when it came to Nik tugged her lips into an ironic, self-mocking smile.

Blind instinct had got her this far and if she had any sense, Chloe reflected, it would take her straight back the way she had come.

She never had had much sense.

'It's very beautiful.'

He didn't react to her comment, so she assumed he already knew she was there. She took a few more steps towards him, in the shade cast by the rocks, which meant it was pleasantly cooler underfoot. But not as cool as standing ankle deep in the water, which Nik was doing in his beautiful handmade leather shoes, although he seemed utterly oblivious.

'Don't worry; I'm not going to ask you if you're all right.'

'Are you moving on to *you probably deserve it*?' he tossed back, thinking grimly that if so, she was right.

Digging his hands deep into the pockets of his tailored trousers, he stared sightlessly in front of him, eyes narrowed at the horizon, trying to remember what it felt like not to carry this constant weight of guilt around with him.

He swivelled around, his short hair catching the breeze as a sudden spurt of stronger wind made it stick up in sexy tufts.

As their eyes connected it struck Chloe with the force of a blow that his expression was exactly the same as the first time she had seen him, dark and tortured. The sight made her heart squeeze in her chest.

The expression he caught on her face stung his pride into painful life, but he didn't want her concern, genuine or otherwise. He didn't deserve concern, and certainly not from her… Hell, life had been easier when she had been filed in his memory banks under the heading of a typical shallow, narcissistic socialite. He had used her once to distract himself from his past and he was doing the same thing now; why didn't she seem able to recognise a lost cause when she saw one?

'No, I don't think you deserved it.' Chloe's first thought had been that she was seeing an ex-lover he'd done the dirty on seeking revenge, and to her shame she had been prepared to be the cheering squad, but the impression had only lasted for seconds as it had almost immediately become obvious that she was seeing something much more complicated.

An expression she couldn't interpret flickered across his face. 'Well, I do.' He flung the words at her like a challenge.

'You must have done something really bad, then,' she said calmly.

A sense of deep self-loathing rushed through him with the force of a forest fire. His chest heaving, he heard a roar inside his skull before the feelings he'd kept locked inside for years finally exploded out. 'I killed a man— my best friend.'

'I'm sorry.'

His head came up with a snap.

'Sorry!' he echoed as he began to walk out of the water towards her with slow deliberate steps. Confession was supposed to be good for the soul but he didn't feel good or cleansed; he felt furious with himself for losing control, especially in front of the last person he wanted to see…see what?

The question brought him to a halt when he was six inches away from her, so close that she had actually closed her eyes to shut out the awe-inspiring image he presented.

She could feel the heat of his body through the narrow gap between them but it was nothing compared to the anger and frustration that the air was practically coloured with that rippled off him in almost tangible waves.

He dragged a frustrated hand roughly across his forehead, but as he scanned her face for a clue to what she was thinking his own expression was cloaked. 'Did you hear what I just said?'

'You said that you killed your best friend. I have no idea what actually happened but, as they put people in jail for murder and you are not there, I'm assuming—'

He interrupted her, speaking through clenched teeth. 'He is dead.' His shoulders sagged as the anger drained away leaving a desolate hollowness inside his chest. 'I am here.'

The emptiness in his flat delivery brought an ache to her throat. Watching him through her lashes, Chloe struggled to hide the dangerous rise of emotions that made her chest tight.

'I know, Nik, I'm not deaf or blind.'

The hand he was dragging back and forth through his hair stilled at the mild reproof. He shot her a look and wondered for the tenth time in as many seconds why, if he was going to have some sort of meltdown, he had to do it in front of this woman who did not seem to have any concept of personal boundaries.

'I am not one of your charity projects!' he snarled, the very idea offending his masculine pride deeply.

Taken aback by the outraged charge, she just blinked.

'Has it ever occurred to you that people who put so much of themselves into worthwhile causes are compensating for something that is missing in their own lives?'

Anger at this outrageous statement replaced her bewilderment. Face flushed, she compressed her lips and arched a brow. 'Let me guess what you think is missing in my life—a man,' she drawled. 'Why do all men assume that they are essential for a woman's happiness and fulfilment? If there is anything missing in my life I'll get myself a dog. They're far more reliable.'

Eyelids half lowered so that all she could see was a glitter of dark brown, he let the silence that developed between them stretch out taut before breaking it with a thoughtful, 'I obviously touched a nerve there.'

He'd managed to change the subject from his own trauma, she realised, which she was assuming had been his intention all along. 'Your friend is dead and I'm sorry. You might feel responsible, you might *be* responsible in some way, I have no idea, but I do know for definite that you didn't kill anyone.'

'How can you possibly know that?' he jeered. 'You don't know me.'

She found herself wondering if anyone did. Did he push the world away or was it just her? 'Who was that woman?' she asked quietly.

He turned to look at the sea again. 'Her name is Helena and she was engaged to Charlie, my best friend.'

'Do you mind if I sit down?' Without waiting for him to respond, she brushed a piece of silvered driftwood to one side with a foot, set down her shoes and sat down on the sand, stretching her long legs in front of her, crossing them at the ankle.

Nik turned as she was leaning back on her hands, just as the breeze lifted her hair, blowing it across her face before it settled in a fine silky mesh down her back except for a few errant strands that stuck to her face. Wrinkling her nose, she pursed her lips and huffed them away.

There was something about her beauty that could touch him in a way he hadn't known he was capable of even at a time like this. He made an effort to resurrect a scowl but gave up on the attempt, deciding instead to sit down beside her.

'Charlie was a cameraman, the best there was. People often forget when they see some correspondent standing there in the middle of a gun battle that there's a man behind the camera too, taking the same risks without the same recognition. We'd worked together for two years in the sort of environment where…well, let's just say that you get to see the best and worst of people.'

Chloe glanced sideways at his face…and wondered what he was seeing as he stared out to sea. For a while there was nothing but the hissing sound of the waves breaking a few feet away, and she had the impression he had forgotten she was there.

When he finally spoke his deep, strong voice held a rusty crack.

'He met Helena through me. Her family are part of the London Greek expat community too, but like us they have relatives who still live here on the island. When I was a kid staying with my grandparents I used to hang around with her brothers. That was one of them with her back at the airport—Andreos. Helena used to tag along with us,' he recalled. 'A nice kid.'

And the nice kid had grown up to be a beautiful young woman with everything to live for, except now she didn't want to live.

'She and Charlie hit it off straight away. I was surprised as they were total opposites. Charlie was an extrovert and she was thoughtful, quiet and...' He swallowed hard, the muscles in his brown throat working.

It really hurt her to see him struggle. 'So it was a whirlwind romance?'

'Actually more of a slow burner,' Nik recalled. 'They had an on-off thing that lasted eighteen months or so, the sort of thing that often fizzles out. But then something changed... I don't know what it was, but they got engaged.'

She watched as he silently wrestled with the emotions inside him. Finally, she prompted softly, 'You were surprised.'

He turned his head, his dark eyes glittering with self-contempt as he contradicted her. 'I was irritated. We were a team and Charlie had announced that he was quitting and moving to a safe job where there was no risk of being kidnapped or shot.

'It was me who persuaded him to take that one last assignment together. I was convinced that he'd realise that he couldn't survive without the adrenaline rush, that he'd resent Helena if he gave up a life he loved for her. Oh, I was a *really* caring friend.' Nik squeezed his eyes closed, still seeing Charlie's dead eyes, his nostrils flaring at the remembered metallic iron scent of blood. 'So it did turn out to be his last assignment after all, and he was only there because of me.'

Chloe swallowed the lump in her throat and turned her head to hide the tears that filled her eyes before picking up a handful of sand and letting the silver particles slide through her fingers, watching them vanish into the billions of identical grains. Risking a look at him through her lashes, she saw his expression was completely remote as though he'd retreated to another place entirely.

She didn't attempt to react to his words until she had full control of her emotions again. Nik didn't want her tears or her sympathy; he'd made that obvious. The only thing he wanted from her was her body, which rather begged the question as to why she was getting involved with his problems, seeing as it was the one thing she couldn't give him.

'What happened was a tragedy.' She winced at the triteness of her comment. 'But how exactly is it your fault?'

He vented a hard laugh and looked at her incredulously. 'Have you listened to a word I said?' He still didn't know why he'd said those words—any of them.

He was already regretting it.

He was a private man living in a world where people were tripping over themselves to expose their innermost thoughts and feelings, mostly for public scrutiny. You couldn't turn on a television or a computer, or open a newspaper, without finding some celebrity *revealing all*, but the idea of turning your personal tragedies and failings into entertainment for the masses made his blood run cold.

Getting to his feet, he brushed the sand off his clothes

and stood there looking down at her. 'Tatiana will be wondering what has happened to us.'

Chloe uncrossed her legs and raised herself gracefully to her feet. 'Do you think you're honouring your friend in some way by beating yourself up for being alive? The way you talk about him, it doesn't make it sound as though your friend Charlie would have approved.'

'Helena might disagree.'

'Come on, you're an intelligent man—it doesn't take a professional to see that the poor woman needs help. She's attacking you because she wants someone to blame.' She shook her head in disbelief as he turned and walked away. 'Nik!' Cursing softly under her breath, she picked up her shoes from the sand and ran after him. 'Fine,' she said, falling breathlessly into step beside him. 'Deal with it by ignoring the problem. That always works, doesn't it? It's very adult of you!' How the hell could you help a man who was too stubborn to admit he needed it?

He stopped and swung around to face her, feeling a twisting feeling in his chest as he looked down into her angry face. 'I did not invite you into my head, so stay out!'

'Or what?' she charged, pitying the woman who one day actually wanted to reach him, whose heart ached to help him.

He reached out and cupped a hand around the back of her head, drawing her up onto her toes until their lips were a whisper apart. 'Or this.'

Her gasp of shock was lost in the warmth of his mouth as it came crashing down hard on hers. He kissed her like a man starving for the taste, kissed her as though he'd drain her. One big hand slid down the curve of her back, coming to rest on the smooth curve of her bottom, dragging her up against the grinding hardness of his erection.

His free hand moved to the back of her head to hold her face up to his as the kiss continued on and on until her head was spinning.

Her body arched against him as her shoes fell from her nerveless fingers. Mouths still sealed, they took a few staggering steps together as the ferocity of their desire intensified. Chloe's knees were on the point of buckling when without warning he suddenly let her go.

She slid down to the sand and sat there, arms wrapped around herself as she looked up at him, her big eyes wide and shocked. Bleeding control from every nerve ending, Nik's hands clenched by his sides… He wanted to shed the pain, lose himself inside her—but he knew he would be using her in exactly the same way he'd used other women…using sex to gain a few moments' oblivion.

Why couldn't he bring himself to use Chloe?

'*That's* my way of dealing with it, *agape mou*,' he told her harshly, staring at the pouting line of her lips, which were still swollen from his kisses. 'So if you're feeling sorry for me and fancy a bit of pity sex…?'

Even as she winced at the deliberate crudity of his suggestion, shameful excitement clenched low in her belly.

'It was just a thought,' he drawled.

She watched him stalk away, wondering how anyone managed to look rock-hard, tough and vulnerable all at the same time, but then he was a man of massive contradictions. Her energy levels felt as though they'd moved into negative territory as she began to slowly slog her way through the sand after him. It wasn't until the car came into view with Nik standing beside it looking impatient that she realised what the tight feeling in her chest was— fear. She had never felt more scared in her life, which was saying something.

She couldn't be in love with Nik. She lifted her chin in defiance at the idea… She *refused* to be in love with him.

As she approached he opened the back door for her.

She tipped her head in acknowledgment and murmured sarcastically, 'What a gentleman,' before slamming the door behind her just in case he thought he was going to ride in the back with her.

CHAPTER NINE

'DO YOU LIKE IT?'

'It's beautiful,' Chloe said honestly as she walked around the room that Eugenie had guided her to. 'What a view,' she exclaimed, walking over to the open French doors. Three steps away was the infinity pool and beyond that the sea.

'It used to be a little tiny cottage, and Granny was born here,' the teenager confided. 'She was poor. That must be awful, I think. When she married Grandpa he wanted to knock it down but she wouldn't let him so he built around it. There wasn't any beach here then, so he brought the sand and made one.'

'What about the big place on the hill?' It had looked Venetian and just gorgeous set against a backdrop of pines.

'Oh, we own that too. Grandpa bought it but Yaya wouldn't live in it and he preferred modern so…' She gave a shrug that made Chloe think of her uncle. 'It's pretty much falling down now.'

'That's sad,' Chloe said, glancing through the doors of a walk-in closet, realising that she didn't have even so much as a toothbrush with her.

The girl seemed to read her thoughts. 'Don't worry. Mum will organise you some stuff.'

'No, really—'

'It's fine. She has closets full of samples.' She looked at Chloe with envy. 'They wouldn't fit anyone else here. Are you sure you won't join us for dinner?'

Chloe resisted the pleading tone and gave a firm shake of her head, adding, 'I'm really whacked.' She escorted Eugenie to the door and closed it behind her reluctant-to-leave guest.

She released a sigh and leaned back against the wall, willing the images that were flashing through her head to stop or at least slow down because they made her dizzy.

Finally summoning the energy to kick off her shoes, she flopped onto the bed and lay there staring at the fan that was whirring silently above her head.

She had pleaded exhaustion when she had been given the option of a tray in her room, which suggested she looked as bad as she felt. The bone-deep weariness felt as if it were crushing her; even lifting a hand to her head was an effort, as was closing her eyes. But when she'd managed it, opening them again was just not an option.

She suspected her weariness was as much emotional as physical. Lack of sleep was the reason, she decided, unwilling to admit the truth even to herself.

She touched her lips, a silent sigh rippling through her body as she remembered the moment Nik's eyes had dropped to her mouth and she'd known he was thinking about kissing her... Had he been able to feel how much she wanted him to? Oh, God, why was she even wasting her time thinking about it? It was just a damned kiss; there was nothing deep and meaningful about it!

She sighed, thinking, *I'll get up in a minute and shower the day and the memories away...* There was no hurry.

* * *

Fighting her way out of sleep was like fighting her way through layers of gauze, convinced when she finally broke through the veil of sleep that she had heard someone crying out.

She lay there listening but it was silent except for the sounds of the night coming in through the open door.

Night!

She sat up abruptly, looking around the room. It was dark but not inky black, as the sky outside the door was tinged faintly with red. She reached for the lamp switch and found it, illuminating the room and revealing a tray on a table, the food covered by domes.

She swung her legs over the side of the bed and the first thing her glance lighted on was a full-length silk kaftan hanging on a hook of the door to the bathroom. She smiled as she got stiffly to her feet. She picked up her phone and glanced at the time, her eyes widening as she saw it was five-thirty in the morning!

She picked up one of the domes and looked at the food, but she was not hungry enough to be tempted by the sad, cold remains of what had, she had no doubt, been a delicious meal.

There were more clothes neatly folded and stacked on the shelves in the wardrobe and hanging on padded hangers. Tatiana had clearly crept in while she was asleep like a petite Greek Santa. She yawned and stretched, wondering about Greek Christmas traditions.

She spent a long time in the shower and emerged feeling half human. Laying out a towel on the bed, she sat down and began rubbing the oil one of her physiotherapists had recommended into the tight tissues of her scars with light but firm strokes.

Maybe its effects were just a placebo but it smelt good

and, while it was no magic cure-all, her skin always felt more supple after she'd applied it. She had got into the habit of carrying it in her handbag.

She waited for it to dry before she put on the kaftan, enjoying the feel of the silk against her skin. She lifted an arm and performed a swishing motion, smiling. Tatiana really was talented. Drawn by the smells and sounds of early morning, she wandered to the open door and pulled aside the mosquito curtain that someone had pulled across while she slept.

Eyes closed, she breathed in deeply before she walked out, the soft scented breeze blowing the kaftan against her body. A tiny lizard disturbed by her tread emerged from a crack in the stone and vanished beneath the glossy, well-trimmed shrubbery.

The swimming pool lit by underwater lights that reflected the mosaic tiles drew her like a magnet; she loved water. She'd learnt to swim at school and if she had been prepared to put in the sort of dedication that involved a relentless early morning training schedule and no social life she might have been able to compete at a high level.

Physical ability and natural talent were no good unless you had the dedication that went with them and Chloe didn't…but she really loved to swim. Apart from the times she had stayed with her sister, as camera lenses and shocked stares were really not an issue in the royal palace, she had not ventured into the water since the accident.

She liked to think that one day she would be brave enough to swim in a public pool and not care about the stares, but that day had not yet come.

Walking to the edge, she hitched the folds of silk around her knees and sat down, dangling her feet in the warm water, thinking about the lovely feeling of it on her skin.

It was tempting to go in for a swim, it really was... Who was around to see?

Nik had been swimming lengths for ten minutes, pushing his body to the limit in an attempt to wash away the personal devils left in his head after the nightmare had visited him yet again. He neared the wall at the deep end, flipped over and had lifted his head to gulp in air when he saw Chloe approach the pool through a watery haze.

He paused, his head just breaking the surface as he trod water, the shimmering image solidifying. He was unable to take his eyes off her as she walked towards the water, the thin floor-length robe she wore blowing tight against her, outlining every supple curve of her long, luscious body.

She obviously wasn't wearing a stitch underneath.

The sound of blood drumming in his ears became deafening as in his head he saw her opening the garment and slipping it off, then standing there naked on the side before diving in... All she actually did was trail her toes in the water, pretty tame by most standards, but Nik felt his dormant libido once more kick into life—hard.

He took a deep breath and slid silently down under the surface of the water.

Her dreamy thoughts drifted as she continued to inscribe circles in the water with her toes.

The sheer unexpectedness of the sudden tug on her foot drew a shrill shriek from her throat. She pulled against the pressure and scooted back, fighting against the restraint and kicking out wildly.

There was a grunt of pain followed by a curse and she was suddenly free. She had curled both legs up protectively against her body when Nik's sleek dark head appeared, water streaming down his face.

'What the hell did you think you were doing? You nearly gave me a heart attack!' she accused shakily.

'I was swimming…it's good; come in and join me.'

The invitation sent a slam of hormonal heat through her body. She shook her head, her heart thudding like a metronome as she stared at him.

'Fair enough.' It took him two lazy strokes to reach the side. 'Then I'll join you.' Hands flat on the mosaic tiles, he casually heaved himself out of the pool, pausing for a moment on the balls of his feet before straightening up to his full impressive height.

Chloe had no control over her stare, and her skin prickled with heat as her helpless gaze travelled up the length of his long legs, taking in the ridges of his flat belly and broad, hair-roughened chest. His shoulders were muscle packed and powerful but he wasn't bulky. There was a streamlined strength to him, no excess flesh at all to blur the symmetry. Each individual muscle stood out defined and perfect beneath the surface of his gleaming golden skin.

Her eyes reached his face and his white grin flashed, making him look like a very smug fallen angel as he lifted one hand and rubbed it hard across his hair, causing more water to stream down his face.

He tilted his head to one side in an enquiring attitude. 'Sure I can't tempt you?' asked her personal embodiment of temptation, the gleam in his eyes suggesting that this was no secret to him.

Even though it was frustrating it was also true— she had zero control over the colour that rushed to her cheeks—but she refused to drop her gaze, or was it she couldn't escape the grip of his black, heavy-lidded stare?

Her insides clenched as she ran her tongue across the outline of her dry lips.

'No, you can't,' she lied, struggling to inject a note of amusement into her response. 'But don't let me stop you.' Hearing the quiver of something near to desperation in her own voice, she half turned and gave an elaborate yawn. 'I was just going back inside.'

He reached for a towel that was slung over a chair, rubbing it over his dripping hair, then blotting the moisture off his face. 'You really should take a swim.' His eyes went to the wet hair that was slicked back to reveal her smooth, high forehead and perfect pure profile. 'Or have you already?'

She lifted a self-conscious hand, dragging it down the damp surface of her wet hair. 'I showered.'

He swallowed, the muscles in his brown throat visibly working, a nerve spasmodically clenching in his lean cheek as his darkened eyes drifted slowly over her face, then down over the soft curves of her lush body outlined beneath the folds of iridescent fabric, his imagination peeling away the fabric, seeing the water streaming down her smooth skin.

It took Chloe a few moments to realise that the noise she could hear was her own breathing, as she struggled to breathe through the sexual tension that hung in the air.

She wasn't sure that Nik was breathing at all. He just stood there, the bands of dull colour running along the slashing angles of his cheekbones emphasising their razor-edged prominence as the moments ticked away. Each passing second made her heart beat faster until she could feel the thuds vibrating throughout her entire body.

'I… I need to go.' Her voice sounded as though it was coming from a long way away.

'Why?'

'I need to book my flight.'

'It's six a.m.'

'Online.'

'Eugenie will be disappointed; she was looking forward to showing you the sights.'

'I need to get back.' There was a hint of a plea in her voice.

He shrugged and looped the towel around his middle, drawing her attention once again to his flat, ribbed belly and the thin directional line of dark hair that vanished into the waistband of the black shorts he wore. 'Are you sure you won't join me for a swim? It'll take the edge off it.'

She didn't make the mistake of asking what *it* was.

How would he react, she wondered, if she pulled the kaftan open and stood there scars and all? *Why are you even asking the question?* she asked herself.

He's not interested in your heart or soul; he only wants the beautiful body—or the one he thinks you still have.

'I don't have a swimsuit.'

His eyes dropped. 'You've never skinny-dipped?'

She stiffened and lowered her lashes over an expression that tugged his dark brows into a straight interrogative line above his hooded stare... *Sadness* seemed an inexplicable reaction for her to have.

'Are you afraid of the water?' he asked gently.

Her eyes slid longingly over the still surface of the pool, but she shook her head.

'Do you often swim at this time of the morning? Are you in training or something?' She'd only been changing the subject, but now that she'd thrown the idea out there she found it wasn't actually a struggle to see him competing in a triathlon or something; he had the body, the fitness levels and undoubtedly the competitive streak it took for such an endurance event.

'No, I usually run.' He bent and picked up a second towel before rubbing his still-wet hair vigorously with it.

'So you are in training?'

He dropped the towel. 'I don't sleep.'

The confession evoked a rush of sympathy in Chloe.

Midway through her hospitalisation, when the heavy doses of analgesia she'd been prescribed for pain had been reduced, she'd suffered badly from insomnia. Though it was not a time she thought about often, choosing instead to focus on the fact she had survived, the experience had left her wary of taking even an aspirin and she'd gained a personal appreciation of the negative impact insomnia could have on a person's daily life.

'I suppose it's hard to switch off sometimes.' *Especially when you have chosen to carry around guilt the size of a planet... Not your problem, Chloe,* she reminded herself, rejecting the stab of empathy that made her chest tighten. People who deserved sympathy were those who actually tried to do something about a problem. 'I settle for warm milk—not very cutting edge, I know, but that usually does the trick for me.'

He gave a sudden hard laugh. 'I don't want to sleep.'

'You mean you don't *need* much sleep?' He fitted the profile of the driven alpha type you generally associated with surviving on two or three hours a night.

'I mean I have nightmares.' The hand he was dragging across his face stilled, shock flickering in his hooded gaze as he asked himself why the hell he had just told her that.

His nightmares were something he had never discussed with anyone. Did he suffer from some form of post-traumatic stress disorder? He was sure there were any number of so-called experts who would be happy to tell him. In Nik's view the label didn't matter. Sharing was not his style and the idea of being an object of pity was something that he rejected on a visceral level.

Charlie was dead because of him and no label was going to change that. He didn't want to feel better... He didn't *deserve* to feel better, he accepted that, but the nightmares were a punishment too far.

She blew out a long fatalistic sigh. She knew that she was issuing an invitation to have her head bitten off but she couldn't bring herself to do *nothing. Story of your life, Chloe.*

'So do you want to talk about it?'

He turned his head and glared at her. 'Can you turn off the empathy for a minute? That's not what I want from you.'

Chloe held her ground. 'You're not responsible for what happened, Nik. Charlie made his own decisions.'

'How the hell can you say that? I told you...' He stopped, his eyes narrowing over an expression of angry bewilderment. Why *had* he told her when he hadn't told anyone else? He didn't like that he couldn't answer the question. He was at her side in three strides, his hand closing around her upper arms as he dragged her into him until their bodies collided. 'Why do you have to be different?'

The emotions pouring off him made her dizzy, or was that the contact with his hard, lean body? The sexual pulse emanating from him and the feverish glitter in his dark eyes made her head spin.

His eyes stayed open and connected with her own as his lips moved across her parted lips, the contact a mere whisper, the progress agonisingly slow.

She shuddered and sank deeper into the suffocating excitement that caused her breath to come in short, shivery little gasps. His face blurred before she closed her

eyes and the ache of hunger low in her pelvis dragged
a sob from her aching throat as she whispered fiercely.

'Please!'

The hoarse, hungry plea snapped whatever shred
of control he retained as, with a moan deep in his own
throat, Nik plunged his tongue into her mouth, plunder-
ing the warm recesses. The kiss grew wild, teeth clashed,
tongues tasting with an escalating passion.

Rising up on her toes, Chloe put her arms around his
neck to hold on for grim death. She could still hear alarm
bells ringing but they were almost drowned out by the excited clamour of her own heartbeat. Her fingers dug into
the smooth muscled skin of his shoulders and back as she
pulled him closer, craving the connection of their bodies.

He'd still been clinging to the idea that making love to
her was some sort of therapy to drive his devils away, but
that illusion burned away the moment his hands began to
move over her body, exploring the soft curves.

This wasn't therapy, this was survival—he felt as
though his life depended on this. He *needed* this; he
needed her. No, it was just sex, he amended as he cupped
one warm breast in his hand and held it, his thumb rubbing across the engorged peak as he kissed his way up
the curve of her neck.

'You make me want you!' he growled, thinking that
all she had to do was breathe and he was out of his mind
with lust. 'I just want to feel your skin on mine. I have
to kiss and taste every inch of you.'

What was she doing? Your skin on mine, he'd said…
In her mind's eye she suddenly saw the puckered flesh of
her thigh and imagined the shocked disgust on his face
when he discovered it. And she couldn't bear it.

'No…no!' She pushed hard against him and his arms
fell away. He stepped back, his chest lifting and falling

dramatically as he appeared to struggle to draw enough
air into his lungs.

'What is happening here, Chloe?'

She gave a tight little smile and thought, *I'm dying.*
'Nothing is happening. I just…changed my mind.'

'You changed your mind?' The lines of colour along
his cheekbones stood out starkly against his blanched,
sweaty pallor. He looked like a man in shock and he felt
like a man in purgatory!

She took a deep, controlling breath. 'You come with
too much baggage for me… I like to keep things simple.'

His head went back as though she'd struck him; he
was aching and hurting and mad as hell. She thought
he was some sort of emotional cripple who needed taking care of and she didn't want the job! The injury to his
pride was almost as painful as the frustration that raged
through his body. 'It's only sex, *agape mou*; I'm not asking you to marry me.'

She knew it was irrational to let the words hurt, but
they did anyway. 'Maybe, but *just sex* can get complicated.'

'I'm a man of simple needs.'

She gave a bitter smile. 'You don't need to tell me
that. As I recall you didn't even manage to say a simple
goodbye…' She regretted the words even before she registered the speculation in his eyes and rushed into further speech. 'I really think you should talk to someone
qualified, about the nightmares, I mean. It's good that
you don't drink to excess now, but the way you were
that night…'

'The night we had sex, you mean.' He saw her flinch
and was glad; she deserved to flinch after her harsh rejection of him just now. 'There hadn't been any nightmares
that night because I hadn't been to sleep.'

There was a beat of silence before a look of shocked comprehension slid across her face, taking with it any trace of colour that had been there. By the time she breathed again even her lips were bloodless and the only colour in her entire face was the burning blue of her eyes.

'Charlie's death had just happened, hadn't it?' But it wasn't a question... Suddenly it all made sense: the darkness in him, the combustible quality of their chemistry, the driving need of his lovemaking—he'd been trying to burn away the pain of his memories in the fire of passion.

He tipped his head in acknowledgment, the weight in his chest painful as he looked at her standing there, frail and defenceless. Wasn't there already enough guilt in his life?

'You used me.' Anger and hurt shimmered through her and she didn't care if she was being rational; she didn't feel rational.

'I was too tired to fight you off,' he shot back.

Chloe flushed. At what point had she thought he would *ever* let her in? 'You really are a bastard.'

He didn't deny it. How could he? It was true. She turned away. 'Where are you going?' He had to clamp his lips tight over the word *stay*! He had never begged a woman in his life, and he wasn't about to start now.

'Going?' She turned back and lifted her chin. 'As far away from you as I can get!' she flung childishly. 'And who knows? If I'm lucky I might find a man who is not afraid to admit he's not perfect.'

'*Agape mou*, you're not looking for a man, you're looking for a cause!' he sneered contemptuously.

'Maybe I am, but you're a *lost* cause,' she flung back. 'You'll never have a future until you forgive yourself for the past. And you don't want me, you want a memory of something perfect... Well, I'm not that. I'm...' Breathing hard, she fought her way out of the kaftan, ripping the silk as she tore it off her body and stood there naked in the light of the breaking dawn.

He sucked in a deep breath, his eyes moving down over her body. She watched his face and saw the exact moment when he reached the area where the skin was badly scarred, saw the shock and horror he couldn't conceal.

That tiny flame of hope died right then and there.

'You see, I'm not what you need. I'm not perfect any more.'

She had no idea how she managed to walk the few steps back to her room, oblivious to the fact he had followed her.

CHAPTER TEN

THE VIOLENCE WITH which she'd slammed the door behind her made it swing back open, but she seemed oblivious to that as he stepped over the torn silk robe that lay crumpled on the floor.

It took him a few dazed seconds to label the emotion that broke loose inside him as tenderness when his gaze lifted to the slim figure standing there, staring blankly straight ahead like a beautiful, flawless marble statue… Except she was not stone, she was blood and flesh and nerve endings, and the flaw on her body that stood out only emphasised how stunning she really was.

He could only imagine what was going through her mind. This woman had more guts in her little finger than a regiment of marines.

'Haven't you seen enough?' she asked, staring at a point over his left shoulder. If he hadn't, she certainly had!

She would never forget that look of horror in his eyes.

Every resource he had was needed to retain his control, but he was straining at the leash so hard he could barely form the word. 'No!'

Her eyes flew to his face as he walked towards her, the fierce tenderness in his eyes making her tummy flip and her throat tighten, as she had no defence against it.

'But…'

'I want to do more than look at you,' he growled out, lifting a big hand to curve his fingers around one side of her face. 'And I think we can do better than just sex!' he declared with arrogant confidence. Holding her startled gaze, he bent his head, closing his eyes only when their mouths were sealed together.

When he raised his head they were both breathing hard, her eyes were bright, her skin was feverishly hot, and every skin cell on her body was bursting with painful awareness.

'Let's even things up a bit, shall we?' he suggested, stepping away but only far enough to slide his wet shorts over his hips.

She swallowed, her eyes dropping to watch his actions, helpless to resist the desire that flowed through her as she observed how the lowering of the fabric revealed the level of his arousal. He flashed a grin at her, but his features were hard and fierce as he held her eyes.

'Come here!' he demanded.

She did and he took her hand, directing it straight onto his groin and curling her fingers around the hardness of his erection. 'That is what looking at you does to me.'

'But… I'm not…'

'You're perfect to me…and you are perfect for me.'

At the stark declaration the muscles deep inside her fluttered and the rapid rise of desire swept over her like a wave, wiping away the last shreds of her self-consciousness. As she tightened her fingers experimentally over his crotch, excitement swirled through her.

'Amazing!' she murmured.

He gave a low, sexy rumble of laughter that made the hairs on the nape of her neck tingle.

Nik caught hold of her hands, raised them to his lips and pressed kisses into each curling palm before lowering his mouth to hers once again.

The kiss began as a slow, sensual tender exploration and then suddenly it became something else, his tongue driving deeper inside her mouth and eliciting an explosion of raw need and desperation as teeth clashed and tongues collided. Chloe moaned deep and raised herself up on her toes, gasping as her aching, sensitised breasts flattened against his iron-hard chest.

By the time they broke apart, they were both breathing as though they'd just crossed the marathon finishing line, and he hooked a hand behind her neck, sliding his fingers into her hairline, the fingertips gently massaging the skin there.

Then he kissed the swan curve of her neck and Chloe's head fell back in rapture, her eyes squeezed closed on a long sigh that became a groan as his hand claimed first one quivering breast and then the other, stroking then kneading… Her head fell back further to allow him greater access, her spine arching back, supported by the iron strength of the arm across her ribs.

Her passion-glazed blue eyes flickered open as he scooped her up as though she weighed nothing and walked towards the bed.

She stroked his face, touching his mouth, his fascinating, pleasure-giving mouth, thinking that she honestly wouldn't have cared if he had laid her down on the floor and taken her there and then… The thought was both shocking and incredibly exciting to her.

As he strode towards the bed, although she wasn't small or delicate he made her feel both, yet at the same time powerful and strong.

He laid her down on the tumbled sheets and stood there looking down at her, nostrils flared, breathing hard, each breath lifting his ribcage.

His body was hard and tanned, warm, bone, sinew

and muscle all so perfect that the desire low in her belly clutched hard as she stared at him, unable to look away.

'You're beautiful,' she whispered. 'Perfect.' Her eyes suddenly filled with tears as she choked out, 'I wish I still was for you too—'

The rush of emotion he felt when he interpreted the expression in her eyes was shocking in its intensity.

She was grieving.

His expression was both stern and tender as he came down beside her, lowering his long body so that they lay thigh to thigh.

'Listen to me. You are beautiful.'

She gave a teary smile, loving him so much it hurt. 'Inside, maybe.'

'Everywhere,' he contradicted. 'Inside and out. And I want to love every part of you. You have lost something, I know, but let me give you something to fill the space…' He took her hand and laid it on his chest where she could feel the heavy thud of his heartbeat, strong and steady. She could feel it vibrating through her own body; it was as if they were one…but she craved an even more intimate joining.

'I want you,' she said simply.

His eyes darkened in response to the husky plea. 'Then, *agape mou*, you shall have me.'

Arms braced above her head either side, he leaned down and kissed her, and she sighed into his mouth, eager for his taste, wanting to fill her senses with it. The heat was searing and she whimpered as she was swept away on a tidal wave of primitive need.

The erotic exploration of tongue against tongue continued as he lowered his body beside her and turned her onto her side to face him. He lifted his mouth from hers, but only to kiss his way down her neck and then over the quivering mounds of her breasts.

A keening cry escaped her lips at the first brush of his tongue over first one nipple and then the other, then when he took one into his mouth and sucked on it sensuously she gasped.

Her damp nipples continued to ache from his ministrations as he slid lower, his tongue leaving a wet trail over the slight mound of her belly while his fingers moved into the soft curls at the apex of her legs, stroking the damp folds gently and then parting them until he found the tight nub nestling inside.

She was so focused on the new, agonisingly blissful sensations he was creating that she didn't realise at first where he was kissing.

She stiffened, rejection making her eyes fly wide open, hating that he was touching the ugly scarred tissue on her thigh, imagining the disgust he had to be feeling. She didn't want him to have to pretend to be enjoying it. 'No!'

'Yes!' he insisted.

For the space of a heartbeat their eyes connected, and she was the first to look away.

Quivering but quiescent now, she lay there as he gently kissed the damaged skin, her face wet with silent tears that slid unnoticed down her face.

'You can't want to do that.'

Her broken whisper felt like a tight fist around his heart. In response, he loosed a low growl and dragged himself up her body until they were face to face. Holding her gaze, he took her hand and curled her fingers around the hard, silky shaft of his erection. His whole body was trembling with need as she stroked him, breathing in the male musk of his warm body.

She looked into his eyes and the desire blazing there burnt away her last doubts and inhibitions; she suddenly felt free.

Kissing her passionately once again, Nik pulled her on top of him and held her there, his hands curved over her bottom, continuing to kiss her into mindless submission until he finally rolled them both over, reversing their position.

Lying beneath him, Chloe gave herself over to the sensations bombarding her. She surrendered to the feelings, as she surrendered to him.

Then he parted her legs and she held her breath and released it in a low, slow sigh when he finally slid into her. She grabbed his hips, her back arching to deepen the pressure, wanting more.

With a groan he obeyed, giving her everything he'd got.

'Put your legs around me, Chloe.'

She did and he sank deeper into her, each strong movement of him inside her sending her deeper into herself, into him. It became one and the same, and they were both at the core of a firestorm, and when it broke the effect on every nerve cell in her body was electric!

She turned her head on the pillow, where beside her Nik lay gasping for air, his chest heaving and the sweat on his skin cooling.

She began to worry that he was cooling towards her because he suddenly seemed so far apart from her, but before the fear could take root he reached out and dragged her against him, as close as possible.

'What are you doing all the way over there?' he asked, propping his chin on the top of her hair-rumpled head as he pulled up a sheet to cover them both.

'Does it still hurt?' he asked quietly when they were both lying still.

She sat up then, dragging the sheet up to her chin, and looked down at him. 'My leg?'

He nodded.

'Only when I laugh… No, seriously, not really, it's kind of numb because the nerve endings were pretty damaged.'

He was pretty sure that her matter-of-fact delivery covered a world of hurt and pain.

'The skin can get tight sometimes.' She reached out and took a bottle from the bedside table. 'If it does, I usually massage this stuff into it.'

'Were you in hospital for a long time?' The image of her lying alone in a hospital bed enduring such pain produced a fresh surge of protectiveness in him.

'Longer than expected, because the grafts didn't take. There was an infection so they had to start all over again. That's why I'm not going back.'

He stiffened. 'They want you to?'

She nodded. 'They have offered me another op, but that's what they said last time…'

'Shouldn't you listen to expert advice?'

'The surgeon says he *might* be able to improve the appearance, but there are no guarantees, and I've had enough of being poked and prodded.'

The way she said it, the defiance in her tone, made his throat ache with emotion, and his arms tightened around her narrow ribs as he rocked her against him.

'But wouldn't it be worth it if they could improve it?' he said against her neck.

She pulled away, her expression wary. 'I still wouldn't be perfect, and it's not about other people, it's about *me*. *I* have to be able to look in the mirror and know I'm still me…' she pressed a hand to her breasts '…inside.'

He watched the tears slide down her cheeks and felt as

if someone had reached a hand into his chest and pulled out his heart. 'Don't cry, *agape mou*.' He smoothed down her hair with a hand and pulled her back into his arms.

Nik felt regret when he saw the warm rays of sunlight filtering through the blinds, certain to wake Chloe up. The irony of his dismay was not lost on Nik, as for a long time he hadn't been able to wait until he could get out of bed.

But morning was already well established now, which meant that he'd have to let her go and lose the incredible sense of peace and *rightness* he'd felt holding her, a peace that had been better than the sleep his body craved, sleep that he had denied himself out of fear that in the grip of a nightmare he might hurt her. It was a fear with foundation, as there were reported incidents of men suffering from PTSD acting out their nightmares and injuring their partners in their sleep.

If he hurt Chloe, even unconsciously, he knew it would kill him.

The time had come to get up, but on the plus side the bright sunlight made it possible for him to study the face on the pillow beside him. Half obscured by the tangle of silky blonde hair, she lay with one arm across his chest and the other tucked under her head like a pillow. He could make out the fact that her eyelashes fanned out lush and curving against her smooth cheek.

If anyone had told him before yesterday that he would say a woman's name just because he wanted, no, *needed* to hear it he would have laughed them out of the building and yet…

'Chloe.'

It was barely a whisper but she must have sensed it because she stirred, whimpering a little and shifting restlessly, then, eyes still closed, she shouted, 'No!' She opened her eyes suddenly, and blinked as the haziness vanished. 'I was dreaming…' she whispered sleepily.

'It sounded like a nightmare.'

'I forgot about my leg and had put on shorts, which is silly because I never forget…' she murmured sleepily. 'People were laughing and pointing at my scars…'

Nik flinched inside. 'I won't let anyone laugh,' he promised fiercely.

Chloe smiled happily as he turned onto his side and pulled her to him, running a hand in long soothing strokes down her back again and again until her breathing evened out once more.

It was a long time since he had spent more than an hour or so in bed with a woman, partly because he didn't want anyone to witness his nightmares. It was ironic, really, that the nightmares this time had been Chloe's.

You don't have exclusive rights on nightmares, Nik.

The memory of her pathetic whimpers cut right to his heart, and he kissed her forehead gently, pleased that her breathing was now soft and easy.

She bore her scars so bravely but how many times had she lifted her chin and pretended not to care…as she had with him earlier this morning? Carefully he leaned across her and pressed the phone that lay on the bedside table, so that the time appeared; it was already nearly ten a.m.

His throat was dry and the glass of water remained out of reach.

He moved, sliding a hand from under her, careful not to disturb her, and levered himself from the bed. Walking through to the kitchen, he closed the door to muffle the sound and turned on the tap. He downed the glass of water greedily.

Then he retraced his steps, making a detour to retrieve his own phone, which was in his jacket pocket, before he stood there gazing at the sleeping figure. While he respected her decision not to have further surgery he wondered if there wasn't another way to help her…a way that would leave her free of nightmares about people pointing at her.

A sense of deep grinding impotence rose up inside him. There *had* to be a way to protect her from all the cruelty out there, the people prepared to gossip and mock.

Chloe woke up and wondered why she felt so good, then she remembered and she felt even better. Eyes still closed, she patted the bed beside her, realising that the sheets were almost as cold as the sudden tightness behind her breastbone. Nik had left her again.

No, Chloe, this is how paranoia starts.

'Good morning.' Nik must have been back to his own room, as he was now wearing an unbuttoned shirt—a very good look on him—and cream linen shorts… Well, you couldn't have everything, she thought naughtily, knowing she preferred him naked. He was carrying a tray that held a cafetière of coffee, buttered toast and some fresh fruit.

'Hello.' She hid the sudden surge of paralysing shyness by grabbing for a piece of toast.

'Hello to you too. Black or white?' Nik asked, nudging the bedside lamp out of the way to balance the tray on the little side table. He sat down on the bed beside her and scanned her face.

She pushed a hank of hair from her eyes. 'Black and thank you, for earlier on.'

'I'd say it was a pleasure, but I hope that was perfectly obvious.'

She blushed, taking a sip of strong, fragrant coffee, and peeped at him over the rim. 'For me too.'

'I've been doing a bit of research online.' He was buzzing with the information he'd discovered and couldn't wait to share it with her.

She took another sip of coffee and thought ruefully that he had more energy than she did, as she felt tired in places she hadn't even known existed!

'I don't know who your consultant is but there is a team of medics in New York who are working on some new plastic surgery techniques. They're still at the trial stages but the results are nothing short of miraculous.'

She listened to him in silence but he had lost her after *your consultant*.

'I'm not interested.'

The coldness in her flat voice acted like cold water on his enthusiasm. He regarded her in frustration but when he spoke to her his tone was all gentle patience. 'I don't think you understand.'

She put down her cup and tightened her grip on the sheet she had gathered across her breasts. 'No, it's you who doesn't understand, Nik. It's you who hasn't been listening.' Or at least understanding. She felt a fool now for believing that he had. 'You really think there is anything you can tell me about possible treatments? Do you think I haven't looked into absolutely everything available?' She pushed her bare leg out from under the covers, shocking a small grimace from him. 'I've been living with this for a long time.'

He shook his head. 'I realise that—'

'Do you think I came to this decision lightly?' she asked him, her anger growing steadily. 'Do you think I didn't agonise over it? I came to a decision that is right for me and I need you to respect it.'

'Obviously, this is an emotional subject,' he began, 'but—'

Her lips tightened. 'Don't patronise me and don't try and change me. You need to accept me as I am, or walk away.'

He held his hands out flat in a pacifying gesture; this conversation was not going at all the way he had anticipated! 'There is no need to overreact.'

She arched a brow. 'No? Well, how would you feel if I brought you a cup of tea and told you all about the PTSD that you are suffering from?' She saw his flinch and ignored it. 'That I suddenly became an expert on your *problem*.' Her mouth tightened as her resentment rose.

'We are not talking about me.'

'Yeah, because unlike you I'm not in denial about my problem…and it isn't a problem for me. The only problem is the attitude of people like you!'

While she had been speaking the colour had gradually leaked from his face and by the time she'd finished his warm skin tone was ivory.

'I'm trying to help you!' he ground out, getting to his feet.

'How about helping yourself first? *I* don't need fixing. You're the one who won't even admit he has a problem!' she flung back, wanting to hurt him as much as he had her. A strange sense of calm settled over her as she looked up at him…this damaged, beautiful man she had grown to love in such a short space of time. This thing between them, whatever it was, had been doomed from the outset. It had never been going to work; she had only been fooling herself.

Why drag it out? she asked herself sadly.

'Until you sort yourself out… I don't want anything to do with you!'

CHAPTER ELEVEN

SHE'D KNOWN THE event was being filmed live but Chloe hadn't expected the cameras to be outside as well.

She could hear the young woman speaking into the mic as she stepped out of the car that bore the royal crest of Vela. She squared her shoulders. If her sister, who absolutely hated being the centre of attention, could do this then so could she…all she had to do was channel her inner show-off.

'And this…yes, that is Lady Chloe Summerville, who is standing in for her sister, the future Queen of Vela. We understand,' the reporter continued with a coy smile for the camera, 'that the princess was unable to attend tonight, and, though there has been no *official* confirmation, I'm sure you recall how the Princess suffered terrible morning sickness during her first pregnancy…?

'Lady Chloe is wearing…' she consulted a sheet of paper she was holding '…yes, I believe she is wearing a creation by Tatiana… Lady Chloe, hello.'

Chloe paused in front of the mic that had been pushed into her face, and smiled. 'Hello.' The personal touch would have been nice but she didn't have a clue who the other woman was.

'That is a beautiful cape,' the reporter said, gazing

at the floor-length velvet fur-trimmed cape Chloe wore. 'Real fur?'

'No, it's not real.'

'You are presenting one of the awards tonight, I believe, to the little girl who, I'm sure our viewers will remember, ran back into a burning house to save her baby sister and was injured herself. Humbling…so humbling…'

'To *Kate*, yes, I got lucky being able to present that particular award.'

'Standing in for your lovely sister? And how is the princess?'

Sabrina was where she spent most evenings at the moment, hanging over a toilet bowl…still asking anyone who'd listen why they called it *morning* sickness.

'She is really sorry she couldn't be here as it's a cause very close to her heart. Heroes so often go unsung and it's good to redress the balance just a little.'

'So why was she—?' The fortuitous arrival of the cast of a famous reality TV programme saved Chloe from fielding any more questions, and as the camera moved to the new arrivals she made her way quickly up the steps and into the theatre's foyer, which was filled with small gaggles of well-dressed people chatting. Tatiana immediately peeled off from one of the nearer groups and came across to where Chloe stood.

Chloe bent to kiss her when almost immediately her phone began to bleep and, fishing it from the minuscule bag she carried, she glanced down. 'A text from Sabrina,' she explained, skimming the message her sister had sent her.

Good luck and chin up! If you change your mind that's fine either way. We'll be cheering you on, so have a glass of fizz for me! And hurry back, please. If my husband asks me if I'm all right one more time I might have to kill him.

Chloe's smile was tinged with wistfulness as she switched her phone off and slipped it back into her bag. What would it be like to have a man be as crazy about you as her brother-in-law was about her sister?

Swallowing the emotional lump in her throat, she knew how lucky she was to have a family like hers, who were aware of her plans and supported any choices she made. It had been a struggle to stop her parents from flying over to offer moral support, and she suspected they were a bit hurt by the rejection, but she knew it was something she had to do alone.

'Is everything all right?' Tatiana asked.

'Fine if you discount the fact that Sabrina can't keep anything down. The doctor says if things don't improve by the end of the week, they'll have to give her IV fluids.'

'Oh, the poor thing!'

'So what happens now?' Chloe asked.

'Well, you're up first so they want you to go straight backstage, and after you've presented the award you'll see Kate back to her table, where they've seated you there for the rest of the dinner.'

Chloe nodded. 'That sounds good.'

'You sure about this?'

'Quite sure.' Chloe was surprised by how calm she felt now the moment was almost here.

'You know there are going to be headlines.'

Chloe nodded again, refusing to give mind space to fear and doubts. Producing headlines was the idea. You couldn't challenge common perceptions from a position of fear. She'd been going around telling the world that they should accept people with scars while hiding her own.

Which made her a big fat hypocrite.

'Tonight is the night of the big reveal.'

'I think you're very brave,' Tatiana husked emotionally.

Chloe felt uncomfortable with the praise. 'No, the people being awarded tonight are brave.'

She'd never thought of herself as brave but she had thought that she had come to terms with her injury. However, watching a filmed conversation with the little girl she was due to present a bravery award to tonight had destroyed that particular illusion for Chloe.

'So what do your friends think about your scars, Kate?' the reporter had asked.

The little girl had put down the doll she was playing with and thought about it.

'Well, I think they thought my arm looked funny at first, and some kept staring. A few people, not my *proper* friends, were mean and made me cry, but everyone's used to it now, so they don't even notice it cos they see it every day and I'm still me.' She'd picked up the doll, applied a comb to its hair and added thoughtfully, 'I still cry sometimes cos I liked my arm the way it was.'

The hard-nosed reporter had had tears in his eyes as he'd wound up the segment and Chloe doubted anyone watching would not have been similarly affected.

She herself had wept gallons but her tears had been partly out of shame. She had been hiding, Chloe realised that now, and if she hadn't, if she'd been truly honest with herself and everyone else, that devastating scene with Nik a few weeks ago on Spetses would never have happened.

Now she'd have to live with the memory for ever, all because she had preferred to be treated like a woman with no imperfections. Of course, there had been a price to pay for her deceit: she'd fallen deeply in love. Flaws and all, she loved Nik Latkis, but he didn't love her in return. Unrequited love had seemed much more romantic when she was a teenager with a lurid imagination, but the reality actually sucked.

It didn't help that her youthful imagination was still hanging in there inventing implausible happy-ever-after scenarios, not that she was ever in any danger of identifying her fantasies as anything other than what they were.

It was the thought of Nik's far more sinister dreams that continued to haunt her. She wondered and worried about the demons that visited him in the night and the eventual toll they would take on his health, both emotional and physical. She longed to comfort him but knew that was never going to happen after what had happened between them. She didn't blame him for that; he'd tried, but her scars were obviously an issue for him and he wasn't interested in helping himself, either.

Would he be watching the awards ceremony?

Would he disapprove of her decision?

She knew full well that her big reveal would go viral on social media, sparking thousands of debates, which was good, and an equal number of cruel comments, which was not, from people who thought anonymity gave them the freedom to say vile things about people they had never met.

She was prepared for the impending blaze of publicity as much as it was possible to be prepared.

'Lady Chloe.' One of the organisers, an efficient-looking woman in a blue evening dress, appeared. 'You look lovely,' she gushed. 'Has Tatiana explained the format to you? Excellent. You really do look amazing. Oh, excuse me.' She stepped to one side as, at a nod from Chloe, Tatiana moved forward to remove her floor-length cape.

'It's OK,' Chloe whispered when the older woman hesitated.

Chloe smoothed down her hair, which tonight she was wearing gathered in a simple jewelled clasp at the base of her slender neck. Her dress was the same bold red as her lipstick, a silk sleeveless sheath cut high at the neck and low at the back, the reverse cowl open almost to her waist, and plain except for the pattern traced in hand-sewn beads along the daring slit that was cut high on the left side that fell open to reveal her thigh.

It wasn't accidental; she had asked Tatiana to do it that way.

'Stunning!' the woman began then stopped; she'd clearly reached the revealing slit. There was a pause before she lifted her eyes and during the slight hiatus Chloe fought the urge to twitch the fabric over the scars.

When the woman did finally speak, her voice was husky. 'That,' she said, looking at Chloe as though she were seeing her for the first time, 'is *beautiful*.' Then, clearing her throat, she waved away the assistant who had clearly been allocated to escort Chloe. 'I'll take Lady Chloe in myself.'

The lift was empty as they stepped in.

As the lift whooshed silently upwards the woman cleared her throat. 'My sister was born with a cleft palate and lip; it's fine now and you'd never know, but I remember the comments she'd get when my mum used to take her out in the pushchair. People can sometimes be very cruel and what you're doing is…good, very good. I'm Jane, by the way.'

Backstage was actually pretty crowded, but Jane found Chloe a seat in a corner that wasn't occupied by what seemed to be the entire cast of a hit West End musical, who were waiting to go out and do the opening number.

Jane left but returned almost straight away with a glass of wine, and stayed with her while the comedienne who was hosting the event introduced the musical stars.

'Your turn.'

Chloe jumped at the touch on her arm.

'Don't worry. Pretend the cameras aren't there.'

Chloe straightened her shoulders and walked out onto the stage.

Nik arrived late, but he was there. He entered the back of the hall and surveyed the tables that had replaced the normal seats in the auditorium, searching for his sister and niece. He had just located them and plotted a course towards them when a ripple of applause made him decide to hang back until there was a break in proceedings so he could slide unobtrusively into his seat and no doubt get an earful for being late.

Maybe he'd slip out to the bar…? He hated this sort of occasion and he'd have been much happier to just make an anonymous donation, but he'd been guilted into coming, not by his sister for once, but his niece, who had gone into Bambi-eyes mode and reminded him that he'd never taken her to the show he had promised for her birthday.

He was in no position to deny it, although he didn't remember the promise or the birthday, so here he was. He hadn't smelt a set-up, not until he heard Chloe's name announced, followed by another ripple of applause.

Nik only heard the name.

Theos, she looked magnificent!

Lust struck through his body as his glance moved from the woman standing on the stage to the larger image on the screen at the side of the stage. Elegant, assured, with the glamour of a siren of the bygone golden Hollywood era, she was wearing a dress that had to have sent every male temperature in the room sky-high… The thought of anonymous males lusting after her drew his brows into a straight line of disapproval above his eyes, but they relaxed when she began to speak.

A sigh of pleasure left his lips…he had missed that sound. The simple admission sent a shock through his body and he didn't catch what she said as he focused instead on the sound of her voice.

She had a beautiful voice; pleasingly low and clear, it filled the room. She must have said something amusing because there was a soft ripple of laughter…except he didn't feel like laughing. There was nothing humorous about the way he was feeling, the *things* he was feeling.

Did an alcoholic feel this way when they found the innocuous orange juice they'd just swallowed was laced with vodka?

What did they say about recovery? Something about the first step was accepting you had a problem…but what if you didn't want to recover—*ever*?

Frustration burned through him as he stood there staring at her, a multitude of clashing emotions swirling inside him. He desired her, he resented her…he had *missed* her.

He had been only trying to help her and she had thrown his actions back in his face, accusing him of being the one with the problem, assigning the worst possible motives to his actions.

Why should he defend himself to this woman?

The woman who had tapped into his deepest fears, the weaknesses he despised in himself, and exposed them all to the light, and she'd made it sound as though he had a choice…?

She was wrong. Knowing it was enough, challenging her mistakes would have made it seem as though he needed to defend his actions, or, as she saw it, his lack of action… Move on, she'd said, but where was he meant to move on to? He couldn't rewrite the past.

A man takes responsibility for his own actions, Nicolaos.

The memory of his father's comment surfaced, smoothing out the creases of uncertainty at the edge of his mind.

Strange how some memories stuck. How old had he been? He couldn't even remember what lie he'd told, or what childish rule he'd broken. Maybe the moment had stood out for him because it was outside the norm. His father had not had a hands-on parenting style; he had seemed as remote a figure as the portrait of his stern-looking great-grandfather that Nik always felt disapproved of him.

He remembered the shame he'd felt and the determination never to disappoint his father again; he'd be a man.

The idea that he hadn't lived by that adage ever since was ludicrous. As for feeling guilty about how he'd handled matters with Chloe, she was the one who had seduced him that night they'd met!

Ah, poor you, the unwilling victim!

His inner dialogue was interrupted by a sudden roar of applause, and Nik realised that he was the only person in the room still looking at the figure in red on the stage. The spotlight, along with everyone else, was focused instead on a table near the front.

The big screen showed a little girl with a woman kneeling beside her, obviously her mother, encouraging her to go up on stage to receive her award, but the little girl was shaking her head emphatically.

There was an awkward silence as the child began to sob loudly then, and it was a heart-rending sound.

He was relieved and pleasantly surprised by the show of sensitivity as the camera moved off her face. No, not sensitivity, he saw then, they were just following the story. It focused on the tall figure in red who was now walking down the steps of the stage.

A murmur of approval went round the room that faded to a silence as Chloe began to weave her way through the tables towards the child. A silence Nik didn't understand until he saw the image of her body on the screen. The camera had dropped to show the long legs, the daring slit and…everything inside him froze.

The lighting was harsh and the camera picked out every detail of the discoloured, twisted flesh.

'Theos…!' His stomach muscles clenched, not in reaction to the sight of the ugly marks, but the pain they represented, the *months* of pain they represented. The explosion of pride he felt drew a raw-sounding gasp from a place deep inside him he hadn't known existed. An emotion he had stubbornly refused to acknowledge.

Like everyone else he watched as she dropped down into a graceful crouch beside the little girl, the big screen showing her smile as she spoke.

There was another faint ripple of sound around the room when the little girl lifted her teary face from her mother's shoulder. Chloe nodded and pointed to her own leg.

The room held its collective breath as the child reached out and touched Chloe's leg, then released it on a sigh as the camera recorded the smile that bloomed on her face.

Chloe said something that made the kid laugh, then she got to her feet and held out her hand. The room erupted when the child took it, and together to the sound of applause they walked back up onto the stage.

Nik wasn't applauding, he was barely breathing… He

felt a maelstrom of pride, shame and an aching desire to run up there and take Chloe in his arms, but he knew that even if he had earned the right to do that, which he hadn't, this was her night.

As the tall, beautiful woman walked onto the stage and turned to face the audience they rose to a man and gave a foot-stamping ovation, which the excited child joined in with…and Nik knew he was looking at tomorrow's front-page headline.

He also knew he was looking at the love of his life.

And he'd blown it.

For once, no heads turned his way when Nik Latsis left the room.

CHAPTER TWELVE

IT WAS NEARLY one in the morning when Chloe got back to her flat.

She rarely received a call on her landline these days, but the red light on her answer machine was flashing, showing her it was full of messages.

She ignored it, as she had already spoken to everyone who mattered, and her mobile phone lay switched off in her bag. She massaged her temples with her fingers to alleviate the tension she could feel gathering behind her eyes.

She could feel the exhaustion bearing down on her like a lead weight, but her mind remained active, not in a productive, problem-solving way, but more of a febrile, hamster-on-a-wheel way.

She kicked off her heels, conscious of a sense of anti-climax. She had been building up to tonight for days, not quite admitting how nervous she was about it, and now it was over and it couldn't have gone better, she should be feeling elated. But instead she felt…oddly flat, and not at all the inspiring figure that people had lined up to tell her she was this evening.

Easing the beautiful cape off her shoulders, she walked through to her bedroom, where she hung it on a hanger before covering it in a protective bag. Hopefully a few people would bid for it at the charity auction her sister had planned for next month.

When Chloe had suggested the timing might not be good for Sabrina to organise an auction, she had quipped, 'Trust me, I'm a doctor. I'll be feeling fine by then.'

As she stripped off the beautiful red gown and ran a bath for herself, she debated having a nightcap, but on balance decided against it, worried it might compete with the champagne she'd drunk earlier that evening.

Lighting the scented candles around the bath, she eased herself into the sweet-smelling water and lay there drifting, feeling deliciously decadent. Slowly the tension began to ease out of her shoulders.

Then the doorbell rang.

Her eyes peered through the open bathroom doorway to the clock on her bedroom wall, and she squinted to make out the time. Who on earth could that be in the middle of the night?

Everyone had warned her to expect some press intrusion after tonight and she thought that was realistic but this was ridiculous. It was getting on for two a.m.!

She decided to ignore it.

But her late-night caller was not giving up, and Chloe lay there, teeth gritted as the tension climbed back into her shoulders. And then the answer to her earlier question popped into her head.

Who did knock on doors at this time of night? The police with bad news.

Leaping out of the water, her pulse racing in panic and still dripping wet, she fought her way into a thick towelling robe and ran to the front door, leaving a trail of wet footprints in her wake. By the time she reached the door her imagination was cranked up to full volume and she was on her fourth awful possible scenario!

Cinching the belt a little tighter, she checked the safety chain was fastened and, as an extra precaution, picked up a heavy pale wood Dala horse from the console table and opened the door a crack.

Her late-night callers weren't wearing uniform and it was one visitor, singular, although she couldn't make out who it was.

Caution replaced dread, though on the plus side if this was a homicidal maniac standing there the walls were very thin in the apartments. Someone would be bound to hear her being murdered, and hopefully report it to the police.

'My neighbour is a black belt in karate!' she called through the crack.

She could only see a sliver of the man standing outside her door in the communal hallway, but as he stepped closer the partial view was more than sufficient to make the colour in her face recede, leaving her dramatically pale, and then return as quickly, dusting her cheeks with rose pink as she stood there frozen.

Her first thought was that she had fallen asleep and this was a new version of her recurring dream. In all the other versions, Nik had been wearing black swimming shorts and nothing else, not a dinner jacket that hung open and a white dress shirt that was pulled open at the neck and seemed to have several buttons missing. There were the remains of a bow tie sticking out of his breast pocket too; he really did not look his usual immaculate self.

'Hello.'

This Nik, with dark shadows under his eyes and stubble on his chin, still looked more sexy than any man had a right to be.

'I need to lie down,' she mumbled, thinking, *And then I need to wake up!*

'Can I come in first?' His mild tone was at stark variance to the glitter in his eyes as he stared at her.

'I thought you were the police! I thought Sabrina had lost the baby or my mum had fallen and broken her hip, or my dad had—'

'Sorry I scared you.'

'You can't really be here because you don't know where I live. I moved.' She'd rented out her old place as part of the entire new change she had decided to adopt on her return from Greece.

'Then you should consider going ex-directory, you know.' He dragged a hand across his hair and sounded tired as he added gruffly, 'Let me in, Chloe, please.'

'All right.' It took her longer than it should to remove the chain. Her hands, she noticed, viewing the phenomenon with a strange out-of-body objectivity, were shaking violently.

Finally she released it.

She stepped back as Nik walked in; he was real after all. Dreams didn't smell this good, carrying with them the scent of outdoors underlain with a faint scent of whisky.

'Beware Greeks bearing gifts,' she murmured.

Especially tall, lean, gorgeous Greeks with pride etched onto every inch of a classically perfect profile and with explosive tension locked into every muscle.

He held out his empty hands and turned them over. 'I don't have any. I wasn't sure if you'd even let me in.'

'I wasn't sure you were real,' she countered huskily. Then, shaking her head to clear the static buzz, she tried to inject a little normality into what was a very surreal situation.

'Do you know what time it is?' She flicked back the

hair from her face, the soggy ends dusting her cheek with dots of moisture.

'I couldn't wait until morning,' he said simply.

Struggling to convey a calm she was a million miles from feeling, Chloe met his eyes. The combustible quality in his heavy-lidded stare dried her throat and made her heart thud harder against her ribcage. She cinched the belt even tighter, suddenly very conscious of the fact that she was naked underneath her robe.

'Why are you here, Nik…?' Her eyes fluttered wider. 'Has something happened to Tatiana… Eugenie…?'

'No, they're fine,' he soothed immediately.

Panic subsiding, Chloe let out a relieved little sigh and arched a brow, folding her arms in an unconsciously protective gesture over her chest as she asked again, 'So why are you here?'

'Why didn't you tell me…?' He stopped and spread his hands. 'Tonight, you… No, you don't have to tell me. I know I've got no right to encourage your confidence in me.' He was the last person she'd turn to for support.

'You saw it on television?'

'I was there,' he said heavily. The pride he had felt for what she'd done was still there but overlaying it now was apprehension for her future. For every voice raised in admiration there would be another writing crude, cruel insults, but he'd be there for her, regardless.

She refused to jump to conclusions. 'Where?'

'At the theatre, for the bravery awards.'

The muscles along his jaw tightened as he realised with a sudden startling insight what she really wanted. She didn't want to be protected from people; she wanted to be released to be the brave, beautiful heroine she was. She might make those who cared for her sick with worry on her behalf, but it was a price they'd have to pay.

Nik knew with a total certainty that he wanted to be one of them, even though the idea of anyone hurting her by word or action left a sour taste in his mouth, and rage in his heart.

All he could do was be there for her—if she'd let him.

'Oh.' What else could she say? 'You didn't stay around for the party, then.' Her attempt at levity fell flat in the face of his grim-featured non-reaction.

For a big man Nik moved very fast.

The weight of his body made her take a staggering step back as he framed her face with his hands and turned it up to him.

'It was the bravest thing I have ever seen,' he rasped in a throaty whisper. 'Can you ever forgive me? I don't want to change you, I swear, but I'll change who I am. I'll—'

'I like you the way you are…'

His kiss silenced her. When he finally lifted his head his forefinger replaced his lips. 'Let me speak without putting words in my mouth…' She nodded dazedly, and he took his finger away. 'Tonight I saw the bravest, most beautiful woman I know…do the bravest, most beautiful thing.'

Her eyelids lowered over the haze of tears that shimmered in the swimming azure depths. 'I was scared stiff,' she admitted. 'I thought you'd be angry with me.'

The expression drawn on his chiselled face was one of astonished incredulity. 'I *am* angry.'

Her head began to lower but he placed a finger under her chin and drew her face inexorably up to his. 'But not with you, *agape mou*. Never with you. I'm furious with *myself* for wasting so much time!' he rasped out throatily. 'I know I have a problem with PTSD, and I'll get help for that. I might never be the man you deserve but, so help me, I'll do whatever it takes, so long as you take me back?'

She blinked in shock as she stared at him. 'Did I ever really have you?'

The shaky laugh dragged from her throat cut off abruptly as she encountered the hard, hungry, slightly unfocused look in his stare.

'From that first moment I met you, I think, but I was too stupid, too much of a stubborn, proud fool to re- alise it.' He dragged a hand through his hair. 'I really don't have any pride left, Chloe, and there hasn't been a day gone by since that morning in Greece that I haven't hated myself for making you think I was ashamed of your scars.'

She put up a hand and cupped his cheek. 'I see now that wasn't the case.'

'It's *my* scars I'm ashamed of,' he admitted heavily. 'Everything you said to me that morning was absolutely right. I knew it then, but I just couldn't admit it. Now I'm asking you to take me, Chloe, scars and all, for better or for worse… I love you, *agape mou*, and I need you.'

He took a deep shuddering breath. 'I know I walked away from you—twice—but I promise that will not hap- pen ever again. Let me into your life and I will always let you be you. I don't want to stifle you. I want to watch you fly.'

With a little sigh, she laid her head on his chest, her eyes squeezing shut as she felt his strong arms close around her. She stood there listening to the thud of his heartbeat, feeling the weeks of loneliness slip away.

Finally she lifted her head. 'I love you too, Nik.'

The kiss he gave her went on and on, his hungry pas- sion leaving her feeling limp yet very happy when they finally came up for air.

She stroked his face lovingly. 'I feel as though a weight has been lifted from me the last few weeks.'

He took her face between his hands. 'I love you, I love every part of you, and, yes, I admit I did want you to reconsider the plastic surgery, but not,' he emphasised, 'for me. For you...'

'I realise that now,' she admitted.

'I don't know if you've fully considered this,' he began tentatively, 'but what you did tonight will make you the target of—'

'Internet trolls and other low-life, yes, I know.' She dismissed them with an impatient click of her fingers.

It took a few moments for the information to filter through to his brain...but when it did his hands fell from her face in astonishment.

'Of course I know that; I'd need to live on Mars not to know,' she said with a rueful smile.

'And you still did it.' He shook his head and gave a laugh. 'You really are the most incredible woman,' he declared with husky pride.

'Is there stuff out there already?'

He nodded.

'We're not going to read it,' she declared.

'I think that is a good move.'

He cleared his throat.

'Nik, why are you looking shifty?' she demanded.

Without a word he picked up his phone, scrolled down the screen and handed it to her. 'There are some other things out there you should probably know about.'

With a puzzled frown Chloe took it and began to read, her expression changing from bemusement to anger as she progressed. 'Oh, my God, who did this? Do you know who the source is? It has to be someone close to you to know all these details. It's a gross invasion of privacy!' she declared indignantly.

'Me!'

Her eyes flew wide. It made no sense. Nik was an intensely private person so why would he feed this story about himself to a journalist? 'I don't understand.'

'I gave this story, this evening. You made me so proud tonight, seeing how courageous you were, not hiding in any sense of the word… You were marvellous and it made me feel completely ashamed of myself. You were right: I've been hiding like a coward. Your name is going to be out there all over the media, and I knew I couldn't stop that, but I could show some solidarity so… I decided to join you and—who knows?—reading about what happened to me might even help someone else. I'm definitely going to do something about it, I promise you.'

'I know you will.'

'I wanted to prove to you that you could give me your heart and I would keep it safe and I am hoping that you would accept mine.'

Chloe's breath caught in her throat.

'And for the record I don't want to change a single thing about you.'

Tears pouring down her cheeks, Chloe flung herself at him, sobbing with sheer joy, and he swung her up into his arms.

Eyes locked on his, she took his hand and placed it on her heart. 'I know you'll keep it safe.'

Three months later

'Another builder has quit,' Nik said, wandering into the office where Chloe was working. 'At this rate we'll never move into the house on Spetses. You have to do something about her.'

'Me!' Chloe echoed. 'I don't think so. She is your grandmother.'

'She is counting nails! We are in the middle of multimillion-pound renovation of a classic sixteenth-century mansion and my grandmother is counting nails.'

'She is thrifty.'

'She is insane, and you know it.'

'She's *your* grandmother...' she reminded him, coming around the table and looping her arms around his neck. Nik kissed her hard.

'At this rate we're not going to be able to move in after the wedding.'

Chloe shrugged. 'I don't care if I start married life in a shoe box, so long as it's with you.'

'Now you tell me, after I've already had to cope with planning officers from hell, contractors who never answer their phones and, of course, let's not forget Yaya.'

'She's excited about us being her new neighbours... well, for some of the time.' Nik had not given up his London house.

'It will all be worth it in the end, you'll see, waking up to the smell of pines and the sound of the sea,' she said dreamily.

'So long as I can see you when I wake up, I don't care. Which reminds me, have you got the shortlist for the new team leader for the charity? I don't want my wife—'

Her eyes widened as she pressed a finger to his lips and looked over her shoulder. 'Hush! You'll give the game away! Imagine how upset everyone will be if they find out we already got married after they've been to so much trouble to arrange this massive wedding.' Somehow she didn't think that people would be that understanding about their impulsive elopement.

He looked at her, eyes glowing with pride and love. 'I couldn't wait to make you my wife. I just wish I saw more of you.'

'I know,' she admitted, stroking his cheek with a loving hand. 'But who knew that the charity would take off this way? We're interviewing for a team leader next week and there are some very strong candidates.' She squeezed his bicep and pretended to faint. 'Obviously not as strong as you, darling.'

Their kiss might have gone on longer if Nik's ninety-five-year-old grandmother, all four feet five of her, hadn't suddenly appeared. 'A man came who said he was a building inspector. In my day there were no such thing; we just build a house with no paper.'

'The good old days,' Nik murmured. 'So where is the building inspector, Yaya?'

'Gone. I told him my grandson and his woman were busy making babies, and if they weren't doing that, then they should be.' Chortling at her own joke, she shuffled out of the room.

'Well, they do say that with age comes wisdom.' Nik extended a hand towards the door through which his grandmother had just exited. 'How about it, wife? Do you fancy a little baby making?'

'Only if you lock the door. If Yaya walks in on us, I might be scarred for life…' As the unintentional play on words hit home she released a loud laugh.

Nik felt pride swell in his chest once more. His wife laughed when others might weep. She had a gift for living life to its utmost, and looking at the world through her eyes had finally brought him the peace he'd never thought he'd feel again.

'Have my children, Chloe.'

Her throat closed up with sheer happiness. 'It's a big house, Nik, and there are lots of bedrooms to fill.'

'So maybe we should get started.'

'You read my mind!'

* * * * *

BLACKMAILED BY
THE GREEK'S VOWS

TARA PAMMI

For all the readers who asked for
Valentina's story.

CHAPTER ONE

SHE WAS DRESSED like a...a hooker.

No...not exactly a hooker.

No hooker he knew possessed the class, the style and the innate grace that imbued every one of his wife's movements.

More of a high-class escort.

It took Kairos Constantinou a few seconds to clear the red haze that descended in front of his eyes.

Dios...of all the stunts he had expected his impulsive, fiery wife to pull, it hadn't been this.

When his PI had informed him that he'd located Valentina and that she'd be aboard Kairos's own yacht for the party tonight, he hadn't been surprised.

Valentina had always been the life of the party scene in Milan.

Lively. Sensual. Like a beautiful butterfly that flits from flower to flower. The minute her brother Leandro had pointed her out to Kairos, standing amidst a gaggle of men, Kairos had decided he wanted her.

Three minutes into Leandro introducing them, he'd known she was going to be his wife.

She had been the best possible incentive Leandro could have offered to reel Kairos into the alliance. Kairos would gain entry into the rarefied old-world alliances that her family the Conti dynasty, swam in, and she would get a rich husband.

Not once had he questioned why Leandro had thought he needed to set up his beautiful sister like that.

All Kairos had wanted was the prize that was Valentina Conti.

Except, a week into his marriage, he had realized his wife was anything but a trophy.

She was emotionally fiery, intensely vulnerable and impulsive as hell.

The best example of which was her deserting him nine months ago without so much as a word.

And to find her here among this crowd now.

With instincts he'd honed among the street gangs of Athens, he noted three Russian investors who operated businesses barely this side of legal—the men his friend Max intended to wine and dine—another man who was a model and a friend of Valentina's, and five women to entertain them, not counting Valentina.

Women of the oldest profession known to man. Not streetwalkers, like some of his earliest friends, but undoubtedly from an escort service.

And the most provocatively dressed among them was Valentina in a flimsy gold dress.

The slinky material pooled at her chest to create a low neckline that left her shoulders and her toned arms bare. It pushed up those small breasts that he had touched and kissed and sucked while she writhed under him, like a lover's hands.

So much golden, soft, silky skin… His jaw tightened like a vise as three other men salivated over her.

But it was the smiles she bestowed on the men as she charmed them, those arms flying about in that way of hers while she narrated some escapade in her accented English, full of fire, the way she put a hand on Max's arm and thanked him when he refilled her drink…that was what caused the ice to stiffen his spine.

The wall of detachment that had always been his armor against anything was his only defense.

No, this was only want. Physical want…nothing more.

He still wanted her, desperately, because she was Valentina and even with her explosive tempers and childish tantrums, she had still snuck under his skin.

He needed her as his wife for a few months. And in those few months, he'd work her out of his blood. Out of his life.

If Valentina Conti Constantinou had indulged in some fantasy delusion that her husband Kairos had arrived on the yacht to achieve some sort of romantic reunion between them, he burned the notion to ashes within the first few minutes.

It had been disturbing enough to find that not only had her photographer friend Nikolai, at whose persuasion she had come to the party, manipulated her into wearing the tackiest outfit, but that she was surrounded by women from an escort service *and* men expected to be *entertained* by them.

She'd squared her shoulders, made Nikolai *claim* her for the evening, and had begun to charm the Russians. The one thing she knew how to do. She might have been living on nothing for months but she had class. Years of practice at playing the perfect socialite—well-versed in fashion and politics.

Until Kairos had walked in.

Barely sipping her G&T, she nodded at something Nikolai whispered in her ear, keeping her effusive smile firmly in place. Her throat was raw with the falsely pitched laughs, and her chest hurt at having to play the unruffled socialite the way she had all her life.

Every inch of her rebelled against the calm she had assumed from the moment Kairos had stepped onto the deck. Every cell in her roared to swat away the woman who was even now cozying up to him, far too pleased with herself.

She wanted to announce to the rest of them that he was hers.

But he had never belonged to her.

Her grip shook, clinking the ice in her tumbler.

Tina put her glass down, fighting for control.

Men scrambled around Max for an introduction to Kairos, and the women—hair fluffed, breasts pushed up to spill out of already plunging necklines—it was as if the rough, rugged masculinity of him was an inviting caress to every woman.

Dios mio, the strength of his sheer masculine appeal hit her like a punch now, shaking her up, turning her inside out.

His white shirt stretched tight across his broad shoulders, enhancing his raw, rugged appeal. His expansive chest tapered down to a narrow waist, over leaner hips and then he was all legs. Hard, muscular thighs followed by those runner's calves that had once driven her crazy.

His hair was cut into that short style he preferred. Her fingers twitched, remembering the rough sensation of it, and she fisted them at her side. His gaze flicked down to her hands and then back up her body, slowly, possessively.

Those silvery eyes lingered on the long stretch of her legs, her thighs, noted the short hem of the dress, up to her waist, lingered again over her breasts, moved up her neck and then settled again on her face.

If he had run those hands over her body with that rough urgency that he'd always mastered before he lost control, she couldn't have felt more owned. With one look, he plunged her into that state of mindless longing, that state of anticipation he had become used to expecting from her.

Shivering inside her skin, forgetting all the misery he had inflicted on her, Tina lifted her chin in defiance.

He had never liked her to dress provocatively. Had never liked her easy attitude with other men, that almost flirty style of talking that was her nature. They had had more than one row on the subject of her dresses, her hair, her shoes, her style, her attitude and even her body.

One of the blondes she had genuinely liked earlier—Stella of the big boobs and even bigger hips—tapped his arm. A smile curving his thin lips, he sliced his gaze away in clear, decisive dismissal.

Tears scratched up Tina's throat and she hurriedly looked away before someone could see her mortification.

Nine months ago, she'd have slapped the woman's face—she cringed at the memory of doing that to her sister-in-law Sophia, having been induced into a jealous, insecure rage. She'd have screamed and made a spectacle of herself, she'd have let her temper get the better of her and proved to everyone and Kairos how crazy she was about him.

Nine months ago, she'd have let the hot emotions spiraling through her dictate her every word, every move.

Nine months ago, she'd been under the stupid delusion that Kairos had married her because he wanted her, because he felt something for her, even if he didn't put it in words.

But no, he had married her as part of an alliance with her brother Leandro. Even after learning that bitter truth, she could have given her marriage a try.

But Kairos didn't possess a heart. Didn't know what to do with one given into his keeping.

She had humiliated herself, she had prostrated her every thought, every feeling at his feet. And it hadn't been enough.

She hadn't been enough.

* * *

"So you're truly over with him…that glowering husband of yours."

"Si," Tina said automatically. And then wished she hadn't.

When the party began winding down, she had slipped below deck with the excuse of visiting the ladies' room and hidden herself away in the lovely gray-and-blue bedroom, her nerves frayed to the hilt at the constant awareness of Kairos.

It was tiring to play the stoic, unaffected party girl. To stuff away all the longing and hurt and anger into a corner of her heart.

But Nikolai had followed her downstairs.

Although over the last couple of months she'd realized that Nikolai was harmless, he was drunk now. Her brother Luca had taught her long ago never to trust a drunken man.

"A taxi for you," she said to Nikolai, pulling her cell phone out of her clutch.

From the foot of the bed where he made an adorably pretty picture, Nikolai stretched his leg and rubbed his leather boot against her bare calf. "Or we could spend the night here, Tina, *mi amore*. Now that things are truly over between you and the Greek thug—"

Using the tip of her stiletto, Tina poked his calf until he retreated with a very unmasculine squeal.

Her head was pounding. She'd barely drunk any water. Her body and mind were engaged in a boxing match over Kairos. The last thing she needed was Nikolai hitting on her.

"Kairos and I are not divorced. Also, I'm not interested in a relationship," she added for good measure.

"I noticed him tonight, *cara mia*. He spared you not a single glance." A claw against her heart. "As if you were total strangers." A bruise over her chest. "He seemed pretty interested in that whore Stella." Bile in her throat.

Just like a man to use the woman and then call her crude names. Oh, why had she come tonight? *"Per favore,* Nik, don't call her that."

"You called Claudia Vanderbilt much worse for marrying a sixty-year-old man."

Tina cringed, shame and regret washing over her like a cold wave.

She had.

She'd been privileged and pampered and had behaved so badly. She should keep Nikolai in her life. If nothing, he'd keep reminding her what a bitch she'd once been.

While Valentina held up her phone and walked around the bedroom looking for a signal—she'd spend the night here if it meant avoiding seeing Kairos leave with one of the women, not that he'd need to pay for the pleasure—Nikolai had moved closer.

Valentina froze when his hands landed on her hips. She arrested his questing hands. "Please, Nikolai. I would like to keep the single friend I have."

"You have really changed, Tina. Transformed from a poisonous viper to a—" his alcoholic fumes invaded her nostrils while he tilted his head, seemingly in deep thought "—an innocent lamb? A lovely gazelle?"

Christo, the man was deeply drunk if he was calling her innocent.

Before Tina could shove Nikolai's hands away—she really didn't want to plant her knee in his groin like Luca had taught her—his hands were gone. Whether he skidded due to his drunken state or was pushed, Tina would never know. He landed with a soft thump against the bed, slid down it and let out a pathetic moan.

Tina whirled around, her breath hitching.

CHAPTER TWO

KAIROS STOOD AGAINST the back door, not a single hair out of place.

There was that stillness around him again, a stillness that seemed to contain passion and violence and emotion.

And yet nothing.

Emotions surged through her, like a wave cresting. But just like a wave broken by the strongest dam, Kairos had come pretty close to breaking her.

Ignoring the fact that her dress climbed up her thighs and she was probably flashing her thong at the inebriated Nikolai, she went to her knees next to him, sliding her fingers through his gelled hair.

Nikolai's hot, alcohol-laden breath fluttered over the expanse of her chest. But it was the silver gaze drilling holes into her back that pebbled goose bumps over her skin.

A sound like a swallowed curse emanated from behind her. She ignored it, just as she tried to ignore her pounding heart.

"What are you doing?"

It had been nine months since she'd seen him. Nine months since he'd spoken to her. The hope that he would come after her had died after the first month. She swallowed to keep her voice steady. "Checking for a bump."

"Why?"

She snorted. "Because he's my friend and I care what happens to him."

Tina stared down at Nikolai's picture-pretty face and sighed. He *was* her friend.

He had gotten her the entry-level job in a fashion agency when she had returned to Milan from Paris, her tail tucked between her legs and ready to admit defeat, and found her a place with four other girls in a tiny one-bedroom hovel.

Not out of the generosity of his heart, but because he'd wanted to see her humiliated, wanted to enjoy how she'd come down in the world. Maybe even to get into her pants.

Whatever his motivations, Nikolai was the only one who'd helped her out, the only one who hadn't laughed at her pathetic attempts.

Unlike the man behind her, whose mocking laugh even now pinged over her nerves. "You have no friends. At least not true ones. Shallow women flock to you for approval of their clothes and shoes. Men flock to you because they…"

Truth—every word was truth. Humiliating, wretched truth.

But it hurt. Like something heavy was pressing down on her chest. "Don't hold back now, Kairos," she said, smarting at the stinging behind her eyes.

"Because they assume that you'll be wild and fiery in bed. That you will bring all that passion and lack of self-control and that volatility to sex. Once your *friend* here gets what he wants, he will be through with you."

If she'd had any doubt what he thought of her, he'd just decimated it.

She had fallen in love with a man who thought she was good for sex and nothing else.

A need to claw back pounded through her. "I'm shallow and vapid, *si,* but what you see is what you get. I don't make false promises, Kairos."

The silence reverberated with his shock. "I've never made a promise to you that I didn't keep. I promised your brother to keep you in style when I agreed to marry you and I did. I promised you on the night of our engagement that I would show you pleasure unlike anything you've ever known and I believe I kept that promise."

I never said I loved you.

His unsaid statement hung in the air.

No…he hadn't said it. Not once.

It had all been her.

Stupid, naive Valentina building castles of love around this hard man.

She found no bump on Nikolai's thick skull and sighed with relief. His head lolling onto her chest, he fell asleep with an undignified snore. She'd have gagged at the sweat from Nikolai's flushed head trickling down her meager cleavage if all her reactions weren't attuned to the man behind her.

The small hairs on her neck stood up before Kairos spoke. "Leave him alone."

Ignoring him, she rose to her feet, and planted her hands under Nikolai's arms.

"Move, Valentina."

Before she could blink, Kairos hefted Nikolai up onto his shoulders and raised a brow at her.

He had carried her like that once, the hard muscles of his shoulders digging into her belly, his big hands wrapped around her upper thighs, after she had jumped into the pool at a business retreat in front of his colleagues and their wives because he'd ignored her all weekend.

He'd stripped her and thrown her into the cold shower, rage simmering in his eyes. And when he'd extracted her from the shower and rubbed her down, all that rage had converted into passion.

She'd been self-destructive just to get a rise out of him.

She looked away from the memory of that night in his eyes.

Masculine arrogance filled his eyes. "Now that the poor fool has served his purpose, shall I throw him overboard?"

"His purpose?"

"You used him to make me jealous—laughing at his jokes, dancing with him, touching him, to rile my temper. It is done, so you don't need him anymore."

"I told you, Nik is my friend." She jerked her gaze to his face and flushed. "And I did nothing tonight with you on my mind. My world doesn't revolve around you, Kairos. Not anymore." She wouldn't ask whether his temper was riled.

She wouldn't.

With a shrug, he dumped Nikolai on the bed like a sack of potatoes.

Nik's soft snores punctured the silence. If she weren't so caught up in the confusing cascade of emotions Kairos evoked, the whole thing would have been hilarious.

But nothing could cut through her awareness of six feet four inches of pure muscle and utter masculinity. She pressed her fingers to her temple. "Please leave now."

"Enough, Valentina. You've got my attention now. Tell me, did you really sign up with the escort service or was that just a dramatic touch to push me over the edge?"

"Are you asking me if I've been prostituting myself all these months?" She was proud of how steady she sounded while her heart thundered away in her chest.

"I thought perhaps no first. But knowing you and your vicious tendencies, who knows how far you went to shock me, to teach me a lesson, to bring me to heel?"

She walked to the door and held it for Kairos. "Get out."

He leaned against the foot of the bed, dwarfing the room with his presence. "You're not staying here with him."

She folded her hands and tilted her head. The sheer

breadth of his shoulders sucked the air from the room. "I've been doing *what* and *who* I want since the day I left you nine months ago, since I realized what a joke our marriage is. So it's a little late to play the possessive husband."

Hadn't she promised herself that she'd never stoop to provoking him like that again?

She cringed, closed her eyes at the dirty, inflammatory insinuation in her own words.

But she saw the imperceptible lick of fire in his gaze, the tiny flinch of that cruel upper lip. At one time, the little fracture in his control would have been a minor victory to her.

Not anymore.

"It is a good thing then, is it not, Valentina—" the way he said her name sent a curl of longing through her "—that I did not believe all your passionate avowals of love, *ne*?"

Something vibrated in the smooth calmness of his tone. The presence of that anger was a physical slap. Her eyes wide, she stared as he continued, his mouth taking on a cruel tilt.

"No more pathetic displays of your jealousy. No grand declarations of love. No snarling at and slapping every woman I'm friends with. Now we both can work with each other on the same footing."

Dios, she'd always been a melodramatic fool. But Kairos, his inability to feel anything, his unwillingness to share a thought, an emotion…it had turned her into much worse. "*Non*, Kairos. No more of that," she agreed tiredly.

She didn't even have cash for a taxi, but if she'd learnt anything in the last nine months of this flailing about she'd been doing in the name of independence, it was that she could survive.

She could survive without designer clothes and shoes, she could survive without the adulation she'd taken as her due as the fashionista that Milan looked up to, she could survive without the Conti villa and the cars and the expensive lifestyle.

She picked up her clutch from the bed, her phone from the floor. "If you won't leave, I will."

He blocked the door with his shoulders. "Not dressed like a cheap hooker, strutting for business at dawn, you're not."

"I don't want—"

"I will throw you over my shoulder and lock you up in the stateroom."

It should have sounded dramatic, emotional. But Kairos didn't do drama. Didn't utter a word he didn't mean. *And if he so much as touched her...*

"Fine. Let's talk." She threw her clutch back on the bed and faced him. "Even better, why don't you call your lawyer and have him bring divorce papers? I'll sign them right now and we won't see each other ever again."

He didn't exactly startle. But again, Tina had the feeling that something in him became alert. She had...surprised him? Shocked him?

What did he think her leaving him had meant?

He stretched out his wrists, undid the cufflinks on his right hand—platinum cufflinks she'd bought him for their three-month anniversary with her brother's credit card—and pushed back the sleeve.

A shiver of anticipation curled around her spine.

He stretched his left hand toward her. Being left-handed, he'd always undone the right cuff link first. But the right hand...his fingers didn't do fine motor skills well. She'd noted it on their wedding night, how they had felt clumsy when he tried to do anything.

For a physically perfect specimen of masculinity, it had been a shock to note that the fingers of his right hand didn't work quite right. When she'd asked if he'd hurt his hand, he'd kissed her instead. The second time she'd asked, he'd just shrugged.

His usual response when he didn't want to talk.

She'd taken his left hand in hers and deftly undone the cufflink on their wedding night. And a thousand times after that.

It was one of a hundred rituals they'd had as man and wife. Such intimacy in a simple action. So much history in an everyday thing.

Tina stared at the blunt, square nails now, her breath ballooning up in her chest; the long fingers sprinkled with hair to the plain platinum band on his ring finger; the rough calluses on his palm because he didn't wear gloves when he lifted weights. It was a strong, powerful hand and yet when he touched her in the most sensitive places, it was capable of such feathery, tender movements.

A sheen of sweat coated every inch of her skin.

Dios, she couldn't bear to touch him.

Without meeting his gaze, she took a few steps away from him. "What do I have to do to make you believe that I'm done with this marriage? That my behavior is not dictated anymore by trying to get you to acknowledge my existence?"

He smirked, noting the distance she'd put between them. "Is that what you did during our marriage?"

She leaned against the opposite wall and shrugged. "I want to talk about the divorce."

"You really want one?"

"*Si*. Whatever we had was not healthy and I don't want to live like that anymore."

"So Leandro enlightened you about the fat settlement you will receive then."

"What?"

"Your brother made sure you would receive a huge chunk of everything I own should we separate. Bloody insistent, if I remember correctly." His shrug highlighted those muscle-packed shoulders. "Maybe Leandro knew how hard you would make it for any man to stay married to you."

"You think that will hurt me? Leandro…" Her voice caught, the gulf she had put between her brothers and her a physical ache. "He practically raised me, he loved me when he could have hated me for our mother deserting him and Luca. And I still cut him out of my life because he thought so little of me that he had to bribe you to marry me. In the grand scheme of things that I've lost and learned, this marriage and anything I get by dissolving it…they mean nothing to me, Kairos."

He was upon her in the blink of an eye. The scent of him—a hint of male sweat and the mild thread of his cologne—hit her first. Awareness pooled low in her belly. He didn't touch her, and yet the heat of his body was a languid caress.

"How will you afford your haute couture and your designer stilettos then?"

"I haven't touched your credit cards in months. I haven't taken a single Euro from Leandro or Luca. Even the clothes I wear belong to Nikolai."

"Ah…" His gaze raked down the length of her body. The edge of cruelty in it stole her breath even as her skin tingled at his perusal. He nodded toward the happily snoring figure behind him on the bed. "Of course, your pimp dresses you now."

"Nikolai is not a pimp and he tricked me into believing tonight was just a party."

"I have to admit, only Valentina Constantinou could make a tacky, slinky dress look stylish and sophisticated.

But that skill is not really helping, is it? Paris chewed you out and threw you back to Milan after a mere two months. Since then, you've been licking the boots of everyone at that fashion magazine. Fetching coffee for those bitchy socialites, when you had once been their queen bee, running errands in the rain for photographers and models that salivated over you for years…" His gaze swept over her in that dismissive way of his. "Have you had enough of reality? Are you ready to return to your life of luxury?"

She wasn't surprised he knew what she'd been up to in the last few months. "I don't care how long it takes, I mean to—"

"Is that why you decided to try your hand at the oldest profession in the world?"

"You're the one who bought me from Leandro, remember? If anyone made me a whore, Kairos, it was you." Every hurt she felt poured out into her words, all her promises to herself to keep it civil forgotten.

"I did not pursue you under false pretenses. I did not take you to bed, hoping that a good performance would bring me closer to the CEO position of the Conti board."

A blaze lit up in his silvery eyes, tight lines fanning around his mouth.

He tugged her and Tina fell onto him with a soft gasp. Hard muscles pushed against her breasts, sending shock waves through her. "Believe me, *pethi mou*, if there is one aspect of our marriage that both of us agree on, it is in bed."

His fingers wrapped around her nape in a possessive hold, a flicker of arousal and something else etched onto his features.

"You're the one who broke our marriage vows, Valentina. You're the one who avowed her love in passionate statements and sensational gestures, *ne*? Again and again. All I wanted was a civil marriage. Then, the fickle, spoilt brat that you are, you ran away because your little fantasy world where you rule as a queen and I fall at your feet crumbled. You leave no note. No message. You tell my security guard you're visiting your damned brothers. I imagined you kidnapped and waited for a ransom note. I imagined your body lying in some morgue because you met with an accident. I imagined one of the women or men you insulted with your cruel words may have been pushed to the limit and wrung your pretty neck."

Heart thundering, Valentina stared.

His fingers dug into her tender flesh with a grip she was sure would leave bruises. She'd never seen him like this, smoldering with a barely banked fire. "Until Leandro took pity on me and informed me that you had simply walked out on me. On our marriage."

Tina sagged against the wall, a strange twisting in her belly. He had been worried about her safety. *Terrified for her.* "I'm… I'm sorry. I didn't think…"

"Too little, too late."

He was right. If nothing else, he deserved an explanation. "I was furious with you and with Leandro. I had just learned that I was not a Conti but a bastard child my mother had with her chauffeur. That you married me as part of a bloody deal. You've had nine months to come after me." The words slipped past her tongue, desperate, pathetic.

And just like that, any emotion she had spied in his eyes was wiped away. He stared at his fingers pressing into her flesh, his other hand kneading her hip.

His eyes widened fractionally before he stepped back. Stopped touching her. "The moment Leandro informed me what you'd done, I stopped thinking of you. I had other matters—*urgent, important* matters—to deal with rather than chase my impulsive brat of a wife through Europe."

A fist to her heart would have been less painful.

But this was good, Tina reassured herself. She'd needed this talk with him. She'd needed to hear these words from Kairos's mouth. Now, she could stop wondering—in the middle of the night, alone in her bed—if she'd made a mistake.

If their marriage deserved another chance.

After tonight, she wouldn't have to see him again. Never hear those hateful words again. "*Bene*. You had important matters and I had enough time to think my decision through. I had nine months to realize what I did on impulse was right. I do not care whether you pay me alimony or not because I would not touch it. I intend to make something out of myself."

"By whoring yourself out to Russian investors? By dressing like a cheap tramp? Admit it, Valentina. You've gotten nowhere in nine months except ending up with that buffoon who wants to get in your pants. You have no talent. No skills. Your connections were the only things of value about you."

"I know that. Believe me, I have learned a lifetime's worth of lessons in these nine months. The only good thing about this is that whatever connections you thought I would bring you as the Conti heiress are now lost."

"Your brothers haven't disowned you."

"I have cut all my connections with them. With that life. I'm of no more use to you."

"Ah…so that is your petty revenge? To deny what I planned to get by cutting yourself off from your brothers temporarily?"

"You give both me and your role in my life too much credit, Kairos. I love my brothers. Every day I spend away from them tears my heart. But it is the price I have to pay to face myself in the mirror."

Finally, it seemed that she was getting through to him.

And still, ruthlessness was etched onto his every feature. "This marriage is not done until I say it is done."

"All I want is a teeny signature on a piece of paper. Ask me to sign away that alimony Leandro set up and I will. I will do anything you ask of me to be released from this marriage. You already wrote me out of your life when you decided not to come after me nine months ago, Kairos. I was nothing but a disappointment to you. So why drag this on? Is it just because your masculine pride is dented? Is it because, once again, I made you lose your rigid self-control?"

"Whether you want it or not, whether you touch it or not, half of what is mine will be yours for years to come. If I'm going to pay through the nose for the mistake of indulging you in your foolish fantasies of everlasting love, for putting up with your temper tantrums, for the pleasure of having you in my bed, I would like three more months of marriage, *agapita*. And maybe, a little more of you for that price tag."

"A little more of me for that price..." Tina whispered, his words gouging through her already battered heart.

Her hand flew at him, outrage filling her every pore.

His lightning-fast reflexes didn't let her slap land. With a gentleness that belied the hard, wiry strength of his body, he held her wrist between them, crowding her body against the wall until it kissed the line of her spine.

Hardness and heat, he was so male. Her five-inch stilettos made up for the height difference between them until she was perfectly molded against him. Muscular thighs straddled hers. His granite chest grazed the tips of her breasts, making her nipples tighten and ache. And against her belly... *Maledizione*, his arousal was lengthening and hardening.

Damp heat uncurled between Tina's thighs. A whimper

flew from her mouth—a needy and desperate plea for more. She clenched her thighs on instinct. "I do not even use my hands or my mouth. Yet you're damp and ready for me, *ne*?"

Breath shallow, she fought for control over her body, over the hunger he lit so easily. "As you said, it's why other men follow me around. I'm hot and uninhibited in bed, *si*? I could always match your sexual appetite and we both know it's insatiable. That I'm like a bitch in heat right now is not a point in your favor. You give good sex, Kairos. It was the one place where I was happy as your wife."

A lick of temper awakened in his silver eyes. "Tell me, Valentina. Do you get hot like this for any other man? For the fool lying in the bed behind us?" He twisted his hips in that way of his.

His erection rubbed against the lips of her sex and she jerked.

Pleasure was a fork in her spine, setting fire along her nerves. She could feel that thick rigidness inside her, could see the tight control etched onto his features as he moved inside her. She craved the softening of his gaze, the few moments of the real Kairos, tender and caring, that she used to glimpse after he found his release.

And she still wanted that man. Like a puppy that had been kicked but still came back for more.

His mouth was at her cheekbone and his stubble chafed her lips. A wet, open kiss at her pulse. "I have other uses for you, wife…along with a few more months in my bed." His hands moved to cup her buttocks and pulled her against his hardness.

His mouth trailed lazily along her jawline, heading for her lips—the depth of her want, the fire along her skin— and she could taste the release in her fevered muscles.

"Admit defeat, Valentina. You can pretend all you want but your best bet is to be a rich man's trophy wife. It is not a bad role for you. Accept your limitations. Adjust your expectations. Just as I did when your brother Luca stood in the way of the Conti board CEO position. I want nothing more from a wife, and who knows? You can maybe even persuade me to give this marriage another try."

He *was angry* she had walked out.

No, not angry, she realized, running shaking hands through her hair.

He was furious with an icy, cold edge to it. Every word and caress of his was meant to provoke her with its cruelty. She'd never seen him like that.

It was more temper than she'd seen of him in all of their relationship so far—and, by God, she'd done every awful thing she could think of to provoke it.

But he wasn't asking her back. He didn't want to give their marriage another chance. He didn't want to give her a chance.

No, all he wanted was a sop to his male ego. All he wanted was to punish her for daring to leave him, for calling him out on his ruthless ambition.

That pain gave her a rope with which to climb out of the sensual haze. To deny herself what she'd never been able to before—his touch.

"Please, Kairos, release me."

The moment the words were out of her mouth, he let her go. Pupils drenched with lust, he stared at her as if he couldn't believe she could put a stop to it.

Shaking but determined to hold herself up, she met his gaze. "What do I have to do to get you to agree to a divorce? To get you to leave me alone?"

He looked taken aback but recovered fast. "Three months as my wife."

"Why? Why do you need me now? Other than because you want to punish me for walking out on you?"

"I have a debt to pay to Theseus."

"The man who brought you home from the streets, the one who adopted you?"

"*Ne.*"

"And for this, you need to have a wife?"

"Yes. His daughter Helena—"

"Is causing trouble between you and him? You want me to take her on? I don't understand how your wife's presence will help..." The words trailed away from her lips as she saw his closed off expression. A mocking laugh rose. "*Non,* I've got it, I think. The daughter wants you and you want to say no without hurting anyone's feelings. How noble of you, Kairos."

His brow cleared, relief dawning in his eyes. "Theseus deserves nothing less from me."

The depth of his sincerity shook Tina. She had never seen Kairos feel that strongly about anyone or anything. Except wealth and power and the amassing of it.

"This is the only way you get your divorce, Valentina."

"You cannot drag me back into that life against my will."

"But I can fight the divorce proceedings. Make your life into the media circus that you suddenly appear to abhor. And even worse, one wrong word or move from me toward you will bring forth your brothers' fury upon me and their interference in your life...if you truly intend to make it on your own, that would be hell."

Tina stared at him, amazed despite the anger pouring through her. He was calling her bluff about all this—the new direction she wanted to take in life.

She was damned if she answered it, damned if she didn't. She didn't want to spend another moment with him and yet he had left her no choice.

She sighed. "You will release me when things are clarified?"

"When things are clarified to *my* satisfaction, yes. No sooner. I'm warning you, Valentina, I want a perfect wife. No tantrums. No reckless escapades. You could even leave with the fat settlement the divorce will award you with the satisfaction that you've truly earned it. A novel feeling, I assure you."

"And if I sleep with you to earn it, you will have truly made me a whore, *si*, Kairos? Will your dented ego be repaired then? Because, hear me out, Kairos. My body might be willing but my heart is not."

The growl he swallowed down filled her with vicious satisfaction.

Valentina smiled for the first time in nine months.

Now all she'd have to do was convince herself of what she had told him.

CHAPTER THREE

WHAT DO I have to do to get you to leave me alone?

She truly wanted out of their marriage.

The realization moved through Kairos like an earth-quake as he stared down at her sleeping form in the rear cabin of his private jet.

He'd only thought of how he would punish her when he found her. How good she would feel under him once again. How he would provoke her temper until she came at him all explosive fury and uncontained passion.

But she'd done nothing of the sort.

Oh, she'd lost control a couple of times and given him back as much as he'd deserved, but that was nothing to the Valentina he had known.

It was as if he was looking at a stranger.

If I sleep with you to earn it, you will have truly made me a whore.

Christos, only she could find such an appalling twist to what he had suggested.

But then since he was blackmailing her into his bed, was it any wonder that she had fought dirty?

He should have been impervious to her passionate, fiery declarations after ten months of living with her and her infamous tempers. Should have been unaffected by the sounds of her moans, the slide of her lithe body against his when he touched her.

That he wasn't, disconcerted him on a level he didn't understand.

His physical need for her and only her, and the fact that neither the sweet Stella nor any of the women who had readily offered him a place in their bed in the nine months since Valentina had walked out on him had remotely even tempted him, he could still somehow explain.

Like she had so crudely pointed out, Valentina was explosive in bed. He had been more than surprised when he'd discovered her virginity on their wedding night.

Valentina, as he'd quickly learned to his tremendous satisfaction, was an utterly sensual creature. Whatever he had taught her in bed, she'd not only taken to it enthusiastically but her innate curiosity for his body, her relentless eagerness to return every pleasure he had shown her. That she had remained untouched had been a shock.

She possessed a quick temper and an even quicker sexual trigger, and *Christos*, he'd reveled in making her explode to his slightest caresses. Tender and drawn-out, or explosive and fast, her passion had matched his own.

No man could be blamed for becoming obsessed like he had.

He needed Valentina with a fervor he didn't care or need to understand, and he would have her.

But the hurt in her eyes as he had dealt one cruel statement after the other, hoping to get her temper to rise, festered like an unhealed wound in the hours since he'd arranged for them to travel to Greece.

He should be grateful that the blinders were torn from her eyes. That she would not look at him anymore as if he were her knight in shining armor. Or the man who'd fulfilled all her romantic fantasies.

Whether they divorced or not, it was a good thing she had finally learned the truth.

He had no familiarity or place in his life for tender feelings or love. They demanded a price he couldn't afford, however wealthy he had become.

But the sight of her huge brown eyes as he'd torn her into shreds with his words wouldn't leave him alone. He hadn't pulled any of his punches and she had taken them as if they were her due.

He didn't believe for a second that Valentina would stick to her chosen path or that she had what it took to succeed in her career.

She was just too undisciplined, too impulsive, too spoilt for the hard work it entailed. But still, for the first time in his life, Kairos felt as if he had stood up to the title that had haunted him all his childhood.

Bastard.

He was a bastard.

For even knowing that she would end up in his bed, even acknowledging that something intrinsic had changed in Valentina and he was the one who had caused it, knowing that he would hurt her, he still couldn't walk away from her.

Neither would he keep her.

For all that she'd professed her love for him, she had proved that she was like the rest—using love as manipulation, and then breaking her word.

No one was important enough for him to risk that, to forget the lesson he had already learned.

Love was nothing but a game.

For all your avowals, you left. You proved how little your words mean.

The words and the sentiment behind them stung Tina as she lathered up in the small shower cubicle.

Had there been an infinitesimal thread of complaint in

Kairos's tone? Was she just reading too much when there was nothing again?

She had, at every available moment and opportunity, prostrated her feelings at his feet. Made a spectacle of herself.

How dare he think she'd given in too easily?

She wrapped a towel around herself, and stepped out.

Designer-label bags in every size and color covered the bed.

Mothership to Valentina... Calling now.

A soft sigh emerged from her lips.

She lasted nineteen seconds before she pulled the soft tissue out of the first bag and discovered a black cold-shoulder blouse and white capri pants. More casual pants and blouses. She counted four dresses ranging from a cocktail dress to a pale pink ball gown that would show off her tan beautifully.

Small, silky tissue bags of underwear and everything in her size. Makeup bags with her favorite lipsticks and perfumes with designer labels.

The bras were from the designer label she loved and sinfully expensive—two of them she had discovered recently would pay for her food for a month. And of the push-up kind she'd always preferred to make the most of her nonexistent boobage.

Sliding to the bed in her towel, Tina fingered the butter-soft cushioning of a push-up bra. In some throwaway remark he had made once when they'd watched an old Hollywood movie, she'd realized her husband had a thing for big breasts.

And hers were meager at best. So, like an idiot female, she'd gone on a rampage with lingerie, bras especially, and in the end there had been more cushioning and padding in her bra than flesh on her body.

One evening, she'd gone with an extreme push-up bra to a party—her boobs, exposed by a low neckline, almost kissing her chin and barely covering her nipples. Kairos had blown his top and called her entire outfit trampy—the first time in their marriage that he'd lost it.

He'd said, in clipped tones, that her need for every man's attention made her the shallowest woman he'd ever met. And then he'd walked out for the night.

She frowned.

For all his smarts, hadn't Kairos realized that she'd gone from one outrageous outfit to the next to get a rise out of him? To make up for what she thought she was lacking, for him? That from the moment Leandro had introduced her to him, she hadn't thought of another man ever again?

Why did she have to go to such extremes to please him?

Why was she even now, making such a big deal about the fact that he'd remembered the size of her underwear, of all things?

Kairos had a mind like a super computer, remembering every small detail that went in. It had no significance.

"A starved dog would look at meat scraps with less hunger," said a dry voice from the doorway.

Tina stood up and tugged the towel up.

He had also changed—a gray V-necked sweater that hugged his biceps and chest and dark jeans that caressed his muscular thighs. She had to swallow the feminine sigh of appreciation that wanted to come out.

"Old dogs can learn new tricks," she said repressively.

His laughter pervaded the small cabin. Grooves etched in his cheeks, his eyes alight with humor. "I think the saying says the opposite."

"I don't want the clothes."

"No choice. My wife, the fashionista of Milan, can't dress in trashy clothes that better suit a street walker or..."

he picked up the worn-out denim shorts and loose T-shirt that she had put out "…hand-me-downs. Wow, you have really taken this role to heart, *ne*? You would have turned your nose up at these a few months ago."

"I would have, *si*. But it is not a joke, Kairos. Those are clothes that I could afford on what I made."

He threw the shirt carelessly aside. "You have to look the part, Valentina. Believe me, you're going to need the armor."

She frowned at the thoughtful look in his eyes. Armor for what? She'd been so caught up in staying strong against his onslaught she hadn't delved too much into the details. "I want to discuss this after I dress."

A brow raised, Kairos stared at her leisurely. Water drops clinging to her skin should burn and singe for the lazy intensity of his gaze. "Still so modest, Valentina? I have seen, touched, licked, sucked every part of you, *ne*?"

She glared at him. "I was willing then. Not anymore."

"But I can see you if I close my eyes." He closed his eyes, leaning against the wall. A wicked smile dancing around his lips. "The mole on the curve of your right buttock. The mark you have on your knee from skinning it. The silky folds of—"

She pressed her palm to his mouth and whispered, "Stop, please."

Unholy humor glinted in his silver eyes. "That's not all. I have the sounds you make, the way you thrust your hips up when I'm deep inside you, I have them all in my head." He tapped his temple, his nostrils flaring. "They're the first things I recall in the morning when I wake up with—"

She drew her hand back, burned. But even beneath the sensual web around them, it was the humor in his eyes that threw her. "You're shameless."

His eyes followed a drop of water from her neck to the

tight cinch of her towel. A devilish smile glinted around his mouth. "You know how I get in the morning, *ne*? You left me with no recourse." He pulled up her left hand and frowned. "Where are your rings?"

"In my bag."

With purposeful movements, he looked through her bag. Stalking back to her, he pushed the rings on her finger. Another sleek box appeared from somewhere.

Her heart thundered as he pulled out a simple gold chain with a diamond pendant.

The pendant was a thumbnail sized V in delicately twisted platinum and gold with tiny diamonds lining up the branches. She had seen it at a jewelry store once—on one rare occasion when they'd been out shopping together to buy a gift for her niece Izzie. Buying it with her credit card—against Kairos's dictate that she stop spending Leandro's money—would have been easy.

But already…something had changed in her back then.

Clothes and shoes and jewelry had begun to lose their allure. Because none of those, she had realized, made a difference in how her reserved husband saw her.

And yet he'd noticed her watching it.

She met his eyes over the fragile chain dangling in his fingers. "I… I have a lot of funky jewelry to dress the part. I can't stand the thought of fake gifts."

"I bought it for you. We might as well use it." With one hand, he pushed the swathe of her hair aside, then his hands were gentle around her neck. His warm breath feathered over her face, his arms a languorous weight over her shoulders. "Throw it away after we're done with this for all I care."

The pendant was cold against her bare skin. Tina licked her lips, warmth pooling in her chest. "When?"

His fingers lingered over the nape of her neck, straightening the chain, but still her heart went thud against her ribcage. "When what?"

"When did you buy it?"

"When you were waiting outside, in the car. I meant to give it to you on—" he laughed, and yet beneath the mockery Tina sensed self-deprecation, even anger "—the ten-month anniversary of our wedding. I feel like a fool even saying that."

"Then why did you buy it?" Her tummy rolled at his proximity, at the revelation. "You called me a sentimental little fool when I bought you gifts on that date. A child who celebrates every little thing."

"Maybe you finally wore me down. But then you left two days after that shopping trip, so maybe it's a good thing I didn't change too much for you, *ne*?" he said, looking away.

This time, there was no doubt that he was angry, even bitter that she had left him. That she had given up on their marriage. She must have changed him a little if he had truly thought of giving her a gift on that date. Maybe just a little.

But still, he hadn't acted on that anger. He had simply written her off, like a bad asset. He had only come for her when he decided he needed her. She had to remember that.

"The clothes, the shoes, everything will stay." He walked away, a faint tension radiating from him. "I want the classy, stylish Valentina. The adoring, loving wife."

"I can't force the last part."

"Pretend then. For months, you did just that anyway. Do you need anything else?"

"Underwear. Bras, to be exact," she said the first thing that came to her lips while her mind whirled. Had he cared about her just a little? Had he bought her the necklace to make her happy?

Did his humiliating proposal that she could persuade him to try again hold a hint of what he wanted?

"The ones I have are plain cotton and will show—"

"Things I'd rather not have anyone but me see in those slinky dresses," he finished for her, possessiveness ringing in his tone. He frowned and looked at the reams of new bras. "I had my PA order those from the boutique you spend a fortune in."

She sighed—she really did like how big those push-up bras made her breasts look. No, what she liked was that they had made her feel like he would like her more. But no more of her crazy shenanigans. "Those don't…fit anymore."

His gaze moved to her chest like a laser beam. The wicked devil! "I can't tell from under that towel."

She picked up a pen and notepad and wrote down her size.

"No underwire, no padding, no lifting. All you're going to get is my tiny boobs as nature made them," she muttered to herself.

He laughed, half choking on it. She jerked her head up, realizing too late he'd been standing far too close. He stared at her as if she had grown two horns. "What?"

She pasted a fake smile to her lips. "My sanity returned nine months ago. I can't wait for the next three months to be over."

He scowled. Didn't even bother to hide it.

"Fortunately, I know you well enough not to trust a word out of your lovely mouth," said the blasted man.

If a shiver claimed her spine, she didn't let it show on her face.

A few more months in my bed…

A rich man's trophy wife…

Kairos would never see her as anything else.

She'd seen how he behaved with her sister-in-law Sophia, one of his oldest friends. A woman he'd proposed to before he'd decided on Tina herself.

Sophia was the smartest woman Tina knew. And she commanded Kairos's respect. Even Leandro's wife Alexis had Kairos's regard.

Both women, so different, and yet they had one thing in common that she did not have.

They were successful in their own right—strong, independent women who were more than enough to take on her powerful brothers Leandro and Luca.

That was what Tina wanted to be. That was what she wanted to see in his eyes when he looked at her.

If he was going to tease and torment her for three months, then she would earn his respect, his regard. She was Valentina Conti Constantinou and she would have her own form of revenge by succeeding beyond his wildest dreams.

She would rub his face in what he was giving up. And only then, only when she had brought him to his knees, would Valentina walk away. Even her Machiavellian grandfather Antonio, who'd only ever accepted her under pressure from Leandro, couldn't deny that she was any less of a scheming Conti now.

She turned around and faced Kairos. "I have been thinking of our deal since last night." Steady, flat, her voice cooperated. "I have a few conditions."

His nostrils flared. "You don't get to negotiate."

That she had shocked him snapped her spine into place.

She let a smile curve her mouth. She hadn't been born a Conti, but her proud, powerful brothers had raised her to be one. "I might be vain and vapid but I'm not *stupido*, Kairos. You came to me last night because you need me. So, *si*, I will negotiate and you will listen."

"What are your conditions?"

"You were right about the industry being a bitch. I didn't get anywhere in nine months. I want word spread that we're back together again. I want the names and numbers of everyone you do business with. And I want your backing."

"I'm a respected businessman, Valentina. I will not give the weight of my name to any harebrained scheme of yours that is sure to embarrass me and sink in a few months. If you want my money, you have to wait until the divorce is final to get your hands on it."

"*Non*! Not money. I want access to your rich friends and their wives. Or their mistresses. I don't care how you put it forward. Tell them your juvenile, impulsive bratty wife is putting together a shoot and you're indulging her. Tell them it's the way I'm whiling away my useless life. Tell them it's your way of indulging my tantrums. I don't care what you tell them. I need to put together a portfolio and a shoot. I need to get word of mouth going that I'm offering my services as a personal stylist to anyone who's got reputation, status and money."

"A personal stylist?"

"*Si.*" She raised her hand, cutting him off. "If you're going to use me, Kairos, I will use you, too. At least, we're finally speaking the same language."

"And what language is that, Valentina?"

"The language of transactions. You never do anything without some advantage to yourself. Our marriage has taught me one useful thing at least."

"You're playing a dangerous game, *pethi mou,* hurling accusations at me. You can only push me so far."

"I know you'll find it hard to believe, but I'm not doing anything to provoke you, Kairos. For the first time in my life, I'm thinking with my head. I've looked past the surface and not liked what I see in myself.

You have made me face reality. And for that, I shall always be grateful to you."

"You want a divorce because you're grateful to me?" The

stony mask of his face belied how angry he was with her again. No, not anger. But he was affected by her decision.

"Just because I've realized what was wrong with me doesn't mean you were right, does it? I will never give you power over me again."

For all her brazen confidence, she'd never stripped before him, because she had thought her body imperfect, not made to his specifications and preferences.

Or maybe because she had always wanted to be perfect to please him—perfect straight hair, perfect dress, perfect posture.

It had got her exactly nowhere with him.

Without waiting for his response, her breath suspended in her throat, she picked some underwear. Her back to him, she dropped the towel. The soft exhale behind her pulled her nerves taut. Somehow, she managed to pull her panties up the right way and hooked her bra on.

The intensity of his gaze on her body burned over her skin, as if he was stroking it with those clever fingers. But she was determined to see this through, to prove to him that he wouldn't always have the upper hand.

With barely a glance in his direction, she pulled on a pair of capri pants and a white silk top.

And then, head held high, she walked out to the main cabin, her heart a deafening roar in her chest.

She was tweaking the tiger's tail, true. But she had to do this. She had to prove to him that she was made of stronger stuff. And then, when the three months were up, she would have his respect and then she would walk away.

CHAPTER FOUR

THEY ARRIVED AT a large estate on the island of Mykonos around six in the evening in a tinted limo.

A grove of dark green olive trees beckoned as the car drove up the curving driveway.

Lush green surrounded the whitewashed villa nestled in a picturesque setting. Blue beaches stretched as far as the eye could see.

But Tina barely took it in for her gaze stuck to the myriad expressions crossing her husband's usually expressionless face.

His chest had risen and fallen with a deep breath at the first sight of the villa. His jaw clenched tight at the sight of a green sports model Beetle. Tenderness and ache and grim determination flashed across his silver eyes at the sight of the three people—an older man and woman and a young woman—waiting at the top of the steps.

Tina felt as if she was standing in a minefield. She'd never seen Kairos show so much emotion, much less such varying reactions.

"Kairos?" she said softly, loath to disturb the glimpse she was getting into a man she'd thought felt nothing, held nothing sacred.

His gaze turned to her from the opposite seat. And in the seconds it took him to focus on her, his expression became blank, as easily as if he'd donned a mask, completely shutting her out yet again.

But she couldn't scream or fight him for his usual response. "What exactly does this debt to Theseus entail, Kairos?"

Hesitation like she'd never seen flickered across his face. "There are some duties I need to fulfill. That's all you need to know."

Curiosity ate through Tina even as she told herself to stay out of it.

In ten months of marriage, all she'd learned about him was that he was an orphan who had grown up on the streets of Athens. That he had had a mentor who had given him an education. That was it, no more.

Getting her husband to talk about himself, his past, or his emotions was like getting blood out of stone. She'd honestly never met a man who talked so little.

Something about the tension wreathed in his face made her say, "You're not going to murder someone and ask me to lie for you in court, are you?"

His mouth twitched. "So you haven't stopped watching American soap operas."

"Sell me to land a business deal like that guy did in *Indecent Proposal*?"

He laughed. The warm sound enveloped her in the dark interior.

"*Oxhi*... No," he clarified. "Even if I wanted to, I don't think there's a man living who'd know how to handle you, Valentina."

"I know *oxhi* means no," she said, trying to think of his statement as a compliment. "I plan to say it quite a lot to you over the next few months. In English, Italian *and* Greek," she added for good measure.

Memories permeated the air between them, bringing a smile to her own lips.

For the first month of their marriage, they had had hilarious moments, teaching each other Italian and Greek. But they had both settled on English in the end.

Except when he made love to her. Then he slipped into Greek—guttural, pithy words that even now sent a shiver through her insides. Words she'd never hear again.

No, words she didn't want to hear, she clarified for herself.

"Cold?" he asked, his head dipping down toward her as she exited the car.

She shook her head but he draped a muscled arm around her shoulders, pulling her flush against his side. A clamor of sensation rose inside her. But still, she was aware of a pair of eyes drilling holes into her.

The younger woman, she knew instinctually.

A sliver of apprehension clamped her spine. "Kairos, this feels—"

He cut her off with the press of his lips.

It began as a soft nuzzle. A tender hold of her jaw. A warning to play along in his eyes. Barely a slide of his body against hers.

A show. He was putting on a show. For that woman, Helena.

And yet, as their lips met, as her chest grazed his, as his hand descended to her hip to keep her steady, everything changed.

Nine months of deprivation came pouring out. Desire rose—swift and spiraling.

Heat and pleasure radiated from where their lips grazed and pressed. Air left her lungs. Her knees wobbled and she clutched his arm. A whimper fell from her mouth when he licked the seam of her lips.

He cursed against her lips and Tina instantly opened up. The masterful glide of his tongue against hers made her moan and press harder into his hard body. Her hands crawled to the nape of his neck, her fingers pushing into his rough hair.

The world around them dissolved. Colors burned behind her eyelids, desire making her blood heavy. She could feel the defined contours of his body digging into hers. Images and sensations from memory drowned the little thread of her will: the cradle of his hard hips bearing her down into the mattress; his rock-hard thighs pushing against the soft flesh of hers; the utterly masculine grunt at the back of his throat when she dug her nails into his back.

Heat bloomed low in her belly as he swept over every inch of her mouth with glorious, knowing strokes. No tenderness. No holding back.

Purely carnal, he thrust in and out of her mouth with his tongue.

Pockets of heat erupted all over her, her clothes caging the sensations against her hot skin.

One hand around her neck and one encircling her hip, he held her the way he needed for his onslaught, only letting her come up for air briefly before he claimed her mouth again. He bit her lower lip with such aggressive possession that she moaned. Pleasure and pain wound around her senses.

Instantly he gentled the kiss, laving the hurt with his tongue.

Softer and slower. Ache upon ache built in her lower belly, spinning and spiraling. Tina whimpered against his mouth, craving release. Craving this closeness with him.

"Enough, Kairos! Introduce us to your little plaything."

The venom in that voice, hidden beneath a vein of sweet playfulness, was ice water over Tina's head. She pulled away, heart thundering a million miles an hour in her ears. Her lips stung, her entire body thrummed with need.

"Helena, please be...polite," came another soft voice.

His fingertips trailing lazily against her jawline, his chest rising and falling, Kairos let out a soft growl that reverberated along her trembling body. Tina sensed his shock as her own senses began to clear.

"Nine months…" he whispered against her mouth, his forehead touching hers in uncharacteristic affection. "Even if I hadn't needed you here for this day, *pethi mou*… You and I are not through."

The words were feral. Possessive. And not meant for their audience.

Tina licked her lips and tasted him there. But all he meant was for sex, she reminded her sinking senses. She frowned. "It is just one kiss."

Masculine arrogance etched into every line of his face. "You will come to me, *pethi mou*. I simply shall not allow it to be otherwise." He rubbed her lips with the pad of his thumb. "I might, however, decide not to give you what you want. As a punishment."

She saw it now. He meant to use these months to work her out of his system. He didn't like it that he still wanted her so much. And then, he would walk away.

And if the kiss had been any indication, he was right. She hadn't even mustered a token protest. "This is a game to you, isn't it? Like who will blink first, or who will draw first and shoot the other person?"

"You're the one who always plays games."

Anger and frustration pulsed through her. "No more," she said, tilting her head toward the woman waiting. She rubbed at a piece of nonexistent lint on his shirt, felt the thundering of his heart under her palm. "My days of fighting for you are over, Kairos. That woman and you are welcome to each other."

"I have never loved you, Valentina. When we were married, I could barely stand your theatrics and tantrums. But believe me when I say the only woman I have desired since I met you, the only woman that drives me insane with lust, is you. I want only you, *glykia mou.*"

The truth of his declaration reverberated through Tina, leaving her shaking. His own disbelief that he still wanted her, his frustration at his inability to understand it, much less control it, saturated his words.

She barely processed it—four sentences about what he felt or didn't feel from Kairos was like a long speech from any other man—before she felt the younger woman right behind them. Her subtle floral perfume carried to them on the air.

His shoulders tensing, Kairos moved them toward the couple who had come down the stairs but who waited at a discreet distance. His arm remained at her waist in a possessive grip.

"Valentina, this is Theseus Markos and his wife Maria. They are—" his Adam's Apple bobbed as he hesitated "—friends of mine." Tension built in the older couple's faces at his label. Jaw tight, he nodded to the younger woman. "And this is their daughter Helena. My wife, Valentina Constantinou." Possession was imbued in the softly spoken words.

He addressed the greeting mainly to the man.

With a head full of thick gray hair, Theseus looked to be in his sixties. He had a heavy, beefy build but even in the afternoon sun there was an unhealthy pallor to his skin. As if he had spent the last few months away from it.

Tina shook his hand, which was warm beneath her fingers. "We have been very curious about you, Valentina," he said genuinely, the wariness melting from his gaze. Unlike Kairos, his accent was thick. "Welcome to our home. We hope you are not angry with us for taking your husband away from you for so long. Kairos has been an immense help here."

"Of course I'm not," Tina said as if she knew all about it.

This was her chance to dig in and ask questions. True to her self-centered mindset, she had simply assumed that Kairos had been away because he hadn't cared about her fleeing their marriage.

But knowing that he had been here in Greece where his presence was needed and appreciated so much, changed her view.

Maria Markos was more subdued in her welcome, though no less honest. She seemed…anxious and distracted.

Tina thanked them for their welcome.

Only then did she allow herself to look at the woman standing at the periphery. She was a striking contrast to her parents—in both health and attitude. And older than Kairos's twenty-nine.

Thick, wavy black hair was expertly styled around contrastingly waif-like features. A pale yellow sleeveless dress hugged every inch of her big breasts and tiny waist, and fell to above her knees. Familiar with the latest fashions, Valentina instantly noted the designer of that dress and the three-inch wedge platforms she wore. A simple gold necklace with a big diamond pendant shone at her neck. As did matching diamond studs at her ears.

She was short and voluptuous, almost overflowing out of her dress.

Instead of meeting Tina's eyes, Helena threw herself at Kairos. Kairos didn't let his displeasure show, but it was there all the same in the tightness of his mouth, in the way he immediately bowed his body so that only their shoulders touched.

She shouldn't have required the evidence after his statement. Yet, something in her calmed to see that he didn't want nor welcome Helena's attention.

Neither did the woman miss it. She still kissed his cheek, and squeezed his biceps, with a long-drawn sigh, as if she were welcoming a long-lost lover home.

Tina looked at Helena's parents and saw their discomfiture at their daughter's unseemly display toward Kairos in front of his wife. She cringed.

Hadn't she behaved just like Helena at one time?

Becoming jealous and irrational every time Kairos had spent one-on-one time with another woman? Hadn't she tried to stake her claim over him—just as Helena had just done—in a party full of guests, because she'd been insecure and impulsive?

Dear lord, she'd slapped her now sister-in-law because she'd learned of Kairos's regard for her. Thankfully, Sophia had been kind, seeing Tina's insecurity and had befriended her despite her awful behavior.

The outline of Helena's lipstick on Kairos's cheek called to her now, invoking her rash temper, that possessive urge to show that he belonged to her. And only her.

She trembled from the will it took to control herself.

Fortunately, before she could make a fool of herself, Theseus claimed Kairos's attention and Maria followed them up the stairs.

The silence became fraught as Helena stared at her openly. There was no overt animosity in her stare, yet it was all there.

"Valentina Conti Constantinou," Helena said her name with a flourish, ignoring the hand Tina offered. "Although the Conti is apparently not quite true, *ne*?" She didn't wait for Tina to reply. "Poor Kairos. He assumed he was getting the rich Conti heiress, and instead ended up with…a talentless, fortuneless hack. I have heard that even your powerful

Conti brothers have deserted you. I wonder why, after all these months, he brings you back into his life."

It shouldn't have hurt. She'd heard the same from countless mouths, people she'd considered friends, who had assumed the same of her situation and his actions innumerable times.

Hearing that Kairos had ended up with a talentless, poor, bastard of a wife—and that it was *her*—hurt like a piece of glass through her flesh.

Because it was all true. It was what she thought about herself in the worst moments.

She'd never taken a fight lying down but no words came. Like the little girl she'd once been, grieving for her mother, she wished her brothers were here, that she had Leandro's arms to cocoon her in safety, that Luca was at her back bucking her up, that more than anything she had the respect and trust of the man she had once loved so desperately to throw back in the spiteful woman's face.

But she had none of them around her. She had nothing but the truth to face.

Swallowing the deep ache in her belly, she considered the woman staring at her.

Again, she saw the similarities between her and Helena. The insecurity beneath the beauty, the expensive clothes and shoes, the pampered, spoilt attitude that screamed that what she wanted, she would have.

But neither did she feel sympathy for Helena. "Maybe Kairos realized that even without all the trappings of wealth and fortune, he still wants me. He needs me desperately." Just saying the false words was a punch to her middle.

As if she hadn't spewed the most hateful things to her face, Helena looped her arm through Tina's and propelled her forward. "In the end, he will discard you again, you know. He will choose me. We have too much history between us. It would be better for you if you accept that."

"What history?" The question escaped her mouth before Tina could bury it forever.

Helena laughed. A gentle, tinkling sound. "He hasn't told you? Then I can't, either."

With a smile, she wandered off, leaving Tina at the entrance, wondering at the sanity of the woman. And her own, as well.

What the hell had Kairos dropped her in the midst of? What was it that he wanted of her? To scratch and scream at the woman who so boldly touched her husband in front of her? And if she did, how much would be for pretense and how much for real?

Unless he did want to win Helena's hand in the end and was only using Tina to make her jealous, to cement his grip over Helena? To get a better deal?

Bile crawled up her throat.

No! She wasn't going to torture herself like this.

He was welcome to the woman, if that was what he really wanted.

Her skin prickling, she looked up.

Kairos was standing at the balcony with a wine glass in his hand, studying her openly while Theseus talked to him from the side. His shirt was undone at the cuffs and to his chest, owing to the summer heat. The sun glinted off the dial of his platinum watch—her six-month anniversary gift to him, bought with Leandro's money.

That he had kept the watch didn't mean anything. All the thousand tiny things didn't mean anything when he hadn't come for her.

It was her mantra.

He raised the wine glass to her in a mocking toast, his brows raised inquiringly.

She knew what he could see in her face—her longing for him, her distress that he might want Helena, her frustration that he still had this much power over her.

She chased away every expression from her face. Took a deep breath. Even affixed a smile to her mouth.

She pulled her phone from her clutch and texted him, then waited for him to see her text.

The shock in his gaze, the smile fighting to emerge around his mouth…it was a balm to her soul.

Shocking Kairos was her barometer in her fight for independence and if him raising his wineglass to salute her was any indication, she had won this round.

CHAPTER FIVE

Your move, Kairos...keep up your side of the bargain.

LIKE A LOVESICK teenager, Kairos stared at Valentina's text for the millionth time since the night they had arrived. Like she used to say when he had taught her chess.

True to form, he was a master at strategizing, never betraying himself with a look or gesture, laying out traps to lure her in. And she, impulsive, bloodthirsty and eager for mayhem, would charge forward with everything she had, would mount attacks without thinking them through and had always walked into his traps.

It had been a delight to teach her, to see her fight her innate nature and try to stay at least one step ahead of him.

But yesterday, the week since he had seen her on the yacht had been nothing like guessing her chess strategy. The woman he had married was nothing if not unpredictable.

He'd expected her to throw a tantrum right in front of the steps when Helena had hugged him and kissed him in a provoking display. Helena's actions had been purely for Valentina's and Theseus's benefit.

And yet Valentina had recovered. Quickly and smoothly. Had kept her composure as he'd never seen her do before.

And there had been no questions. At all. About his past. About his past relationship with Helena. About his history with Theseus and Maria.

Nothing.

He'd seen her during dinner, then kissed her cheek good-night. Like the quiet, poised wife he'd always wanted, she'd retired without a word at the appropriate time. When he had finally gone to bed around midnight, she'd been asleep.

When he'd gone outside at five the next morning for his run, he had found her running laps around the house already. When he'd quietly joined her, she'd barely blinked.

It had been the same for four days. Since he'd been gone for more than a week to fetch her, work had piled up. So he had left her mostly in Maria's care, knowing that she would treat Valentina with kindness, at the least.

Even as he wondered how long this new serenity would last, he missed the Valentina he'd married. The Valentina that had given voice to every feeling that had crossed her mind, the Valentina that lived through every emotion fearlessly, the Valentina that had, again and again, vowed that she'd always love him.

The Valentina that he only realized after she had left him had brought so much color and noise to his life.

The realization unsettled him.

Designer clothes, haute couture heels and reigning over her little clique—that had been the extent of her interests.

You have made me face reality, she had claimed.

And the weight of that statement hung around his neck. He hadn't wanted the weight of her love nine months ago and he didn't want the burden of the new direction her life had taken now, either.

Attachment and affection only brought the worst out in all people, as Theseus had taught him seven years ago. And Kairos never wanted to experience the pain that came from people letting him down. Of people taking away what they had given, when it was not convenient anymore.

But of course, all this was dependent on the fact that Valentina had changed. And *that* he still could not believe.

Just as he was about to check where she was, Valentina walked into the sunlit breakfast room.

Desire punched him anew, a sharp pulse of longing that he didn't quite understand beneath the voracious hunger.

She stilled at the buffet laid out on the side table, like a doe caught in the sights of a predator. Slowly, her breath evened out, her expression assuming that calm he was beginning to detest.

There were a lot of changes in his wife and this was the most aggravating. She'd never been able to hide her emotions before. *Christos*, there'd been moments when her open longing for him had embarrassed him, when he'd wished she had a little control over herself.

Only now, when he couldn't decipher what was running through her mind, did he appreciate how refreshingly guileless and unflinchingly honest she had been. Only now when she was scrunched up in a corner of the bed did he realize how much he'd missed her warmth in his bed.

"*Kalimera*, Valentina," he said, his tone husky.

"*Buongiorno*, Kairos," she greeted sharply, and turned away toward the food.

He didn't drop his gaze from the delectable picture she made. The tight clench of her shoulders covered in thin straps told him she was aware of his gaze.

Black trousers followed the line of her long legs lovingly—legs that she had wrapped around his shoulders more than once. An emerald green blouse showed off her toned arms.

The wide V-neck gave no hint of a cleavage—had she finally abandoned those ghastly bras that had hidden the curve of her soft flesh from his fingers but exposed the bones in her chest?

She had always been more muscled than soft or fleshy because of her runner's build but she bordered on scrawny now. Even last night, as she had cozied up to him unknowingly in sleep, he had noted she was all sharp angles and bones. Not that it had made any difference to the erection he had sported in a matter of seconds. It was as if he had no control over his lust when it came to her. Lust he needed to address soon.

She had fashioned her glorious hair into some kind of tight braid, pulling it away from her face. It only made her features sharper.

He frowned at her grapefruit and coffee. And the way she settled down at the chair farthest from his. "You have lost weight."

She shrugged, raising those bony shoulders. "I didn't eat much in the last few months."

"Or sleep much?" The dark shadows under her expressive brown eyes were still there after a week. "You missed me so much that you couldn't eat and sleep?" he said, wanting to see a smile on her lips. Wanting that wariness in her eyes gone.

"I didn't know you were capable of cracking a joke," she taunted. Then sighed. "I would think you wouldn't want to engage in a discussion about our marriage where Theseus or his family could walk in or overhear."

"Theseus took Maria and Helena out first thing in the morning for a tour of the estate as it's Saturday. To give us the privacy we've been denied for the past week."

"That was kind of him," she replied. "Is he well? He looks like my grandfather—" she shook her head, a raw glitter in her eyes "—like Antonio did after his heart attack."

A tightness gathered in his chest at the clear distress in her gaze. "Antonio said words to you about your mother?"

He knew how much importance the Conti patriarch put on his bloodline.

"He didn't dare say a thing to me. Not in front of Leandro and Luca." The flat tone in which she spoke revealed how much it really did matter to her. "But I finally realized why he'd always been reserved with me. I always wondered if it were the fact that I was a girl that he cared so little for me.

"Now I know it's because I'm not really his blood." She pushed a lock of hair behind her ear. "Tell me about Theseus."

Why did her pain reach him like a hand into his chest when nothing she'd ever done had? Because he'd never even thought her capable of this depth? Kairos cleared his throat. He didn't know how to handle her emotion. Or maybe he didn't know how to handle this new Valentina at all.

"Theseus had a heart attack nine months ago. Maria says his health had been suffering for a while. An almost successful hostile takeover at his company, I think, precipitated the attack. For a while there, we weren't sure he'd make it through."

"He sent for you then?"

"Something like that."

"You've been here all these months?"

"Yes."

"And the hostile takeover?"

"I stopped it."

"He thinks the world of you, doesn't he?"

He shrugged. "Doesn't matter what he thinks. I…have a duty to him, that's all."

Kairos waited for a question about Helena to come his way. He waited for the cloak of zen around her to disappear now that she knew they'd have no audience.

Time ticked on, seconds gathering into minutes. Only silence.

Disappointment curdled in his stomach.

She took a sip of her coffee. "I…wasn't making enough to buy nice meals and afford the rent on the flat," she said, answering his earlier comment. "Even shared four ways, it was steep."

Her guilelessness in openly admitting failure after he had taunted her shamed him. Scraped him raw, too. "Was it so awful to remain married to me that you preferred walking away from every luxury I offered? From the penthouse suite and an unlimited credit card to live in some hovel with three other women and barely enough to eat?"

"*Si,* it was."

Blunt, and without the theatrics. Everything about this… *new her* unsettled him.

"I'm to believe that neither of your overprotective brothers smothered you in money and comforts? Not even a care package from Luca?"

"Luca respects my wishes. Leandro…" Her throat moved, her knuckles tight around her coffee cup.

Longing vibrated in her voice. This—this rift with her brothers, obviously enforced by her, more than anything else made him wonder about the change in her.

Leandro, Luca and Valentina shared a bond unlike anything he'd ever seen before. Even more astonishing, for it had been revealed that Valentina only shared a mother with her brothers.

Was that why he had gravitated toward Leandro's offer when there had been so many?

No, he hadn't been looking for a ready-made family. He had been burned enough with the one he had considered his.

It was Valentina that had caught his attention from the

first moment Leandro had pointed her out to him. Valentina whom he had wanted to possess.

She rose, put away her untouched grapefruit. "I told Leandro our rift will be permanent if he interferes in my life again."

That she meant it was clear. That it tore at her was also clear.

He had wished so many times that she was more intellectual, more contained…more everything she was not. Yet now that she was like a shadow of her former self, he felt protective of her. "You barely ate anything."

"Since when do you—"

He watched, fascinated, as she shook her head, took a deep breath that made her chest rise invitingly and then met his gaze. "I want to talk about what you're going to do for me. I made a list of—"

"I can do a lot of things for you, Valentina, if only you'd quit this whole 'Independent Valentina' project."

"Wow! Jokes and innuendoes, I don't know if you're the Kairos I married or not. All I usually got were nods and sighs and grunts. And oh, that look you used to get when you wanted sex."

Seeing Kairos disconcerted was like an adrenaline shot to her body.

Dark color stole under his cheeks and for the first time in months, Valentina laughed.

He pushed his chair back and stretched his long legs. His running shorts pulled back, exposing the hard muscle of his thighs. Greedily, she drank in the hair-roughened legs, and the calves. Her breath halted in her throat. Until she'd seen Kairos's muscled calves, she hadn't thought of a man's calves as sexually arousing.

But then, every inch of him was made to be appreciated. Touched. Stroked. Licked…not that he'd ever given her a chance to do all those things. Even in that arena, he had held the strings.

"I don't know what you're talking about." His words tugged her out of the sensual haze. "In my defense, you usually talked so much, fought so much, bitched so much that all I could interject was nods and grunts."

Even his cruel remark couldn't dampen her spirits. "You would get this strange glitter in your eyes. First, you would fight it. As if wanting to sleep with your wife was an urge you had to conquer. Then a run, followed by a shower. Then you would walk into our bedroom and stare at me. For a while there, I thought you found my pajamas distasteful. Then you—"

"You thought I found those little shorts with bows on the sides and sleeveless, braless tops you wore distasteful?"

"You'd sit in the chaise, elbows on your knees, and rub your neck," Tina continued as if his words hadn't sent a shiver of pleasure down her spine. "If you ran your fingers through your hair three times, I knew I was going to get laid that night. If you swore during all this aforementioned waiting time, it meant…"

Stillness surrounded him. Dark slashes of color in his cheeks. "It meant what?"

"Never mind," she dodged.

"What did it mean, Valentina?"

"It meant you would be demanding and a little…rough. It meant you would draw it out until I had no breath left in me. Until I was begging for you to grant me release."

It meant he would punish her. For his own loss of self-control as he saw it. For pushing him to the edge, Tina realized, trembling from head to toe. *Because he couldn't even put into words how much he needed her.*

Why hadn't she realized how much of his true self Kairos had revealed during sex? The power balance in their relationship—had it been more fluid than she'd thought?

She'd never really tried to understand him, never tried to look beneath the surface. She'd expected grand gestures and sweeping statements. And like a little girl denied what she wanted, she'd made his life hell for it.

But—thinking about it now—he had been twenty-seven when they had married, had been estranged from his adoptive family. He had had a rough upbringing, and neither of them had much experience with romantic relationships.

Had she taken any of that into account? Had she ever tried to reach him in a different way?

Non. All she had wanted was a fairy tale without putting any work into the relationship.

A long, filthy curse exploded from him, polluting the sunlit breakfast room. "*Dios*, Valentina! You should've told me if hurt you."

"You didn't. You never hurt me, Kairos. Whatever we did in bed, I was a willing, enthusiastic participant. So don't…don't make it a thing you did *to* me. Instead of with me. I craved the…" *the intimacy I found with you there* "…the pleasure you gave me. I told you that enough times."

His gaze darkened, a faint tension enveloping his muscular frame. Things she didn't say swirled in that cozy glowing room.

He knew now how much she'd watched his every move, every gesture for meaning. How deprived she'd been for a single word of affection. Even a simple statement of his desire for her. For a word of praise—even if it was about those blasted pajamas she'd spent hours choosing. Or about her hair. Or her readiness for him whenever he wanted sex.

That he'd even liked her sexual appetite for him, was something she'd only realized when he'd cruelly commented on it on the yacht.

"You cannot doubt I found satisfaction with you." His gaze held hers in defiance and something else. As if only now he realized how much he had hurt her.

Legs shaking, she walked to the buffet table and poured herself another cup of coffee she didn't want. She took a sip just to force the lump in her throat down.

"I do not find relationships easy to manage."

Stunned that he would even make that concession now, she stared at him. If the consequences of that hadn't hurt her so much, she would have laughed at his mulish explanation.

"Those words would have meant a lot back then," she said sadly. "All I ever heard from you was criticisms."

"And every time I criticized you or compared you to Sophia or Alex, you fought back with an outrageous act," he said slowly, as if he was finally figuring it out.

"Si." Her cup rattled loudly when she put it down on the table. "It's all in the past anyway."

If he had forced the discussion to continue, she'd have fled the room.

He went to the buffet. The clatter of cutlery behind her calmed her nerves.

Her relief was short-lived when he reached her, clasped her wrist in his rough fingers, tugged her and pushed her into the chair. The plate he deposited in front of her overflowed with fresh strawberries, a slice of toast and scrambled eggs.

Her stomach growled.

Without thanking him, Tina dug into it. Within minutes, she had polished off most of the breakfast.

She noticed only as she swallowed the last piece of the toast. Toast *he'd* prepared for her. Almost blackened, slathered in butter.

Just the way she preferred it.

Warmth bloomed in her chest. He'd noted that much

about her. She tried to remind herself that it was too little. But the truth was there now that she wasn't in a fairy tale but real life.

Kairos had cared about her. It had been in all the little things he'd done for her. In the silences after they made love and the way he had held her as if she was precious, in the unsaid words between them after one of her escapades, in the way he had always encouraged her to come out from under her brothers' protective umbrella and make something of herself.

But how could she ever overcome the fact that she hadn't been enough? That she might never be good enough?

CHAPTER SIX

It SEEMED IT was a day of shocks. No, a week of shocks.

From the moment he had set foot on the yacht and seen his wife dressed like a hooker to now, looking at the spreadsheet she showed him on her laptop screen.

Even the slide of her thigh against his couldn't distract his attention this time.

There were reams and reams of data in her pretty pink sketchbook and laptop.

While she pulled up different files—her lower lip caught anxiously between her teeth—he took a huge notebook and flipped it open.

Maybe two hundred pages were filled with sketches—dresses and accessories. Outfits put together from cutouts of dresses and hats and handbags. Pictures of people they had both known—Conti board members' wives and daughters and whatnot. And next to each person's photo cutout from some society pages were notes about how they were dressed wrong. Little corrections to their outfits, makeup, hair, shoes... Kairos idly flipped through the book, then picked up four more like the first one.

There were eight sketchbooks in all. It was years and years of work, he realized, shock vibrating through him.

"When did you start doing these?"

She shrugged, juxtaposing two different spreadsheets on her screen. "When I was eleven, twelve? About two years after I came to live with Leandro and Luca.

"I didn't really have a lot of clothes and accessories to play with until then. When they took me on that first shopping spree to this designer boutique..." Unadulterated joy filled her voice. She leaned back against the chair and closed her eyes, a smile playing at her lips. "It was like I was in heaven. I spent the whole day picking out dresses and shoes and hairbands and bows and belts and pins and more shoes... Leandro says I kept looking behind me every minute."

"Why?" Kairos asked automatically, even as he understood.

An uncomfortable tightness descended in his chest.

He'd forgotten that she hadn't always been this spoilt, rich Conti Heiress. It was the one time he'd wanted to go back for her after she'd walked out on him—when he'd heard the vicious rumor mill repeat the dirty truth.

Valentina Conti wasn't truly a Conti, but her mother's bastard with a chauffeur after she'd left the maniac Enzo Conti after years of abuse.

He had wondered who had leaked the news when the patriarch Antonio Conti and his grandsons Leandro and Luca Conti had hidden the truth for years; he wondered what it had cost Valentina to learn the truth.

A shimmer of doubt nagged at him.

"According to Luca, I was worried they would abandon me at the store and disappear. He says I was this little scrawny thing that would dig my nails in if he even loosened his grip around my hand." She straightened in her chair, her tone so devoid of emotion that the hair on the back of his neck prickled.

"Why?" he asked again.

He'd been married to her for nine months and he'd known nothing about her. *Christos*, he hadn't even been interested. He hadn't loved her, but he also knew firsthand what came of negligence. Of how simply holding back belief in someone could destroy one's belief in oneself.

Theseus had done that to him. And he had never recovered.

"I don't remember clearly actually. Even the bits I do, it's only because Luca would prod me softly. To make me remember. He said I would come running into his room or Leandro's in the middle of the night, crying and in panic. That for years, they would find me sleeping at the foot of his bed, one of my hands on his ankle.

"All I know is that there were months after my mom's accident before someone came looking for me. When Leandro found me and told me he was my older brother, he said I clung to him like a rabid dog."

When she seemed to be lost in the memories of the past, he tugged her hand into his. She returned the tight clasp before she opened her eyes and met his.

Such strength shimmered in her eyes that he felt singed by it. He could see why her brothers were so protective of her. Could see that little feral thing in her eyes. Could see the vulnerability that had always lurked beneath her dramatic personality.

Before he could say a word, she pulled her hand away.

"Valentina, who leaked the fact that you were not…a Conti?"

"I did," she replied instantly, her dark gaze holding his.

He sat back in his chair, reality as he knew it shifting and sliding. "Why?" It seemed to be the only word he could speak around her today. "How did you find out?"

"Sophia knew I was…miserable with you.

"Luca had told her about the circumstances of his birth, about how our mother left his father after his monstrous actions for years. About how Leandro sought to protect me from the truth. About why you married me.

"For the first time in my life, I had a friend who truly cared about me, who trusted me to have the courage to face the truth."

"What did she think it would solve?" He had always liked Sophia, but right now, he could happily wring her neck for interfering in his marriage.

"She thought the truth would free me from that downward spiral I was in because you…" Again that shrug. "She was right. When I learned I wasn't a Conti, I realized how tightly I had clung to it because it had given me an identity when I'd been so scared and alone. When I learned about the alliance between you and Leandro…everything fell apart. If I wasn't Valentina Conti Constantinou, I was nothing. Something you told me again and again. It would only be a matter of time before you learnt the truth too, before you realized you hadn't gotten quite what you wanted. So I left."

Before you left me, the unspoken words reverberated between them.

That he measured so little in her estimation burned his gut. "I didn't leave you after Luca thwarted my fight to be the Conti CEO," he said, knowing it was the utter truth, "and I wouldn't have left you for not being the Conti heiress."

Instead of pacifying her, his words just caused a flash of that old temper to glitter in her eyes. "Do you even realize how arrogant that sounds? As if you were doing me a favor by keeping me on? I wasn't willing to find out what *would* drive you to leave me."

"Valentina—"

"Kairos, please don't pretend as if my leaving—once you get over your dented ego—didn't fill you with relief. It was a circus and it is done. Let it go."

It took every ounce of his self-control to let it go. Every

inch of his pride to give in and admit failure. But her accusation that he was relieved…how dare she?

No, their marriage hadn't been great. Not even close to normal. They hadn't known each other at all.

But it was something he had begun to count on, even with her ridiculous, outrageous theatrics day after day.

She had become a constant in a life that had never known one.

The strength of the urge to punish her for disappointing him, for breaking her word to him, for thinking so little of him…the hurt driving that urge…it stunned him.

He fought the urge to swallow it away, to let it fester. If they were pulling skeletons out of the closet… "For what it's worth, I did hold our marriage sacred, Valentina. I counted on you sticking with me for the next fifty years or more. To have children with me, to build a family of our own… You showed me a glimpse of a future I'd never wanted before. And when it didn't work the way you wanted it to, you took it away, without even bothering to tell me. So don't you dare tell me what I felt when you walked away."

She had acted just as Theseus had once done. He had given Kairos everything and then snatched it away in the blink of an eye.

Maybe he should be glad that it was over with Valentina.

In nine months, he'd proved to himself—and her—that he didn't need her.

He wouldn't have seen her except for the divorce proceedings, if Theseus's situation hadn't forced him to seek her out.

And as she was so wisely reminding him, *she* had walked out. *She* had broken her promise. And that meant she wasn't worth all this thought, much less his regard.

His wife was what he had thought her initially—impulsive, immature and without loyalty.

"Let's just focus on the future like adults," he finally said.

* * *

Her throat stung as Kairos's words penetrated her defenses. For him to admit that her leaving had dented more than just his ego…

Her leaving had hurt him. So he had lashed out on the night at the yacht with cruel words. It didn't excuse it, but it explained so much.

She had been right. Kairos felt so much more than he ever let on.

What was she supposed to do with that knowledge? Why hadn't they ever talked like this before?

When she had talked about her childhood, she'd seen understanding.

Even a little flash of respect when she'd said *she'd* leaked that she wasn't a Conti. As if he hadn't thought her capable of shedding that safety blanket, that position of privilege. It was respect she craved with every cell in her body.

For a few minutes, he'd been kind. Understanding. Interested in her past and how it had shaped her. Interested in her—the person she was beneath the Conti tag—beyond what she could be for him.

But the admission about her leaving had cost him. The walls were back up, as if he had given her far too much.

Now, as she pointed to him several rows and columns, all she got was a polite stranger. The hard press of his thigh against hers, the graze of his corded forearm against the sides of her breasts as he pointed to the screen made her supremely aware of every inch of her body.

"What are all these names?" he asked pointing to the calls she'd highlighted.

"These are the names of the personnel I called at different couture houses—assistant buyers, vendors, designers' assistants and more."

He pulled the laptop to himself and browsed down.

"There are almost…one hundred entries here. With times and dates."

She tried to shake off the vulnerability that descended on her. This was almost a year's worth of work. And she had nothing to show for it. For months, she would finish working a nine-hour workday, and then settle down to make calls. Humiliating chitchat, answering gossip about herself—she'd endured everything in the hope of getting the answer she wanted.

Nothing. Nada. Zilch.

"I kept a very thorough record."

"I see that. But what is it a record of?"

"Calls I made to different people over the last few months."

"You called all these people?" Disbelief rang in his tone, making her all prickly. When she tried to take the laptop from him, he resisted. "Answer me, Valentina."

"*Si.* I called all of them."

He ran a square-nailed finger against the column of Yes/No and the paltry maybes peppered through. "And what does this column mean?"

"It means whether they agreed to let me borrow the piece of clothing, the accessory or the shoes I called about. These are people who have access to the latest designer wear. Magazines and fashion houses and distributors and vendors, etc…"

"Why do you need all these? I thought you turned your back on things you couldn't afford? To attend parties with your pimp?"

That he still thought so little of her made her want to thump him. "I need a portfolio. As a stylist, whether a personal client or a house of design, it's the first thing clients and businesses want to see.

"I roped Nikolai into helping me do the photoshoot, and

even enlisted an up-and-coming model to pose for me. But I don't have access to any clothes or shoes. Without that I have nothing."

"Weren't some of these people your friends? That one and that one…that guy?"

"Sì."

"But it says no against their names."

Tina gritted her teeth. "Are you being dense on purpose?"

One look at him told her he wasn't.

She sighed and rubbed her temple. "It's because they said no. They didn't say no to my face. Half of them wouldn't return my calls. And when I showed up at their workplace anyway, they had their minions tell me they were busy."

"Why?"

"I guess because word had spread that Leandro and Luca had abandoned me and that you dumped me after learning that I wasn't the esteemed Conti heiress. Only Nikolai would even talk to me. He got me that job. It took me a month to understand that none of my so-called friends were really friends. Just as you pointed out. Sophia, of course, offered the Rossi connections but I said no."

"That was foolish. The business world is nothing without connections and networking. You think I chose to ally myself with Leandro because I lacked business acumen? That I chose to head the CLG board because of the politics? Your brothers and Antonio have connections unlike anything I've ever known. I knew that if I wanted to go further in the business world, I needed more. I needed the powerful connections Leandro brought with him. I needed the old families to accept me into their circle."

It was the first time he had mentioned the agreement he had come to with Leandro. The agreement that had led to their marriage. It didn't sound as ruthless a transaction as she'd imagined.

"Are you giving me an explanation for why you did what you did? Perhaps asking for my forgiveness?" *Dios*, she was such a fool.

"No. The agreement we entered into is not that unusual. Leandro knew me. He knew that I would treat you well. And I—"

She glared at him. "But you didn't treat me well."

"Name one thing I deprived you of during our marriage."

"Respect. Affection. Regard." *Love*.

His silence was answer enough for Tina. "If I let Sophia help, then Luca would get involved, too. And if Luca got involved, Leandro would move heaven and earth to open every door for me. And soon, I would be drowning once again in my brothers' favors. I would forget why I started all this. I would become *that* Valentina."

He closed the laptop with a soft thud. With a glare, she hugged the thing to her chest. He took the laptop back from her clenched hands with exaggerated patience and set it down on the table. "Why *did* you start all this?"

She felt like an insect being examined under an industrial microscope. "I told you. I want to make something of myself."

His silver eyes pinned her to the spot. "What I'm asking is why you want to make something of yourself? What is this sudden need to prove yourself? Why all this hardship when before you couldn't even be bothered to understand anything beyond the little circle you were queen of?"

She couldn't tell him that he was the reason.

That she wanted his respect, his regard more than anything else in the world. That she wanted him to be proud of her. That she wanted him to regret—at length and at great pain—what he had lost by letting her go. Of course, she hadn't shed her vindictiveness.

"It's high time I took responsibility for myself. For my happiness, for my life," Tina repeated the lines she'd remembered Sophia spouting at her when she had been at her lowest.

All those things had significance, yes, but not in comparison to what she wanted to see in Kairos's eyes.

"So now that you have seen what I have done so far—" she opened her notepad and drew a couple of bullet points "—tell me the different ways you can help me. I know we talked about you putting word out to different friends of yours. But even if you succeeded in letting them hire me as their personal stylist, I would still need this portfolio to impress them, to gain their business. Now, with Nikolai and Marissa, I have a photographer and model lined up. All I need—"

"You're not working with that Russian joker anymore."

"You don't get to dictate who I talk to or not. You're not my husband anymore."

He pulled her left hand into his and awareness exploded through her. Callused fingers gripped hers, the pad of his thumb wiggling her wedding ring. "Officially, I am."

She pulled her hand away. "Nikolai's talented and he's proved that he has my best—"

"He wants to get in your pants, Valentina."

"I know he does. It doesn't mean he'll get there. Or that I want him there."

"You're not attracted to him."

The statement, which was really a question, arrested the millions of neurons firing away in her brain. Like complex machinery coming to a screeching halt.

Was that doubt in his question? A minute fracture in his arrogant confidence?

She wanted to lie and say she was attracted to Nikolai, to give him a taste of that uncertainty that had been her companion all during their marriage.

No games, Tina!

"I've never been interested in Nikolai. Not even before I met you." She cringed. "But I… I don't think I was kind in my rejection of him."

"What if he had attacked you that night on the yacht?"

The flippant response that rose to her lips arrested as Tina saw the whiteness of his knuckles. "I know him, Kairos. He's all bluster, and believe me, he has punished me enough with innuendoes and insults over the last few months. He's had his petty revenge. I have confidence that he'll be here when I ask him."

"I will not tolerate his sniffing around about you. You will entertain only me."

If her outrage could have been given action, Valentina would have had smoke coming out of her ears. She picked up her laptop and stood up. "I was a fool to think you'd take me seriously."

He gripped her arm and arrested her. "Even if I let you work with him, you still have no access to all the designer clothes and accessories you need. Unless you were thinking of asking me to buy them for you. As long as you—"

She covered his mouth with her palm. And instantly realized the foolishness of the move. His breath was warm against her palm, sending a rush of heat to her breasts and lower belly. As if he was touching his sensuous mouth to those places.

"*No,*" she said and then cleared her throat. "I don't want you to buy anything for me. I only agreed to have my wardrobe back because my role as your loving wife demands it."

Was she never going to solve this Catch-22? What would she show prospective clients if she didn't have a portfolio to interest them, and how would she develop a portfolio if she never had clients?

Kairos pulled her hand away from his mouth but held it against his chest. His heart thundered against her fingertips. "You could join Theseus's company and try to achieve it that way. Go at your goal in a different way."

"Theseus's company?"

"He owns an advertising agency among the group. They put together a lot of shoots here and abroad to design the catalog for the luxury boutiques the Markos group holds all over Greece. A styling internship with such a company could get you valuable experience and contracts."

"And you can get me a position at his company just like that?"

"The woman who runs that department is a friend of mine. It'll be unpaid. Chiara's a no-nonsense go-getter who will only hold it against you that I got you the position."

"I'm willing to do any kind of work if it means I'm a step closer, Kairos. Being here with you when I'd rather mop floors at the fashion agency should prove that."

He ignored her petty barb. "But... Helena is in charge of that division. The moment she figures out you're there, she'll interfere."

"*No!*" Refusal escaped her lips even before she could process his words.

One thing she'd realized in the last week in his company was that she'd always be vulnerable when it came to Kairos. This proximity was bad enough without adding a woman who wanted him. A woman who shared history with him.

A woman who provoked every one of Valentina's baser, jealous instincts to the fore.

He tilted her chin up. "You do not have to be afraid of her, Valentina. She will not harm you, not while I'm here."

"That you have to reassure me of that speaks volumes."

"It's me she's after."

"I know that," she said, her voice going to that whiny octave she hated so much. That Helena wanted Kairos had been written in every malicious smile, every cruel remark of the past few days.

The whole situation twisted her gut. "I'll ask only this one question. Please, Kairos, answer it honestly."

He scowled, his fingers inching into the hair behind her ear tightly. The pad of his thumb pressed at her lower lip roughly. "I've never lied to you."

"Is this—" she waved her hand between them "—some elaborate ploy to make her jealous or to prove your power over her? To make her want you even more?"

At least, that was what Helena had hinted at over last night's dinner. That this thing between her and Kairos was a minor lovers' tiff. That he was using Valentina for any number of purposes.

"I have never played those kinds of games. With anyone."

No, those stupid games had been her forte. Observing Helena's antics was seeing a mirror version of her worst self.

"That doesn't answer my question."

"I don't want Helena."

"You never—"

"*Oxhi!* I wouldn't dishonor Theseus and Maria like that."

The depth of relief that spread in her chest scared the hell out of Tina. This was so not the time to discover Kairos's honorable streak or any other fine qualities. *Dio mio*, he was not for her. "But Theseus and Maria…they want you for their daughter. They think of you as their son. It was clear they—"

"Thinking of me as their son and being their son is

different, Valentina. In the end, blood wins." His nostrils flared, the topic clearly hitting a nerve. "At least, that's been my experience."

Because Theseus had chosen Helena to head the company over him the last time? Tina had gathered that much from the hints Helena had dropped over the last few days. And from the obvious tension between Theseus and Kairos every time the discussion shifted to the companies.

She pushed out of his hold, needing to think clearly. "I can't work with Helena."

"Opportunities like this internship won't come your way often."

"I'll somehow—"

"You won't. If it's not this job, it will be a troublesome client. If not Helena, someone else to whom you would have to grovel. The fashion industry, whether here or in Milan, is cutthroat. Full of pitfalls and backstabbing men and women. There's no shame in knowing your shortcomings. No shame in giving up."

Tina stared at him. "Giving up?"

"Aren't you? You'll be here for at least three months, and you're turning down a position in the field you want to work in. Not that I'm surprised."

"Your pride—which is a monumental thing—got bruised because I left you. And for that, you're punishing me by making me work for her."

His mouth twitched. "Actually, I have always thought you and Helena were cast from the same mold. All glitter and no substance."

She'd thought the same, yet the laughingly delivered comment punched Tina hard. Her chest tightened. Did he think so little of her? Still?

All glitter and no substance.

No words could encompass her so well. No one had

ever stripped all pretense, all her armor, and laid her bare like that.

This intimacy, his admission that their marriage had been sacred to him, it was making her forget what kind of a man he was. Making her forget that there was no place in his life for anything but ambition.

"You know, from the moment you told me you 'needed' your wife, I've been wondering why." She stilled at the wide doors to the courtyard, the sun caressing her bare arms. The villa, the grounds, everything was paradise. Sharing a room with the man she'd given her body and soul to, pretending that they adored each other, was incredibly seductive.

A thin line of tension appeared between his brows. "I told you why."

"But not all of it."

Silence stretched. She waited, wanting him to offer to tell her. Wanting him to want her to know the truth about his present, his past. About the ruthless choices that seemed to define his life.

To want to make her understand him.

"And what did you figure out?" Pure steel in his voice.

"Maria said that you flew to Theseus's side the moment you heard of his heart attack. That you held off a hostile takeover on his board that would've wrenched control from Theseus. And Helena mentioned that you had almost been engaged. She clearly adores you still. But there's tension between all of you. It's clear that you had a falling out, something that prevented you and Helena from being together the last time around. You saved his life and his company…"

A brow rose on his face, his hip cocked out at a jaunty angle, but still he waited. Ruthlessness dripped from his very pores. "Make your point, *pethi mou*."

"I think you saw an opportunity."

Any hint of charm disappeared from his eyes. "What opportunity would that be, Valentina?"

Even as he asked the question, there was a warning in his words.

Not to voice it. Not to give form to her thoughts. But she wanted to fracture that icy control, that smooth, uncaring facade. Bloodthirsty by nature, she wanted him to tell her the whole truth. To admit that her accusations hurt.

"You want to take over Theseus's company but not his daughter, so you produced me to pretend we have a perfect marriage. I haven't quite figured out why you can't get rid of me and marry her, and then you would have everything you want. But what I know is that when you have the company in hand, you'll discard me, leash Helena and become the CEO. What else would motivate you to put your life on hold except the fact that you can gain power by this move?"

A cold smile sliced his cruel mouth upwards. "And here I worried that Helena would twist your mind with lies."

There was such a wealth of emotion in his tone that Tina's heart pounded. "Will you deny that at the end of all this you'll own Theseus's company?"

"No."

"That you brought me here to deceive that sweet couple, to avoid Helena's attentions?"

"No."

"Then where is the lie in what I said, Kairos?" She waited for him to deny her accusation, to give her another reason. Anything for her to hold onto, a chance for them.

"Everything you do, every decision you make, it's to acquire more wealth. More power. More connections." She thought she was over the worst but it only hurt to see the coldness in his eyes. "Why should this be any different, when all that ever motivates you is ambition?"

CHAPTER SEVEN

EVERYTHING YOU DO is motivated by ambition.

Valentina's words played like a broken record through his mind even after a month. Taking another sip of his throat-burning Scotch, Kairos admitted it grated still.

For years after he had walked away from Theseus, all he had been able to think of was how to advance, how to prove to Theseus—and himself—that he could make it work without his former mentor's help. And without Theseus's legacy.

In that blind drive, he had developed a reputation for ruthless deals and an expertise in getting rid of broken parts of a company. He had forgotten that there was more to life than business deals and the next takeover. A fact Leandro had pointed out when he had first met him.

He smiled. The man was a master strategist if ever there was one. But his words had sunk in. And once he had seen Valentina, he had wanted her. The idea of marriage, settling down, making a family of his own…had held appeal.

He'd seen it as another forward move in his life, not an adjustment.

Or maybe his mistake had been to let his libido choose the wrong wife. Maybe if he hadn't been so obsessed with winning Valentina, hadn't reveled in how artlessly she had fallen for him, he would have said no to Leandro's offer.

Leaning back into his seat, he swept his gaze around the nightclub. His tension deflated a little when he found

Helena dancing with one of the younger board members on Markos's board of directors.

Valentina's accusation had been correct…and yet also not correct at the same time. It rankled that she thought so little of him, that he would take advantage of Theseus in his feeble state. And yet he had balked at explaining himself.

The more she delved beneath his surface, the more he wanted to hide himself away.

Why did it feel like giving Valentina a piece of the past was giving her a part of his soul? Why didn't the damn woman revert to what he had considered her default?

Restlessness slithered in his blood. Even the brutal three-hour-a-day training he had been pushing on his body, in preparation for a triathlon, was still not enough to rid his body of that simmering energy.

And his sweet, little wife was the cause.

It was close to a month now since she had accepted that position in the ad agency. A month of waiting to receive a call from Chiara that Valentina had slapped someone, or fought with someone, or that she had stormed out because she had had to work too hard.

Not a peep from his wife's boss or Helena or Valentina about her job. Not a single complaint.

They had sort of fallen into a routine as husband and wife far too easily—they had started running together in the morning, breakfasting together, and then he gave her a lift to work and they parted ways. Most evenings, they dined with Theseus and Maria until either he or she went back to work again.

And then came the long torturous nights.

His balls, he was afraid, were permanently going to shrivel if he had to take one more cold shower, if he had to untangle Valentina from himself in the middle of one more night.

She thought him a ruthless bastard anyway. So what stopped him from taking what he wanted like he'd always done?

If he waited on some twisted notion of honor, he'd have had nothing in life. He'd have still been foraging through some dumpster in the back alleys of Athens, ended up either dead or pimping some poor prostitute to make a life. It was only by taking what he wanted he'd gotten this far in life.

He wanted sex—*Christos*, it was all he could think of—and he had a wife who matched him in his fervor for sex if nothing else. So what the hell was he feeling guilty about?

She was changing how he saw her, and she was changing him from the inside out.

Why else did his gut clench when he saw the shadows under her eyes, when he saw her weave tiredly through dinner? Why else did he want that adoration, that love back in her eyes?

Was celibacy making him sentimental?

Andaxi!

He ordered another glass of Scotch—his second, which was one more than he ever allowed himself, when he heard the soft hush around his table. The hairs on the back of his neck prickled.

Desire came at him in that same visceral punch when his gaze found her. But with that ever-present hum came a bubble of laughter bursting out of his throat. The shocked silence around the table was enough proof that he rarely laughed like that.

He should have known she would do something like that. Knew the subdued shadow she was making herself into was...unnatural for her.

Thrown into brilliance by the multicolored strobe lights from the bar, her copper-colored sheath dress with a million metallic chips contrasted dazzlingly against her golden skin tone. The material clung to her chest and waist like a lover's hands and then ended just below the thin flare of her hips.

His mouth dried. Her gaze swept through the club, landed on him.

The long, toned muscles of her thighs when she moved… it was pure sensuality in motion. Five-inch stiletto heels made her legs go on for miles. Her hair was in its usual braid.

Only he knew how the silky mass would caress a man's face or how it provided an anchor to hold on to when he was driving into her wet heat. She wore no jewelry except those plain diamond studs at her ears that were a gift from Luca, and the pendant he'd given her. A foolish piece of sentimentality he'd indulged in.

His knuckles gripped the seat as she reached their table and every man's gaze in the vicinity devoured her.

A subtle thread of her fragrance wafted over him as she bent and kissed his cheek.

"Hello, Kairos," she said, wrapping her arms around him from behind. Her breasts pressed against his neck. Sensations assaulted him, his muscles curling with the control it took not to clamp his mouth over hers.

Slowly, that initial roar of desire settled into a simmering hum. Clarity came.

For a month, she'd been so careful around him. Never touching him unless necessary and unless they had an audience. Even then, he could feel the tension in her frame every time he came near her. Could feel her flinch every time he touched her.

Now, she was all over him. And instead of leading her into one of the backrooms specifically reserved for couples who wanted private space and taking her against the wall as every instinct was riding him to, he found himself frowning.

One elbow over the back of his seat, she looked down at him. Shadows swirled in her eyes, hiding what he wanted to see.

"Are you drunk?"

"I had three glasses of white wine while I dressed in Chiara's personal suite after your high command."

He noted the jut of her collarbone, the bluish shadows under her eyes. "Did you remember to eat before the wine?"

She scrunched her forehead. "No wonder it went straight to my head. You'll have to put it down to the shock that you ordered me to meet you in a nightclub, of all places. That's like—" she frowned, her lower lip jutting out "—the old me going to a sale in a department store, or being kind to Claudia Vanderbilt. Or the new me succeeding at something." She laughed.

Beneath the low, husky sound, Kairos found something disconcerting. A hint of pain.

It wasn't just the dress. Her lips were painted a dark voluptuous red—the only feature she possessed that was plump and lush. It was a color he'd once forbidden her to wear.

Because, throughout the formal dinner with his new business partners one night, all he'd been able to think of was kissing that mouth, of wanting his innocent wife's lush mouth wrapped around his cock even as she goaded his temper by flirting outrageously with another man across the table.

Something was wrong. Because whenever something went wrong in his wife's little world, she acted like a teenage rebel.

It had taken him this long to understand the pattern. For a smart man, he lost all capability for logic and rationality when it was Valentina.

She'd slapped Sophia when he'd refused to define his relationship with her.

She'd stripped and jumped into a pool in her underwear at a venture capitalist's retreat in Napa Valley because he'd told her in no uncertain terms that they weren't there for fun but business. A fact she'd been made aware of well in advance.

When he'd forced her to return the Bugatti she'd had delivered for his birthday present—bought with her brother's money no less—she'd decided to return it recklessly and almost hit a tree in her anger.

All actions that had infuriated him.

Was this another ploy?

But what he saw this time was vulnerability in her gaze. The tremble in her fingers as she picked up his drink and took a sip. The fine lines of tension around her forehead.

Valentina never indulged in spirits at least. Something to do with her mother's accident. And yet, here she was, not completely sloshed but without the wariness and inhibition he'd spied in her eyes in the last month.

The booth was U-shaped and he was sitting at the end. "Let me see the back of your dress," he taunted, some devil in himself goading him.

She turned around obligingly, moving with an innate grace that had captured his attention the first time he'd met her. He gritted his teeth. He was right.

The fabric barely covered her buttocks. But *Christos*, his palms ached to cup them, to pull her flush against him until she felt what she did to him.

"You asked me to join you at a nightclub." Her gaze swept over the club and landed on Helena leaning against the bar and watching them with a smirk. The glitter in his wife's eyes brightened as her gaze swept over the cool blue knee-length dress Helena wore. In contrast to Valentina, he noticed now, she looked elegant, refined.

His wife's tension doubled. "I assumed it was to put on a show for Helena."

He pulled her down to sit beside him. "How has she been treating you?"

"Nothing I can't handle. Except the little snippets of your history that she keeps dropping around the team. How many favors Theseus did you. How many disappointments you've had to face in life. I think everyone on the team realized she was talking about me."

"Valentina—"

"She doesn't bother me, Kairos."

"No?"

She shrugged. "All the scenarios she desperately tries to plant in my head would have driven me crazy if…you still meant something to me." She looked up then and smiled. But the smile didn't touch her eyes. "Anyway, I came armed with the weapons I possess."

"Weapons?" he said, his mouth twitching. For all he tried, he couldn't muster disappointment or anger that she'd shown up dressed like a…delectable morsel he wanted to consume.

He felt anticipation and tenderness. For something was definitely not right and he wanted to fix it for her.

"She flaunts her breasts in your face every opportunity she gets. I don't have big breasts or flaring hips. My legs are my weapons and I decided to showcase those."

He rubbed his fingers over his face, fighting the urge, but laughed out loud anyway. He had a feeling it would hurt her feelings. And it had, if the way she gripped the table showing white knuckles was anything to go by.

"Twisted, *si*? That my insecurity about my body has finally found your sense of humor?"

Just like that, his smile disappeared. "What in God's name are you talking about now?"

"The fact that I obsessed for nine months over your fascination with my lack of melons."

"Melons?" he said, almost choking on the sip of his whiskey.

She mock-cupped her hands in front of her chest like men did when they talked about big breasts. "You know... jugs. Bazookas."

His mind roiled, came to a jarring conclusion. "*Christos*, is that why you took to wearing those obscenely ridiculous push-up bras? Because you assumed I was into big breasts?"

Color streaked along her cheekbones. "*Si.* I wanted to please you. I was naive and foolish enough to believe that the illusion of big breasts would somehow make you appreciate me more. Make your nonexistent heart beat."

"I hated those bras. When I touched you...all I could feel was padding." He muttered another oath. "Where in hell would you get the idea that I liked big breasts?"

"From things you said when we watched old Hollywood movies. From the way all your love interests were built in the front. From the way you never..." She looked away, her throat bobbing up and down.

He turned her to his side until she faced him. Strips of light caressed the high sweep of her cheekbones. The narrow blade of her nose. She licked her lips nervously. He couldn't be distracted. At least not yet.

"I never what, Valentina?"

She shuffled her legs under the table but he wouldn't let her budge. In the end, she ended up piling her legs above and around his. It was the closest he'd been to her in months. Fever took root in his muscles.

"I don't know why we're talking about this."

"Because I want to know."

"Francesca Pellegrini told me that her husband was obsessed with her breasts." Her cheeks burned. "But when we made lo—when we had sex, you never…spent a lot of time with my breasts. So I assumed you didn't like them. There? Are you happy? Or would you like more humiliating details from our marriage?"

"Did it not occur to you that I might have just been in a hurry to get to other places? That unlike Francesca Pellegrini's husband—who by the way always gawks at you, the old pervert—I might be a leg man?" he whispered, not knowing whether to laugh or groan.

She had built up so many things in her head and it was his fault. He had incessantly found fault with her.

Shame settled in his chest. He ran his knuckles over the lean line of her leg, and her breath hitched.

"You have legs that go on for miles, *glykia mou*. You're so tall that I don't get a crick in my neck when I kiss you. You fit so perfectly against me that I could hold you against the wall and be inside you in a second. When I'm inside you and you wrap your legs around me…" He cleared his throat, forgetting where he was going for a second. "But of course, forgive me for my oversight." He let his gaze rove over the deep V plunge of her neckline. His blood became sluggish, his erection an insistent ache in his trousers. "I promise to spend more time with your breasts in the near future."

A choking gasp fell from her mouth. Her eyes sparked outrage. "You're not getting anywhere near my breasts."

He raised a brow, loving the warm flush on her cheeks. "We'll see about that."

A waiter brought some appetizers he had ordered. He picked up a piece of cheese and held it to her mouth. "Eat."

She shook her head, held his gaze defiantly and took another sip of his Scotch.

"You're acting like a child. You'll be sick if you chase wine with Scotch. You don't do well with alcohol."

She pouted, leaning back against the seat. "You don't like dancing, you don't want me to drink and you don't like for me to have any fun. Why am I here then? If it's for Helena's sake, you should know she doesn't buy our reunion."

"Let Helena think whatever she pleases."

"Please, Kairos. The truth, for once. Why are you here?"

"When one of the board members suggested we check out the new club, I joined them. Georgio," he said nodding at the man standing close to Helena, his angelic features visible even from here, "is—"

"Alexio Kanapalis's son," she said, shocking him into stupefied silence. "Alexio tried to get the vote to oust Theseus from his own board. You booted him out instead. But Georgio stayed. So you wonder if Georgio's loyalty lies with his father or with Theseus. Of course, that he's so… chummy with Helena goes in its own column of uneasy matters."

He stared at her.

She laughed. "I'm not stupid. Georgio visits my department all the time. All the ladies swarm around the pretty boy cooing over his perfectly symmetric features and all that dark blond hair. Not counting his charm and wit, he reminds me a bit of Luca."

"Stay away from him, Valentina."

She sighed. "How many men will you order me to stay away from?"

He ignored her question, but didn't quite succeed at ignoring the jealousy in his gut, however, when Tina looked at the other man and his damned perfect features. "In nine months of living together, you never once had an inkling of my business affairs."

She scrunched her nose at him. "Because I didn't care. Not because I didn't lack intellect."

"And now you're interested?"

"Si."

"Why?"

"Because as soon as you figure out who's behind all this, Theseus and you will come to an agreement, and the sooner I'll be out of your life. Forever this time."

Her eagerness to be done with their charade made him grit his teeth. "It wasn't just to keep an eye on Georgio and Helena," he admitted. She was always so damned honest with him. Was he such a coward that he couldn't even admit small things to her? "You've been working far too hard. I thought you would like to have a change of pace for one night."

"Did Theseus comment that you've not shown me any sights? Has Helena poked a hole in our happily-ever-after?"

The brittleness in her smile tugged at him. "Does there have to be a reason to want to see my wife?"

"Ah…you want sex. What did you assume—you'd spend two hours being nice to me and I'd let you screw me in the back room? I'm sure there are any number of women, including Helena, who'll be happy to be your screw toys."

He gripped her chin in his hand, anger and hurt riding him hard. *Christos*, only Valentina could turn him into a little boy. "Your insults to my character are getting annoying, Valentina. Is it so hard to believe that I wanted to give you a night away from the villa? From work?"

"Si, it is. You don't do anything without a motive or a goal, Kairos."

Yes, he meant to keep an eye on Helena and Georgio, but he'd wanted to give Valentina a night out on the town, too.

But his wife was as receptive as a porcupine.

Whose fault is that? Have you ever treated her as a partner, as an equal?

He slid the small package he'd had delivered the minute he'd finished his call with her brother, and pointedly ignored the awkward silence that fell when she saw it.

Leaning toward her, he kissed her cheek. Her shoulders tensed, a sudden stillness enveloping her.

God, she had such silky soft skin. All over.

His favorites were the incredible sensitive skin of her inner thighs, the neatly delineated curve where her tiny waist flared into hips, and the skin right below her right buttock where she had another mole.

He remembered her body like it was a map to some treasure.

"Happy birthday, Valentina."

She went still. "Who reminded you?"

When he didn't answer, she turned to him. "I know you're not big on remembering or celebrating birthdays and anniversaries."

His laughter when she'd joyously given him the platinum cuff links for one month of their marriage reverberated between them. He'd thought it hilarious that she bought expensive gifts for him with her brother's money without batting an eyelid.

She'd pouted prettily, argued that he was laughing at a romantic gesture.

He remembered the crushed look in her eyes when he'd blithely stated that it had probably cost her nothing to charge her brother's card.

Dios, he'd been an uncaring jerk of the first order. If she'd been juvenile and volatile, he'd been cruel and ruthless.

When he'd realized the wife he had acquired as part of

a merger was not the elegant, refined socialite he could be proud of, not the political asset he could count on, but a living, breathing creature with feelings and wishes, he'd resented her.

When she'd avowed love for him, he'd pitied her for her grand delusions. Become indifferent to her, waited for her to grow out of it.

When she'd started acting out, he'd been infuriated.

Not once had he realized how much vulnerability she had hidden beneath the fiery temper and impertinence. How honest she'd always been.

He wouldn't have fallen in love with her, but he could have been kinder to her. He was a man who thrived and succeeded in actively hostile environments—he could have molded her to what he wanted in a wife with one kind word or a romantic gesture.

Yet, he'd rigidly shut her out. As a clever business man, his own actions didn't make sense to him. He had used her for only one thing. And he'd made up his mind to do it again before discarding her for good.

Her slender fingers fiddled with the strings on the small package. "Kairos?"

He cleared his throat. "Leandro called me last night. He said it was the first birthday in years that you were spending away from them. He asked where you were and what I had dragged you into."

She pushed the gift away from her with such force that the small package flew off the other end of the table. She pinned him with a furious gaze. "I told him to stay out of my life." Her chest fell and rose with her harsh breaths. "I told you our deal was off if you even spoke to one of them behind my back."

When he'd have calmly walked away before, he said, "I told him this was between you and me."

He tugged her wrist when she'd have walked away. "They're simply worried about you. About what you're doing back with me. About your job and even about your safety—"

"Because no one thinks I can take care of myself. That I'm capable of being anything other than a naive sister or a trophy wife. No, wait, you've made it clear that I failed at even that. Not much of a trophy, am I?"

Somehow, she loosened his grip on her and walked away. She cut a wide swathe through the crowd, her hips swaying.

It was only one of her tantrums, he told himself.

He was not going to chase her like some lovesick boyfriend.

She had lasted a month—a miracle in itself—before that cloak of serenity had been ripped. Just what he had expected.

There had been innumerable occasions when she'd lost it just like that. And Kairos had always let her stew in it. He'd always set the boundaries so she would understand that he would never indulge her juvenile temper.

She would come back to him. She always had done. She would walk back in, and he'd pretend like nothing was wrong.

Until one day, she had left. Walked out, a voice mocked.

Until now, he'd attributed it to her foolish, romantic delusions but for the first time, he had to consider the possibility that he had driven her away. That he hadn't been the man she needed.

Punishing Valentina for walking out on him, seducing her and then discarding her...the very idea felt wrong now. Without honor. Yet what was the alternative?

Running his hands through his hair, he cursed long and hard.

Did he want to keep her? Knowing now that she'd always want something he couldn't give. Something he didn't know how to do.

And even if he did, his blind confidence all these days that Valentina would come back to him smacked of arrogance.

All he knew was that he was far from done with her. And she... *Christos*, even without trying this past month, the woman still had her hooks in him. There was passion between them and if he allowed it, there could be respect and even affection maybe.

Was there a chance for them?

Right now, all he knew was that she was hurt, that she needed a friend. And for once, he wanted to be everything Valentina needed.

CHAPTER EIGHT

TINA KNEW SHE was acting childishly, just as Kairos had predicted. She knew she was letting her emotions rule her head once again.

But she couldn't just sit there, with the pity gift he'd probably had his assistant order for her, mocking her. God, she hated herself for the leap in her pulse when he'd kissed her cheek, the hope bubbling in her throat when he'd placed the present in front of her.

She couldn't face him knowing that sooner or later he was going to find out what a spectacular failure she was; couldn't pretend anymore that being around him—seeing him day in and day out—wasn't wearing her down.

She walked away from the dance floor into the interior of the nightclub.

Black marble gleamed at her feet. Slowly, the music and noise from the crowd faded. She reached a door marked VIP lounge and hesitated.

When the six-foot-tall guard let her through without raising a brow, she slipped into the room.

The silence in the room was absolute. It was properly soundproofed. Black leather sectionals lined the entire back wall. Except for soft recessed lighting, the room was all shadows. She opened the refrigerator built discreetly into the wall. More wine and champagne.

It was so tempting to have some more. To bury the sensation of sinking, the bitterness of knowing that Kairos was right about her.

Instead she took out a bottle of water. She picked up one of the remotes. The music system, built into the walls, came on. Alicia Keyes crooned out a love song.

Sighing, she turned to the wall that was completely glass and looked down to the dance floor.

She sensed Kairos's presence behind her even before she heard him. Her spine felt like it would crack in two at the rigidness she infused into it. For a man who was six foot four and built like a bouncer, he'd always moved with such economy of movement. She chanced a quick look.

He was leaning against the door. Black dress shirt and black trousers—he could have blended into the shadows if didn't have such an electric presence. Goose bumps rose over her arms, remembered sensations zigzagging over her skin.

It had been foolish to think he wouldn't follow her. Right now, she was sort of an important asset to his complex machinery. Why had she trapped herself in here with him? Especially in the reckless mood she was in.

Even though they had shared a bedroom for the last month, she had left herself no chance to be alone with him. He worked late most nights, closeted in the study with Theseus and after sixteen-hour days with barely a break for dinner, she had been falling into exhausted sleep.

Now they were enclosed in the dark room—every sound and sight of the outside world cut off, electricity charging the air. His desire was like a scent she couldn't escape and every cell in her responded to it.

He'd never given her anything as a husband—not a word of praise, not a token gift, not a gesture of affection. But the knowledge of his desire for her, and that it seemed unquenchable, was a powerful aphrodisiac. It filled her with a false feeling of power over him, over this situation between them.

She turned and faced him, the harsh beauty of his face stealing her breath away. "Go back to your…strategies. Christian will drive me back to the house."

He prowled into the dark room, picked up the bottle she had left on the table and emptied it within seconds. "You're upset. You've been upset from the minute you walked into the nightclub. What happened?"

His concern, shockingly, was genuine. And it would only make her weak. "I won't run away in the middle of the night, if that's what you are worried about."

His growl was soft yet so loud in the soundproofed room. Goose bumps broke out on her skin. "Forget about the damned company for a second, Valentina. Forget about Theseus and Maria and Helena. Forget about our godforsaken pretense of a marriage. I'm asking you to tell me what's bothering you. Whatever it is, I will solve it for you."

"I don't want your help or your damn pity gift, or your concern."

"It is not a pity gift. I feel any number of things for you, Valentina, but pity is not one of them."

"I don't want any more clothes or jewelry or shoes. Giving me those things when I insist that they don't matter to me anymore only hurts me. Deeply." She hugged her middle. "I never thought you were a particularly cruel man. Heartless, but not cruel."

"It is not any of those things." His breath hissed out. "And I don't… I don't like hurting you. I never wanted to. Well, except for that night when I found you on the yacht."

"What is it then? The gift?"

"A subscription to an American network channel that streams Westerns. All you have to do is plug in the serial number on that card and you can stream an unlimited number of shows and movies." His mouth pursed at her silence.

"I heard you and Theseus discuss them the other day. It would be a good way to pass Saturdays. He loves it when you join him to watch those movies."

Shock enveloped her, followed by a rush of such powerful joy that she felt dizzy. "I…don't know what to say." She felt vulnerable, small. The strength of what she felt for him…she shook from it.

A flash of light illuminated his face. His nostrils flared, his mouth tightened. "I was cruel and harsh toward you that night. All through our marriage, really. I don't know diplomacy with you. I don't know how to soften my words. You…you weren't what I expected. Your days were filled with shopping and parties. You dressed outrageously. You flirted with every man you met—"

"I only did that after we were married," she shouted into the dark.

"How is that better?" He spoke more and more softly, gritting the words out.

With every step he took toward her, she stepped back. "I flirted to make you jealous. I flirted to get your attention. I flirted with friends who knew why I was doing it and who pitied my pathetic efforts. Because I was married to an uncaring beast."

He stilled. And if she weren't so miserable, Valentina could have laughed at the absurdity of it all. Hadn't he realized such a small thing?

"I didn't succeed even then, did I? You had no regard for me, I knew—"

He continued as if she hadn't interrupted him. But any hint of warmth she'd seen earlier was gone. His eyes were chips of the coldest frost. His jaw set into a granite cast.

"You drove me crazy, Valentina. I couldn't concentrate in meetings for worry of which party you would show up at that night, or with whom you would flirt all evening, or what hijinks you would get up to because I refused to cut the single friend I had. I canceled my trips abroad because I was worried what scandal you'd get into behind my back. I couldn't sleep when I went to Beijing because I was so worried you'd stay out too long with those useless friends of yours in some damn club with no one to look after you. I wanted a wife—instead you were like a child, who wanted the latest, shiniest, most expensive toy.

"I didn't know when you would decide you'd had enough of me. When you would ask your bloody brothers to purchase you a new man. When you would decide that you didn't want me in your bed anymore. When you would decide to welcome another man into your body—"

Her hand flew at his cheek. The sound reverberated in the silence like the crack of thunder.

Valentina gasped, waves of pain radiating up her arm. Still, that pain was nothing compared to the hurt in her chest. His head jerked back but he didn't even touch his cheek.

Her chest heaved, her breath rattling against the outrage she felt. "I've never looked at, much less thought of, another man since the first evening I saw you. Yes, I was shallow, naive, I had no purpose in my life. But what I gave to you, I gave it with conviction, with loyalty. You wanted a robot you could screw at night, a trophy you could display to the world during the day. You don't know how to give, Kairos. But you don't know how to receive, either. That first month… God, I was deliriously happy because of the orgasms you doled out. You shouldn't have married me when you don't know how to have a simple relationship."

She made to get away from him but his arm snagged around her waist. She fell into his side, her breasts and belly pressed up against his hard body. Her breath was punched out of her, shallow and serrated. One hard thigh tangled between hers, rubbing at the center of all the ache. Wetness pooled at her sex, soaking into her flimsy thong.

A whimper fell from her mouth as she tried to move back and rubbed up a little more against him. One arm stayed tight around her waist while he lifted her chin with the other.

His silvery eyes glowed with unbanked desire. Both his hands gripped her hips now. Such large hands that his fingers could always easily span her waist. Her breath fell in soft pants, which seemed amplified in the room.

"It's been more than ten months, now, Valentina. I've been going crazy with wanting you."

Her eyes widened. "I don't believe you. You…"

"Because I'm so dishonorable that I would bed another woman while my wife is missing? Because one woman is the same as the next for an ambitious, ruthless man like me? Because I didn't miss you in bed with a longing that eats at me, a hunger that I can't control?"

"Then why didn't you come after me?"

"Because I don't need you, Valentina."

He growled the words out loud as if he could make them true and yet Tina knew that he meant them. Everything seemed to tilt and shift, the flash of hurt in his eyes when she'd called him a robot, not imagined but real.

For the first time, he felt like a flesh-and-blood man. He was determined to prove to her, and more important, to himself, that he didn't need her.

Why was he so determined to keep her out, to pretend that he didn't care? The gift, this night, his care for her when she was exhausted—everything said he did care.

Further thought was extinguished when his mouth fell onto hers with a rapacious hunger. Relief poured through her, twisting with need. She missed his body, the sense of excitement and danger as he toppled her inhibitions one by one. She missed his bruising kisses, his insatiable appetite that drew out her pleasure until she was begging him, even the epithets that flew from his lips during sex.

His tongue plunged into her mouth, sliding and stroking around her own. Power. Passion. Possession. His mouth stamped all of them over hers. His stubble rasped roughly against her jaw, her lips stinging from the torturous pleasure.

Her hands roamed all over him—the broad shoulders, the muscled arms, the defined chest. The thud of his heart filled her with a reckless urgency. Just tonight, she promised herself. Just a few kisses.

His hands sunk into her hair, pulling at it roughly as he tilted her face up. Rough and hard, he kissed her as if he meant to devour her. As if she had finally pushed him over the edge.

She reveled in the pain and the pleasure his grip forced on her. Moans and whimpers, the sounds she made filled the quiet room. Her eyelids fell, her breath was not her own. An explosion of color filled her body as his mouth left hers to trail down her jaw. Featherlight kisses alternated with hard, guttural words from him in Greek.

She tugged at his hair, desperate to be closer. She shuddered as he sank his teeth into the crook of her neck. Her pulse beat fervently against his tongue. He closed his mouth against the tender skin and sucked. Tremors raced across her skin, pooling between her legs. He swept his tongue over the tender hurt. "Look at me, *pethi mou*. Look at what you drive me to, still. Look at what you turn me into."

Raw desire glittered in his eyes. Tina gasped as cold glass pressed against her bare buttocks. And in front of her he was a cauldron of desire. Heat blasted up her neck and into her cheeks as she realized he had walked her to the back of the room. Shock and desire made her voice strange, husky. Fingers bunching into his shirt, she fought the sensual haze. "We're…they can…"

"No one can see you but me, Valentina. No one knows this body except me, *ne*? Let them be witness to what you drive me to. Let me take you here, in a public place with nothing but a flimsy piece of glass separating us from the crowd. Does this tell you how much control I have? Does that tell you what insanity you drive me to?"

His hands tugged her dress up. Madness filled her body. Rough hands pulled her leg up to wrap it around his hip. She moaned loudly. Her aching sex pressed into his pelvis like that. So close. So hard. Head thrown back into the glass, Tina let herself drown in the sensation.

Nothing else remained anyway. Nothing she was good for. She wanted to gorge on the sensations he created. One calloused hand cupped her buttock while one hand roughly pushed her thong out of the way. Gaze holding hers, he simply covered her mound with his palm. All the roughness, all the urgency faded. Soft and exploring, his fingers stroked the lips of her sex.

The intimacy of it in such a public place pushed her arousal to the edge. Her heart pounded, she was past rationality.

Slowly, his fingers separated her folds and dipped inside.

"You're wet. So ready for me. Always ready for me."

It was a statement that rang with masculine pride. Her palms flat against the glass, she shivered as he spread the dampness around her opening in mind-numbing circles with a thoroughness that cinched her body into a tight knot.

"Please, Kairos," she whispered, burying her mouth in his neck. Roughly, she dragged the lapels of his shirt apart, until a button popped. She was ravenous for him. For his skin, For his taste. She licked the strong column of his throat. Tasted the sweat and masculinity of him.

He growled, the sound bursting out of his chest. His hand left her buttock. Valentina moaned in protest. But he only laughed. With deft movements, he undid the knot at the back of her neck.

The silky strings fell over her chest. His silver gaze held hers, a wicked smile curving his sensuous mouth. Slowly, he pulled the strings down.

Down, down, down until the dress flopped at her waist. It bunched around her hips, leaving her breasts and her sex exposed to his devouring gaze.

He looked like a marauder from the dark ages, the stamp of desire on his hard features. His gaze moved to her breasts. They were brown tipped and tight from the cold air kissing their pert tips. His breath fell in hot strokes. Their gazes held. Breath was fire in her throat. Callused fingers cupped their meager weight. Molded and cupped. He drew maddening circles around the aching tips.

And he bent, licking one engorged tip. Again and again. This breast and then that breast. He cupped them and pushed them up, his tongue flicking around and around. "You were right. I was a selfish bastard to have ignored these. To have overlooked what pleasure I could bring you by touching you here. Never again, *pethi mou*. Never will I neglect these again." And then, as if to seal his promise, he opened his mouth and closed it over one turgid peak.

Tina shook and shuddered, coming off the wall as he suckled her deep into his mouth. Pleasure forked down from the tips of her breasts to her pelvis in deep, sharp arrows. He pressed his tongue against the tip and began the torturous pleasure all over again. Just when she thought she couldn't bear it anymore, he started on the other breast.

The tremors coursing through her were constant now. Dampness coated her skin. His mouth still at her breast, he moved his hand down to her sex and penetrated her with a finger while his thumb pressed against her clit. Her head banged against the glass pane, Tina thrust her pelvis into his hand. Release was so close now, a shimmer of heat all over her skin, building and building.

"Open your eyes, *agapita*," Kairos whispered huskily. His words vibrated against her skin, pulling that knot in her belly tighter. "I know what brings you over the edge."

Tina looked down. His mouth was at her breast, his silver eyes darkened to a dark gray that happened only when he was aroused. His fingers didn't stop their rhythm but it was the heat in his gaze that pushed her. He rubbed his cheek against the wet, glistening nipple. His thumb and forefingers pinched her clit just as he commanded, "Come for me, Valentina."

Her orgasm broke over her, rolling and rippling through her in a flurry of waves that kept coming and coming. But he didn't stop. His fingers kept her at that high, riding that swollen, sensitive bundle.

The aftershocks shook her muscles until she flopped her forehead onto his shoulder and arrested his wrist. She felt boneless, as if she were nothing but a conduit for pleasure and sensations. "Stop, please, Kairos. No more."

His big hand remained between her thighs, soothing the tremors in her muscles. The other pushed back a damp tendril from her forehead. Tenderness. He'd always shown her tenderness in bed. For the span of a few minutes.

The last flutters of her release left her body, leaving an aching void behind. She'd challenged him so boldly that she would resist him. That she would never again fall into his arms. And here she was, her dress bunched up around her waist, against a glass wall while a crowd danced beneath them.

Still, there was a physical ache inside her where she wanted him. Needed him.

His mouth moved from her temple to her cheekbones to her jaw. His mouth was warm and hard, hungrier now. She thrust her tongue into his mouth, determined to pull him into the same sinking well of pleasure. He growled, his chest vibrating with it when she dug her teeth into his lower lip. Hard. And again.

He'd always controlled their sex life—when, where, how—all of it. Enslaved by the pleasure he gave, she'd allowed him to lead, blindly following. But no more.

Her hands automatically locked at his nape, pulling him closer.

His hard chest crushed her sensitive breasts. His hands were filled with her buttocks. Lifting her against the glass, he brought her pelvis closer to his erection.

Moans erupted from their mouths as he rocked into her. Thick and long, his erection pressed against her sensitized clit, sending a quiet flutter of sensation through her again.

"Put your hands up."

A shiver went through her at the raw lust in the command. Denial whispered at her lips yet no words came out.

A rigid line to his mouth, he gripped her wrists and pulled her arms up. The arch of her spine pushed her breasts toward him. He didn't let go of her wrists. As if he didn't trust her. But his other hand, palm down, moved from her forehead to her nose, to her mouth.

When his fingers stilled at her lips, she instantly opened her mouth. She knew what he liked. He had trained her well enough. Though he had never let her take him in her mouth, even when she'd offered. But it wasn't just that he had taught her what pleased him.

She was addicted to his pleasure. Drunk on the power she felt for the few minutes when he needed her so desperately. When his control balanced on a serrated edge.

And she needed that tonight. She needed him to want her as desperately as she'd needed his touch.

His features hardened when she sucked his finger into her mouth. A shudder went through him at her caress. The raw pleasure etched on his hard, implacable features turned her on as if he had touched her again at her core.

She had lived for those moments. She took each callused finger into her mouth one after the other, knowing that it drove him crazy.

His silvery gaze devouring her, he undid the clasp of his belt buckle. The soft rip of the zipper punctured the sound of her harsh breaths. His trousers fell from his hips with a shy whisper.

She had no will left. Her gaze dipped down to his groin. Heat broke out over her skin again, instant, explosive, like lightning appearing over a dark sky in the blink of an eye. She stared, greedy for the sight of him.

Reaching out boldly, she pushed his shirt up until a patch of his ripped abdomen was visible. Dark skin stretched taut over defined musculature delineated with a line of hair. Even the V at the juncture of his groin was well defined.

His cock—she blushed at thinking the word he'd made her say in the second week of their marriage—thickened and lengthened under her hungry gaze, the soft head already glistening wet.

He hustled her back toward the glass again, his hands kneading her buttocks. His mouth buried in her neck again. Her nipples, hard once again, poked at his chest. His hands were everywhere. Even after he'd given her release, he wouldn't just take her. No, he built her body into a frenzy all over again.

If he had been a selfish lover, if he'd denied her pleasure even once, maybe she wouldn't have become such a slave to it. And to him. But no, he pushed her again and again to the edge. To release.

Rough hands pushed her dress all the way down. "I need to be inside you. Now. Valentina."

The question in his statement jerked her head up. He wouldn't assume, he wouldn't take.

"*No!*" The stillness that came over him had such restrained violence in it that she shivered.

In a fluid move, she sank to her knees.

His curse ripped the heavy silence when she wrapped her fingers around his hardness. Velvet-coated steel, he was so soft and yet so hard at the same time. His thigh muscles tensed like rocks when she braced her hands on them.

"Valentina, you don't—"

"Will you give up control for a few minutes? Will you let me in?"

She didn't wait for his answer. Bracing herself for the taste of him, she licked the soft head.

Salty and masculine. She looked up, her mouth open and ready. Tension etched onto every angle of his face. Such raw need and longing written on every hard plane of it that satisfaction pulsed through her.

Tilting her head down, she took him in her mouth this time. Another curse burst through the air. His hips jerked forward until he was filling her mouth.

Instantly, he pulled back. He was losing control. The thought spurred her on like a wild fire in the forest. *Bene,* she wanted him to lose control.

She repeated the movements of her mouth and hands. He said nothing, made no demands. When she glanced a look up at him, he growled an animalistic sound that sent shivers up and down her spine. But his body spoke for him. His hands had reached into her hair at some point. Every time she clasped him harder, he thrust a little into her mouth. Every time he hit the roof of her mouth, his thighs clenched a little more.

His body betrayed him, his need took over just as hers had done earlier. Using it, Tina sucked him harder, faster, intent on blowing his mind apart.

Her mouth felt hollow, her knees dug into the hard marble, her wrists were beginning to hurt from the repeated action but she didn't care.

Every discomfort was worth it for now her husband had no control left. His hands in her hair directed her mouth where and how he wanted it. Deeper and faster and harder.

And then suddenly, he pulled out of her mouth. Rough hands grasped her under her shoulders and pulled her up. She swayed, her knees shaky, and he held her fiercely close with one arm while he stroked himself.

His roar of pleasure vibrated around them as he came against her belly.

Tina looked up, a fever of arousal in her muscles at how completely undone he looked. Silence beat down around them, punctured only by his harsh breaths. His head bent against her shoulder, his breath hit her in warm strokes. His powerful body was still shuddering against hers.

She had no idea how long they stood like that. The scent of his release and hers cloyed the air, leaving her no escape from it. When he looked up at her, she closed her eyes. His thumb traced the line of her jaw softly, almost with reverence.

Her eyes flew open when she felt his fingers on her belly. He wiped her tummy with a napkin he produced from somewhere and then gently righted her dress. Heat swamped her cheeks.

His hands shook as he zipped up his trousers and buckled his belt. She tucked her hands to the side but the little tremors wouldn't subside.

She couldn't pretend that the whole experience hadn't shaken her. She truly was naive. Drawing satisfaction by seeing his control shatter, by bringing him to his knees like that, the raw intimacy of his actions…it had only seared him deeper into her psyche.

She looked away from him just as his gaze turned toward her. She walked over to the refrigerator on trembling legs and poured herself a glass of water. She drank the whole thing in one gulp, her mouth parched.

She felt him come to a stop right behind her. Hesitation, so uncharacteristic of him, charged the air. "Valentina—"

"Please, Kairos. Take me home."

He stared at her for what felt like an eternity before he nodded.

CHAPTER NINE

She had barely reached their room and changed out of the stupid dress, then come down for a cup of hot tea when he cornered her.

"I want to sleep. I'm… I can already feel the headache beginning."

He took hold of her wrist, tugging her into the study he had taken over from Theseus.

The smell of wood and cigars instantly reminded her of her grandfather Antonio. Another man who had thought she would amount to nothing.

While she stared into the empty fireplace, Kairos came back with steaming black coffee, cheese and perfectly cut apples.

"Eat."

Her stomach roiled so she took the plate from him and dutifully ate. He sat down on the step of the fireplace, his long legs bumping into hers until she shifted and the line of them grazed hers.

"Valentina, look at me."

Concern and something else glinted in his silver gaze. She forced a fake smile to her mouth. "My knees are a little the worse for wear, but, *si*, I'm perfectly fine."

He flinched then, whatever he saw in her eyes making him draw back. *As if she could hurt him!*

"I've never… I didn't ask you to do that for me."

"You did it for me." Just mentioning the day when he

had put his mouth to the most intimate part of her sent shivers through her.

He scowled. "Why today?"

She looked at him and then away, afraid of what he would see in her eyes. "I was frustrated, feeling reckless." She looked down at her locked fingers. "The release you gave me took the edge off before I did something stupid. So I returned the favor."

A dangerous glint appeared in his eyes. One brow arched on his arrogant face. "Took the edge off? Was that what I did?"

His gaze dared her to shrug, to cheapen it.

He pinned her to the spot with his penetrating stare, as if he could see into her soul.

She swallowed and looked away. The endless silence, his painful indifference—it was all gone and there was a different man watching her. A man she'd always sensed beneath his ruthlessness but could never touch.

She struggled to make her voice casual. "Compared to my history of making a spectacle of myself every time I get upset, giving my almost separated husband a blow job is probably of minor consequence, *si*?"

"You do not fool me, Valentina. What happened at the nightclub couldn't have left you untouched—" he placed a broad palm over her chest "—in here."

Her heart pounded away under his touch. "Because only you can be casual about sex? Not I?"

"I've slept only with two women in my entire life. You and one other girlfriend. It was a convenient relationship I fell into and we went our separate ways when it wasn't more. I have never been casual about sex. I told you I don't fall into relationships easily. I had Theseus's support but when I left him, I had to start all over with little to my name. Careers like that don't leave room for relationships."

"You proposed to Sophia."

"Because I thought we would suit. Because we were friends and I admired her." He blew a breath, the light from the chandelier caressing his rugged features. "She was wiser than I was, which is why she said no. I realize now she had felt like a safe choice."

Every word out of his mouth mocked the wall she had erected.

She couldn't bear his tenderness, this concern. She couldn't fight her own need for him like this. Especially not today. "If I had known a blow job was all it would take to get you to open to me, I would have gone down on my knees long ago," she said flippantly.

When she would have shuffled away from him, he clasped her arms. "Stop being so glib! Stop acting as if that didn't mean anything."

"What did it mean then, Kairos?"

He looked as if she had slapped him, not asked a simple question. But when she thought he would shut down and walk away, he looked thoughtful. "It meant that you and I are not done with each other. And not just sexually. It meant that…this is not just about Helena and Theseus and our stupid deal or the divorce anymore. It is about us."

Her breath left her, her heart thudding against her ribcage. When he opened up like that, when he let her see what he was feeling, thinking, she… *No!* She couldn't.

Tina had never been so terrified by her own vulnerability, by her own stupid hope.

She wanted to break through the barriers he had erected between them, wanted to find the sweet man who had bought her a gift he knew she would love.

She wanted that Kairos in all the moments, not just every now and then. She would always want him. But would the way he saw her ever change? Could she give herself to him completely if he didn't respect her?

No. She couldn't.

She strolled onto the veranda, trying to get a grip on herself.

He settled down next to her on the small wicker sofa. Hesitation shimmered in his eyes. "I...shouldn't have kissed you today. I shouldn't have lost control. I want you every minute of every day. But only today I realized that what I...planned for you is wrong. What I thought about you is wrong."

"What did you plan for me?"

"I thought I would work you out of my system in these three months. I was angry... I felt betrayed when you left. My ego was definitely bruised."

Laughter burst out of her. "Oh, please...don't look so guilty. I meant to bring you to your knees by rubbing your nose in my fabulous self. I was going to make you regret ever leaving me."

Elbows on his knees, he bent forward. He sighed and studied his hands. One thick lock of hair fell forward onto his forehead, his shoulders bunched into a tight line. It was a rare glimpse into his true self that she couldn't help but drink in.

Her heart clenched when he looked up and smiled.

"I knew, even that night when I couldn't find you, that it wasn't just your fault our marriage had failed. I just... my pride wouldn't let me accept it, accept that while we both have flaws, what you gave me is priceless. You didn't throw it away on a whim or an impulse."

It felt as if they had reached a crossroads. "Look at us, all grown up, *si*?" she said trying to lighten the moment. "Being adult about a breakup. Maybe we can be friends like they show in American sitcoms?"

A blaze lit up in his eyes and she looked away. Of course, it was a foolish suggestion. But the thought of having to walk away all over again, especially when she was finally getting to see beneath the rigid exterior…the very thought of it made her shiver.

"Will you please tell me what happened, Valentina?" He exhaled roughly. "I promise you I won't be cruel or mocking. I want to understand."

With one promise, he knocked all her barriers down. For Kairos never promised anything he didn't mean. "Chiara fired me. Only *I* could get fired from an unpaid internship, *si*?" The words fell over themselves to come out now.

"What? Today?"

"Right before you called me. I was…putting away my stuff. I feel like such a failure."

His arm came around her gently.

Tears pooled in her eyes and she inhaled noisily. "Don't be kind to me."

"What was the stupid thing you would have done today? Run away again?"

"Crawl back to my brothers. I miss them today." She swallowed the ache down. "I miss Leandro's tight hugs. Luca's corny jokes. I miss Alex's calm acceptance, Izzie's wet kisses. I miss Sophia's quiet support."

"They adore you, don't they?" he said softly.

"For years after Leandro brought me to live with them, every time something went wrong in my world, I would throw one hell of a tantrum." She laughed through the tears, realizing how insecure she'd been to doubt her brothers' love for her. "I'd push them to the edge as if to test them."

"To see how far you could push them before they rejected you? And if that was going to happen, you'd rather know sooner?"

The depth of his perception stunned her. "*Si.* If there's one thing I've learned through the debacle of our marriage, it's that I process everything that doesn't go my way by acting out. I think I did it at regular intervals—either when I thought Leandro was distant or when Luca disappeared for weeks. I would wreak hell and they would rush to reassure me that I was indeed loved and wanted. I was so... needy and vulnerable and they spoiled me to make up for losing my mother, for how terrified I had been when they found me after her death.

"There was nothing I wanted that couldn't be mine. Leandro even tried to protect me from the truth, *si*? And then I met you and you wouldn't dance to my tune...and all my insecurities came pouring out."

"Today, you wanted your brothers to tell you that it was okay to get fired at a job?"

"Yes. That I wasn't a useless waste of space. I wanted them to protect me from you."

He groaned and she laughed at the regret pinching his mouth. "I was such a—"

"Uptight, self-righteous ass?" she supplied. When he nodded and laughed, her heart slipped a little out of her reach. "Sophia's words."

"The last time I spoke to Chiara, she told me that your team all adore you. That you're taking them by storm."

She nodded. "I've been enjoying it. Chiara's not easy to work for but she's so talented. You were right, I was learning so much. We've been preparing for the fall collection. I've been liaising with designers and their assistants, and PR people to put a marketing campaign together. She let me put the outfits and accessories together. I even handpicked the models to showcase each different outfit. I talked to the photographers, the lighting assistants. A hundred different things have to come together perfectly for the collection to be showcased. I…honestly don't know how it happened. I double-checked and triple-checked everything. I spent most of the previous evenings calling every personal assistant and designer checking to make sure things would go smoothly. I…"

"What went wrong?"

"Honestly, I've no idea. I must have messed up something because we ended up with ten boxes of swimwear. Which is a *disaster* because it's October and the same order was shipped to about eleven different stores. Instead of Burberry coats, we have Bermuda shorts. Instead of designer pantsuits, we have sleeveless tops and shorts. Everything was wrong. The catalogs are not even ready. Chiara had a nightmare to fix on her hands and no inventory. Her phones kept going off. I tried to stem the panic from store managers waiting to figure out what to do. I… When I went into her office, one of the vice presidents was ripping into her. I told him it was my fault, not Chiara's. I… I quickly put together a letter of resignation and walked out."

"So she didn't really fire you then?"

He squeezed her fingers softly. "She was so buried that she didn't get a chance. We were alone for a moment in her office. She looked up and said she knew she shouldn't have taken me on. She knew I would only bring trouble."

"Valentina—"

"I… I had a simple job to do. And I messed it up." She rubbed the base of her palms around her eyes. "You were right. I should just accept that I'm not good for anything—"

Kairos tilted her chin up until she looked at him. "That's not true. I was a cruel bastard to say that." He'd always thought her weak-spined, a slave to suggestion, but only now could he see the strength that had always been there. "Valentina, listen to me. Making a mistake in a job is not the end of the world. What you do after is what matters.

How many times you pick yourself up after you fall…that's what matters."

"Then I failed in that, too, *si*?" She laughed and the sound couldn't hide the frustration she felt. "Don't you see, Kairos? Letting you kiss me, touch me, letting myself get physically close to you…what I did today was not cheap, *no*. Was not meaningless. Seeing you undone—" her gaze landed on his mouth, his eyes, and he felt burned by the intensity of it "—it's a high I could chase again and again. But it is self-destructive behavior. It is harmful to me. *You are harmful to me.* Every little bit of your past you give me, every small admission you make about what you feel for me…it comes at a high price. It comes with a fight, it feels like squeezing blood out of a stone. I think that's just how you're made. And if I've learned anything by watching my brothers and their wives, I know it shouldn't be this hard. You broke my heart last time and if I give you half a chance, you will do it again.

"So please…if you have ever cared for me, even a little bit, don't touch me. Don't kiss me." A ghost of a smile flitted over her face as her brown gaze moved over his. "Don't follow through on your nefarious plans."

"This…what happened between us tonight—" he moved his hand between them, a fine tension in his body "—is nothing shameful. This is not something that I would ever use against you."

"And yet this—my sexual desire for you—is what made you think I wouldn't hesitate before falling into another man's bed. That I would betray our vows."

He clasped her jaw, forcing her to look at him. "I was lashing out. I knew you wouldn't betray me. I just…on the best of days, you're like a hurricane. All I wanted was to contain you, contain the damage you did to—"

"Your reputation? Your business alliances?"

"Damn it, Valentina! *Damage to me!* To the way I wanted to live my life. I've never in my life cared about anyone. The only way I learned to survive was by being in control of myself. Even after I came to live with Theseus and Maria… I don't know how to let someone close. I don't know how to handle emotion and all that it entails. I can't bear the pain that comes from loving someone. I just…can't. And you…every day you made me insane. You mocked my rules, you teased my attention even when you weren't trying and when you got up to one of your spectacles, you threatened every ounce of my control."

"But you never lost it," she whispered, his confession searing through her.

Every time Kairos thought he had a grip on her, Valentina showed him a new side. Unraveled him anew. What they had done tonight at the nightclub had not just been physical release.

Christos, it only showed again how open she was. How much he could hurt her, if he wasn't careful.

And suddenly the idea of hurting Valentina was unconscionable.

"The more you pushed me for a reaction, I see now, the more I retreated. It became a matter of my will against yours. I couldn't…let you…have so much control over me. Being married to you—it was like asking a man who doesn't know how to walk to swim an ocean. You are right, though. It shouldn't be this hard. But I can't… I don't know if it will ever be different, either. I can't change what I am."

I won't love you.

Kairos knew she understood what he'd said because she paled and nodded. If there were tears in her eyes, she hid them by looking down at her clasped hands.

He should have felt an ease of the weight that had been cinching tight around his neck. Instead of relief that he had set the score right, that he had told her what the future could be, all he felt was an ache in his chest. An unnamed longing.

"The fault is not all yours, Kairos, I know that."

The vulnerability in her eyes, the lovely picture she made in the moonlight melted something near his heart. That she thought herself a failure because of his cruel words was unacceptable.

He knelt in front of her, took her hands in his, looked her in the eye. "I'm...sorry for making you feel like you're less than what you are. Even if Chiara fired you, you're not a failure. You're the most courageous woman I know. It took guts to walk away from your brothers, from me, from the lap of luxury. Guts to face all the people who mocked you, who treated you so horribly and to go to work at that place all these months. It took guts to try again and again to put together that blasted portfolio, guts to stand up to your blackmailing husband and make a deal of your own.

"You live your life with all your passion poured into it. You take risk after risk with yourself. And maybe there's no way forward for us, but *Christos,* I still want you. Desperately. Like I have never wanted anything else in life. But I won't touch you. Not unless your heart and mind both want me to."

Tina took a long, hot shower, took even longer to dress and finally walked back into the bedroom. She wasn't going to fall asleep anytime soon. She was too wired, too many thoughts whirling through her head. And she definitely didn't want to have the confrontation that was coming.

It was ironic since she'd always been the one that had pushed for it.

Since the nightclub a week ago, she'd been avoiding Kairos, faking sleep when he came to bed, running around the estate like the very devil was chasing her in the evening when he was home.

As always, he'd given it to her straight. Told her he would never change, never open himself up to her. Which should have sent her running for the hills.

Instead, his words seemed to have burrowed deep into her soul. She had seen the respect she'd wanted in his eyes. She'd seen the glitter of regret and pride when he had told her it had taken guts to stand up for herself.

That should have been enough. But all she wanted was more of him, more of the Kairos who saw the true her, the Kairos who kissed her as if he couldn't breathe, the Kairos who—

Dios, had she no self-preservation instinct?

"Couldn't hide any longer in the bathroom?"

Kairos's low voice halted her hand toweling her hair. She shrugged. Taking a deep breath, she finished brushing her hair, trying her hardest not to let her gaze settle on him in the mirror.

Turning to the dresser, she pulled out her running shorts, a T-shirt and a sports bra. She pulled her hair back into a high ponytail.

She barely took two steps before he was in front of her. Blocking her. Breath halted in her throat.

"Where are you going?"

She kept her gaze on his chest. The olive skin shadowed through his white dress shirt, which wasn't tucked quite neatly into his trousers. Every time she looked at him, she remembered him undone now. Heat swarmed her face again. *Dios*, what had she been thinking to be so...bold with him? That was a memory she wouldn't forget to her dying days. Nor did the image of him climaxing fail to arouse her. "I... I'm going for a run. I'm too restless to sleep."

"It's eleven thirty at night. And if you run anymore, you will disappear into thin air."

Before she could even blink, he took the clothes from her and threw them on the bed. A finger under her chin tilted her face up. "Is it working, Valentina?"

"What?"

"Avoiding me. Is it making the ache to be with me any less? Because if it is, you have to share the secret with me."

"I don't know... *No*. It is not helping. You're like that slice of chocolate cake that you can't resist even knowing that it will go to your hips and buttocks."

He laughed, lovely crease lines fanning out near his eyes. "I talked to Chiara today."

Hurt punched through her. "I can't go back to a job where not only am I not wanted, but can't even do anything properly, Kairos. How can I face my colleagues when they all see that I returned because of my powerful husband's recommendation? I will have no more value than a mannequin."

"Fine," he said, releasing her. Something like humor shone in his eyes. "Maybe I'm wrong in assuming you would want to hear what Chiara told me involved Helena."

Having dropped the bomb, the devilish man casually strolled to the balcony attached to the bedroom.

"What do you mean Helena was involved?"

"Sit down and maybe I will tell you."

She glared at him. And sat down.

He pulled her closer to him and she went unwillingly.

His thighs pressed against hers and instantly that awareness slammed into her. But beneath that ever-present hum was something else, something new between them.

Tenderness. Rapport. The connection she had craved for so long with him. As if all the cacophony and noise in their relationship had been cleared away and they could see each other clearly for the first time.

And the more she saw of Kairos, the more Valentina liked him. Genuine like, not the I-want-to-rip-his-clothes-off kind. Although that was there, too.

"I have been thinking on what you said to me."

Instantly, he tensed. "Which part?"

Tina could literally feel his stillness. The way it contained his rumbling emotions. He thought she had made a decision about them, their future. And he was hanging on an edge just as she was any time she thought about it. "About picking myself up, planning my next move. I will find another way to achieve my goals. Working with Chiara gave me the confidence that I'm in the right field, that I can work as hard as it takes. That I have a natural talent for fashion. It's just a matter of finding the right outlet, the right opportunity."

The smile he shot her was full of joy and admiration. "I'm glad to hear that."

"So…anyway, *efharisto*, Kairos."

"You needn't thank me, I did nothing."

"Thank you for seeing me through that first hurdle. For…just being there." And since she had to fight the glittering desire she saw in his eyes, she quipped, "For showing me that when I hit the next hurdle, all I have to do is get drunk, go to a nightclub and maybe find a guy to—"

"You finish that sentence at serious threat of harm to yourself, Valentina."

His growl made laughter explode from her mouth. She leaned back into her seat, and took a deep breath of the scented air.

When Kairos had handed her a glass of red wine, she took a sip and sighed.

"No more than one glass," she added.

He smiled, slanted a teasing, hot glance her way. "I was hoping you wouldn't count. I was hoping to get you drunk and have my wicked way with you. I like you drunk."

"Ha ha…not funny. You like what I do when I'm drunk." *Dios mio*, he was even more irresistible when he teased her like that.

"Too horny for it to be a joke?" There was a flash of his white teeth and that rakish smile. Tina wondered if her panties could melt by how hot and wet she was.

"Something like that, *si*," she replied haughtily and had the pleasure of being enveloped by his deep laughter again.

"I have always loved your honesty, *agapita*." Her heart thudded against her ribcage. "Fine, no more than one glass."

As far as the eye could see, darkness blanketed the grounds. Crickets chirped. The scents of pine and ocean created a pungent yet pleasant perfume on the air. For a long while, neither of them spoke.

His arm came around her shoulders, his fingers drawing lazy circles on her bare skin. There was nothing sexual about his touch and still her breath hung on a serrated edge. The intimacy of the moment was even more raw than what they had shared at the nightclub.

"Do you realize we've never once…spent time like this? Without fighting, without ripping each other's clothes off?" The words escaped her—wistful, poignant—before she could lock them away.

Moonlight threw shadows on her hand clasped in his. His thumb passed back and forth over the veins on the back of her hand. She sensed he was as loath to disturb the moment as she was. "Hmmm. Although I always liked the ripping-clothes-off part, too."

She snorted and he snorted back.

"Today is my mother's birthday," he said suddenly into the silence.

"I...do you miss her?"

"Yes. She would have liked you. She was like you—fierce, bold."

She laced her fingers through his and brought his hand to her mouth, pressing a soft kiss to the veins on the back of his hand. Strength and willpower and vulnerability—she was only beginning to realize what a complex man he was.

"I would like to know more about her, please."

He remained quiet for so long that Tina sighed. She couldn't force him to share pieces of himself with her. She couldn't forever be the one who took that first step. Not because of pride but because she couldn't bear the hurt of it when he left her standing again.

Until he started speaking. "She was a prostitute. I know how they're forced into those choices firsthand, the wretchedness of that life. She fed me from the money she made through her...job. Until she fell sick and drifted into nothing."

Even in the slivers of moonlight, Kairos saw how pale Valentina became. She blinked until the sheen of tears dimmed. Only then did he realize he'd revealed something he'd told only one other person. Theseus.

"I'm sorry that you..."

"That I came from such a dirty past?"

"That you lost a mother you loved." Pure steel filled her voice, daring him to mock her sympathy. "No matter her choices. I know what it feels like to lose a loved one."

Why did he forget that beneath the sophistication and good humor, Valentina's childhood hadn't been smooth, either? That she, more than anyone, understood the ache that came with loving someone?

It was as if he still, willingly, refused to look beneath the impulsive, reckless woman he had initially assumed she was.

"Are you ashamed of who she was?" The question was soft, tentative.

He scowled. "No. Never. Why the hell would you think that?"

"Because," she said with a sigh, "you play your cards pretty close to your chest, Kairos. Even when they did that exposé on you for that business magazine, there was nothing about your background. Top businessman under thirty and it was as if you had sprouted from nowhere as a full-grown businessman at the age of twenty-three."

He grimaced, recognizing the truth in Valentina's summation.

The journalist who'd done that interview had been so frustrated. More than once, she'd tried to steer the conversation to his childhood and he'd bluntly steered her away, keeping his answers to his successes and the companies he had fixed.

He wasn't ashamed, but for years, he *had* hidden his roots. He'd pushed away men who could have been friends because he'd felt separate, isolated. Felt as if he hadn't belonged because of where he had come from.

His mind whirled as thoughts poured through him.

"How did you come to live with Theseus and Maria?"

He braced himself, knowing what it was building to. Knowing that Valentina wouldn't stop until all of him was stripped before her. His illusions and his control. "He and Maria came to one of the most impoverished areas of Athens and he caught me as I cut the strings to Maria's purse and started running."

He heard her soft gasp and clenched his heart—or what remained of it—against the pity. Memories came at him like swarming bees. The poverty. The filth. The fight to survive another day. As if she was losing him to the past,

Valentina tightened her fingers around his, brushed a soft kiss against the underside of his jaw.

"Do not pity me, Valentina. This is why I wouldn't reveal my background before. Because it skews people's perception of me. Instead of a powerful businessman, they see a man who's crippled by his roots."

She snuggled into him as if he hadn't just snarled at her. "Or they see a man who made something of himself even when the odds were stacked against him. You keep treating me as if I'm unfamiliar with anything in life but designer couture and privilege, Kairos. If Leandro hadn't persuaded Antonio that I belonged with them, if he hadn't found me and brought me to live with him and Luca, where do you think I would be today? You think I've forgotten the fear that no one will care about me. Just because I pretend as if that doesn't matter it doesn't mean it's not there every day within me."

He looked at her and this time only saw understanding. Again, the realization, that this understanding had always been there for him to reach for, filled him.

The realization that Valentina was more than he'd ever wanted in a wife. It was as if his subconscious had been aware of it all along.

Was that why he'd always kept her at a distance? Why he'd retreated in the face of her passionate declarations, treated her with cold indifference?

She cupped his palm tenderly, her thumb tracing his jawline back and forth. It was comfort, it was affection. And still the jolt of that contact rang through him. Neither was he unaware of the different kind of intimacy the night and their discussion had wrought on them.

She was stealing away pieces of him. He tried to fight it, a sense of dread blanketing him, but her tender touch anchored him to the here, to the now. To her.

"How old were you?"

"Eleven? Twelve?" He rubbed his free hand over his face. "I was this...feral animal that would have done anything to survive another day. I was terrified he'd turn me in to the police. Theseus was really built in those days. He restrained me for fifteen minutes while I tried to break his hold and run. I stopped fighting when he said he would not turn me in. I was shocked when he brought me to his home. That first year I was terrified he would change his mind and throw me out. By the time, I was thirteen, Theseus and Maria adopted me officially."

"Then why did you leave them?"

The question came at Kairos like a fist, smashing through the walls he hadn't even known he'd need against her. "You know the answer to that."

"*No*, I don't." Something almost akin to desperation rang in her voice. "All I have is conjecture based on the little tidbits Helena hints at. Based on what you show me and the world at large."

Jaw tight, he stared at Valentina. Felt a visceral tug at the genuine concern in her eyes. Not pity. Not disgust. But a real emotion that had always been there. That he chose not to embrace, not to want.

He still couldn't make himself want it. If he went that last step... "It was time to see the world, time to stretch my wings. To reach for bigger and greater things."

"You mean find a richer and maybe slightly less crazy heiress compared to Helena?"

He laughed. And she laughed. But they both knew he was skating over the issue. A part of him wanted her to push, like she did, relentlessly. One part of him wanted never to see her again.

It was the same torment he faced night after night.

Every cell in him wanted to tie Valentina to his side. To

seduce her, to chain her to him with his touch, to promise her whatever she wanted. To build a family with her, to fill his life with laughter and drama and everything she brought into it. He wanted to be selfish and take what he wanted, despite the aching vulnerability in her eyes.

Another part of him cringed at the very idea, his self-preservation instinct coming to the fore. His subconscious had known even back then.

Valentina was dangerous to him. She would send him down a path where only pain waited.

And soon he was going to have to make a decision. For he had no doubt that she would leave him when their deal was up if he didn't reach for her.

The idea of Valentina forever walking out on him this time…he couldn't bear it.

CHAPTER TEN

TINA HAD PLANNED on escaping the party Kairos and Helena had arranged to celebrate Theseus and Maria's fiftieth wedding anniversary by hiding behind her workaholic boss.

The truth was that she was afraid to face what was happening between her and Kairos. To face what was happening to her.

After he had told her how Helena was the one who had messed up the purchase orders—something Chiara had realized from the beginning—she had returned to work. Despite Kairos's worry that Helena's antics were escalating and against his wishes.

Of course, he hadn't let her confront Helena.

Loath to disturb the truce they seemed to have achieved, she had quietly gone back to work.

Seeing him night after night stretched her nerves to the end. They couldn't look at each other without plunging into sexual tension. It was like waiting for a rumbling volcano to erupt. She sensed his hesitation, too, the way he studied her as if he wanted to devour her, the way he barely even touched her, as if his control were hanging by a thread.

The way he talked about everything but the future.

There was a friendship of sorts between them, however much he didn't like the label. They talked about her job, his work, about mutual friends. About their livelihoods.

She wanted to hide tonight. From him, from Theseus

and Maria and Helena and from every board member that wanted to meet Valentina Constantinou.

She wanted the world to disappear and leave her alone with Kairos so that she could…

She could what? Figure out where it was that they were heading? Figure out if she wanted to take a step toward him again?

Was she willing to put herself through all that heartache again? Was she prepared to wait forever if she wanted him to take that step toward her?

Kairos had, of course, in his usual commanding tone ordered Tina's presence at the party. She was, he'd decreed this morning over breakfast, required as his wife.

Keep up your side of the bargain, Valentina, were his parting words without so much as a look in her direction. He hadn't even taken her calls the rest of the day so she couldn't offer him excuses.

In the end, she'd decided she didn't want another argument with him. She didn't want to push him for she had a feeling they were both treading a fine line.

She arrived at Markos Villa with the dress and shoes she'd purchased with his credit card on her lunch break, to find a mass of activity in the huge acreage behind the villa.

Sunset was still a couple of hours away but the orange light lent a golden glow to the white silk marquees being put up. Tables were being dressed with lanterns and orchids in little glass jars. An extensive wine bar was set up on one end while a small wooden dance floor had been erected in the middle of all the small tents.

Fifty years! Theseus and Maria were celebrating fifty years of marriage. Of being together, of knowing one another inside out. Of belonging to one another.

Something she still wanted with the Kairos she was slowly discovering.

With a sigh, she made her way up the stairs outside the villa.

An eerie calm dwelled inside the high-ceilinged walls, in contrast to the hubbub of activity outside. A line of sweat poured down between her shoulder blades. Something felt wrong. As she walked through the airy villa, poured herself a glass of water in the kitchen, the sense of unease only got stronger.

Where were Theseus and Maria and Helena?

Apprehension sitting like lead in her gut, Tina took the stairs up. Suddenly, all she wanted was to see Kairos. To reassure herself that he was okay. On the first-floor landing, she was walking past the main master suite—Theseus and Maria's rooms—when she heard the argument.

She hadn't meant to pause and overhear, but over the last month, she had only become more and more attached to the older couple. Whatever the tension between their daughter, Kairos and them, there was a bond of steel between the husband and wife. An unshakeable love that Tina wanted in her own life. A bond made of respect, humor and utter affection. She'd even wondered how such a lovely couple could have given birth to such a brittle woman like Helena. She wouldn't have dreamed of eavesdropping but it was Maria's voice raised, close to breaking, and uttering Kairos's name that halted her steps.

She had a good grasp of Greek now and yet Maria's impassioned argument was hard to follow. She was imploring Theseus not to cut their own daughter out. To give Helena one more chance to prove the truth? To come to see the proof of it with his own eyes.

Kairos's true nature? Proof?

Wait, Theseus was going to cut Helena out of the company? How could he do that to his own daughter? Had Kairos persuaded him to it finally?

Tina's thoughts whirled and collided, a cold chill sweeping over her skin. What kind of proof was Maria talking about? What did Helena mean to prove to her parents?

She had tried to fill Valentina's mind with the supposed love between Kairos and her. It hadn't worked. She had tried to get her to leave by ruining her work. It hadn't worked.

What new scheme was she cooking now?

Heart racing a thousand miles a minute, Tina reached the vast bedroom she'd been sharing with Kairos. She dropped the bags on the floor, her gaze sweeping over the furniture and contents.

Kairos's huge desk was littered with papers, as was customary, but nothing seemed out of place. She could hear the shower running. And then she saw it—a flash of blue silk from the connecting door that led to the shared veranda. The other door from the veranda, she'd discovered the first evening, led to Helena's bedroom.

When she'd laughingly inquired of Theseus, he had told her that the house had been originally designed for a husband and a wife to share different bedrooms. With a wink at Kairos, the older man had gruffly announced he'd never want Maria to sleep in a separate bedroom. Maria had charmingly blushed.

Tina knew who would walk in to their bedroom in a few seconds. She could already hear the gruff baritone of Theseus's voice and Maria's pleading one—still close to tears. She didn't wait to see who would emerge from the veranda.

Unbuttoning her dress shirt, she pushed it off her shoulders. Next her trousers. By the time she reached the huge, rectangular glass-enclosed shower, she was in matching black bra and lace panties. The shape of a muscular flank made her hesitate.

With a deep breath, she pulled off her bra, then pushed down her panties and entered the shower.

To say her husband was stunned would have been the understatement of the year. To say she had forgotten how the sight of his naked body made her feel would be the understatement of the century.

All she could do was stare at him.

Water poured down Kairos's muscular body in rivulets. His dark hair pasted to his scalp made his rugged features harsher. His nose was broken and bent. His mouth a wide, cruel line. His neck was corded and muscled. Every inch of him was a feast to her starving senses.

Sparse hair covered a broad chest. His skin was like rough velvet—a sharp contrast to her own soft skin.

A line of hair arrowed down over his ridged abdomen, becoming thicker near his hips and then his pelvis. Legs built like a gladiator's clenched at her leisurely perusal.

Then, and only then, did she let her gaze drift to his arousal. He lengthened and hardened until it was curved up toward his belly.

A soft moan flitted from her mouth as she remembered the sensation of him moving inside her. For a man who didn't dance, he made love with a sensuality that made her eyes roll.

"If you don't stop looking at me like that, I will be inside you in two seconds. I will not give a damn if it is harmful or a weakness or what promises you drew from me." He sounded ragged, at the end of his rope. "I'm but a man, Valentina."

Her skin prickling, she pulled her gaze to his. The heat she saw there blasted through her meager defenses. Her nipples tightened into painful points, her breasts ached to be cupped.

Her breath came in serrated puffs as his gaze took in the plump points of her nipples, down her midriff to the junction of her thighs where wetness suddenly rushed, the scent coating the moisture-laden air around them.

Legs trembling, Tina turned away.

One more second of his gaze traveling down her length and she would have begged him to take her.

From the moment he'd slowly peeled off her wedding dress on that night, she'd realized she loved sex. That she had an appetite to match his own voracious one. And yet today, enclosed in the glass cubicle with his hard body mere fingertips away, all she felt was a longing. To belong to him. To possess him in equal measure—mind, body and soul.

To love him for the rest of their lives.

She touched her forehead to the glass wall, hoping to cool off. Willing her body to find a thread of reason as to why this wasn't a good idea.

She felt him move in the small space. He didn't touch her yet the heat radiating from his body was like a blanket over her skin.

"Valentina?" In his husky voice, her name was both an order and a request. He touched her then, his palm around her neck, while his other hand traveled down her bare back to her spine. To her hips.

With a deep groan, he pulled her closer, until his erection settled against her buttocks. Their guttural gasps rent the air.

"Wait," she managed, the scrape of his chest against her tightening her hunger.

"Now who's punishing whom, *pethi mou*?"

"I would never tease you like that," she whispered hurriedly. "She…planned something, Kairos. I don't know what. I just couldn't… I couldn't let them think that of you."

Instantly, she felt the change in the air. He was still warm and hard but it was as if he had turned off a switch. "Who planned what?"

She didn't have to answer the question. They could hear voices just outside the bathroom—Maria urging Theseus.

The silence raging behind her had such a dangerous quality to it that she turned.

Rage filled Kairos's face, making it so harsh that Valentina instantly clasped his cheeks. What could she say? What platitude could she offer when she had willfully believed the worst of him? Wouldn't she have believed her own eyes, too, if she'd been but a few minutes late?

He pushed her palms away as if they burned him. Cold dawned into his silver eyes, making them into a winter wasteland. "Did you see her?"

Valentina shook her head. "Only a flash of her dress. That turquoise blue silk she'd chosen for tonight."

He said nothing in reply.

Valentina shut the shower off and grabbed the towel from behind her. "I will go out first," she said softly, afraid of touching him.

He wouldn't harm Helena however angry he got, but she was also aware of his struggle to control his temper. She'd never seen him like this, so ragged at the edges.

What Helena had attempted to do, what Theseus and Maria would have seen if Valentina hadn't acted quickly… it was dirty, disgusting. And it had shaken him to the core.

She could see his frustration, his anger, but also for the first time since she'd met him, the depth of his affection for Theseus. He loved that old man and his wife. It was written in the torment on his face.

Becoming the company's CEO meant nothing to him. Only Theseus's love, his good opinion of him mattered.

It would have hurt him immeasurably if Theseus and Maria had found him in the shower with Helena. Finally—a true glimpse of the man she had married. A deeply caring man beneath the hard shell, the ruthless ambition.

All she felt were his emotions—raw and bleeding in that moment. And her own answering ones—desperate and potent. Everything to do with him and not her.

It was the first time in her life Tina felt someone else's pain. The first time she felt this overwhelming urge to reach out. To do anything she could to take that pain from him.

She wanted to hold him and never let go. But she understood him now. He would reject any comfort she offered. "Don't...do not embarrass them," he said between gritted teeth.

Confused for a few seconds, she stared at him. Then nodded, another realization hurtling through her.

He would do anything to protect them from embarrassment, from hurt. Even if it was heaped upon them by their own daughter. He would go to any lengths to hide Helena's reality from Theseus, to protect Theseus.

Even pretending to love the impulsive, juvenile wife that had walked out on him without doing the courtesy of telling him face to face.

She wrapped the towel around herself, pasted a smile to her face and stepped out. The pristine marble tiles were cold beneath her feet, jerking her into this moment.

Grabbing a smaller towel, she wiped the water dripping from her hair. Took a few deep breaths to clear the lump from her throat. Forced a cheery tone into her voice and said loudly, "Wait until you see my dress, Kairos. You're not going to want to leave the bedroom."

CHAPTER ELEVEN

ALL THROUGH THE party Tina waited for the explosion of Kairos's temper to come.

Maybe not in front of Theseus and Maria. It was after all their wedding anniversary celebration.

Maybe not in front of the guests who were extended family and board members from the Markos company and even employees and their families.

But in private maybe. Just between them? Would he confront Helena at least to see if what they'd assumed was right?

No!

Her husband acted as if nothing untoward had happened.

Helena appeared a few minutes after her parents and Kairos and Valentina had started welcoming the guests together.

Like a queen finally drifting down to meet her citizens. Like she hadn't tried to spread poison among people who cared about her.

Kairos's fingers clamped tight around her bare arm. "Stay out of this, Valentina."

Her hackles rose at his whispered warning. "But she—"

His fingers drifted to her hips, his grip so tight as he turned her that she had to smother a pained gasp. Instantly, he released her, a flash of something in the silvery gaze. "It doesn't concern you."

"How can you say that? If I hadn't—"

"You played the role I brought you here for, *ne*? You went out of your way to keep up your side of the bargain. For that I thank you. But Helena is my business and mine alone."

Hurt festered like an unhealed wound but for once in her life, Tina tried to put her own hurt aside for a moment and think of him.

He was in pain and he was lashing out at her. But she wouldn't let him. She wouldn't let him shut her out again. With all the guests' gazes on them, she clasped his jaw and pulled him until his mouth was a bare inch from her. Until he was all she saw, all she felt. Until everything she felt was mirrored in her gaze.

Until there was no escape from the truth in her eyes. "I did it because I care about you, because I couldn't bear to see you hurt. Don't shut me out tonight, not after everything we have shared the last couple of months. Please, Kairos. Don't turn away from me. From us."

She didn't wait for his reply. She had said what she meant to say, what she meant to do.

Helena was dressed in an exquisite blue, knee-length cocktail dress that made her look like a voluptuous baby doll. A diamond choker glittered at her throat. She looked innocent, beautiful—a façade.

Tina smoothed a hand down her own emerald green dress that left her shoulders bare and fell to her ankles, with a slit on one side. Her hair—since she hadn't even washed it properly in that shower—was neatly tied into a French braid.

Much as she tried to separate herself from the occasion and the people, Tina was drawn into the warmth of the celebration. She danced with Theseus, another older man with a bulbous face and kind eyes, a younger man who told her in Greek she was beautiful and that Kairos didn't deserve two beautiful women drifting about him.

Kairos had danced with Maria first, and then he'd

twirled Helena around the dance floor. Which had lasted four minutes and fifty-two seconds, too.

But he hadn't asked her. He'd watched her all evening with that consuming gaze—until Tina had felt as if she were standing naked in front of him again. As if he was testing her words, as if he didn't trust them. As if he loathed believing her.

Defiant and resolved, she met his gaze every time he looked at her. Let him see that this time she wasn't backing out, let him see the decision she had already made. The awareness between them was underscored by something heavier, darker.

Soon, she was surrounded by both men and women as she regaled them with the stories of growing up around her powerful brothers.

Unlike Conti Luxury Goods, however—which was a much more powerful and bigger conglomerate than the Markos Group, thanks to Leandro—Theseus's company was smaller and possessed a close-knit community feeling. Most of the board members and employees had been with the company for over twenty or even thirty years. And intensely loyal to Theseus, which made the attempted hostile takeover that much worse.

Even after a gap of seven years—Kairos had left when he'd been twenty-one—their trust and confidence in him was absolute. That he would naturally succeed Theseus as the CEO a foregone conclusion. She heard tales of Kairos's kindness, his leadership, his work ethic as he'd learned the ropes of the business under Theseus's guidance. Something she had learned herself in the last few weeks.

As night drove away the remnants of the lovely day, small lanterns lit on the tables threw faces into shadows. Strings of lights illuminated the grounds, marking paths.

Dinner was a lavish affair, with guests calling out for speeches. Theseus made one about Maria while she looked up at him adoringly and smiled. Helena made one, though it was mostly about the legacy Theseus would leave, as if he were already gone.

When Kairos raised his glass, a palpable hush fell over the crowd. "To Theseus and Maria…you are…" His Adam's apple bobbed up and down. Clearly, he was battling with his own emotions. "To another fifty years," he finished simply.

Maria burst into tears, her arms loosely wrapped around Kairos's waist from the side. The entire party came to a silence as if the moment were frozen in time. Helena frowned. Theseus kept his hand on his wife's back, concern lighting his eyes.

But it was Kairos's reaction that made Tina's chest so tight that she could barely breathe.

He had become utterly still the moment Maria had wrapped her arms around him. His shoulders painfully rigid, his jaw so tight that he might have been cast from marble. Only his eyes glittered with such raw emotion, such depth of pain that Tina had to look away. Seconds piled on into minutes as Maria silently sobbed, her face buried in Kairos's chest.

Tina took his free hand in hers and shook him slightly. "Kairos?"

Awakening from whatever held him in its ragged grip, Kairos awkwardly patted Maria's back while Theseus pulled her to him.

Theseus stood up again, raised his wineglass and announced his retirement. A pin dropped could have sounded like thunder in the thick silence.

"It is something I should've done years ago," he said, holding Kairos's gaze, an apology and something else in his tone. "I announce Kairos Constantinou as the new CEO of the Markos group of companies."

Applause thundered around them and yet as she saw Helena's face, dread curled around Tina's spine.

Helena hated Kairos and the depth of it terrified Tina. But even beneath that fear throbbed the sinking realization that he had what he wanted.

He was the CEO.

Which meant he had no need of Tina anymore.

While she…she had only just realized how desperately she was in love with him.

Midnight had come and gone by the time Tina went upstairs. Theseus had tired soon and Tina had convinced him and Maria to retire. Since Helena had been missing in action for several hours, she had taken over as the hostess. And stayed with a smile on her face until the last guest had departed.

But now as she dragged herself up the stairs, her feet hurt and a headache was beginning to throb at her temples. The staff had already cleaned up most of the debris from the party. Utter silence reigned over the villa.

Kairos was nowhere to be seen.

She took a quick shower and dressed in pajamas. Urgency and anxiety together made a nasty cocktail in her head. But she held onto the belief that he would come to her. He had to. He felt something for her and she would make that enough. She would make it work. They belonged together.

She drifted into sleep, the same thought running circles around her head.

Tina awoke suddenly, consumed with a feverish sense of urgency.

Pure darkness blanketed the room. The curtains that would have let in the moonlight were closed. Her skin prickled with awareness. She scooted up in the bed and turned on the lamp on the night stand.

Kairos was seated in the armchair in the corner. A bottle

of whiskey lay unstoppered next to him. Half empty. And no glass. Tall legs stretched in front of him drew her gaze to his muscular thighs. His tie was gone. Jacket discarded.

The white shirt was unbuttoned all the way to his abdomen. Golden olive skin dotted with sparse dark hair beckoned her touch.

And yet it was his face, wreathed in shadows, that drew her breath in serrated puffs. Dark brows winged over deep-set silver eyes perfectly framing his face. The thin, cruel slash that was his mouth. The strong column of his throat. His nostrils flared as he seemed to wait for her to acknowledge him.

"Kairos?"

"Your negligee is loose."

"What?" It took her a few seconds to comprehend his words. Heat swarming her cheeks, she tugged the strap that had fallen off her shoulder, baring most of her breast. "What are you doing here?"

"I'm not allowed in our bedroom?"

"Of course you are," she said, swallowing down the panic rising through her. Something was wrong. The way he stared at her, the stillness... He hadn't looked like that even when she'd told him what Helena had planned. Now... whatever had happened in the evening since, he looked unraveled. Completely undone.

And yet he had sought her out. He had been waiting for her in the dark, pain etched on every feature.

"I meant, why are you sitting there? In the darkness. Alone."

His tongue flicked over his lower lip. Her pulse raced. He stared at her for a long time before he responded. "I was wondering if I should wake you or not."

"Wake me?" she repeated, still grappling with the dangerous quality surrounding him. It seemed as if her mind couldn't concentrate on his words. Only on the vibe that radiated from him. "Is something wrong with Theseus or Maria? She did seem off all evening, I wondered if she was ill or if…"

Her words fell away as she reached him. Something about his stillness discouraged touch. Her hands hung loosely at her sides.

Silvery eyes raked down the length of her with a thoroughly possessive intent. She hadn't brushed out her hair before falling into bed. Now her braid was half undone, thick strands falling over her shoulders.

The negligee she'd picked was one she had bought after their wedding, a soft pink silk that hung loose around her chest now. Falling several inches above her knees, however, it bared most of her thighs and legs.

A sharp laugh from him startled her and she instinctively jumped back.

Her hand shot to her chest, rising and falling heavily. "What is funny?"

"Your legs."

"My legs are funny?"

"Did you pick that negligee on purpose?"

Her cheeks heated as the memory of all the provocative nightwear she'd worn to entice him. "I…was too exhausted and honestly I didn't think you'd be coming to bed anytime soon."

"You make it hard, Tina. You always make it so damn hard," he whispered, almost to himself.

She could no more stop her gaze from moving to his crotch than she could stop breathing. The shape of his arousal spiked her heartbeat.

He laughed, again, and she hurriedly pulled up her gaze to his. "That, too, *glykia mou*." Wicked lights danced in his eyes. "I always rise to the occasion, *ne*?"

"*Si*, always."

It was impossible not to laugh, even in the fraught moment. He looked young and charming and careless then, as if the tight grip he held over himself had snapped finally. It was a stark contest to the focused, always strategizing man she'd come to know.

What had snapped it?

"Kairos, how much have you drunk?"

Without answering her, he took the heavy bottle and took a huge gulp again. "You don't drink," she said softly.

"Usually, I don't. My mother…" His words didn't quite slur, though he seemed to lose focus. "I told you about her, *ne*?"

Her throat burned at the affection in his voice. "*Si*, you did."

"She hated what she was forced to do to…feed me. So every evening, as she got ready for work, she would drink. She would drink after she came back. For years, she drank to drown out her reality. In the end, her liver was so damaged that she drifted away into nothing. I hate alcohol. How it promises to dull things down and yet it doesn't."

He stared at the bottle in his hand, and plunked it down with such force on the side table that the thick glass instantly shattered, and his hand plunged into the broken shards with the force of it.

Valentina gasped and reached for him.

"*Oxhi, Valentina!*" His hands held her hips in a bruising grip. "There are shards everywhere. Your feet are bare."

Blood from the cut on his hand painted his shirt. "Kairos?"

"Yes, *agapita*?"

"Your hand…will you please let me dress it?"

He nodded and released her.

Tina darted into the bathroom, and came back with the first-aid kit. In silence that pulled her nerves, she finished dressing the deep cut, and wound it with gauze. She put the kit away, and pushed the broken fragments under the table and stared down at him.

He was staring at her as if he meant to devour her. And didn't know where to begin.

She was arrested between his wide legs, his face scant inches from her belly. Heat from his body hit her in powerful waves, the thin silk of her negligee no barrier.

"*Christos*, you smell like heaven," he said, pulling her closer. "Like you're the only place I can land, Valentina. But that is a mirage, too, *ne*? You're dangerous, *glykia mou*. Always a threat to my sanity."

Tina sank her hands into his hair to steady herself while he buried his face in her belly. He nuzzled her, as if he meant to burrow into her, setting every nerve ending on fire.

"Kairos?"

"I need you, *agapita*. So badly… I need you tonight." There was a ragged question underneath the demand that twisted her heart. He was not sure of her and she had only herself to blame for it.

"I'm here, Kairos. I've always been here, for you."

But there was no tenderness left in the moment. No humor. Only his need. Only the pain in his eyes and the frantic urgency she felt in his breath, in his movements to escape it.

His hands circled her waist restlessly, settling on her buttocks, and pressed her harder into his face. Molten heat spread from his mouth. The wet patch stuck to her skin. A heaviness filled her breasts, pooling into damp warmth at the juncture of her legs. The tension in his frame multiplied as he held her like that.

Then his hands were teasing the backs of her legs and thighs. Sneaking under the silky hem, cupping her buttocks, dragging her higher up against him. Higher, higher, lifting her with those sinewy arms. Until she was half standing, half draped over his shoulders.

Until his face was flush with her mound.

Tina swallowed the sound that rose to her lips, her trust absolute. Willing him to take whatever he needed.

His hot breath fell in puffs against her.

She jerked at the sudden surge of sensation so sharp that she almost fell backwards. But he didn't release her. He held her as if he would never let go.

As if she were his salvation.

Her fingers crawled from his hair to his neck. When he pressed a warm, wicked kiss against the silk pooling at her sex, she dug her nails into his neck.

He growled and burrowed his mouth into her folds. Her spine arched, the knot in her lower belly so tightly wound. Her breath became fire. His fingers bit into her hips, the pain coating the pleasure with a sharp contrast that made it unbearable.

A thousand little tremors exploded when he opened his mouth, when his teeth dug into the lips of her sex. Violent shivers that she couldn't contain. Moans and whimpers that she couldn't swallow. Up, up, up went the silk. Until she was bared to him utterly and there was not even a flimsy barrier between his wicked mouth and her willing flesh.

Rough fingers dragged over her hips, her buttocks, stroking, kneading, clutching. No thoughts marred the pure lights of sensation darting up and down her body.

And then his tongue was there at the place where she ached for him. Always. Stroking, licking, laving. Pushing her higher, higher, higher onto the cliff. Driving away everything else from her body except him, and what his mouth, and his wicked tongue did to her.

Insistent. Raw. Relentless. She moaned and rocked into his mouth, clutching onto him as if he were her everything.

She was transported to that wanton place only Kairos could take her. And then the knot in her belly broke apart, her muscles clenched long and deep, pleasure splintering through her. Her thighs shook from the pressure, every inch of her trembling.

Arching into the warmth of his body, she pulled the negligee off and threw it away. His cheeks were flushed with stripes of color. Fingers trembling, she somehow undid the clasp of his belt. Unzipped his trousers. And then he was in her palm. Hard and hot. Thick. Lengthening.

"Inside you, Valentina, now." The open need in his words was a balm to her soul.

Straddling his thighs that spread her indecently wide, she pushed down. His hips jerked up, and he thrust into her with one smooth stroke, fingers holding her hips grounded against him.

A long curse ripped out from his sinful mouth.

Tina gasped. Her body felt invaded even after the release he had given her, shivers of a different kind building over her skin. He was so deep. So hard inside her. Entrenched inside her body just as he always was in her heart.

A slow panic began to build inside her. She would never be free of him now. Never come out of this intact if he pushed her away.

"Shh…*agapi mou*…" he whispered against her temple. Long fingers stroked her damp skin softly. Soothingly. Until the tremors quieted.

A soft kiss against her damp lips. A featherlight stroke against her cheek. He nuzzled his stubble into her neck as if he had all the time in the world. As if just being inside her was enough.

"I didn't forget for one second how tight you feel around me. But I didn't realize that after so many months…you would be…" He sounded so adorably puzzled that Tina laughed. "Am I hurting you?"

Arms wrapped around his shoulders, she looked at him. His hair was damp and sticking to his forehead. His mouth pinched with the control he exercised. Skin pulled taut over his hard features, the depth of his need glimmered in his eyes. "*Si*," she whispered, unable to stem the truth from falling from her lips. She'd forgotten how huge he felt inside her, but it was the panic running amok that she wanted to control. "Give me a moment."

His hands tightened around her hips. "Do you want me to stop?"

"*No!* I… I just need to get used to you again." She wriggled her hips in a small movement. The tightness was still there but something else fluttered beneath it.

A soft kiss against her breastbone. "Take all the time you need."

She hid her face in his shoulder, blinking back the tears that rose. Did they have time? Did he want forever, like she did?

Anchoring her hands on his shoulders, Valentina arched her spine, then moved up and down. The tightness eased. In its wake came little flutters of sensation. She pushed against the sensation, chasing it. Lips pulled first at one nipple and then other, sharpening the little jolts that went to her groin.

Clasping his stubbled jaw, she took his mouth, hard and possessive, letting her kiss speak what she couldn't say. "I want your skin, Kairos. All of you."

In a blink of movement, he brought her to the bed. In the next, he had stripped his shirt, boxers. And then he was prowling on to the bed and she watched him to her heart's content.

The sleek lines of his body. Velvet-rough skin stretched taut over rippling muscles. When he covered her body with his, when he thrust into her, Tina was ready this time.

The drag of their sweat-slicked bodies against each other brought familiar pleasure racing along her nerves. When he thrust, she raised her hips. His grunt of satisfaction made her growl in response.

Hands on her hips, he held her down and yet he was slow, taking his time.

Driving her out of her own skin.

"Faster, please, Kairos. Harder," she urged him on, knowing what he needed. What he desperately craved. Wanting to be everything he needed.

No, not wanting to be.

She *was* everything Kairos needed already. She understood him, she loved him so much, and there wasn't anything she wouldn't face for him. No one she wouldn't fight to be by his side.

All she needed was to make him realize that. To make him understand that she belonged with him.

The realization flew through her veins, turning the moment into so much more than pleasure. He was hers and she would do anything to keep him.

She stroked his broad shoulders, his chest, dug her fingers into his buttocks, tasted the saltiness of his skin. Bit the arch between his neck and shoulders. Possessively, she drank him in.

He pressed a kiss to her temple, his rough thighs grazing her soft ones. "I don't want to hurt you."

"You won't. I can take whatever you give me, Kairos. Don't you know that already?"

As his thrusts became rougher and faster, as his breath hitched, as he growled and his body shuddered on top of her, Tina kissed his temple, breathing the sweat and scent of him.

Whatever his ambitions, whatever had made him into what he was today, she loved all of him. And she would fight for him.

CHAPTER TWELVE

KAIROS COULDN'T HELP HIMSELF. Gathering Valentina to him, he kissed the slope of her shoulder, the skin still damp from their shower an hour ago.

He had pushed her body relentlessly tonight, craving release after release, a need for escape riding him hard. He'd barely soaped her and himself after he'd pushed her against the wall and taken her. Much less toweled them both dry before they had tumbled into bed.

He felt like he had run a triathlon, so sore was his body.

Valentina had, as usual, fallen asleep and nuzzled into him but sleep had evaded him. He'd wanted to leave the bed and her.

Intimacy was always hard on him and the more he'd been determined to limit his increasing need for Valentina to bed, the more she had undone him there.

But last night he hadn't wanted to go. He hadn't wanted to be alone. No, that wasn't right. He was not going to lie to himself now.

He hadn't wanted to leave *her*. The haven she provided against the cruelty of the world. Against the pain that had filled him.

She was warmth and fire and heaven.

He'd seen her slave hour after hour to make it up to Chiara, to find her place in the fashion world.

He'd seen her care for Theseus and Maria in the last month, responding to their kindness. Worrying about Theseus's health. Persuading a reluctant but smiling Maria into letting her redo her entire wardrobe, because she'd declared impishly to a stunned Theseus that being married to a grouchy bear like him for fifty years, Maria deserved to be dripping in diamonds.

The laughter that had boomed out of Theseus, the shock and gratitude in Maria's eyes that Valentina could make her husband laugh like that again... Theseus had ordered a stunning diamond necklace for Maria on Valentina's advice and when he'd asked Tina to pick something for herself for a present, she'd ask to be counted among his friends, no matter what.

"You like him," he'd said to her later in the privacy of their bedroom. "And he likes you."

"Most people like me, Kairos. I'm fun to be around most of the time. And who wouldn't adore Theseus? Helena is truly poor that she doesn't care for such loving parents. I never knew my father but now I know how to imagine him, at least.

"Theseus...he reminds me of you."

He'd looked at her, shocked. "What?" She couldn't have known what that meant to him.

"Or rather I see what you will be forty years from now. If you..."

He'd backed her against the wall then, something in her expression goading him. "If I what, Valentina?"

"If you learn to be more fun and communicative and a little less brooding."

Before he could punish her for such insolence, she'd slipped away from him.

And in that glimpse of longing and adoration in her eyes when she looked at Theseus, he saw the similarities between them.

Just like him, she had never left that scared, little girl

behind. And yet there was fire inside her and for a night, he had wanted what she could give him.

Words never came easily to him and this strange vulnerability she'd created in him robbed him of what little did come.

So, when morning dawned, he had woken her up with kisses and soft caresses, needing to be inside her desperately. Needing to hold her close one more time, needing that intimacy where he could show that he did appreciate her. The only place he could do so.

She had whimpered when he had filled his hands with her breasts.

Arched her behind into him sleepily and whispered, 'Si...' in that husky tone when he'd hoarsely asked if he could take her like that. So he had slowly stroked himself into her with her back pressed to his chest, her legs caught between his, played with her clit until the need for release was riding her just as hard as it did him. And when her muscles had clenched him even tighter in blissful climax, when she had clung to him, and whispered his name against his own lips again and again, only then did he claim his own release.

And every time his release rushed at him, and he was lost to the pleasure inside her, it felt as if she was stealing some other part of him. As if he was not whole anymore.

But the truth he had learned today, the renewed pain—it was a reminder. He couldn't love Valentina, and he couldn't bear it if...she did the same thing as people who claimed to love him had done.

He would rather hurt her now, keep her whole, than destroy her later, all in the name of love.

When he had woken up this time, she was sitting in the chair he had sat in last night. Freshly showered and dressed in his shirt, she looked the perfect mixture of innocent and siren, a woman capable of tenderness and guts.

Their gazes met and held, the air in the room redolent with the scent of sex and them. Poignant. So much emotion in her eyes that he felt inadequate.

"Come back to bed," he said, pulling the duvet up.

Without a word she crawled back into bed, her trust in him complete.

A faint tension shimmered over her. He kept his arm around her, unwilling to let her retreat from him. Her fingers gripped his forearm, whether asking him to release her or not, he didn't care.

He buried his face in her hair. Tugged her so close that his groin pressed into her buttocks. His chest crushed her back to him. His arm cushioned under her breasts.

"You're not going to ask me about last night?" he whispered.

She pulled his palm to her mouth and pressed a soft kiss. "You will tell me when you're ready."

He stiffened. "What does that mean?"

He felt her exhale, as if she was striving to be patient. "Are you asking to know or to annoy me?"

He swatted her buttocks and she laughed.

Just hearing that sound made his chest lighter.

"It means that whether you share your past or not, whether you continue to act like a gruff bear or a fluffy unicorn, whether you lose your temper or subject me to these heavy silences…nothing changes how I see you, how I think of you. I think, finally—" her voice wobbled and she pressed her face into his hand tightly, before releasing it "—I know the true you, Kairos. Nothing and no one will shake my belief in you. Not even you."

"And if you had seen me in that shower with her?" The question slipped from him, his tone ragged.

"Then I would have dragged her out by her lovely hair and slapped her face. Like I wanted to before you stopped me."

"Your trust in me is that absolute, Valentina?"

"*Si*, it is. Even when I taunted you that you want Theseus's company. I knew the truth, I was just too scared to acknowledge it."

And that implicit trust in her voice broke Kairos down. Words no one had ever heard from him came pouring out. "She told them that I…was the one who got her pregnant."

Valentina jerked, moved in his hold as if to turn around. But he arrested her movement, for he didn't know if he could speak if she pitied him. Slowly, the rigidness in her shoulders eased. A long exhale left her but she gripped his fingers tighter. "Helena?"

"Yes. She… I…one of her high-flying friends, he ran the moment she told him. She and I…we never were close but mostly she tolerated me. Theseus wanted her to show interest in the company and she did, as long as it allowed her extravagant lifestyle. When he learnt that she was pregnant, he became extremely angry. Helena's recklessness never knew bounds but this was too far for him. He threatened to cut her off if she didn't change her ways, if she didn't settle down. She realized that he meant to give me control of everything."

"So she told her parents that you were the one who got her pregnant?"

He could feel her heart racing. Could almost see the conclusions she was running through. He held onto her, long beyond the point where he could fool himself into thinking the comfort was for her.

"Kairos, what did Theseus do?" He felt her kiss his wrist, hold it to her face as if she were bracing herself. For him. Everything she felt—the fear, the worry—it was all for him.

He let it wash over him, let himself bask in it.

"Theseus—" he cleared his throat, wishing for her sake that he was a different man "—decided that Helena and I would marry and possess equal power over the company. He trusted me to keep her in line, I suppose."

"What did you say to his proposal?"

"I agreed. I told him I would do whatever he asked of me."

"You were willing to be a father to some other man's child?"

"Yes. I asked only that he believe that I had never even touched her."

This time, there was no stopping Valentina. She turned in his arms, her gaze peering into his, as if she meant to own everything of him. A bright shine made them glitter. "And he didn't believe you?"

"No. He wouldn't even look at me. I don't think he even cared if Helena and I had been…together. But, however many times I insisted, he wouldn't say that he believed me. By denying his trust…he…he took away everything he had ever given me.

"It felt as if I was that orphan boy again looking through a glass window into what a family looks like." His voice shook. "I don't even remember being angry with Helena's blatant lies. Only crushed by his silence. I…felt betrayed. I told him I didn't want the company if I didn't have his… respect. His trust." His love.

Theseus had chosen Helena's lies over Kairos's truth, and that was what had broken Kairos's heart, why he had left.

Unable to stay still, Tina pulled herself up on the bed and the sheet with it. Every muscle was tense in his body as if he was living through the ghastly moment again. The anguish in his eyes only showed that she had been right. There was a heart that beat under all that ruthless exterior.

She clasped his jaw and pulled him close. He became

still, too rigid, as if he could physically will himself to reject her concern. But she didn't care. All she wanted was to tell him he wasn't alone. That she understood his pain. That it was okay to have loved Theseus so much that it still hurt after all these years.

That he was a good man, one of the best she had ever met. That her brother Leandro, as always, had made the right decision, that he had chosen for her the best man she could ever have asked for.

But she felt too fragile, stretched far too thin after everything they had shared in the last few days.

So she did the only thing she could.

She crawled to him on her knees, the sheet barely covering her breasts and her legs. He watched her with glittering eyes, as if daring her to come closer. Hands on his shoulders, she bent until their noses were touching.

Softly, slowly, she took his mouth. So rigid and hard and yet capable of such tender kisses. Mouth slanted over his, licking the seam of his lips, she willed him to accept it. The sheet slithered down her body, and she heard the hitch in his breath when her nipples grazed his chest.

When he suddenly opened up for her, she plunged her tongue inside. And just like that, the tempo of the kiss changed as he took over.

Even with her body sore in so many places, pleasure inched over her like petals unfurling ever so gently. His fingers wrapped around her neck and he kissed her back hungrily. As if he needed the taste of her to get through this moment. It took but one touch, one stroke, one moment for their hunger to rise, to sweep them away. Their harsh breaths reverberated as he pulled away.

His nostrils flared as he fought for control. He got off the bed, pulled on the shorts he had thrown off some time during the night and looked out the French windows.

She swallowed the words rising through her throat. She would not beg but neither would she retreat. Limbs heavy with exhaustion, she pulled on his discarded shirt and buttoned it down.

Slowly, as if she were dealing with a wounded animal, she reached him and tucked herself into his side until he had to relent. Until he wrapped his hand around her shoulders and pulled her close.

"What happened at the party? Something…changed." It wasn't what Theseus did seven years ago that had cut him.

"I figured out why Theseus didn't believe me seven years ago. Or why he let himself be convinced that Helena was telling the truth."

Breath on a serrated edge, Valentina wrapped her hands around his waist, refusing to be pushed out. Her heart ached for him. His words, his voice reverberated with the depth of his love for Theseus. The rawness of his wound created by Theseus's refusal to trust his word.

"You still came back," she whispered. "You came back when you heard he was sick."

"How could I not? He…" His voice broke and he looked away. "He…gave me the world, Valentina. How could I not rush to his side when he had need of me? When after years of living on the streets, he had shown me compassion, affection? When he made me into everything I am today?"

"You figured out who backed the hostile takeover. That's why you were…" She didn't want him hurt anymore. The notion of him closing down the part of him that cared, it terrified her.

He ran a hand through his hair, his bare chest falling and rising. "Helena was in cahoots with Alexio all along, yes. But it was Maria's stock that tilted the whole thing."

"Maria would have gone against Theseus? But why?" Maria was devoted to her husband. The absolute love and trust between the couple…through everything, they had held together.

Whereas she had avowed love again and again to Kairos, and then run way at the first obstacle.

"I think Theseus wouldn't…didn't believe me over Helena back then because Maria had told him that she'd seen Helena and me…together. In bed."

Tina gasped. "Maria backed Helena's story knowing it was a lie?"

"Helena was desperate and Maria couldn't say no to her daughter. She's always been kind to me and I can almost see how she would think I was getting not a bad deal out of it, that I would be able to control Helena's wildness if we married."

He spoke as if it didn't matter but it was the clear lack of emotion that told Tina how much it had hurt him to realize what Maria had done.

"You are making excuses for her. And all the guilt, it has been too much for her. That's why she cried on your shoulder like that. That's why she kept saying she was sorry."

Kairos nodded.

"Why give her stock to Helena? Why deceive Theseus?"

"Theseus is stubborn to the core. He…he knew his health was deteriorating, he wouldn't slow down, the company was doing badly. Maria told me that first day she'd been begging him to ask me for help. She'd been terrified about his health. So, coupled with Helena's insistence that it was for the best, I think Maria signed over the proxy on her stock to Helena, which gave Alexio the boost, the vote of confidence to begin turning men loyal to Theseus toward him. Men who were genuinely worried about the company. Men who thought Alexio was the better of two bad choices. Instead, it precipitated Theseus's heart attack."

"But how did you stop it when Maria had already

signed it over?" She frowned and then it came to her. "They see you as Theseus's true successor. So when they saw that you had returned, they decided not to back Alexio's coup."

He smiled faintly, but it didn't reach his eyes. "Again, I'm the better choice for the company."

"You can't seriously believe that, Kairos. They treated me like I was part of a family, as if being Kairos Constantinou's wife was something in itself.

"Their trust in you, their confidence is absolute. It is you who always holds himself separate. Who isolates himself. I wish I could make you see it. I wish I could…"

He pulled up their laced fingers and kissed her knuckles. The intimate gesture sent a ray of hope through her. "What?"

"I wish I could change you, just a little."

"Valentina…your trust in me about everything after the way I treated you…it has meant a lot to me. It's a gift I never expected."

"I'm full of surprises like that," she added, trying to lighten the atmosphere. "What happened then?"

"When Maria saw me at Theseus's side within a few hours of his attack, when she saw that all Helena cared about was the company and not her father… I think she started having second thoughts."

"So Helena changed tack, told them that she truly loved you all these years. Since you will not tell Theseus the truth, you had to bring me here. Did you tell him Maria's part in all this? How she deceived him, too?"

Any hesitation she saw in him vanished. His mouth took on that stubborn, uncompromising tilt. "I will not do anything that could harm him. And I forbid you to tell him anything."

"What if Maria will forever continue to assist Helena?

Kairos, you didn't see the look in her eyes when he made the announcement. What if, even this evening, Helena had Maria's backing in that...disgusting move?"

White lines fanned around his mouth, and Tina knew that the very real possibility had struck him, too. "It will never be good for both Helena and me to be here. She will only hurt them to get to me, to cut the little trust that there still is between me and Theseus. I can't put Theseus through that. I can't face seeing disillusionment in his eyes again. I will not tell him that his wife of fifty years lied to him to protect their daughter."

"Maria was supposed to protect you, too."

"Listen to me, Valentina. You have to leave what I told you here in this room. I've already started a head hunt for another CEO. An impartial outsider will be good for the company. Helena will be terminated from her position at the company. As soon as I locate her, I will inform her that her stock options will be set up in a trust fund from which she can draw an income, a more than comfortable one. But going forward, she will have no stake in the company. Hopefully that will stop her from trying...to ruin her parents' lives. What she planned two nights ago...it would have broken Theseus. In so many ways." He became again that ruthless man she had lived with for nine months. "I will cut away everything she wants if she doesn't behave."

"And when this is all settled to your satisfaction?"

"I will remain on the board since Theseus insists on signing over his stock to me, and I will oversee things from time to time. Other than that, I'm finished here."

Finished here?

If he could have slammed a door down between them, the message couldn't have been more absolute.

Hands around her waist, Tina swayed against the wall. Even the scent of his skin, the radiating warmth of his body…it felt like they could sear her skin. Tears lumped in her throat, and she breathed deeply, trying to keep them in. "You mean you don't need me anymore in this role," she said almost absently, as if it were happening to someone else.

As if the crack of her heart was outside, not within her.

"*Ne.*"

She moved her hand to point behind her toward the once-again rumpled bed. Sometime before or after he had made love to her for the third time, he had carried her to the armchair, pulled the sheets off and made the bed again with clean, crisp bedlinen. When she had looked askance at him, he had winked at her and told her he was nowhere near done.

"What was that then? The four orgasms were parting gifts to remember you by?"

He rubbed a hand over his face. "That was me being selfish, being weak. Needing escape." He looked away and then back, as if he found it hard to focus on her. His features could have been carved in granite for the emotion in them. "Dealing with Maria's lies, Helena's deceit…it has reminded me I have no stomach for this."

"Lie to yourself all you want, Kairos, but don't equate what I feel for you with them."

"Don't make this hard, Valentina. I… I have an upcoming trip to Germany in four days. I'll be gone for almost three weeks. I'm trying to tie up everything before I leave. But even then, I… I think you should return to…"

"To whatever hole I crawled out from?"

He flinched. "Like you pointed out, Helena is going to be furious. She's focused all her anger on me now. I've no idea what she's going to throw at me next and I would rather you were a thousand miles away than here when that happens."

"*Per piacere,* Kairos! Treat me with respect and give me the real reason." Pain crystallized, morphed into fury and Tina embraced it with everything she had. "Shall I send you divorce papers then? Shall I have my powerful brothers throw everything they have at you so that I can take half of everything you own? What does leaving here mean, Kairos? You will damn well spell it out for me!"

When he stayed silent, her heart slipped from her chest.

He simply stared at their clasped hands as if they were talking about the weather. "It will mean divorce. It will mean you can take me for everything I have. You can bring me to my knees."

"You're a bastard!"

"You have no idea how close to the truth you are."

"That's not what I meant. You could have left me well alone. You shouldn't have…you should have let me think you were nothing but a ruthless jerk, Kairos."

He clasped her cheeks with such reverent tenderness that her heart broke a little more. "But I am, Valentina. What I feel for Theseus is gratitude. Don't you see? You were right. It is only a transaction for me. He gave me everything so I repay as much as I can."

"That's not true." She fought against his grip even as he was kicking her out of his life.

"But you… I was wrong about you." Another hard kiss, another piece of her heart forever lost to her. "When Leandro said any intelligent man would know that you are worth more than a hundred companies, he spoke the truth. You deserve everything a man can give you, Valentina. You deserve more than I can give you."

"You're just choosing not to."

"No," Kairos repeated, steeling himself against the bright sheen in her eyes. "I don't know how to love you, Valentina. And I do not wish to learn. Go back to your brothers, *pethi mou*. Tell Leandro, for once in his life, he made a bad bet. Tell him he was wrong about me. Tell him—" Kairos ran his thumb over her lower lip, a cold void opening up inside him "—that I do not deserve the precious gift he gave me."

If only he could embrace it...*this, her*. If only he was capable of giving her what she deserved. Needed.

She felt like home. Like warmth and acceptance. Like a splash of color to his gray canvas. After years of near starving, of no companionship, that was how Maria and Theseus's home had felt. He had been so cautious at first, but eventually they had won him over. He hadn't asked for anything but they had given kindness, care and love again and again, in so many ways.

Until he had believed it all. Until he had forgotten the cautiousness he had learned on the streets. Until he had forgotten the wretchedness of being alone.

Until he had started loving them, until they had simply become a part of him.

And then everything had been taken away. In one moment, everything had been lost. Seven years ago and now again...

If he trusted Valentina, if he opened himself up to everything she made him feel and things fell apart...it would be so much worse. A million times more painful. And he would break this time. If she took it away like Theseus and Maria had done, if suddenly he found himself all alone after having had a taste of...

Oxhi!

That was a fate he couldn't even indulge in.

He was not ready for the weight of her love.

He was never going to be ready for her.

For this.

For them.

She would only starve for affection with him. He'd already trampled her spirit. If he broke her because he couldn't love her, he couldn't bear it.

"You're right." She pushed the silky mass of her hair away angrily, the innate sensuality of the gesture stealing his breath. "You don't deserve me. I always thought I was not good enough for you. That I had to earn your love some-how. But this has nothing to do with me. *You're* the coward, Kairos. You're unworthy of me, not the other way around. You want to choose a miserable existence instead of trust-ing me, instead of taking a chance on us, fine. Then please stay in the other bedroom until you leave for your trip."

Her words hit him hard. "I can have you flown back to Milan tonight."

She backed out of his reach, a fiery tenacity to her ex-pression. His shirt hung on her, baring most of her sleek thighs. Curves he'd never touch or feel wrapped around himself again. "I'm not leaving, you are."

He jerked his gaze back up, the void in his gut only deep-ening. "Valentina—"

"I have three more weeks left with Chiara. People are counting on me to do my job. I will not let them down, I will not let myself down because you've decided you've had enough of playing marriage. I will not disappear in the middle of the night from Theseus and Maria's lives as if I had done something wrong. As if I'm responsible for this debacle."

"I don't want you here," Kairos said before he could stop himself. Her mouth pinched into a thin line. "Helena—"

"I can handle Helena. At the least, I know what to expect from her. I want to finish my work here, work the contacts I made. Maria will need someone to look after her, too." She gazed at him for a few seconds that felt like an eternity. He couldn't bear the disillusionment in her eyes. Broken hope.

He took a step toward her, but she shook her head and backed away. "Goodbye, Kairos."

CHAPTER THIRTEEN

K<small>AIROS</small> <small>STARED AT</small> the society pages of a leading online fashion magazine, his breath hurtling through his chest and throat like a hurricane.

Valentina was laughing in this picture, standing in between her friend Nikolai and Ethan King—an American textile magnate whose burgeoning alliance with Conti Luxury Goods was all the rage in the news.

He'd known Leandro had been hunting for a new CEO for the board of CLG for months now. The initial prize he had promised Kairos himself. The prize Kairos had thought important enough to take Valentina on.

Thee mou, he'd been such an arrogant fool.

Leandro had stepped down himself after he had discovered he had a child with Alexis seven years ago. When Kairos had looked askance, he'd laughed and said that he would understand one day.

Luca had married Sophia, who headed her stepfather's company Rossi's. The playboy genius still did his own thing, as he had always done. He'd never had any interest in CLG except to thwart Kairos because Luca had assumed that Kairos would only hurt their sister. He'd been right.

Ethan King was a good choice. For the CLG board.

His gaze returned to her in the picture.

She'd fashioned her silky hair to fall over one side. A pink pantsuit made everything of her long legs. A thin chain glittered at her neck and disappeared into the neck-line of her blouse.

Frantically, he clicked through more pictures to see if she'd kept the pendant he had bought for her. But he couldn't spot it.

Christos! What was he doing?

Her arms around Nikolai and Ethan, her eyes glittering with laughter, she looked gorgeous.

She looked…*happy*.

Seven weeks since he'd last seen her. Since she'd told him defiantly that she'd finish her position before she left. Since he'd walked out of her life for good.

By the time he had returned from Germany, she'd been gone. Every trace of her removed from their bedroom, from the villa.

The first time she had left he'd been so angry.

This time, it felt like she had taken a part of him with her. As if she'd ripped him apart, never to be whole. Everything was so blank, so dull since he'd returned. As if all the color in the world had been leached out.

He'd been so sure that he'd done the right thing by her. For once, he'd put her happiness, her well-being before his. Before his own ambitions.

Somehow, he'd been getting through his days.

Until she'd sent him divorce papers.

Until suddenly, she'd exploded into the news again in true Valentina fashion. She'd partnered with Sophia to launch a full-service fashion boutique—for clients who had personal styling needs and a host of other services.

She had collaborated with major fashion brands to launch an online vlog in which she had models of different sizes showcase the latest creations from designer brands.

The camera loved Valentina. She was a natural.

The vlog had exploded within a week of launching,

drawing more than a million hits on the internet and her business had taken off.

She'd already hosted a fashion show on a morning talk show to advertise her services. Stylish and sophisticated, she was already adored by the media. She had appeared in numerous TV style segments.

His heart in his throat, he clicked Play on a small news clip that had been recorded on another talk show.

"I always used to think my talent was useless. But then I learned that I was wasting my potential by denying myself the connections I did have. So I partnered with my sister-in-law and launched the boutique. It was she who gave me the idea. Sophia, for example, is an exceptional businesswoman but had always had problems dressing herself because she—" a fond laugh here "—she wasn't as she says, 'a giraffe with legs that go on forever.' She's curvy and sexy, and it was my pleasure to help her find clothes that showcased her body, to make her feel confident in her own shape.

"I love dressing people and now I can put my expertise into making someone else feel comfortable in their own skin. Be confident in themselves while they go out to capture the world. Everyone needs fashion advice…" She hesitated and then laughed—that husky full-bodied sound—when her brothers walked onto the stage in matching dark gray suits. She stood up and walked to them until they were both standing on her sides. "Even my handsome, powerful brothers, the legendary Conti men."

Kairos closed his laptop hard. He had watched the same damn clip a hundred times.

Leandro and Luca had walked onto the show to give their support to their sister—a spectacular publicity move he was sure had been orchestrated by Sophia, to thrust Valentina's fashion venture into the limelight. With their backing, with Sophia's business acumen and Valentina's own talent, he had no doubt her business would reach unprecedented heights.

She had found her place in the world.

He should be happy that she had taken his advice. That she had used what was at her disposal to fuel her dream, to launch her dream career.

He should be happy that he hadn't…damaged her permanently.

But then Valentina had an unquenchable spirit, a fierce strength, a generous heart. She drew people to her wherever she went.

If not today, if not this month, if not this year, she would find that happily-ever-after that she so desperately wanted. Some man would see what a beautiful person she was, inside and out, and love her as she deserved.

Suddenly the picture of Ethan King and her laughing into the camera at some new nightclub he was launching flashed in his mind's eye.

With a curse, he strolled to the bay windows.

Would Leandro go down that path again? Would Valentina let him find her a husband again? Or had she already found someone who did appreciate what an extraordinary woman she had grown into?

Had she finished with him already?

Bile rose through his throat at the thought of the man holding his wife, touching her, kissing her. At the thought of Valentina surrendering all that passion, surrendering her heart to another man.

A breeze ruffled the papers he had left on the side table. He should just sign the divorce papers and be done with her.

Give her whatever she wanted.

Release her from this marriage. Release himself from the grip she seemed to have on his heart. Be done with it.

He'd made the safe choice, for once in his life, so why couldn't he just live with it? Why couldn't he accept it and move on?

"Kairos?"

He turned around to see Maria standing at the door, wary and hesitant.

He frowned, wondering how long she'd been standing there. He'd mostly avoided her since the night of their anniversary party and she had let him.

"Does Theseus need something?"

"*Oxhi.* He's resting." She looked at her hands and then back up again. "I… I wish to speak to you. Do you have a few minutes for me?"

"Of course," he said, forcing himself to move from his spot.

He watched her silently as she flitted around the room restlessly. As always, she was elegantly dressed in a dark sweater and neatly pressed white capri pants. Her nails had been done with that signature red color for as long as he could remember. Her hair had grayed considerably, still cut into a short bob.

Only now did he realize how much weight she had lost in the last year. She'd been tirelessly caring for Theseus for so many months now. Not to mention whatever hell Helena had put her through.

He poured out water from a jug and placed a glass for her on the side table.

"Is everything okay?" he prompted, her restlessness increasing his own anxiety.

"No. It is not."

"What can I do to help?"

"You would help, Kairos, still?"

Something in her gaze made him uncomfortable. "Of course, I would, Maria. You have but to command me."

A brittle laugh fell from her mouth. "Theseus is right. I am a foolish woman."

He hardened himself against the emotion twisting his gut. It had to be about Helena, about all the decisions he'd been making about the company.

He could take whatever she threw at him, he reminded himself. He could take it and still stay standing. After all, Helena was her daughter and he was…an outsider.

Since the minute Theseus had decided he would adopt Kairos, Maria had welcomed him unflinchingly. She had only ever shown him kindness. And he would pay it back a million times over.

"Maria, whatever it is, you can say it to me without hesitation. I understand how hard this must be for you. And whatever you request for Helena, I promise I will try to do my best to accommodate it. I just can't… I can't let her be a part of the company anymore. Not if I have to do what's best for the business. And for Theseus and you."

She flicked another wary glance at his face and then away. Then she sat down and gestured for him to do the same. Her head down, she looked at her clasped fingers. When she looked up, there were tears in her eyes.

Tears that cut through his heart.

"He's so angry with me. So angry. But it was the right thing to do," she half muttered to herself.

Any walls he had erected against her crumbled at the sight of her tears. He took her hands in his. "Maria, what are you talking about?"

"Can you believe it…in fifty years of marriage, today is the first time he wouldn't look at me. The first time he said he was disappointed in me. He is ashamed of me, and I deserve it."

He sat back, shocked. "You and Theseus never fight."

"I told him everything. Everything Helena ever did. Everything I shielded from him. Everything she…lied about. About the pregnancy. About the stock and the takeover. About…my part in it. About all the disgusting things she'd planned to do to discredit you in his eyes."

"What?" Shock robbed his words. "Is…is Theseus okay? *Thee mou,* Maria! What would that accomplish except jeopardize his health? The last thing he needs just when he is finally recuperating is to learn that you—"

"That I betrayed him. That I betrayed everything he has always stood for." All the hesitation was gone from her face. "That I treated you so horribly."

"You didn't. You…only ever showed me kindness." He walked away, unable to look into her eyes. Unable to stop the dam within him from bursting. "Theseus brought me home, yes, but you welcomed me with open arms. You encouraged me when I thought I would never leave behind my dirty roots. You…gave me everything, Maria. More than I had a right to."

"But I didn't love you like I should love a son. When he told me that day that he wanted to raise you, that he had decided it, in true arrogant Theseus fashion—" laughter burst through the tears running down her cheeks "—that you were our son now, I promised him I would love you like one. That I would embrace you in every way. But I did not. I…was weak. I let my love for Helena blind me. She came so late into our lives…when I had given up on the idea of a child completely that I didn't see how much I was spoiling her."

"You don't need to explain."

"I do. I need to. I didn't just let Theseus down, and you down. I let myself down, too."

He felt her stand next to him, the subtle floral perfume she always wore twisting through him. His belly clenched, the scent of her enveloping him in kindness, filling him with longing. Filling him with an endless need for acceptance, for love.

His jaw clenched, a lump of emotion in his throat. "She is your daughter. I do not begrudge you your love for her. I never expected to be the same. Believe me, I understand. I…never expected more." But he hadn't been able to stop himself from wanting it anyway. From needing it.

"Oh, but it is your right to have everything, Kairos. It is your right to be loved unconditionally, not to be second to her. It is what I promised myself that day we brought you home with us. I'm sorry for forgetting that. You're everything Theseus said you would be. You are not just his. You're *my* son, too, and I am so sorry for…my actions."

"Please—"

"Will you forgive me, Kairos? Will you forgive my foolish hope in thinking that she would change, for thinking she deserved one more chance every time? Will you forgive me for not loving you as I should have?"

She was openly sobbing now, and the sight of it broke his heart.

Kairos took her in his arms and she came with a soft cry. Tears pooled in his own eyes and he held them back by sheer will. "Shh… Maria. I cannot bear to see you like this. I forgive you. Of course, I forgive you." His words rushed out of him, a jagged crack in his heart healing over.

A lightness he had never known filled his chest. "I… I've been fortunate enough to have two mothers, Maria. I never realized how fortunate I was. I… Please, calm yourself. I can't bear to see you cry. I did everything to shield you and Theseus from her. I… She's left me no other way to stop her. I never wanted anything that should have been hers. All I wanted was to make you and Theseus proud of me. All I wanted was…" He forced himself to speak the words he'd always denied himself. To acknowledge the need inside. To admit that loving Theseus and Maria had only made him stronger, not weaker, as he had always believed. "...your love."

She wiped her tears and looked at up at him with sad eyes.

"I know, Kairos. I know you did more than a flesh-and-blood brother would have done for her. I know all the allowances you made for Helena. I know that, despite all the stupid games she played with you, you've never spoken a word against her to Theseus. You took your cue from me. You gave me even more loyalty and love than you gave Theseus. I didn't realize that until he pointed out. Until he said we did have a child who loved us more than anything in the world. You don't owe her anymore.

"There's a certain freedom in letting go, isn't there? She came to see me yesterday, you know. I told her in no uncertain terms that I would be part of her crazy schemes no more. Theseus told me about the trust fund idea you set up and you've been more generous than even he would have been. So let us hope this time she will truly change, *ne*?"

Kairos simply nodded, unable to form words. Unable to staunch the love that flowed within his veins. His world already felt different, lighter, brighter. He felt as if he were a new man, as if everything was possible now.

As if he could let himself—

"What is this?" Maria said, taking the sheaf of documents he had left on the table. "Divorce proceedings? You and Valentina are separating?" Shock punctured very word. "I thought she left because she missed her brothers. She promised Theseus she would see him for Christmas. She..."

He had no idea what she'd seen in his eyes before he looked away. "She left me even before I came back here, before Theseus's heart attack."

"You said it had just been a small misunderstanding. Why did you bring her here then? Oh…to tell us that you were already taken." Her hand on his shoulder turned him. "Did she want to leave again when you'd accomplished everything?"

"No." Even then, she had willed him to understand. Even then, she had given him another chance. Then another chance. What a heartless man he was to have turned her away! What a coward! "I sent her away."

"And she went away dutifully? For some reason, that doesn't suit her. Why did you send her away?"

"It was for her own good. I… Valentina…she's like a storm that ravages everything in its path, in a good way. I… I have nothing to give her, Maria. She deserves better than a man like me."

Something sad flitted in Maria's eyes. She took his hands in hers, and the simple touch calmed the furor in his gut. But nothing could ever fill the void his wife had left in his life. In his heart.

"A more honorable, kinder man, Kairos? A man who could love her more than you already do? A man who needs her so desperately that he walks around like an empty shell?"

Something jerked in the deep crevices of his being. His denial froze on his lips. He could not lie. Not to her, and not to himself.

For he did love Valentina. With every breath in him. With every cell in his body.

He had fallen for her long before he had even understood what it meant.

"I rejected her one too many times. I starved her when all she'd needed was a kind word. I hurt her again and again until whatever she might have felt for me died. I don't know how to love her, Maria. I don't know if I can give her what she needs. I don't know if I could bear it if she…if she stopped loving me. She would destroy me then."

Maria enfolded her arms around him. It was a mother's embrace, something he had longed for for so long, something he had needed for so long. The fear and anguish he had been fighting for weeks flooded him.

"Oh… Kairos. Trust yourself, trust the bond between you two. And trust her love for you."

He nodded, hope unfurling within him. His wife had a generous heart. He had to trust his into her keeping. He had to take the biggest risk of his life if he wanted her.

And he did want her.

Pulling back from the hug, Maria laughed. "How about you and I make a pact? We shall be brave and beg for forgiveness from the ones we love, *ne*?"

He laughed at her suggestion, sobered at the wary glance she cast toward Theseus's bedroom. He kissed her cheek, breathing in her scent one more time. Willing her to lend him a fraction of the courage she had.

"We will be brave in love, together," he whispered.

She nodded, kissed both his cheeks. "You will not stay away for another seven years, will you, Kairos?"

"No, I won't. This is not goodbye, Maria. Valentina and I will spend Christmas here."

She nodded and hugged him again, and in her embrace, Kairos found the strength he needed.

The strength to love the woman who had stolen his heart a long time ago.

CHAPTER FOURTEEN

THE LAST THING Kairos wanted to face, when all he wanted was to see and touch Valentina, was a battalion of over-bearing, interfering, annoying Contis.

Yet when he had finally bulldozed his way into Villa De Conti on the banks of Lake Como almost three weeks later, on a crisp November evening, the family, including the patriarch Antonio, were assembled around the ornate dining table, all staring up at him, mostly with varying degrees of anger, mistrust and doubt.

Except Leandro's little girl Isabella, who instantly wrapped her arms around him for a quick hug.

"Hello, Isabella," he said returning her hug.

Sophia stared at him with searching eyes. Whatever she had seen there, she pushed her chair back and embraced him.

"I'm not going to ask you how you are," she whispered, only for his ears. "You look awful."

"You know what she's capable of," he answered in kind, not even pretending to misunderstand.

"You deserved it."

Suddenly, panic-fueled urgency filled him. "Do I have a chance, Sophia?"

She betrayed nothing. "That's for her to tell you, Kairos." She smiled fondly then. "Always calculating the odds before you take the leap, *si*? It will not work in this."

He could never understand how smart, sensible Sophia

could tolerate the charming scoundrel that was the Conti Devil, but then he still didn't understand what his vivacious wife had ever seen in him to love.

"Being married suits you," he said with a smile.

She blushed before going back to her place next to her husband.

"What the hell do you want now?" Luca growled at him from the top end of the table, sitting exactly opposite Leandro on the other side.

"I wish to speak to my wife."

"She's not here."

"You're lying. And I will beat you to a bloody pulp and mar that pretty face if you get in my way again."

Utter silence descended over the table.

"Don't you think you've hurt her enough?" Again from the crazy genius. "Not counting the fact that you endangered her by letting loose that woman on Tina."

Kairos didn't know what he was doing until he had Luca's shirt bunched in his shoulders. The fear inside him knew no bounds. "What the hell are you talking about?"

Something in his tone must have communicated itself to him, because Luca's voice softened. "Helena came to see Valentina at work and caused a huge scene. I was there thankfully, and I think Tina talked some sense into her."

"Also, Tia Tina told me she slapped that horrible woman," Izzie piped up. "Oops, I wasn't supposed to tell you guys that."

Thee mou, what had Helena done to hurt Valentina?

Luca loosened his shirt from Kairos's grip. "I honestly don't think you're right for her. All you have caused her so far is pain."

The barb stuck home but Kairos forced himself to ignore Luca. Instead he addressed Leandro, who had always been the more sensible one.

"I have been trying for three weeks to see her. To contact her. She's still my damned wife. I should have been told Helena was here. It is I who brought Valentina into her focus. I should have been—" He couldn't even get the words out.

"Tina forbade us, Kairos," Sophia added softly.

"You've no right to stop me. To block my attempts." The stunt that Luca had pulled a week ago when he had ferried Valentina away on his beastly bike while Kairos had been waiting in the front lounge made his blood boil.

Leandro sighed. "She doesn't want to see you. And I will not lose her by interfering again, just when she is back in our lives."

"I'm not asking for your interference. I'm asking you to stay out of this. She is mine—to protect and to hold on to." The ragged words escaped before he could stop them.

Every gaze looked upon him with varying degrees of shock and pity now.

Leandro's wife, Alexis, shrugged. "He has a point, Leandro. You're still protecting her."

"Have you seen the look she gets in her eyes when she thinks no one's looking at her?" Luca demanded of Alexis.

"*Si*, Luca. We have all seen it," Sophia responded, with a hand over his shoulder. "And that tells me more than anything that we should give Kairos a chance. We all make mistakes."

"Not the same one, twice," Luca added meaningfully.

"She's in the garden," Alexis added hurriedly. "And she has a guest, so maybe you should wait."

"Who?"

"Ethan King," Luca said with a wicked smile, twisting the knife a little in Kairos's gut.

Sophia sent him a warning glance. "He's been talking to her about investment opportunities in her new boutique."

Kairos had heard enough. With a muttered curse, he made his way to the garden when Izzie pointed out, "They're not in the garden anymore. I saw them going up the stairs, into her bedroom."

Valentina had barely settled in the sitting room of her suite and pulled up her website analytics with Ethan when her hand hit the glass of white wine she had poured for him.

Cursing to herself, she mopped up the wine from the sofa and was about to hand him the napkin when the door of her bedroom opened with a hard slam. It hit the wall, then swung forward until Kairos stopped its momentum.

His gaze took in her outstretched hand over Mr. King's shirt and thunder dawned in the silver gaze.

Before she could think, she guiltily snatched her hand back. And then regretted the move.

He had no rights over her. She had done nothing to be guilty about, either.

He stared at her with such naked emotion shining in his eyes that it took her a few minutes to process the surge of her own feelings. And then pathetically, once again, she landed on hope in the end.

Her heart pounded with that same eagerness that she had tried to curb since the moment she had realized he was back in Milan. That he had been trying to see her.

But she was so tired of that hope. Exhausted from the weight of it.

"I would like to speak with you," he said, almost successful in packing away all the emotion radiating from him. "In private. At length."

"I'm not free right now," she offered softly. "Ethan only has this one hour before he leaves for the States. I've been waiting for weeks for a chance to speak with him."

His gaze flew to her open laptop and then back to her.

Uncertainty and hesitation and something else flickered in his gaze. He had never looked so vulnerable.

"Take as long as you need. I will wait outside," he said and her heart slipped a little.

Over the next few minutes, she tried to corral her thoughts. But the business proposal she had put together with Sophia's help blurred. The statistics she meant to show Ethan zigzagged, her heart focused on the man waiting outside the door for her.

He had never waited for her. He had never looked at her as if his heart was in his eyes.

Sick of the turmoil in her gut, she finally apologized to Ethan and the gentleman that he was, he was nice about it and excused himself from the room.

The door had barely closed behind him when Kairos reached her.

A white shirt and black trousers hugged his powerful physique. Dark shadows circled his eyes and instead of the satisfaction she wanted to feel, all she suffered was a soft ache.

He looked so tired. She knew how hard he worked. But more than that, she knew what a toll it would have taken on him to finish what he had started with Helena and the company.

She ached to hold him, to love him, to offer him the comfort he desperately needed. But he wouldn't allow it. He needed her but he would never admit it.

"Why is it that I always have to chase you—" his nostrils flared "—and then find you with a man in some intimate situation?"

"Maybe the question you should be asking is why is it that you're always chasing me," she countered. "What is it that you do that makes me run from you in the first place?"

He flinched and she wrapped her arms around herself.

She had promised herself she wouldn't do this. She wouldn't beg. She wouldn't complain. She would want nothing from him.

But seeing him after so many weeks, she could barely breathe, barely keep herself together.

How had she forgotten how he dwarfed everything with his presence? How he took over her very breath when he was near?

"I saw the clip from the talk show. And the vlog...that was a stroke of genius."

"*Si?*"

"I knew you had it in you. I'm glad for your success, Valentina."

"I owe it to you," she said softly.

"That internship with Chiara—"

"No, it was your criticism that I was doing nothing with my life that egged me on. I wanted to prove you wrong. To show you that I could be successful, too. Only I realized how much I enjoy it. That I'm good at it. You did teach me that I could be more than the shallow, vapid Valentina, more than what the Conti genes amount to. But you also made me realize that my value as a person doesn't depend on whether I'm a success or a failure. That I'm my own person and it is your loss if you can't love me."

How many times could one's heart break?

When she tried to step back, he clasped her arm to stop her. "Don't—" he cleared his throat "—do not retreat from me, Valentina."

Her heart crawled into her throat at the rough need he couldn't hide in his voice. "Why are you here, Kairos?"

"First, please tell me Helena didn't hurt you."

"Is that why you're here? To make sure she didn't do me lasting damage? Out of guilt?" She couldn't keep the disappointment out of her voice.

"No, I didn't know until Luca told me a few minutes ago. I'm sorry, Valentina. I should have realized—"

"She didn't hurt me, Kairos. I was actually recording the vlog when she stormed into the studio at Conti Towers. I don't think even she realized how far gone she was. She ranted that you were cutting her off, that she would make you pay for it. And that she knew how to make you suffer. I couldn't take it. I slapped her so hard that my arm still hurts. It was dramatic, almost soap-opera-like, but sometimes that's what it takes, *si*?

"I told her I would tell Theseus everything she had ever done if she didn't quietly accept what you were giving her. And then she would truly be on the streets. I told her I would set my powerful brothers loose on her if she ever came near you again. If she ever hurt you again. And I think it was helpful that Luca looked exceptionally scruffy and dangerous that day—he'd been on one of his days-without-sleep composing binge, and I think for once my threats got through—"

"I love you."

"Got through to her and she…she…" Words stuck in her throat, lodged beneath her heart. Had she imagined the words? Had she… "What did you say?"

"*S'agapao*, Valentina. So much that it terrifies me. So much that I can't sleep or eat or drink."

He fell to his knees in front of her, and Tina thought she might be hallucinating. She was afraid that she was only imagining this, that it was another dream haunting her sleep…no words came.

Until he wrapped his arms around her and buried his face in her belly. So tight that she could barely breathe.

The scent of him hit her like a thunderstorm, sinking into her pores.

He was real, this was real. The arms holding her…the

soft kisses he was planting on her belly, the huffs of his breath feathering over her skin, it was all real.

He looked up then and the love shining in his eyes stole her breath all over again. "I'm crazy about you. I love your teasing smiles, your penchant for drama, your unswerving loyalty, your generous heart." His palm rested on her chest. The thud of her heart was loud enough to roar through the room. "I love your long legs, your small breasts, your perfect skin, but more than anything I love you, *agapi mou*. I love how you love me. I love that you fight so bravely for the ones you love. I love that you make me a better man, that you fill my life with so much color and drama and noise—"

She laughed at that and he laughed and then she was in his arms. Kissing him hungrily amidst sobbing. He tasted of love and acceptance and home. Palms clasping his jaw, she kissed him until she couldn't breathe anymore. But the tears refused to stop.

She knew how much he hated tears so she buried her face in his neck. The scent of him, the taste of his skin finally calmed her.

"Shh, *moru mou*. No more tears. I would rather cut out my heart then be apart from you ever again. I was a fool not to understand how much you love me. How much I already loved you. A coward to believe that you would take it away on a whim.

"I was so afraid of hurt that I didn't even realize how long I have loved you.

"I think it started the first time even. You wore an emerald green dress that bared your entire back and you had been standing amidst your admirers and when Leandro called for you, there had been such unconditional love in your eyes, such open affection… I think I was struck immediately." His words made her gasp and she fought for her breath.

They didn't come easily to him, she knew. And she loved him all the more for it.

His palm stroked up and down her back tenderly, a torrent of endearments rushing out of him amidst a million apologies.

She felt his kiss at her temple, his shallow breaths as if, just like her, he was still unsure that she was here in his arms. "Valentina?"

"*Si?*"

"I should like to hear you say it, *pethi mou*. I am dying inside with the fear that I might have pushed you away one too many times, that finally you have realized that—"

She placed her finger on his lips.

"I love you, Kairos. I always will. I love you, knowing that you are stubborn, and ruthless and reserved. But I also love you knowing that you're kind, wonderful and extremely generous when it comes to orgasms. I recently read in some magazine that very few men actually go down on a woman whereas they expect the return all the time?"

Only his wife could insert the statistics about blow jobs into the conversation while he was pouring his heart out.

Kairos laughed, picked her up and followed her down to her bed.

He tugged her to him and kissed her some more. A lot more. Hard, consuming kisses. Soft, needy kisses. Tongues and teeth, they clung to each other until the need for air forced them apart.

He stripped her clothes and his with an urgency that devoured him.

And then she was naked for him. Long, sleek limbs toned with muscle. Small pouty breasts with lush nipples. She was perfect and she was his.

She reached out her hand to him, no shadows in her eyes. Nothing but abiding love and sultry temptation. "Come to me, please. I have missed you."

"Not more than I missed you." He growled against her mouth. "I can't be slow, *pethi mou*. Not today. I... I don't want to hurt you."

"You won't, Kairos. Trust me. Trust this thing between us, *si*?"

"Si." But there was nothing he could do to stem his urgent need.

He kissed her breasts, her belly, her legs, every inch of her perfect skin. When she scratched his back, just as frantic as him, he pushed his fingers into her wet heat. As deep as she could take him.

The need riding her, her body arching off the bed when he massaged her clit, the sheen of her skin...that calmed his need.

The scent of her arousal, that she had always wanted him, that she had again chosen him to love...it calmed the furor in his blood.

He sucked on her nipples, relentlessly pushing her to the edge until she fractured around his fingers. Until tremors built and ebbed in her slender body.

And then when the edge of their hunger for each other had been taken off, when she had calmed enough to believe that he wasn't going anywhere, he sat up, pulled her into his embrace until she was straddling him and then he thrust into her snug heat.

Arms around his back, mouths glued to each other's, they made slow, lazy love. All he wanted was to be inside her. To be surrounded by her warmth. To love her for as long as there was breath in his body.

"I love you, Valentina," he whispered, before he increased his thrusts, before release claimed his soul.

Hours later, Kairos emerged from deep sleep. His hand shot out instantly searching for his wife.

When he found her, his heartbeat returned to normal.

After he had toppled them both off the edge and into exhaustion for the third time, she had snuck down to the kitchen and had assured her family that he hadn't killed her, for she had heard them outside the door, muttering and arguing,

They had devoured the cheese and fruit plate she had brought upstairs. The white wine—he had lapped it off her breasts, her tummy and her soft folds. Whatever he did, however many times release clashed through him, it wasn't enough.

He pulled her down to lie alongside him. Her back to his chest, she cozily nuzzled into him. "I'm never going to get enough of you, I'm never going to let you go," he said, unable to cover the fierceness of his tone.

"Nor will I you," she said in a low, sleep-mussed voice. "We will have a big family, maybe four, five kids…boisterous, dramatic, noisy kids like me and we will drive you up the wall."

"That sounds like paradise."

"Kairos?"

The uncertainty still in her voice gutted him. "Yes?"

"Are you still looking for a job?"

He laughed and turned her over until she was facing him. Propping himself up on an elbow, he placed a lazy kiss on her mouth. "I am. I have offers from a few MNCs to do some house cleaning but nothing I'm interested in. We can live wherever you want. Do whatever we want. I'm not in a particular hurry to return to work."

"No. I know you're busy and that's fine but I just want to spend time with you. Have those four or five kids after a couple of years maybe?"

"*Si*. I…told Maria that we would spend Christmas with them." He frowned. "I'm sorry. I should have realized that you might want to spend it with your family."

"How about New Year with the Contis instead?"

This time, she rose up and claimed him for a soft kiss. "Hopefully by then Luca and I will be able to tolerate being in the same room."

She laughed, and then sobered. "You and Maria talked?"

"She told Theseus everything."

Her tight hug said so many things words could not. He let himself bask in the warmth of it. A hundred years together and he wouldn't have enough of Valentina.

She combed her fingers through his hair and sighed. "I have a proposal for you. But you don't have to accept it."

"Sounds important," he said trying to sound encouraging.

"I would like to live in Milan for a bit, with the boutique taking off it seems like a perfect fit."

"Valentina, we can live wherever you want, as long as we're together."

"Leandro is still looking for a CEO. He's—"

"*Oxhi!*"

"Kairos, please listen to me. He told me you've always been the perfect candidate. He trusts you. And I think…as the Conti heiress's loving husband, it is your right."

"I never wanted to do anything that would make you doubt my love for you."

"You won't. This doesn't. *Ti amo*, Kairos, and no job you take, no woman who wants you, will change that."

Joy suffusing his very soul, Kairos said yes to his wife.

And he meant to say yes for a very long time—to everything she asked.

* * * * *

THE SECRET
BENEATH THE VEIL

DANI COLLINS

To you, Dear Reader,
for loving romance novels as much as I do.

I hope you enjoy this one.

CHAPTER ONE

THE AFTERNOON SUN came straight through the windows, blinding Viveka Brice as she walked down the makeshift aisle of the wedding she was preventing—not that anyone knew that yet.

The interior of the yacht club, situated on this remote yet exclusive island in the Aegean, was all marble and brass, adding more bounces of white light. Coupled with the layers of her veil, she could hardly see and had to reluctantly cling to the arm of her reviled stepfather.

He probably couldn't see any better than she could. Otherwise he would have called her out for ruining his plan. He certainly hadn't noticed she wasn't Trina.

She was getting away with hiding the fact her sister had left the building. It made her stomach both churn with nerves and flutter with excitement.

She squinted, trying to focus past the standing guests and the wedding party arranged before the robed minister. She deliberately avoided looking at the tall, imposing form of the unsuspecting groom, staring instead through the windows and the forest of masts bobbing on the water. Her sister was safe from this forced marriage to a stranger, she reminded herself, trying to calm her racing heart.

Forty minutes ago, Trina had let her father into the room where she was dressing. She'd still been wearing this gown, but hadn't yet put on the veil. She had promised Grigor she would be ready on time while Viveka had kept well out of sight. Grigor didn't even know Viveka was back on the island.

The moment he'd left the room, Viveka had helped Trina out of the gown and Trina had helped her into it. They had hugged hard, then Trina had disappeared down a service elevator and onto the seaplane her true love had chartered. They were making for one of the bigger islands to the north where arrangements were in place to marry them the moment they touched land. Viveka was buying them time by allaying suspicion, letting the ceremony continue as long as possible before she revealed herself and made her own escape.

She searched the horizon again, looking for the flag of the boat she'd hired. It was impossible to spot and that made her even more anxious than the idea of getting onto the perfectly serviceable craft. She hated boats, but she wasn't in the class that could afford private helicopters to take her to and fro. She'd given a sizable chunk of her savings to Stephanos, to help him spirit Trina away in that small plane. Spending the rest on crossing the Aegean in a speedboat was pretty close to her worst nightmare, but the ferry made only one trip per day and had left her here this morning.

She knew which slip the boat was using, though. She'd paid the captain to wait and Stephanos had assured her she could safely leave her bags on board. Once she was exposed, she wouldn't even change. She would seek out that wretched boat, grit her teeth and sail into the sunset, content that she had finally prevailed over Grigor.

Her heart took a list and roll as they reached the top of the aisle, and Grigor handed her icy fingers to Trina's groom, the very daunting Mikolas Petrides.

His touch caused a *zing* of something to go through her. She told herself it was alarm. Nervous tension.

His grip faltered almost imperceptibly. Had he felt that static shock? His fingers shifted to enfold hers, pressing warmth through her whole body. Not comfort. She didn't fool herself into believing he would bother with that. He was even more intimidating in person than in his photos, exactly as Trina had said.

Viveka was taken aback by the quiet force he emanated, all chest and broad shoulders. He was definitely too much masculine energy for Viveka's little sister. He was too much for *her*.

She peeked into his face and found his gaze trying to penetrate the layers of her veil, brows lowered into sharp angles, almost as if he suspected the wrong woman stood before him.

Lord, he was handsome with those long clean-shaven plains below his carved cheekbones and the small cleft in his chin. His eyes were a smoky gray, outlined in black spiky lashes that didn't waver as he looked down his blade of a nose.

We could have blue-eyed children, she had thought when she'd first clicked on his photo. It was one of those silly facts of genetics that had caught her imagination when she had been young enough to believe in perfect matches. To this day it was an attribute she thought made a man more attractive.

She had been tempted to linger over his image and speculate about a future with him, but she'd been on a mission from the moment Trina had tearfully told her she was being sold off in a business merger like sixteenth-century chattel. All Viveka had had to see were the headlines that tagged Trina's groom as the son of a murdered Greek gangster. No *way* would she let her sister marry this man.

Trina had begged Grigor to let her wait until March, when she turned eighteen, and to keep the wedding small and in Greece. That had been as much concession as he'd granted. Trina, legally allowed to marry whomever she wanted as of this morning, had *not* chosen Mikolas Petrides, wealth, power and looks notwithstanding.

Viveka swallowed. The eye contact seemed to be holding despite the ivory organza between them, creating a sense of connection that sent a fresh thrum of nervous energy through her system.

She and Trina both took after their mother in build, but Trina was definitely the darker of the two, with a rounder face and warm, brown eyes, whereas Viveka had these icy blue orbs and natural blond streaks she'd covered with the veil.

Did he know she wasn't Trina? She shielded her eyes with a drop of her lashes.

The shuffle of people sitting and the music halting sent a wash of perspiration over her skin. Could he hear her pulse slamming? Feel her trembles?

It's just a play, she reminded herself. Nothing about this was real or valid. It would be over soon and she could move on with her life.

At one time she had imagined acting for a living. All her early career ambitions had leaned toward starving artist of one kind or another, but she'd had to grow up fast and become more practical once her mother died. She had worked here at this yacht club, lying about her age so they'd hire her, washing dishes and scrubbing floors.

She had wanted to be independent of Grigor as soon as possible, away from his disparaging remarks that had begun turning into outright abuse. He had helped her along by kicking her out of the house before she'd turned fifteen. He'd kicked her off this island, really. Out of Greece and away from her sister because once he realized she had been working, that she had the means to support herself and wouldn't buckle to his will when he threatened to expel her from his home, he had ensured she was fired and couldn't get work anywhere within his reach.

Trina, just nine, had been the one to whisper, *Go. I'll be okay. You should go.*

Viveka had reached out to her mother's elderly aunt in London. She had known Hildy only from Christmas cards, but the woman had taken her in. It hadn't been ideal. Viveka got through it by dreaming of bringing her sister to live with her there. As recently as a few months ago, she had pictured them as two carefree young women, twenty-three and eighteen, figuring out their futures in the big city—

"I, Mikolas Petrides…"

He had an arresting voice. As he repeated his name and spoke his vows, the velvet-and-steel cadence of his tone held her. He smelled good, like fine clothes and spicy aftershave and something unique and masculine that she knew would imprint on her forever.

She didn't want to remember this for the rest of her life. It was a ceremony that wasn't even supposed to be happening. She was just a placeholder.

Silence made her realize it was her turn.

She cleared her throat and searched for a suitably meek tone. Trina had never been a target for Grigor. Not just because she was his biological daughter, but also because she was on the timid side—probably because her father was such a mean, loudmouthed, sexist bastard in the first place.

Viveka had learned the hard way to be terrified of Grigor. Even in London his cloud of intolerance had hung like a poison cloud, making her careful about when she contacted Trina, never setting Trina against him by confiding her suspicions, always aware he could hurt Viveka through her sister.

She had sworn she wouldn't return to Greece, certainly not with plans that would make Grigor hate her more than he already did, but she was confident he wouldn't do more than yell in front of all these wedding guests. There were media moguls in the assemblage and paparazzi circling the air and water. The risk in coming here was a tall round of embarrassed confusion, nothing more.

She sincerely hoped.

The moment of truth approached. Her voice thinned and cracked, making her vows a credible imitation of Trina's as she spoke fraudulently in her sister's place, nullifying the marriage—and merger—that Grigor wanted so badly. It wasn't anything that could truly balance the loss of her mother, but it was a small retribution. Viveka wore a grim inner smile as she did it.

Her bouquet shook as she handed it off and her fingers felt clumsy and nerveless as she exchanged rings with Mikolas, keeping up the ruse right to the last minute. She wouldn't sign any papers, of course, and she would have to return these rings. Darn, she hadn't thought about that.

Even his hands were compelling, so well shaped and strong, so sure. One of his nails looked… She wasn't sure. Like he'd injured it once. If this were a real wedding, she would know that intimate detail about him.

Silly tears struck behind her eyes. She had the same girlish dreams for a fairy-tale wedding as any woman. She wished this were the beginning of her life with the man she loved. But it wasn't. Nothing about this was legal or real.

Everyone was about to realize that.

"You may kiss the bride."

* * *

Mikolas Petrides had agreed to this marriage for one reason only: his grandfather. He wasn't a sentimental man or one who allowed himself to be manipulated. He sure as hell wasn't marrying for love. That word was an immature excuse for sex and didn't exist in the real world.

No, he felt nothing toward his bride. He felt nothing toward anyone, quite by conscious decision.

Even his loyalty to his grandfather was provisional. Pappoús had saved his life. He'd *given* Mikolas this life once their blood connection had been verified. He had recognized Mikolas as his grandson, pulling him from the powerless side of a brutal world to the powerful one.

Mikolas repaid him with duty and legitimacy. His grandfather had been born into a good family during hard times. Erebus Petrides hadn't stayed on the right side of the law as he'd done what he'd seen as necessary to survive. Living a corrupt life had cost the old man his son and Mikolas had been Erebus's second chance at an heir. He had given his grandson full rein with his ill-gotten empire on the condition Mikolas turn it into a legal—yet still lucrative—enterprise.

No small task, but this marriage merger was the final step. To the outside observer, Grigor's world-renowned conglomerate was absorbing a second-tier corporation with a questionable pedigree. In reality, Grigor was being paid well for a company logo. Mikolas would eventually run the entire operation.

Was it irony that his mother had been a laundress? Or appropriate?

Either way, this marriage had been Grigor's condition. He wanted his own blood to inherit his wealth. Mikolas had accepted to make good on his debt to his grandfather. Marriage would work for him in other ways and it was only another type of contract. This ceremony was more elaborate than most business meetings, but it was still just a date to fix signatures upon dotted lines followed by the requisite photo op.

Mikolas had met his bride—a girl, really—twice. She was young and extremely shy. Pretty enough, but no sparks of attraction had flared in him. He'd resigned himself to affairs while she grew up and they got to know one another. *Therein might be another advantage to marriage*, he had been thinking distantly, while he waited for her to walk down the aisle. Other women wouldn't wheedle for marriage if he already wore a ring.

Then her approach had transfixed him. Something happened. *Lust.*

He was never comfortable when things happened outside his control. This was hardly the time or place for a spike of naked hunger for a woman. But it happened.

She arrived before him veiled in a waterfall mist that he should have dismissed as an irritating affectation. For some reason he found the mystery deeply erotic. He recognized her perfume as the same scent she'd worn those other times, but rather than sweet and innocent, it now struck him as womanly and heady.

Her lissome figure wasn't as childish as he'd first judged, either. She moved as though she owned her body, and how had he not noticed before that her eyes were such a startling shade of blue, the kind that sat as a pool of water against a glacier? He could barely see her face, but the intensity of blue couldn't be dimmed by a few scraps of lace.

His heart began to thud with an old, painful beat. *Want.* The real kind. The kind that was more like basic necessity.

A flicker of panic threatened, but he clamped down on the memories of deprivation. Of denial. Terror. Searing pain.

He got what he wanted these days. Always. He was getting *her*.

Satisfaction rolled through him, filling him with anticipation for this pomp and circumstance to end.

The ceremony progressed at a glacial pace. Juvenile eagerness struck him when he was finally able to lift her veil. He didn't celebrate Christmas, yet felt it had arrived early, just for him.

He told himself it was gratification at accomplishing the goal his grandfather had assigned him. With this kiss, the balance sheets would come out of the rinse cycle, clean and pressed like new. Too bad the old man hadn't been well enough to travel here and enjoy this moment himself.

Mikolas revealed his bride's face and froze.

She was beautiful. Her mouth was eye-catching with a lush upper lip and a bashful bottom one tucked beneath it. Her chin was strong and came up a notch in a hint of challenge while her blue, blue irises blinked at him.

This was no girl on the brink of legal age. She was a woman, one who was mature enough to look him straight in the eye without flinching.

She was *not* Trina Stamos.

"Who the hell are you?"

Gasps went through the crowd.

The woman lifted a hand to brush her veil free of his dumbfounded fingers.

Behind her, Grigor shot to his feet with an ugly curse. "What are you doing here? Where's Trina?"

Yes. Where was his bride? Without the right woman here to speak her vows and sign her name, this marriage—*the merger*—was at a standstill. *No.*

As though she had anticipated Grigor's reaction, the bride zipped behind Mikolas, using him like a shield as the older man bore down on them.

"You little bitch!" Grigor hissed. Trina's father was not as shocked by the switch as he was incensed. He clearly knew this woman. A vein pulsed on his forehead beneath his flushed skin. "Where is she?"

Mikolas put up a hand, warding off the old man from grabbing the woman behind him. He would have his explanation from her before Grigor unleashed his temper.

Or maybe he wouldn't.

Another round of surprised gasps went through the crowd, punctuated by the clack of the fire door and a loud, repetitive ring of its alarm.

His bride had bolted out the emergency exit.

What the *hell*?

CHAPTER TWO

VIVEKA RAN EVERY DAY. She was fit and adrenaline pulsed through her arteries, giving her the ability to move fast and light as she fled Grigor and his fury.

The dress and the heels and the spaces between planks and the floating wharf were another story. *Bloody hell.*

She made it down the swaying ramp in one piece, thanks to the rails on either side, but then she was racing down the unsteady platform between the slips, scanning for the flag of her vessel—

The train of her dress caught. She didn't even see on what. She was yanked back and that was all it took for her to lose her footing completely. *Stupid heels.*

She turned her ankle, stumbled, tried to catch herself, hooked her toe in a pile of coiled rope and threw out an arm to snatch at the rail of the yacht in the slip beside her.

She missed, only crashing into the side of the boat with her shoulder. The impact made her "oof!" Her grasp was too little, too late. She slid sideways and would have screamed, but had the sense to suck in a big breath before she fell.

Cold, murky salt water closed over her.

Don't panic, she told herself, splaying out her limbs and only getting tangled in her dress and veil.

Mom. This was what it must have been like for her on

that night far from shore, suddenly finding herself under cold, swirling water, tangled in an evening dress.

Don't panic.

Viveka's eyes stung as she tried to shift the veil enough to see which way the bubbles were going. Her dress hadn't stayed caught. It had come all the way in with her and floated all around her, obscuring her vision, growing heavier. The chill of the water penetrated to her skin. The weight of the dress dragged her down.

She kicked, but the layers of the gown were in the way. Her spiked heels caught in the fabric. This was futile. She was going to drown within swimming distance to shore. Grigor would stand above her and applaud.

The back of her hand scraped barnacles and her foot touched something. The seabed? Her hand burned where she'd scuffed it, but that told her there was a pillar somewhere here. She tried to scrabble her grip against it, desperately thinking she had never held her breath this long and couldn't hold it any longer.

Don't panic.

She clawed at her veil with her other hand, tried to pull it off her hair. She would never get all these buttons open and the dress off in time to kick herself to the surface—

Don't panic.

The compulsion to gasp for air was growing unstoppable.

A hand grabbed her forearm and tugged her.

Yes, please. Oh, God, please!

Viveka blew out what little air she still had, fighting not to inhale, fighting to kick and help bring herself to the blur of light above her, fighting to reach it…

As she broke through, she gasped in a lungful of life-giving oxygen, panting with exertion, thrusting back her veil to stare at her rescuer.

Mikolas.

He looked murderous.

Her heart lurched.

With a yank, he dragged her toward a diving ramp off the back of a yacht and physically set her hand upon it. She slapped her other bleeding hand onto it, clinging for dear life. Oh, her hand stung. So did her lungs. Her stomach was knotted with shock over what had just happened. She clung to the platform with a death grip as she tried to catch her breath and think clear thoughts.

People were gathering along the slip, trying to see between the boats, calling to others in Greek and English. "There she is!" "He's got her." "They're safe."

Viveka's dress felt like it was made of lead. It continued trying to pull her under, tugged by the wake that set all the boats around them rocking and sucking. She shakily managed to scrape the veil off her hair, ignoring the yank on her scalp as she raked it from her head. She let it float away, not daring to look for Grigor. She'd caught a glimpse of his stocky legs and that was enough. Her heart pounded in reaction.

"What the *hell* is going on?" Mikolas said in that darkly commanding voice. "Where is Trina? Who are you?"

"I'm her sis—" Viveka took a mouthful of water as a swell bashed the boat they clung to. "*Pah.* She didn't want to marry you."

"Then she shouldn't have agreed to." He hauled himself up to sit on the platform.

Oh, yes, it was just that easy.

He was too hard to face with that lethal expression. How did he manage to look so action-star handsome with his white shirt plastered to his muscled shoulders, his coat and tie gone, his hair flattened to his head? It was like staring into the sun.

Viveka looked out to where motorboats had circled to see where the woman in the wedding gown had fallen into the water.

Was that her boat? She wanted to wave, but kept a firm grip on the yacht as she used her free hand to pick at the buttons on her back. She eyed the distance to the red-and-gold boat. She couldn't swim that far in this wretched dress, but if she managed to shed it…?

Mikolas stood and, without asking, bent down to grasp her by the upper arms, pulling her up and out of the water, grunting loud enough that it was insulting. He swore after landing her on her feet beside him. His chest heaved while he glared at her limp, stained gown.

Viveka swayed on her feet, trying to keep her balance as the yacht rocked beneath them. She was still wearing the ridiculously high heels, was still in shock, but for a few seconds she could only stare at Mikolas.

He had saved her life.

No one had gone out of their way to help her like that since her mother was alive. She'd been a pariah to Grigor and a burden on her aunt, mostly fending for herself since her mother's death.

She swallowed, trying to assimilate a deep and disturbing gratitude. She had grown a thick shell that protected her from disregard, but she didn't know how to deal with kindness. She was moved.

Grigor's voice above her snapped her back to her situation. She had to get away. She yanked at her bodice, tearing open the delicate buttons on her spine and trying to push the clinging fabric down her hips.

She wore only a white lace bra and underpants beneath, but that was basically a bikini. Good enough to swim out to her getaway craft.

To her surprise, Mikolas helped her, rending the gown

as if he cursed its existence, leaving it puddled around her feet and sliding into the water. He didn't give her a chance to dive past him, however. He set wide hands on her waist and hefted her upward where bruising hands took hold of her arms—

Grigor.

"Nooo!" she screamed.

That ridiculous woman nearly kicked him in the face as he hefted her off the diving platform to the main deck of the yacht. Grigor was above, taking hold of her to bring her up. What did she think? That he was throwing her back into the sea?

"Noooo!" she cried and struggled, but Grigor pulled her all the way onto the deck where he stood.

She must be crazy, behaving like this.

Mikolas came up the ladder with the impetus of a man taking charge. He hated surprises. *He* controlled what happened to himself. No one else.

At least Grigor hadn't set this up. He'd been tricked as well, or he wouldn't be so furious.

Mikolas was putting that together as he came up to see Grigor shaking the nearly naked woman like a terrier with a rat. Then he slapped her across the face hard enough to send her to her knees.

No stranger to violence, Mikolas still took it like a punch to the throat. It appalled him on a level so deep he reacted on blind instinct, grabbing Grigor's arm and shoving him backward even as the woman threw up her arm as though to block a kick.

Stupid reaction, he thought distantly. It was a one-way ticket to a broken forearm.

But now was not the moment for a tutorial on street fighting.

Grigor found his balance and trained his homicidal gaze on Mikolas.

Mikolas centered his balance with readiness, but in his periphery saw the woman stagger toward the rail. Oh, hell, no. She was not going to ruin his day, then slip away like a siren into the deep.

He turned from Grigor's bitter "You should have let her drown" and provoked a cry of "Put me down!" from the woman as he caught her up against his chest.

She was considerably lighter without the gown, but still a handful of squirming damp skin and slippery muscle as he carried her off the small yacht.

On the pier, people parted and swiveled like gaggles of geese, some dressed in wedding regalia, others obviously tourists and sailors, all babbling in different languages as they took in the commotion.

It was a hundred meters to his own boat and he felt every step, thanks to the pedal of the woman's sharp, silver heels.

"Calm yourself. I've had it with this sideshow. You're going to tell me where my bride has gone and why."

CHAPTER THREE

VIVEKA WAS SHAKING right down to her bones. Grigor had
hit her, right there in front of the whole world. Well, the
way the yacht had been positioned, only Mikolas had
probably seen him, but in the back of her mind she was
thinking that this was the time to call the police. With all
these witnesses, they couldn't ignore her complaint. Not
this time.

Actually, they probably could. Her report of assault and
her request for a proper investigation into her mother's
death had never been heeded. The officers on this island
paid rent to Grigor and didn't like to impact their personal
lives by carrying out their sworn duties. She had learned
that bitter lesson years ago.

And this brute wouldn't let her go to do anything!

He was really strong. He carried her in arms that were
so hard with steely muscle it almost hurt to be held by
them. She could tell it wasn't worth wasting her energy
trying to escape. And he wore a mask of such controlled
fury he intimidated her.

She instinctively drew in on herself, stomach churning with reaction while her brain screamed at her to swim
out to her hired boat.

"Let me go," she insisted in a more level tone.

Mikolas only bit out orders for ice and bandages to a

uniformed man as he carried her up a narrow gangplank, boarding a huge yacht of aerodynamic layers and space-ship-like rigging. The walls were white, the decks teak, the sheer size and luxury of the vessel making it more like a cruise liner than a personal craft.

Greek mafia, she thought, and wriggled harder, signaling that she sincerely wanted him to put her down. *Now.*

Mikolas strode into what had to be the master cabin. She caught only a glimpse of its grand decor before he carried her all the way into a luxurious en suite and started the shower.

"Warm up," he ordered and pointed to the black satin robe on the back of the door. "Then we'll bandage your hand and ice your face while you explain yourself."

He left.

She snorted. *Not likely.*

Folding her arms against icy shivers, she eyed the small porthole that looked into the expanse of open water beyond the marina. She might fit through it, but even as the thought formed, a crewman walked by on the deck outside. She would be discovered before she got through it and in any case, she wasn't up for another swim. Not yet. She was trembling.

Reaction was setting in. She had nearly drowned. Grigor had hit her. He'd do worse if he got his hands on her again. Had he come aboard behind them?

She wanted to cry out of sheer, overwhelmed reaction. But she wouldn't.

Trina was safe, she reminded herself. Never again did she have to worry about her little sister. Not in the same way, anyway.

The steaming shower looked incredibly inviting. Its gentle hiss beckoned her.

Don't cry, she warned herself, because showers were

her go-to place for letting emotion overcome her, but she couldn't afford to let down her guard. She may yet have to face Grigor again.

Her insides congealed at the thought.

She would need to pull herself together for that, she resolved, and closed the curtain across the porthole before picking herself free of the buckles on her shoes. She stepped into the shower still wearing her bra and undies, then took them off to rinse them and— Oh. She let out a huff of faint laughter as she saw her credit card stuck to her breast.

The chuckle was immediately followed by a stab of concern. Her bags, passport, phone and purse were on the hired boat. Was the captain waiting a short trot down the wharf? Or bobbing out in the harbor, wondering if she'd drowned? Grabbing this credit card and shoving it into her bra had been a last-minute insurance against being stuck without resources if things went horribly wrong, but she hadn't imagined things would go *this* far wrong.

The captain was waiting for her, she assured herself. She would keep her explanations short and sweet to Mikolas and be off. He seemed like a reasonable man.

She choked on another snort of laughter, this one edging toward hysteria.

Then another wave of that odd defenselessness swirled through her. Why had Mikolas saved her? It made her feel like— She didn't know what this feeling was. She never relied on anyone. She'd never been *able* to. Her mother had loved her, but she'd died. Trina had loved her, but she'd been too young and timorous to stand up to Grigor. Aunt Hildy had helped her to some extent, but on a quid-pro-quo basis.

Mikolas was a stranger who had risked his life to preserve hers. She didn't understand it.

It infused her with a sense that she was beholden to him. She hated that feeling. She had had a perfect plan to get Hildy settled, bring Trina to London once she was eighteen and finally start living life on her own terms. Then Grigor had ruined it by promising Trina to this... *criminal*.

A criminal who wasn't averse to fishing a woman out of the sea—something her stepfather hadn't bothered doing with her mother, leaving that task to search and rescue.

She was still trembling, still trying to make sense of it as she dried off with a thick black towel monogrammed with a silver *M*. She stole a peek in his medicine chest, bandaged her hand, used some kind of man-brand moisturizer that didn't have a scent, rinsed with his mouthwash, then untangled her hair with a comb that smelled like his shampoo. She used his hair dryer to dry her underwear and put both back on under his robe.

The robe felt really good, light and cool and slippery against her humid skin.

She felt like his lover wearing something this intimate.

The thought made her blush and a strange wistfulness hit her as she worked off his rings—both the diamond that Trina had given her and the platinum band he'd placed on her finger himself—and set them on the hook meant for facecloths. He was *not* the sort of man she would ever want to marry. He was far too daunting and she needed her independence, but she did secretly long for someone to share her life with. Someone kind and tender who would make her laugh and maybe bring her flowers sometimes.

Someone who wanted her in his life.

She would *not* grow maudlin about her sister running off with Stephanos, seemingly choosing him over Viveka, leaving her nursing yet another sting of rejection. Her sister was entitled to fall in love.

With a final deep breath, she emerged into the stateroom.

Mikolas was there, wearing a pair of black athletic shorts and towel-dried hair, nothing else. His silhouette was a bleak, masculine statue against the closed black curtains.

The rest of the room was surprisingly spacious for a boat, she noted with a sweeping glance. There was a sitting area with a comfortable-looking sectional facing a big-screen TV. A glass-enclosed office allowed a tinted view of a private deck in the bow. She averted her gaze from the huge bed covered with a black satin spread and came back to the man who watched her with an indecipherable expression.

He held a drink, something clear and neat. Ouzo, she assumed. His gaze snagged briefly on the red mark on her cheek before traversing to her bare feet and coming back to slam into hers.

His expression still simmered with anger, but there was something else that took her breath. A kind of male assessment that signaled he was weighing her as a potential sex partner.

Involuntarily, she did the same thing. How could she not? He was really good-looking. His build was amazing, from those broad, bare shoulders to that muscled chest to those washboard abs and soccer-star legs.

She was not a woman who gawked at men. She considered herself a feminist and figured if it was tasteless for men to gaze at pinup calendars, then women shouldn't objectify men, either, but seriously. *Wow.* He was muscly without being overdeveloped. His skin was toasted a warm brown and that light pattern of hair on his chest looked like it had been sculpted by the loving hand of Mother Nature, not any sort of waxing specialist.

An urge to touch him struck her. Sexual desire wasn't

something that normally hit her out of the blue like this, but she found herself growing warm with more than embarrassment. She wondered what it would be like to roam her mouth over his torso, to tongue his nipples and lick his skin. She felt an urge to splay her hands over his muscled waist and explore lower, push aside his waistband and *possess*.

Coils of sexual need tightened in her belly.

Where was the lead-up? The part where she spent ages kissing and nuzzling before she decided maybe she'd like to take things a little further? She never flashed to shoving down a man's pants and stroking him!

But that fantasy hit her along with a deep yearning and a throbbing pinch between her legs.

Was he getting *hard*? The front of his shorts lifted.

She realized where her gaze had fixated and jerked her eyes back to his, shocked with herself and at his blatant reaction.

His expression was arrested, yet filled with consideration and—she caught her breath—yes, that was an invitation. An arrogant *Help yourself.* Along with something predatory. Something that was barely contained. Decision. Carnal hunger.

The air grew so sexually charged, she couldn't find oxygen in it. The rhythm of her breaths changed, becoming subtle pants. Her nipples were stimulated by the shift of the robe against the lace of her bra. She became both wary and meltingly receptive.

This was crazy. She shook her head, as if she could erase all this sexual tension like an app that erased content on her phone if she joggled it back and forth hard enough.

With monumental effort, she jerked her gaze from his and stared blindly at the streak of light between the curtains. She folded her arms in self-protection and kept him in her periphery.

This was really stupid, letting him bring her into his bedroom like this. A single woman who lived in the city knew to be more careful.

"Use the ice," he said with what sounded like a hint of dry laughter in his tone. He nodded toward a side table where an ice pack sat on a small bar towel.

"It's not that bad," she dismissed. She'd had worse. Her lip might be puffed a little at the corner, but it was nothing like the time she'd walked around with a huge black eye, barely able to see out of it, openly telling people that Grigor had struck her. *You shouldn't talk back to him,* her teacher had said, mouth tight, gaze avoiding hers.

Grigor shouldn't have called her a whore and burned all her photos of her mother, she had retorted, but no one had wanted to hear *that*.

Mikolas didn't say anything, only came toward her, making her snap her head around and warn him off with a look.

Putting his glass down, he lifted his phone and clicked, taking a photo of her, surprising her so much she scowled.

"What are you doing?"

"Documenting. I assume Grigor will claim you were hurt falling into the water," he advised with cool detachment.

"You don't want me to try to discredit your business partner? Is that what you're saying? Are you going to take a photo after you leave your own mark on the other side of my face?" It was a dicey move, daring him like that, but she was so *sick* of people protecting *Grigor*. And she needed to know Mikolas's intentions, face them head-on.

Mikolas's stony eyes narrowed. "I don't hit women." His mouth pulled into a smile that was more an expression of lethal power than anything else. "And Grigor has discredited himself." He tilted the phone to indicate the photo. "Which may prove useful."

Viveka's insides tightened as she absorbed how cold-blooded that was.

"I didn't know Grigor had another daughter." Mikolas moved to take up his drink again. "Do you want one?" he asked, glancing toward the small wet bar next to the television. Both were inset against the shiny wood-grain cabinetry.

She shook her head. Better to keep her wits.

"Grigor isn't my father." She always took great satisfaction in that statement. "My mother married him when I was four. She died when I was nine. He doesn't talk about her, either."

Or the boating accident. Her heart clenched like a fist, trying to hang on to her memories of her mother, knotting in fury at the lack of a satisfactory explanation, wanting to beat the truth from Grigor if she had to.

"Do you have a name?" he asked.

"Viveka." The corner of her mouth pulled as she realized they'd come this far without it. She was practically naked, wearing a robe that had brushed his own skin and surrounded her in the scent of his aftershave. "Brice," she added, not clarifying that most people called her Vivi.

"Viveka," he repeated, like he was trying out the sound. They were speaking English and his thick accent gave an exotic twist to her name as he shaped out the *Vive* and added a short, hard *ka* to the end.

She licked her lips, disturbed by how much she liked the way he said it.

"Why the melodrama, Viveka? I asked your sister if she was agreeable to this marriage. She said yes."

"Do you think she would risk saying no to something Grigor wanted?" She pointed at the ache on her face.

Mikolas's expression grew circumspect as he dropped his gaze into his drink, thumb moving on the glass. It was the only indication his thoughts were restless beneath that rock-face exterior.

"If she wants more time," he began.

"She's marrying someone else," she cut in. "Right this minute, if all has gone to plan." She glanced for a clock, but didn't see one. "She knew Stephanos at school and he worked on Grigor's estate as a landscaper."

Trina had loved the young man from afar for years, never wanting to tip her hand to Grigor by so much as exchanging more than a shy hello with Stephanos, but she had waxed poetic to Viveka on dozens of occasions. Viveka hadn't believed Stephanos returned the crush until Trina's engagement to Mikolas had been announced.

"When Stephanos heard she was marrying someone else, he asked Trina to elope. He has a job outside of Athens." One that Grigor couldn't drop the ax upon.

"Weeding flower beds?" Mikolas swirled his drink. "She could have kept him on the side after we married, if that's what she wanted."

"Really," Viveka choked.

He shrugged a negligent shoulder. "This marriage is a business transaction, open to negotiation. I would have given her children if she wanted them, or a divorce eventually, if that was her preference. She should have spoken to me."

"Because you're such a reasonable man—who just happens to trade women like stocks and bonds."

"I'm a man who gets what he wants," he said in a soft voice, but it was positively deadly. "I want this merger."

He sounded so merciless her heart skipped in alarm.
Gangster. She found a falsely pleasant smile.

"I wish you great success in making your dreams come
true. Do you mind if I wear this robe to my boat? I can
bring it back after I dress or maybe one of your staff could
come with me?" She pushed her hand into the pocket
and gripped her credit card, feeling the edge dig into her
palm. Where was Grigor? she wondered. She had no desire
to pass him on the dock and get knocked into the water
again—this time unconscious.

Mikolas's expression didn't change. He said nothing,
but she had the impression he was laughing at her again.

Something made her look toward the office and the
view beyond the bow. The marina was tucked against a
very small indent on the island's coastline. The view from
shore was mostly an expanse of the Aegean. But the boats
weren't passing in front of this craft. They were coming and going on both sides. The slant of sunlight on the
water had shifted.

The yacht was moving.

"Are you kidding me?" she screeched.

CHAPTER FOUR

MIKOLAS THREW BACK the last of his ouzo, clenched his teeth against the burn and set aside his glass with a decisive *thunk*. He searched for the void that he usually occupied, but he couldn't find it. He was swirling in a miasma of lascivious need, achingly hard after the way Viveka had stared at his crotch and swallowed like her mouth was watering.

He absently ran a hand across his chest where his nipples were so sharp they pained him and adjusted himself so he wouldn't pop out of his shorts, resisting the urge to soothe the ache with a squeeze of his fist.

His reaction to her was unprecedented. He was an experienced man, had a healthy appetite for sex, but had never reacted so immediately and irrepressibly to any woman.

This lack of command over himself disturbed him. Infuriated him. He was insulted at being thrown over for a gardener and unclear on his next move. Retreat was never an option for him, but he'd left the island to regroup. That smacked of cowardice and he pinned the blame for all of it on this woman.

While she stood there with her hand closed over the lapels of his robe, holding it tight beneath her throat. Acting virginal when she was obviously as wily and experienced as any calculating opportunist he'd ever met.

"Let's negotiate our terms, Viveka." From the moment she had admitted to being Trina's sister he had seen the logical way to rescue this deal. Hell, by turning up in Trina's gown she'd practically announced to him how this would play out.

Of course it was a catch-22. He wasn't sure he wanted such a tempting woman so close to him, but he refused to believe she was anything he couldn't handle.

Viveka only flashed him a disparaging look and spun toward the door.

He didn't bother stopping her. He followed at a laconic pace as she scurried her way out to the stern of the mid-deck. Grasping the rail in one hand, she shaded her eyes with the other, scanning the empty horizon. She quickly threw herself to the port side. Gazing back to the island, which had been left well behind them, she made a distressed noise and glared at him again, expression white.

"Is Grigor on board?"

"Why would he be?"

"I don't know!" Her shoulders relaxed a notch, but she continued to look anxious. "Why did you leave the island?"

"Why would I stay?"

"Why would you take me?" she cried.

"I want to know why you've taken your sister's place."

"You didn't have to leave shore for that!"

"You wanted Grigor present? He seemed to be inflaming things." Grigor hadn't expected his departure, either. Mikolas's phone had already buzzed several times with calls from his would-be business partner.

That had been another reason for Mikolas's departure. If he'd stayed, he might have assaulted Grigor. The white-hot urge had been surprisingly potent and yes, that too had been provoked by this exasperating woman.

It wasn't a desire to protect *her*, Mikolas kept telling himself. His nature demanded he dominate, particularly over bullies and brutes. His personal code of ethics wouldn't allow him to stand by and watch any man batter a woman.

But Grigor's attack on this one had triggered something dark and primal in him, something he didn't care to examine too closely. Since cold-blooded murder was hardly a walk down the straight and narrow that was his grandfather's expectation of him, he'd taken himself out of temptation's reach.

"I had a boat hired! All my things are on it." Viveka pointed at the island. "Take me back!"

Such a bold little thing. Time to let her know who was boss.

"Grigor promised this merger if I married his daughter." He gave her a quick once-over. "His stepdaughter will do."

She threw back her head. "Ba-ha-ha," she near shouted and shrugged out of his robe, dropping it to the deck. "No. 'Bye." Something flashed in her hand as she started to climb over the rail.

She was fine-boned and supple and so easy to take in hand. Perhaps he took more enjoyment than he should in having another reason to touch her. Her skin was smooth and warm, her wrists delicate in his light grip as he calmly forced them behind her back, trapping her between the rail and his body.

She strained to look over her shoulder, muttering, "Oh, you—!" as something fell into the water with a glint of reflected light. "That was my credit card. Thanks a *lot*."

"Viveka." He was stimulated by the feel of her naked abdomen against his groin, erection not having subsided much and returning with vigor. Her spiked heels were gone, which was a pity. They'd been sexy as hell, but when it came to rubbing up against a woman, the less clothes the better.

She smelled of his shampoo, he noted, but there was an intriguing underlying scent that was purely hers: green tea and English rain. And that heady scent went directly into his brain, numbing him to everything but thoughts of being inside her.

Women were more subtle than men with their responses, but he read hers as clearly as a billboard. Not just the obvious signs like the way her nipples spiked against the pattern of her see-through bra cups, erotically abrading his chest and provoking thoughts of licking and sucking at them until she squirmed and moaned. A blush stained her cheeks and she licked her lips. There was a bonelessness to her. He could practically feel the way her blood moved through her veins like warm honey. He knew instinctively that opening his mouth against her neck would make her shiver and surrender to him. Her arousal would feed into his and they'd take each other to a new dimension.

Where did that ridiculous notion come from? He was no sappy poet. He tried to shake the idea out of his head, but couldn't rid himself of the certainty that sex with her would be the best he'd ever known. They were practically catching fire from this light friction. His heart was ramping with strength in his chest, his body magnetized to hers.

He was incensed with her, he reminded himself, but he was also intrigued by this unique attunement they had. Logic told him it was dangerous, but the primitive male inside him didn't give a damn. He *wanted* her.

"This is kidnapping. And assault," she said, giving a little struggle against his grip. "I thought you didn't hurt women."

"I don't let them hurt themselves, either. You'll kill yourself jumping into the water out here."

Something flickered in her expression. Her skin was very white compared with her sister's. How had he not noticed that from the very first, veil notwithstanding?

"Stop behaving like a spoiled child," he chided.

She swung an affronted look to him like it was the worst possible insult he could level at her. "How about you stop acting like you own the world?"

"This *is* my world. You walked into it. Don't complain how I run it."

"I'm trying to leave it."

"And I'll let you." Something twisted in his gut, as if that was a lie. A big one. "After you fix the damage you've done."

"How do you suggest I do that?"

"Marry me in your sister's place."

She made a choking noise and gave another wriggle of protest, heel hooking on the lower rung of the rail as if she thought she could lift herself backward over the rail.

All she managed to do was pin herself higher against him. She stilled. Hectic color deepened in her cheekbones.

He smiled, liking what she'd done. Her movement had opened her legs and brought her cleft up to nestle against his shaft. She'd caught the same zing of sexual excitement that her movement had sent through him. He nudged lightly, more of a tease than a threat, and watched a delicate shiver go through her.

It was utterly enthralling. He could only stare at her parted, quivering mouth. He wanted to cover and claim it. He wanted to drag his tongue over every inch of her. Wanted to push at his elastic waistband, press aside that virginal white lace and thrust into the heat that was branding him through the thin layers between them.

He had expected to spend this week frustrated. Now he began to forgive her for this switch of hers. They would do very nicely together. Very. Nicely.

"Let's take this back to my stateroom." His voice emanated from somewhere deep in his chest, thick with the desire that gripped him.

Her eyes flashed with fear before she said tautly, "To consummate a marriage that won't happen? Did you see how Grigor reacted to me? He'll never let me sub in for Trina. If anything would make him refuse your merger, marrying me would do it."

Mikolas slowly relaxed his grip and stepped back, trailing light fingers over the seams at her hips.

Goose bumps rose all over her, but she ignored it, hoping her knickers weren't showing the dampness that had released at the feel of him pressed against her.

What was *wrong* with her? She didn't even *do* sex. Kissing and petting were about it.

She dipped to pick up the robe and knotted it with annoyance. How could she be this hot when the wind had cooled to unpleasant and the sky was thickening with clouds?

She sent an anxious look at the ever-shrinking island amid the growing whitecaps. It was way too far to swim. Mikolas might have done her a favor taking her out of Grigor's reach, but being at sea thinned her composure like it was being spun out from a spool.

"You're saying if I want Grigor to go through with the merger, I should turn you over to him?" he asked.

"What? *No!*" Such terror slammed into her, her knees nearly buckled. "Why would you even think of doing something like that?"

"The merger is important to me."

"My *life* is important to me." Tears stung her eyes and she had to blink hard to be able to see him. She had a feeling her lips were trembling. Where was the man who had saved her? Right now, Mikolas looked as conscience-less as Grigor.

Crushed to see that indifference, she hid her distress by averting her gaze and swallowed back the lump in her throat.

"This is nothing," she said with as much calm as she could, pointing at her face, trying to reach through to the man who had said he didn't hurt women. "Barely a starting point for him. I'd rather take my chances with the sharks."

"You already have." The flatness of his voice sent a fresh quake of uncertainty through her center.

What did it say about how dire her situation was that she was searching for ways to reach him? To persuade *this* shark to refrain from offering her giftwrapped to the other one?

"If—if—" She wasn't really going to say this, was she? She briefly hung her head, but what choice did she have? She didn't have to go all the way, just make it good for him, right? She had a little experience with that. A very tiny little bit. He was hard, which meant he was up for it, right? "If you want sex…"

He made a scoffing noise. "*You* want sex. I'll decide if and when I give it to you. There's no leverage in offering it to me."

Sex was a basket of hang-ups for her. Offering herself had been really hard. Now she felt cheap and useless.

She pushed her gaze into the horizon, trying to hide how his denigration carved into her hard-won confidence.

"Go below," he commanded. "I want to make some calls."

She went because she needed to be away from him, needed to lick her wounds and reassess.

A purser showed her into a spacious cabin with a sitting room, a full en suite and a queen bed with plenty of tasseled pillows in green and gold. The cabinetry was polished to showcase the artistic grains in the amber-colored wood and the room was well-appointed with cosmetics, fresh fruit, champagne and flowers.

Her stomach churned too much to even think of eating, but she briefly considered drinking herself into oblivion. Once she noticed the laptop dock, however, she began looking for a device to contact…whom? Aunt Hildy wasn't an option. Her workmates might pick up a coffee or cover for her if she had to run home, but that was the extent of favors she could ask of them.

It didn't matter anyway. There was nothing here. The telephone connected to the galley or the bridge. The television was part of an onboard network that could be controlled by a tablet, but there was no tablet to be found.

At least she came across clothes. Women's, she noted with a cynical snort. Mikolas must have been planning to keep his own paramour on the side after his marriage.

Everything was in Viveka's size, however, and it struck her that this was Trina's trousseau. This was her sister's suite.

Mikolas hadn't expected her sister to share his room? Did that make him more hard-hearted than she judged him? Or less?

Men never dominated her thoughts this way. She never let them make her feel self-conscious and second-guess every word that passed between them. This obsession with Mikolas was a horribly susceptible feeling, like he was important to her when he wasn't.

Except for the fact he held her life in his iron fist.

Thank God she had saved Trina from marrying him. She'd done the right thing taking her sister's place and didn't hesitate to make herself at home among her things, weirdly comforted by a sense of closeness to her as she did.

Pulling on a floral wrap skirt and a peasant blouse—both deliberately light and easily removed if she happened to find herself treading water—Viveka had to admit she was relieved Mikolas had stopped her from jumping. She *would* rather take her chances with sharks than with Grigor, but she didn't have a death wish. She was trying not to think of her near drowning earlier, but it had scared the hell out of her.

So did the idea of being sent back to Grigor.

Somehow she had to keep a rational head, but after leaving Grigor's oppression and withstanding Aunt Hildy's virulence, Viveka couldn't take being subjugated anymore. That's why she'd come back to help Trina make her own choices. The idea of her sister living in sufferance as part of a ridiculous business deal had made her furious!

Opening the curtains that hid two short, wide portholes stacked upon each other, she searched the horizon for a plan. At least this wasn't like that bouncy little craft she'd dreaded. This monstrosity moved more smoothly and quietly than the ferry. It might even take her to Athens.

That would work, she decided. She would ask Mikolas to drop her on the mainland. She would meet up with Trina, Stephanos could arrange for her things to be delivered, and she would find her way home.

This pair of windows was some sort of extension, she realized, noting the cleverly disguised seam between the upper and lower windows. The top would lift into an awning while the bottom pushed out to become the railing on a short balcony. Before she thought it through, her finger was on the button next to the diagram.

The wall began to crack apart while an alarm went off with a horrible honking blare, scaring her into leaping back and swearing aloud.

Atop that shock came the interior door slamming open.

Mikolas had dressed in suit pants and a crisp white shirt and wore a *terrible* expression.

"I just wanted to see what it did!" Viveka cried, holding up a staying hand.

What a liability she was turning into.

Mikolas moved to stop and reverse the extension of the balcony while he sensed the engines being cut and the yacht slowing. As the wall restored itself, he picked up the phone and instructed his crew to stay the course.

Hanging up, he folded his arms and told himself this rush of pure, sexual excitement each time he looked at Viveka was transitory. It was the product of a busy few weeks when he hadn't made time for women combined with his frustration over today's events. Of course he wanted to let off steam in a very base way.

She delivered a punch simply by standing before him, however. He had to work at keeping his thoughts from conjuring a fantasy of removing that village girl outfit of hers. The wide, drawstring collar where her bra strap peeked was an invitation, the bare calves beneath the hem of her pretty skirt a promise of more silken skin higher up.

Those unpainted toes seemed ridiculously unguarded. So did the rest of her, with her hair tied up like a teenager and her face clean.

Some women used makeup as war paint, others as an invitation. Viveka hadn't used any. She hadn't tried to cover the bruise, and lifted that discolored, belligerent chin of hers in a brave stare that was utterly foolish. She had no idea whom she was dealing with.

Yet something twisted in his chest. He found her nerve entirely too compelling. He wanted to feed that spark of energy and watch it detonate in his hands. He bet she scratched in bed and was dismayingly eager to find out.

Women were *never* a weakness for him. No one was. Nothing. Weakness was abhorrent to him. Helplessness was a place he refused to revisit.

"We'll eat." He swept a hand to where the door was still open and one of the porters hovered.

He sent the man to notify the chef and steered her to the upper aft deck. The curved bench seat allowed them to slide in from either side, shifting cushions until they met in the middle, where they looked out over the water. Here the wind was gentled by the bulk of the vessel. It was early spring so the sun was already setting behind the clouds on the horizon.

She cast a vexed look toward the view. He took it as annoyance that the island was long gone behind them and privately smirked, then realized she was doing it again: pulling all his focus and provoking a reaction in him.

He forced his attention to the porter as he arrived with place settings and water.

"You'll eat seafood?" he said to Viveka as the porter left.

"If you tell me to, of course I will."

A rush of anticipation for the fight went through him. "Save your breath," he told her. "I don't shame."

"How does someone influence you, then? Money?" She affected a lofty tone, but quit fiddling with her silverware and tucked her hands in her lap, turning her head to read him. "Because I would like to go to Athens—as opposed to wherever you think you're taking me."

"I have money," he informed, skipping over what he intended to do next because he was still deciding.

He stretched out his arms so his left hand, no longer wearing the ring she'd put on it, settled behind her shoulder. He'd put the ring in his pocket along with the ones she had worn. Her returning them surprised him. She must have known what they were worth. Why wasn't she trying to use them as leverage? Not that it would work, but he expected a woman in her position to at least try.

He dismissed that puzzle and returned to her question. "If someone wants to influence me, they offer something I want."

"And since I don't have anything you want…?" Little flags of color rose on her cheekbones and she stared out to sea.

He almost smiled, but the tightness of her expression caused him to sober. Had he hurt her with his rejection earlier? He'd been brutal because he wasn't a novice. You didn't enter into any transaction wearing your desires on your sleeve the way she did.

But how could she not be aware that she *was* something he wanted? Did she not feel the same pull he was experiencing?

How did she keep undermining his thoughts this way?

As an opponent she was barely worth noticing. A brief online search had revealed she had no fortune, no influence. Her job was a pedestrian position as data entry clerk for an auto parts chain. Her network of social media contacts was small, which suggested an even smaller circle of real friends.

Mikolas's instinct when attacked was to crush. If Grigor had switched his bride on purpose, he would already be ruined. Mikolas didn't lose to anyone, especially weak adversaries who weren't even big enough to appear on his radar.

Yet Viveka had slipped in like a ninja, taking him unawares. On the face of it, that made her his enemy. He had to treat her with exactly as much detachment as he would any other foe.

But this twist of hunger in his gut demanded an answering response from her. It wasn't just ego. It was craving. A weight on a scale that demanded an equal weight on the other side to balance it out.

The porter returned, poured their wine, and they both sipped. When they were alone again, Mikolas said, "You were right. Grigor wants you."

Viveka paled beneath her already stiff expression. "And you want the merger."

"My grandfather does. I have promised to complete it for him."

She bit her bottom lip so mercilessly it disappeared. "Why?" she demanded. "I mean, why is this merger so important to him?"

"Why does it matter?" he countered.

"Well, what is it you're really trying to accomplish? Surely there are other companies that could give you what you want. Why does it have to be Grigor's?"

She might be impulsive and a complete pain in the backside, but she was perceptive. It *didn't* have to be Grigor's company. He was fully aware of that. However.

"Finding another suitable company would take time we don't have."

"A man with your riches can't buy as much as he needs?" she asked with an ingenuous blink.

She was a like a baby who insisted on trying to catch the tiger's tail and stuff it in her mouth. Not stupid, but cheerfully ignorant of the true danger she was in. He couldn't afford to be lenient.

"My grandfather is ill. I had to call him to tell him the merger has been delayed. That was disappointment he didn't need."

She almost threw an askance look at him, but seemed to read his expression and sobered, getting the message that beneath his civilized exterior lurked a heartless mercenary.

Not that he enjoyed scaring her. He usually treated women like delicate flowers. After sleeping in cold alleys that stank of urine, after being tortured at the hands of degenerate, pitiless men, he'd developed an insatiable appetite for luxury and warmth and the sweet side of life. He especially enjoyed soft kittens who liked to be stroked until they purred next to him in bed.

But if a woman dared to cross him, as with any man, he ensured she understood her mistake and would never dream of doing so again.

"I owe my grandfather a great deal." He waved at their surroundings. "This."

"I presumed it was stolen," she said with a haughty toss of her head.

"No." He was as blunt as a mallet. "The money was made from smuggling profits, but the boat was purchased legally."

She snapped her head around.

He shrugged, not apologizing for what he came from. "For decades, if something crossed the border or the seas for a thousand miles, legal or illegal, my grandfather—and my father when he was alive—received a cut."

He had her attention. She wasn't saucy now. She was wary. Wondering why he was telling her this.

"Desperate men do desperate things. I know this because I was quite desperate when I began trading on my father's name to survive the streets of Athens."

Their chilled soup arrived. He was hungry, but neither of them moved to pick up their spoons.

"Why were you on the streets?"

"My mother died. Heart failure, or so I was told. I was sent to an orphanage. I hated it." It had been a palace, in retrospect, but he didn't think about that. "I ran away. My mother had told me my father's name. I knew what he was reputed to be. The way my mother had talked, as if his enemies would hunt me down and use me against him if they found me...I thought she was trying to scare me into staying out of trouble. I didn't," he confided drily. "Boys of twelve are not known for their good judgment."

He smoothed his eyebrow where a scar was barely visible, but he could still feel where the tip of a blade had dragged very deliberately across it, opening the skin while a threat of worse—losing his eye—was voiced.

"I watched and learned from other street gangs and mostly stuck to robbing criminals because they don't go to the police. As long as I was faster and smarter, I survived. Threatening my father's wrath worked well in the beginning, but without a television or computer, I missed the news that he had been stabbed. I was caught in my lie."

Her eyes widened. "What happened?"

"As my mother had warned me, my father's enemies showed great interest. They asked me for information I didn't have."

"What do you mean?" she whispered, gaze fixed to his so tightly all he could see was blue. "Like...?"

"Torture. Yes. My father was known to have stockpiled everything from electronics to drugs to cash. But if I had known where any of it was kept, I would have helped myself, wouldn't I? Rather than trying to steal from them? They took their time believing that." He pretended the recollection didn't coat him in cold sweat.

"Oh, my God." She sat back, fingertips covering her faint words, gaze flickering over her shoulder to where his left hand was still behind her.

Ah. She'd noticed his fingernail.

He brought his hand between them, flexed its stiffness into a fist, then splayed it.

"These two fingernails." He pointed, affecting their removal as casual news. "Several bones broken, but it works well enough after several surgeries. I'm naturally left-handed so that was a nuisance, but I'm quite capable with both now, so…"

"Silver lining?" she huffed, voice strained with disbelief. "How did you get away?"

"They weren't getting anywhere with questioning me and hit upon the idea of asking my grandfather to pay a ransom. He had no knowledge of a grandson, though. He was slow to act. He was grieving. Not pleased to have some pile of dung attempting to benefit off his son's name. I had no proof of my claim. My mother was one of many for my father. That was why she left him."

He shrugged. Female companionship had never been a problem for any of the Petrides men. They were good-looking and powerful and money was seductive. Women found *them*.

"Pappoús could have done many things, not least of which was let them finish killing me. He asked for blood tests before he paid the ransom. When I proved to be his son's bastard, he made me his heir. I suddenly had a clean, dry bed, ample food." He nodded at the beautiful concoction before them: a shallow chowder of corn and buttermilk topped with fat, pink prawns and chopped herbs.

"I had anything I wanted. A motorcycle in summer, ski trips in winter. Clothes that were tailored to fit my body in any style or color I asked. Gadgets. A yacht. Anything."

He'd also received a disparate education, tutored by his grandfather's accountant in finance. His real estate and investment licenses were more purchased than earned, but he had eventually mastered the skills to benefit from such transactions. Along the way he had developed a talent for managing people, learning by observing his grandfather's methods. Nowadays they had fully qualified, authentically trained staff to handle every matter. Arm-twisting, even the emotional kind he was utilizing right now, was a retired tactic.

But it was useful in this instance. Viveka needed to understand the bigger picture.

Like his grandfather, he needed a test.

"In return for his generosity, I have dedicated myself to ensuring my grandfather's empire operates on the right side of the law. We're mostly there. This merger is a final step. I have committed to making it happen before his health fails him. You can see why I feel I owe him this."

"Why are you being so frank with me?" Her brow crinkled. "Aren't you afraid I'll repeat any of this?"

"No." Much of it was online, if only as legend and conjecture. While Mikolas had pulled many dodgy stunts like mergers that resembled money laundering, he'd never committed actual crimes.

That wasn't why he was so confident, however.

He held her gaze and waited, watching comprehension solidify as she read his expression. She would not betray him, he telegraphed. Ever.

Her lashes quivered and he watched her swallow.

Fear was beginning to take hold in her. He told himself

that was good and ignored the churn of self-contempt in his belly. He wasn't like the men who had tormented him.

But he wasn't that different. Not when he casually picked up his wineglass and mentioned, "I should tell you. Grigor is looking for your sister. You could save yourself by telling him where to find her."

"No!" The word was torn out of her, the look on her face deeply anxious, but not conflicted. "Maybe he never hit her before, but it doesn't mean he wouldn't start now. And this?" She waved at the table and yacht. "She had these trappings all her life and would have given up all of it for a kind word. At least I had memories of our mother. She didn't even have me, thanks to him. So no. *I* would rather go back to Grigor than sell her out to him."

She spoke with brave vehemence, but her eyes grew wet. It wasn't bravado. It was loyalty that would cost her, but she was willing to pay the price.

"I believe you," he pressed with quiet lack of mercy. "That Grigor would resort to violence. The way he spoke when I returned his call—" Mikolas considered himself immune to rabid foaming at the mouth. He knew first-hand how depraved a man could act, but the bloodlust in Grigor's voice had been disturbing. Familiar in a grim, dark way.

And educational. Grigor wasn't upset that his daughter was missing. He was upset the merger had been delayed. He was taking Viveka's involvement very personally and despite all his posturing and hard-nosed negotiating in the lead-up, he was revealing impatience for the merger to complete.

That told Mikolas his very thorough research prior to starting down this road with Grigor may have missed something. It wasn't a complete surprise that Grigor had kept something up his sleeve. Mikolas had chosen Grigor because he hadn't been fastidious about partnering with the Petrides name. Perhaps Grigor had thought the sacrifice to his reputation meant he could withhold certain debts or other liabilities.

It could turn out that Viveka had done Mikolas a favor, giving him this opportunity to review everything one final time before closing. He could, in fact, gain more than he'd lost.

Either way, Grigor's determination to reach new terms and sign quickly put all the power back in Mikolas's court, exactly where he was most comfortable having it.

Now he would establish that same position with Viveka and his world would be set right.

"Even if he finds her, what can he do to her?" she was murmuring, linking her hands together, nail beds white. "She's married to Stephanos. His boss works for a man who owns news outlets. Big ones. Running her to ground would accomplish nothing. No, she's safe." She seemed to be reassuring herself.

"What about you?" He was surprised she wasn't thinking of herself. "He sounded like he would hunt you down no matter where you tried to hide." It was the dead-honest truth.

Dead.

Honest.

"So you might as well turn me over and save him the trouble? And close your precious deal with the devil?" So much fire and resentment sparked off her it was fascinating.

"This deal *is* important to me. Grigor knows Pappoús is unwell, that I'm reluctant to look for another option. He wants me to hand you over, close the deal and walk away with what I want—which is to give my grandfather what he wants."

"And what I want doesn't matter." She was afraid, he could see it, but she refused to let it overtake her. He had to admire that.

"You got what you wanted," he pointed out. "Your sister is safe from my evil clutches."

"Good," she insisted, but her mouth quivered before she clamped it into a line. One tiny tear leaked out of the corner of her eye.

Poor, steadfast little kitten.

But that depth of loyalty pleased him. She was passing her test.

He reached out to stroke her hair even though it only made her flinch and flash a look of hatred at him.

"Are you enjoying terrorizing me?"

"Please," he scoffed, taking up his glass of wine to swirl and sip, cooling a mouth that was burning with anticipation as he finalized his decision. "I'm treating you like a Fabergé egg."

He ignored the release of tension inside him as what he really wanted moved closer to his grasp.

"Grigor makes an ugly enemy. You understand why I don't want to make him into one of mine," he said.

"Is it starting to grate on your conscience?" she charged. "That he'll beat me to a pulp and throw me into the nearest body of water? I thought you didn't shame."

"I don't. But I need you to see very clearly that the action I'm taking comes at a cost. Which you will repay. I will not be leaving you in Athens, Viveka. You are staying with me."

CHAPTER FIVE

VIVEKA'S VISION GREW grainy and colorless for a moment. She thought she might pass out, which was not like her at all. She was tough as nails, not given to fainting spells like a Victorian maiden.

She had been subtly hyperventilating this whole time Mikolas had been tying his noose around her neck. Now she'd stopped breathing altogether.

Had she heard him right?

He looked like a god, his neat wedding haircut finger-combed to the side, his mouth symmetrical and unwavering after smiting her with his words. His gray eyes were impassive. Just the facts.

"But—" she started to argue, wanting to bring up Aunt Hildy.

He shook his head. "We're not bargaining. Actions have consequences. These are yours."

"You," she choked, trying to grasp what he was saying. "*You* are my consequence?"

"It's me or Grigor. I've already told you that I won't allow you to hurt yourself, so yes. I have chosen your consequence. We should eat. Before it gets warm," he said with a whimsical levity that struck her as bizarre in the middle of this intense, life-altering conversation.

He picked up his spoon, but she only stared at him.

Her fingers were icicles, stiff and frozen. All of her muscles had atrophied while her heart was racing. Her mind stumbled around in the last glimmers of the bleeding sun.

"I have a life in London," she managed. "Things to do."

"I'm sure Grigor knows that and has men waiting."

Her panicked mind sprang to Aunt Hildy, but she was out of harm's reach for the moment. Still, "Mikolas—"

"Think, Viveka. Think hard."

She was trying to. She had been searching for alternatives this whole time.

"So you're abandoning the merger?" She hated the way her voice became puny and confused.

"Not at all. But the terms have changed." He was making short work of his soup and waved his spoon. "With your sister as my wife, Grigor would have had considerable influence over me and our combined organization. I was prepared to let him control his side for up to five years and pay him handsomely for his trouble. Now the takeover becomes hostile and I will push him out, take control of everything and leave him very little. I expect he'll be even more angry with you."

"Then don't be so ruthless! Why aggravate him further?"

His answer was a gentle nudge of his bent knuckle under her chin, thumb brushing the tender place at the corner of her mouth.

"He left a mark on my mistress. He needs to be punished."

Her heart stopped. She jerked back. "Mistress!"

"You thought I was keeping you out of the goodness of my heart?"

Her vision did that wobble again, fading in and out. "You said you didn't want sex." Her voice sounded like it was coming from far away.

"I said I would decide if and when I gave it to you. I have decided. Are you not going to eat those?" He had switched to his fork to eat his prawns and now stabbed one from her bowl, hungrily snapping it between his teeth, but his gaze was watchful when it swung up to hers.

"I'm not having sex with you!"

"You've changed your mind?"

"*You* did," she pointed out tartly, wishing she was one of those women who could be casual about sex. She'd been anxious from the get-go, which was probably why it had turned into this massive issue for her. "I'm not something you can buy like a luxury boat with your ill-gotten gains," she pointed out.

"I haven't purchased you." He gave her a frown of insult. "I've earned your loyalty the same way my grandfather earned mine, by saving your life. You will show your gratitude by being whatever I need you to be, wherever I need you to be."

"I'm not going to be *that*! If I understand you correctly, you want to live within the law. Well, pro tip, forcing women to have sex is against the law."

"Sex will be a fringe benefit for both of us." He was flinty in the face of her sarcasm. "I won't force you and I won't have to."

"Keep. *Dreaming*," she declared.

His fork clattered into his empty bowl and he shifted to face her, one arm behind her, one on the table, bracketing her into a space that enveloped her in masculine energy.

She could have skittered out the far side of the bench, but she held her ground, trying to stare him down.

His gaze fell to her mouth, causing her abdominals to tighten and tremble.

"You're not thinking about it? Wondering? *Dreaming*," he mocked in a voice that jarred because he did *not* sound angry. He sounded amused and knowing. "Let's see, shall we?"

His hand shifted to cup her neck. The caress of his thumb into the hollow at the base of her throat unnerved her. If he'd been forceful, she would have reacted with a slap, but this felt almost tender. She trusted this hand. It had dragged her up to the surface of the water, giving her life.

So she didn't knock that hand away. She didn't hit him in the face as he neared, or pull away to say a hard *No*.

Somehow she got it into her head she would prove he didn't affect her. Maybe she even thought she could return to him that rejection he'd delivered earlier.

Maybe she really did want to know how it would be with him.

Whatever the perverse impulse that possessed her, she sat there and let him draw closer, keeping her mouth set and her gaze as contemptuous as she could make it.

Until his lips touched hers.

If she had expected brutality, she was disappointed. But he wasn't gentle, either.

His hold firmed on her neck as he plundered without hesitation, opening his mouth over hers in a hot, wet branding that caused a burn to explode within her. His tongue stabbed and her lips parted. Delicious swirls of pleasure invaded her belly and lower. Her eyes fluttered closed so she could fully absorb the sensations.

She *had* wondered. Intrigue had held her still for this kiss and she moaned as she basked in it, bones dissolving, muscles weakening.

He kissed her harder, dismantling her attempt to remain detached in a few short, racing heartbeats. He dragged his lips across hers in an erotic crush, the rough-soft texture of his lips like silken velvet.

All her senses came alive to the heat of his chest, the woodsy spice scent on his skin, the salt flavor on his tongue. Her skin grew so sensitized it was painful. She felt vulnerable with longing.

She splayed her free hand against his chest and released a sob of capitulation, no longer just accepting. Participating. Exploring the texture of his tongue, trying to compete with his aggression and consume him with equal fervor.

He pulled back abruptly, the loss of his kiss a cruelty that left her dangling in midair, naked and exposed. His chest moved with harsh breaths that seemed triumphant. The glitter in his eye was superior, asserting that *he* would decide *if* and *when*.

"No force necessary," he said with satisfaction deepening the corners of his mouth.

This was how it had been for her mother, Viveka realized with a crash back to reality. Twenty years ago, Grigor had been handsome and virile, provoking infatuation in a lonely widow. Viveka's earliest memories of being in his house had been ones of walking in on intimate clinches, quickly told to make herself scarce.

As Viveka had matured, she had recognized a similar yearning in herself for a man's loving attention. She understood how desire had been the first means that Grigor had used to control his wife, before encumbering her with a second child, then ultimately showing his ugliest colors to keep her in line.

Sex was a dangerous force that could push a woman down a slippery slope. That was what Viveka had come to believe.

It was doubly perilous when the man in question was so clearly not impacted by their kiss the way she was. Mikolas's indifference hurt, inflicting a loneliness on her that matched those moments in her life that had nearly broken her: losing her mother, being banished from her sister to an aunt who should have loved her, but hadn't.

She had to look away to hide her anguish.

The porter arrived to bring out the next course.

Mikolas didn't even look up from his plate as he said, "What is the name of the man who has your things? I would like to retrieve your passport before Grigor realizes it's under his nose."

Viveka needed to tell him about Aunt Hildy, but didn't trust her voice.

Mikolas said little else through the rest of their meal, only admonishing her to eat, stating at the end of it, "I want to finish the takeover arrangements. You have free run of the yacht unless you show me you need to be confined to your room."

"You seriously think I'll let you keep me like some kind of pirate's doxy?"

"Since I'm about to stage a raid and appoint myself admiral of Grigor's corporate fleet, I can't deny that label, can I? You call yourself whatever you want."

She glared at his back as he walked away.

He left her to her own devices and there must have been something wrong with her because, despite hating Mikolas for his overabundance of confidence, she was viciously glad he was running Grigor through.

At no point should she consider Mikolas her hero, she cautioned herself. She should have known there'd be a cost to his saving her life. She flashed back to Grigor calling her useless baggage. To Hildy telling her to earn her keep.

She wasn't even finished repaying Hildy! That hardly put her in a position to show "gratitude" to Mikolas, did it?

Oh, she hated when people thought of her as some sort of nuisance. This was why she had been looking forward to settling Hildy and striking out on her own. She could finally prove to herself and the world that she carried her own weight. She was not a lodestone. She wasn't.

A rabbit hole of self-pity beckoned. She avoided it by getting her bearings aboard the aptly named *Inferno*. The top deck was chilly and dark, the early night sky spitting rain into her face as the wind came up. The hot tub looked appealing, steaming and glowing with colored underwater lights. When the porter appeared with towels and a robe, inviting her to use the nearby change room, she was tempted, but explained she was just looking around.

He proceeded to give her a guided tour through the rest of the ship. She didn't know what the official definition for "ship" was, but this behemoth had to qualify. The upper deck held the bridge along with an outdoor bar and lounge at the stern. A spiral staircase in the middle took them down to the interior of the main deck. Along with Mikolas's stateroom and her own, there was a formal dining room for twelve, an elegant lounge with a big-screen television and a baby grand piano. Outside, there was a small lifeboat in the bow, in front of Mikolas's private sundeck, and a huge sunbathing area alongside a pool in the stern.

The extravagance should have filled her with contempt, but instead she was calmed by it, able to pretend this wasn't a boat. It was a seaside hotel. One that happened to be priced well beyond her reach, but *whatever*.

It wasn't as easy to pretend on the lower deck, which was mostly galley, engine room, less extravagant guest and crew quarters. And, oh, yes, another boat, this one a sexy speedboat parked in an internal compartment of the stern.

Her long journey to get to Trina caught up to her at that point. She'd left London the night before and hadn't slept much while traveling. She went back to her suite and changed into a comfortable pair of pajamas—ridiculously pretty ones in peacock-blue silk. Champagne-colored lace edged the bodice and tickled the tops of her bare feet, adding to the feeling of luxuriating in pure femininity.

She hadn't won a prize holiday, she reminded herself, trying not to be affected by all this lavish comfort. A gilded cage was still a prison and she would *not* succumb to Mikolas's blithe expectation that he could "keep" her. He certainly would not *seduce* her with his riches and pampering.

I won't force you and I won't have to.

She flushed anew, recalling their kiss as she curled up on the end of the love seat rather than crawl into bed. She wanted to be awake if he arrived expecting sex. When it came to making love, she was more about fantasy than reality, going only so far with the few men she'd dated. That kiss with Mikolas had shaken her as much as everything else that had happened today.

Better to think about that than her near-drowning, though.

Her thoughts turned for the millionth time to her mother's last moments. Somehow she began imagining her mother was on this boat and they were being tossed about in a storm, but she couldn't find her mother to warn her. It was a dream, she knew it was a dream. She hadn't been on the other boat when her mother was lost, but she could feel the way the waves were battering this one—

Sitting up with a gasp, she sensed they'd hit rough waters. Waves splashed against the glass of her porthole and the boat rocked enough she was rolling on her bed.

How had she wound up in bed?

With a little sob, she threw off the covers and pushed to her feet.

Fear, Aunt Hildy would have said, was no excuse for panic. Viveka did not consider herself a brave person at all, but she had learned to look out for herself because no one else ever had. If this boat was about to capsize, she needed to be on deck wearing a life jacket to have a fighting chance at survival.

Holding the bulkhead as she went into the passageway, she stumbled to the main lounge. The lifeboat was on this deck, she recalled, but in the bow, on the far side of Mikolas's suite. The porter had explained all the safety precautions, which had reassured her at the time. Now all she could think was that it was a stupid place to store life jackets.

Mikolas always slept lightly, but tonight he was on guard for more than old nightmares. He was expecting exactly what happened. The balcony in Viveka's stateroom wasn't the only thing alarmed. When she left her suite, the much more discreet internal security system caused his phone to vibrate.

He acknowledged the signal, then pushed to his feet and adjusted his shorts. That was another reason he'd been restless. He was hard. And he never wore clothes to bed. They were uncomfortable even when they weren't twisted around his erection, but he'd anticipated rising at some point to deal with his guest so he had supposed he should wear something to bed.

He'd expected to find release *with* his guest, but when he'd gone to her room, she'd been fast asleep, curled up on the love seat like a child resisting bedtime, one hand pillowing her cheek. She hadn't stirred when he'd carried her to the bed and tucked her in, leaving him sorely disappointed.

That obvious exhaustion, along with her pale skin and the slight frown between her brows, had plucked a bizarre reaction from him. Something like concern. That bothered him. He was impervious to emotional manipulations, but Viveka was under his skin—and she hadn't even been awake and doing it deliberately.

He sighed with annoyance, moving into his office.

If a woman was going to wake him in the night, it ought to be for better reasons than this.

He had no doubt this private deck in the bow was her destination. He'd watched her talk to his porter extensively about the lifeboat and winch system while he'd sat here working earlier. He wasn't surprised she was attempting to escape. He wasn't even angry. He was disappointed. He hated repeating himself.

But there was an obdurate part of him that enjoyed how she challenged him. Hardly anyone stood up to him anymore.

Plus he was sexually frustrated enough to be pleased she was setting up a midnight confrontation. When he'd kissed her earlier, desire had clawed at his control with such savagery, he'd nearly abandoned one for the other and made love to her right there at the table.

His need to be in command of himself and everyone else had won out in the end. He'd pulled back from the brink, but it had taken more effort than he liked to admit.

"Come on," he muttered, searching for her in the dim glow thrown by the running lights.

This was an addict's reaction, he thought with self-contempt. His brain knew she was lethal, but the way she infused him with a sense of omnipotence was a greater lure. He didn't care that he risked self-destruction. He still wanted her. He was counting the pulse beats until he could feel the rush of her hitting his system.

Where *was* she?

Not overboard again, surely.

The thought sent a disturbing punch into the middle

of his chest. He didn't know what had made him throw off his jacket and shoes and dive in after her today. It had been pure instinct. He'd shot out the emergency exit behind her, determined to hear why she had upended his plans, but he hadn't been close enough to stop her tumble into the water.

His heart had jammed when he'd seen her knock into the side of the yacht, worried she was unconscious as she went under.

Pulling her and that whale of a gown to the surface had nearly been more than he could manage. He didn't know what he would have done if the strength of survival hadn't imbued him. Letting go of her hadn't been an option. It wasn't basic human decency that had made him dive into that water, but something far more powerful that refused, absolutely refused, to go back to the surface without her.

Damn it, now he couldn't get that image of her disappearing into the water out of his head. He pushed from his office onto his private deck, where the rain and splashing waves peppered his skin. She wasn't coming down the stairs toward him.

He climbed them, walking along the outer rail of the mid-deck, seeing no sign of her.

Actually, he walked right past her. He spied her when he paused at the door into the bridge, thinking to enter and look for her on the security cameras. Something made him glance back the way he'd come and he spotted the ball of dark clothing and white skin under the life preserver ring.

What the hell?

"Viveka." He retraced his few steps, planting his bare feet carefully on the wet deck. "What are you doing out here?"

She lifted her face. Her hair was plastered in tendrils

around her neck and shoulders. Her chin rattled as she stammered, "I n-n-need a l-l-life v-v-vest."

"You're freezing." *He* was cold. He bent to draw her to her feet, but she stubbornly stayed in a knot of trembling muscle, fingers wrapped firmly around the mount for the ring.

What a confounding woman. With a little more force, he started to peel her fingers open.

The boat listed, testing his balance.

Before he could fully right himself, Viveka cried out and nearly knocked him over, rising to throw her arms around his neck, slapping her soaked pajamas into his front.

He swore at the impact, working to stay on his feet.

"Are we going over?"

"No."

He could hardly breathe, she was clinging so tightly to his neck, and shaking so badly he could practically hear her bones rattling. He swore under his breath, putting together all those anxious looks out to the water. This was why she hadn't shown the sense to be terrified of *him* today. She was afraid of boats.

"Come inside." He drew her toward the stairs down to his deck.

She balked. "I don't want to be trapped if we capsize."

"We won't capsize."

She resisted so he picked her up and carried her all the way through his dark office into his stateroom, where he'd left a lamp burning, kicking doors shut along the way.

He sat on the edge of his bed, settling her icy, trembling weight on his lap. "This is only a bit of wind and freighter traffic. We're hitting their wakes. It's not a storm."

There was no heat beneath these soaked pajamas. Even in the dim light, he could see her lips were blue. He ran his hands over her, trying to slick the water out of her pajamas while he rubbed warmth into her skin.

"There doesn't have to be a storm." She was pressing into him, her lips icy against his collarbone, arms still around his neck, relaxing and convulsing in turns. "My mother drowned when it was calm."

"From a boat?" he guessed.

"Grigor took her out." Her voice fractured. "Maybe on purpose to drown her. I don't know, but I think she wanted to leave him. He took her out sailing and said he didn't know till morning that she fell, but he never acted like he cared. He told me to stop crying and take care of Trina."

If this was a trick, it was seriously good acting. The emotion in her voice sent him tumbling into equally disturbing memories buried deep in his subconscious. *Your mother died while you were at school.* The landlord had made the statement without hesitation or regret, casually destroying Mikolas's world with a few simple words. *A woman from child services is coming to get you.*

So much horror had followed, Mikolas barely registered anymore how bad that day had been. He'd shuffled it all into the past once his grandfather had taken him in. The page had been turned and he never leafed back to it.

But suddenly he was stricken with that old grief. He couldn't ignore the way her heart pounded so hard he felt it against his arm across her back. Her skin was clammy, her spine curled tight against life's blows.

His hand unconsciously followed that hard curve, no longer just warming her, but trying to soothe while stealing a long-overdue shred of comfort for himself from someone who understood what he'd suffered.

He recovered just as quickly, shaking off the moment of empathy and rearranging her so she was forced to look up at him.

"I've been honest with you, haven't I?" Perhaps he sounded harsh, but she had cracked something in him. He didn't like the cold wind blowing through him as a result. "I would tell you if we were in danger. We're not."

Viveka believed him. That was the ridiculous part of it. She had no reason to trust him, but why would he be so blunt about everything else and hide the fact they were likely to capsize? If he said they were safe, they were safe.

"I'm still scared," she admitted in a whisper, hating that she was so gutless.

"Think of something else," he chided. The edge of his thumb gave her jaw a little flick, then he dipped his head and kissed her.

She brought up a hand to the side of his face, thinking she shouldn't let this happen again, but his stubble was a fascinating texture against her palm and his lips were blessedly hot, sending runnels of heat through her sluggish blood. Everything in her calmed and warmed.

Then he rocked his mouth to part her lips with the same avid, possessive enjoyment as earlier and cupped her breast and she shuddered under a fresh onslaught of sensations. The rush hurt, it was so powerful, but it was also like that moment when he'd dragged her to the surface. He was dragging her out of her phobia into wonder.

She instinctively angled herself closer, the silk of her pajamas a wet, annoying layer between them as she tried to press herself through his skin.

He grunted and grew harder under her bottom. His arms gathered her in with a confident, sexual possessiveness while his knees splayed wider so she sat deeper against the firm shape of his sex.

Heat rushed into her loins, sharp and powerful. All of

her skin burned as blood returned to every inch of her. She didn't mean to let her tongue sweep against his, but his was right there, licking past her lips, and the contact made lightning flash in her belly.

His aggression should have felt threatening, but it felt sexy and flagrant. As the kiss went on, the waves of pleasure became more focused. The way he toyed with her nipple sent thrums of excitement rocking through her.

She gasped for air when he drew back, but she didn't want to stop. Not yet. She lifted her mouth so he returned and kissed her harder. Deeper.

Her breast ached where he massaged it and the pulse between her legs became a hungry throb as he shifted wet silk against the tight point of her nipple.

His hand slid away, pulling the soggy material up from her quivery belly. He flattened his palm there, branding her cold, bare skin. His fingers searched along the edge of her waistband and he lifted his head, ready to slide his hand between her closed thighs.

"Open," he commanded.

Viveka gasped and shot off his lap, stumbling when her knees didn't want to support her. "What—no!"

She covered her throat where her pulse was racing, shocked at herself. He kept turning her into this…*animal*. That's all this was: hormones. Some kind of primal response to the caveman who happened to yank her out of the lion's jaws. The primitive part of her recognized an alpha male who could keep her offspring alive so her body wanted to make some with him.

Mikolas dropped one hand, then the other behind him, leaning on his straight arms, knees wide. His nostrils flared as he eyed her. It was the only sign that her recoil bothered him.

Contractions of desire continued to swirl in her abdomen. That part of her that was supposed to be able to take his shape felt so achy with carnal need she was nearly overwhelmed.

"You said you wouldn't make me," she managed in a shaky little voice.

It was a weak defense and they both knew it.

He cocked one brow in a mocking, *I don't have to*. The way his gaze traveled down her made her afraid for what she looked like, silk clinging to distended nipples and who knew what other telltale reactions.

She pulled the fabric away from her skin and looked to the door.

"You're bothered by your reaction to me. Why? I think it's exciting." The rasp of his arousal-husky voice made her inner muscles pinch with involuntary eagerness. "Come here. I'll hold you all night. You'll feel very safe," he promised, but his mouth quirked with wicked amusement.

She hugged herself. "I don't sleep around. I don't even know you!"

"I prefer it that way," he provided.

"Well, I don't!"

He sighed, rising and making her heart soar with alarmed excitement. It fell as he turned and walked away to the corner of the room.

She had rejected *him*, she reminded herself. This sense of rebuff was completely misplaced.

But he was so appealing with his tall, powerful frame, spine bracketed by supple muscle in the way of a martial artist rather than a gym junkie. The low light turned his skin a dark, burnished bronze and he had a really nice butt in those wet, clinging boxers.

She ought to leave, but she watched him search out three different points before he drew the wall inward like an oversize door. The cabinetry from her stateroom came with it, folding back to become part of his sitting room, creating an archway into her suite.

"I haven't used this yet. It's clever, isn't it?" he remarked.

If she didn't loathe boats so much, she might have agreed. As it was, she could only hug herself, dumbfounded to see they were now sharing a room.

"You'll feel safer like this, yes?"

Not likely!

He didn't seem to expect an answer, just turned to open a drawer. He pawed through, coming up with a pink long-sleeved top in waffle weave and a pair of pink and mint green flannel pajama pants. "Dry off and put these on. Warm up."

She waved at the archway. "Why did you do that?"

"You don't find it comforting?"

Oh, she was not sticking around to be laughed at. She snatched the pajamas from his hand, not daring to look into his face, certain she would see mockery, and made for the bathroom in her own suite. *Infuriating* man.

She would close the wall herself, she decided as she clumsily changed, even though she preferred the idea of him being in the same room with her. He was not a man to be relied on, she reminded herself. If she had learned nothing else in life, it was that she was on her own.

Then she walked out and found a life vest on the foot of her bed. When she glanced toward his room, his lamp was off.

She clutched the cool bulk of the vest to her chest, insides crumpling.

"Thank you, Mikolas," she said toward his darkened room.

A pause, then a weary "Try not to need it."

CHAPTER SIX

Viveka was so emotionally spent, she slept late, waking with the life vest still in her crooked arm.

Sitting up with an abrupt return of memory, she noted the sun was streaming in through the uncovered windows of Mikolas's stateroom. The yacht was sailing smoothly and she could swear that was the fresh scent of a light breeze she detected. She swung her feet to the floor and moved into his suite with a blink at the brightness.

He didn't notice her, but she caught her breath at the sight of him. He was lounging on the wing-like extension from his sitting area. It was fronted by what looked like the bulkhead of his suite and fenced on either side by glass panels anchored into thin, stainless steel uprights. The wind blew over him, ruffling his dark hair.

She might have been alarmed by the way the ledge dangled over the water, but he was so relaxed, slouched on a cushioned chair, feet on an ottoman, she could only experience again the pinch of deep attraction.

He had his tablet in one hand, a half-eaten apple in the other and he was mostly naked. Again. All he wore were shorts, these ones a casual pair in checked gray and black even though the morning breeze was quite cool.

Her heart actually panged that she had to keep fighting

him. He looked so casually beautiful. It wasn't just about her, though, but Aunt Hildy.

He lifted his head and turned to look at her as though he'd been aware of her the whole time. "Are you afraid to come out here?"

She was terrified, but it had nothing to do with the water and everything to do with how he affected her.

"Why are you allowed to have your balcony open and I got in trouble for it?" she asked, choosing a tone of belligerence over revealing her intimidation, forcing her legs to carry her as far as the opening.

"I had a visitor." He nodded at the deck beside his ottoman.

Her bag.

Stunned, she quickly knelt and rifled through it, coming up with her purse, phone, passport… Everything exactly as it should be. Even her favorite hair clip. She gathered and rolled the mess of her hair in a well-practiced move, weirdly comforted by that tiny shred of normalcy.

When she looked up at him, Mikolas was watching her. He finished his apple with a couple of healthy bites and flipped the core into the water.

"Help yourself." He nodded toward where a sideboard was set up next to the door to his office.

"I'm in time-out? Not allowed out for breakfast?"

No response, but she quickly saw there was more than coffee and a basket of fruit here. The dishes contained traditional favorites she hadn't eaten since leaving Greece nine years ago.

Somehow she'd convinced herself she hated everything about this country, but the moment she saw the *tiganites*, nostalgia closed her throat. A sharp memory of asking her mother if she could cut up her sister's pancakes and pour the *petimezi* came to her. Nothing tasted quite like grape molasses. Her heart panged, while her mouth watered and her stomach contracted with hunger.

"Have you eaten?" she called, hoping he didn't hear the break in her voice. She glanced out to see he didn't have a plate going.

"Óchi akóma." Not yet.

She gave him a large helping of the smoked pork omelet along with pancakes and topped up his coffee, earning a considering look as she served him.

Yes, she was trying to soften him up. A woman had to create advantages where she could with a man like him.

"Efcharistó," he said when she joined him.

"Parakaló." She was trying to act casual, but she had chosen to start with yogurt and thyme honey. The first bite tasted so perfect, was such a burst of early childhood happiness, when her mother had been alive and her sister a living doll she could dress and feed, she had to close her eyes, pressing back tears of homecoming.

Mikolas watched her, reluctantly fascinated by the emotion that drew her cheeks in while she savored her breakfast. Pained joy crinkled her brow. It was sensual and sexy and poignant. It was *yogurt.*

He forced his gaze to his own plate.

Viveka was occupying entirely too much real estate in his brain. It had to stop.

But even as he told himself that, his mind went back to last night. How could it not, with her sitting across from him braless beneath her long-sleeved nightshirt? The soft weight of her breast was still imprinted on his palm, firm and shapely, topped with a sensitive nipple he'd longed to suck.

Instantly he was primed for sex. And damn it, she'd

been as fully involved as he had been. He wasn't so arrogant he made assumptions about women's states of interest. He took pains to ensure they were with him every step of the way when he made love to them. She'd been pressing herself into him, returning his kiss, moaning with enjoyment.

Fine, he could accept that she thought they were moving too fast. Obviously she was a bit of a romantic, flying across the continent to help her sister marry her first love. But sex would happen between them. It was inevitable.

When he had opened the passageway between their rooms, however, it hadn't been for sex. He had wanted to ease her anxiety. She had been nothing less than a nuclear bomb from the moment he'd seen her face, but he'd found himself searching out the catch in the wall, giving her access to *his* space, which had never been his habit with any woman.

He didn't understand his actions around her. This morning, he'd actually begun second-guessing his decision to keep her, which wasn't like him at all. Indecision did not make for control in any situation. He certainly couldn't back down because he was *scared*. Of being around a particular *woman*.

Then the news had come through that Grigor was, indeed, hiding debts in two of his subsidiaries. There was no room for equivocating after that. Mikolas had issued a few terse final orders, then notified Grigor of his intention to take over with or without cooperation.

Grigor had been livid.

Given the man's vile remarks, Mikolas was now as suspicious as Viveka that her stepfather had killed her mother. Viveka would stay with him whether he was comfortable in her presence or not.

Whether she liked it or not. At least until he could be sure Grigor wouldn't harm her.

She opened her dreamy blue eyes and looked like she was coming back from orgasm. Sexual awareness shimmered like waves of desert heat between them.

Yes. Sex was inevitable.

Her gaze began to tangle with his, but she seemed to take herself in hand. She sat taller and cleared her throat, looking out to the water and lifting a determined chin, cheekbones glowing with pink heat.

He mentally sighed, too experienced a fighter not to recognize she was preparing to start one.

"Mikolas." He mentally applauded her take-charge tone. "I *have* to go back to London. My aunt is very old. Quite ill. She needs me."

He absorbed that with a blink. This was a fresh approach at least.

She must have read his skepticism. Her mouth tightened. "I wish I was making it up. I'm not."

If he expected her trust—and he did—he would have to trust her in return, he supposed. "Tell me about her," he invited.

She looked to the clear sky, seeming to struggle a moment.

"There's not much to tell. She's the sister of my grandmother and took me in when Grigor kicked me out, even though she was a spinster who never wanted anything to do with children. She had a career before women really did. Worked in Parliament, but not as an elected official. As a secretary to a string of them. She had some kind of lofty clearance, served coffee to all sorts of royals and diplomats. I think she was in love with a married man," she confided with a wrinkle of her nose.

Definitely a sentimentalist.

She shrugged, murmuring, "I don't have proof. Just a few things she said over the years." She picked up her coffee and cupped her hands around it. "She was always telling me how to behave so men wouldn't think things." She made a face. "I'm sure the sexism in her day was appalling. She was adamant that I be independent, pay my share of rent and groceries, know how to look after myself."

"She didn't take her own advice? Make arrangements for herself?"

"She tried." Her shoulder hitched in a helpless shrug. "Like a lot of people, she lost her retirement savings with the economic crash. For a while she had an income bringing in boarders, but we had to stop that a few years ago and remortgage. She has dementia." Her sigh held the weight of the world. "Strangers in the house upset her. She doesn't recognize me anymore, thinks I'm my mother, or her sister, or an intruder who stole her groceries." She looked into her cooling coffee. "I've begun making arrangements to put her into a nursing home, but the plans aren't finalized."

Viveka knew he was listening intently, thought about leaving it there, where she had stopped with the doctors and the intake staff and with Trina during their video chats. But the mass on her conscience was too great. She'd already told Mikolas about Grigor's abuse. He might actually understand the rest and she really needed it off her chest.

"I *feel* like I'm stealing from her. She worked really hard for her home and deserves to live in it, but she can't take care of herself. I have to run home from work every few hours to make sure she hasn't started a fire or caught a bus to who knows where. I can't afford to stay home with her all day and even if I could..."

She swallowed, reminding herself not to feel resentful, but it still hurt. Not just physically, either. She had tried from Day One to have a familial relationship with her aunt and it had all been for naught.

"She started hitting me. I know she doesn't mean it to be cruel. She's scared. She doesn't understand what's happening to her. But I can't take it."

She couldn't look at him. She already felt like the lowest form of life and he wasn't saying anything. Maybe he was letting her pour out her heart and having a laugh at her for getting smacked by an old lady.

"Living with her was never great. She's always been a difficult, demanding person. I was planning to move out the minute I finished school, but she started to go downhill. I stayed to keep house and make meals and it's come to this."

The little food she'd eaten felt like glue in her stomach. She finished up with the best argument she could muster.

"You said you're loyal to your grandfather for what he gave you. That's how I feel toward her. The only way I can live with removing her from her home is by making sure she goes to a good place. So I have to go back to London and oversee that."

Setting aside her coffee, she hugged herself, staring sightlessly at the horizon, not sure if it was guilt churning her stomach or angst at revealing herself this way.

"Now who is beating you up?" Mikolas challenged.

She swung her head to look at him. "You don't think I owe her? Someone needs to advocate for her."

"Where is she now?"

"I was coming away so I made arrangements with her doctor for her to go into an extended-care facility. It's just for assessment and referral, though. The formal arrangements have to be completed. She can't stay where she is and she can't go home if I'm not there. Her doctor is expecting me for a consult this week."

Mikolas reached for his tablet and tapped to place a call. A moment later, the tablet chimed. Someone answered in German. They had a lengthy conversation that she didn't understand. Mikolas ended with, *"Dankeschön."*

"Who was that?" she asked as he set aside the tablet.

"My grandfather's doctor. He's Swiss. He has excellent connections with private clinics all over Europe. He'll ensure Hildy is taken into a good one."

She snorted. "Neither of us has the kind of funds that will underwrite a private clinic arranged by a posh specialist from Switzerland. I can barely afford the extra fees for the one I'm hoping will take her."

"I'll do this for you, to put your mind at ease."

Her mind blanked for a full ten seconds.

"Mikolas," she finally sputtered. "I *want* to do it. I definitely don't want to be in your debt over it!" She ignored the fact that he had already decided she owed him.

Men expect things when they do you a favor, she heard Hildy saying.

A lurching sensation yanked at her heart, like a curtain being pulled aside on its rungs, exposing her at her deepest level. "What kind of sex do you think you're going to get out of me that would possibly compensate you for something like that? Because I can assure you, I'm not that good! You'll be disappointed."

So disappointed.

Had she just said "you'll"? Like she was a sure thing?

She tightened her arms across herself, refusing to look at him as this confrontation took the direction she had hoped it wouldn't: right into the red-light district of Sexville.

* * *

"If that sounds like I just agreed to have sex with you, that's not what I meant," Viveka bit out, voice less strident, but still filled with ire.

Mikolas couldn't think of another woman he'd encountered with such an easily tortured conscience or with such a valiant determination to protect people she cared about while completely disregarding the cost to herself.

She barely seemed real. He was in danger of being *moved* by her depth of loyalty toward her aunt. A jaded part of him had to question whether she was doing exactly what she claimed she wasn't: trying to manipulate him into underwriting the old woman's care, but unlike most women in his sphere, she wasn't offering sex as compensation for making her problems go away.

While he was finding the idea of her coming to his bed motivated by anything other than the same passion that gripped him more intolerable by the second.

"Let us be clear," he said with abrupt decision. "The debt you owe me is the loss of a wife."

She didn't move, but her blue eyes lifted to fix on him, watchful and limitless as the sky.

"My intention was to marry, honeymoon this week, then throw a reception for my new bride, introducing her to a social circle that has been less than welcoming to someone with my pedigree when I only ever had a mistress du jour on my arm."

Being an outsider didn't bother him. He had conditioned himself not to need approval or acceptance from anyone. He preferred his own company and had his grandfather to talk to if he grew bored with himself.

But ostracism didn't sit well with a nature that demanded to overcome any circumstance. The more he worked at growing the corporation, the more he recognized the importance of networking with the mainstream. Socializing was an annoying way to spend his valuable time, but necessary.

"Curiosity, if nothing else, would have brought people to the party," he continued. "The permanence of my marriage would have set the stage for developing other relationships. You understand? Wives don't form friendships with women they never see again. Husbands don't encourage their wives to invite other men's temporary liaisons for drinks or dinner."

"Because they're afraid their wives will hear about their own liaisons?" she hazarded with an ingenuous blink.

Really, no sense of self-preservation.

"It's a question of investment. No one wants to put time or money into something that lacks a stable future. I was gaining more than Grigor's company by marrying. It was a necessary shift in my image."

Viveka shook her head. "Trina would have been hopeless at what you're talking about. She's sweet and funny, loves to cook and pick flowers for arrangements. You couldn't ask for a kinder ear if you need to vent, but playing the society wife? Making small talk about haute couture and trips to the Maldives? You, with your sledgehammer personality, would have crushed her before she was dressed, let alone an evening trying to find her place in the pecking order of upper-crust hens."

"Sledgehammer," he repeated, then accused facetiously, "Flirt."

She blushed. It was pretty and self-conscious and fueled by this ivory-tusked, sexual awareness they were both pretending to ignore. Her gaze flashed to his, naked and filled with last night's trance-like kiss. Her nipples pricked to life beneath the pink of her shirt. So did the flesh between his legs. The moment became so sexually infused, he almost lost the plot.

That's how he wanted it to be between them: pure reaction. Not installment payments.

He reined himself in with excruciating effort, throat tight and body readied with tension as he continued.

"Circulating with the woman who broke up my wedding is not ideal, but will look better than escorting a rebound after being thrown over. Since you'll be with me until I've neutralized Grigor, we will be able to build that same message of constancy."

"What do you mean about neutralizing Grigor?"

"I spoke to him this morning. He's not pleased with my takeover or the fact you're staying with me. You need some serious protections in place. Did you have your mother's death investigated?"

That seemed to throw her. Her face spasmed with emotion.

"I was only nine when it happened so it was years before I really put it all together and thought he could have done it. I was fourteen when I asked the police to look into it, but they didn't take me seriously. The police on the island are in his pocket. The whole island is and I don't really blame them. I've learned myself that you play by his rules or lose everything. Probably the only reason he didn't kill me for making a statement was because it would have been awfully suspicious if something happened to me right after my complaint. But stirring up questions was one of the reasons he kicked me out. Why?"

"I will hire a private investigator to see what we can find. If something can be proved and he's put in prison, you'll be out of his reach."

"That could take years!"

"And will make him that much more incensed with

you in the short term," he said drily. "But as you say, if he's under suspicion, it wouldn't look good if anything happened to you. I think it will afford you protection in the long term."

"You're going to start an investigation, take care of my aunt and protect me from Grigor and all I have to do is pretend to be your girlfriend." Her voice rang with disbelief. "For how *long*?"

"At least until the merger completes and the investigation shows some results. Play your part well and you might even earn my forgiveness for disrupting my life so thoroughly."

Her laugh was ragged and humorless. "And sex?"

She tossed her head, affecting insouciance, but the small frown between her brows told him she was anxious. That aggravated him. He could think of nothing else but discovering exactly how incendiary they would be together. If she wasn't equally obsessed, he was at a disadvantage.

Not something he ever endured.

With a casual flick of his hand, he proclaimed, "Like today's fine weather, we'll enjoy it because it's there."

Did a little shadow of disappointment pass behind her eyes? What did she expect? Lies about falling in love? They really were at an impasse if she expected that ruse.

Her mouth pursed to disguise what might have been a brief tremble. She pushed to stand. "Yes, well, the almanac is predicting heavy frost. Dress warm." She reached for her bag. "I'm going to my room."

"Leave your passport with me."

She turned back to regard him with what he was starting to think of as her princess look, very haughty and down the nose. "Why?"

"To arrange travel visas."

"To where?"

"Wherever I need you to be."

"Give me a 'for instance.'"

"Asia, eventually, but you wanted to go to Athens, didn't you? There's a party tonight. Do as you're told and I'll let you off the boat to come with me."

Her spine went very straight at that patronizing remark. Her unfettered breasts were not particularly heavy, but magnificent in their shape and firmness and chill-sharpened points. He was going to go out of his mind if he didn't touch her again soon.

As if she read his thoughts, her brows tugged together with conflict. She was no doubt thinking that the return of her purse and arrival in Athens equaled an excellent opportunity to set him in the rearview mirror.

He tensed, waiting out the minutes of her indecision. Oddly, it was not unlike the anticipation of pain. His breath stilled in his lungs, throat tight, as he willed her to do as he said.

Do not make me ask again.

Helplessness flashed in her expression before she ducked her head and drew her passport out of her bag, hand trembling as she held it out to him.

A debilitating rush of relief made his own arm feel like it didn't even belong to him. He reached to take it.

She held on while she held his gaze, incredibly beautiful with that hard-won determination lighting her proud expression. "You *will* make sure Aunt Hildy is properly cared for?"

"You and Pappoús will get along well. He holds me to my promises, too."

She released the passport into his possession, averting her gaze as though she didn't want to acknowledge the significance. Clearing her throat, she took out her phone. "I want to check in with Trina. May I have the WiFi code?"

"The security key is a mix of English and Greek characters." He held out his other hand. "I'll do it for you."

She released a noise of impatient defeat, slapped her phone into his palm and walked away.

CHAPTER SEVEN

MIKOLAS HAD SET himself up in her contacts with a selfie taken on her phone, of him sitting there like a sultan on his yacht, taking ownership of her entire life.

She couldn't stop looking at it. Those smoky eyes of his were practically making love to her, the curve of his wide mouth quirked at the corners in not quite a smile. It was more like, *I know you're naked in the shower right now.* He was so brutally handsome with his chiseled cheekbones and devil-doesn't-give-a-damn nonchalance he made her chest hurt.

Yet he had also forwarded a request from the Swiss doctor for her aunt's details along with a recommendation for one of those beyond-top-notch dementia villages that were completely unattainable for mere mortals. A quick scan of its website told her it was very patient-centric and prided itself on compassion and being ahead of the curve with quality treatment. All that was needed was the name of her aunt's physician to begin Hildy's transfer into the facility's care.

Along with Trina's well-being, a good plan for Aunt Hildy was the one thing Viveka would sell her soul for. It was a sad commentary on her life that it was the only thing pulling her back to London. She had no community there, rarely had time for dating or going out with friends.

Her neighbor was nice, but mostly her life had revolved around school, then work and caring for Aunt Hildy. There was no one worrying about her now, when she had been stolen like a concubine by this throwback Spartan warrior.

She sighed, not even able to argue that her job was a career she needed to get back to. One quick email and her position had been snapped up by one of the part-timers who need the hours. She'd be on the bottom rung when she went back. If she went back. She'd accepted that job for its convenience to home, and in the back of her mind, she'd already been planning to make a change once she had Hildy settled.

But Aunt Hildy had faced nothing but challenges all her life and, in her way, she'd been Viveka's lifeline. The old woman shouldn't have to suffer and wouldn't. Not if Viveka could help it.

And now that Mikolas had spelled out that sex wasn't mandatory...

Oh, she didn't want to think about sex with that man! He already made her feel so unlike herself she could hardly stand it. But she couldn't help wondering what it would be like to lie with him. Something about him got to her, making her blood run like cavalry into sensual battle. Sadly, Viveka had reservations that made the idea of being intimate with him seem not just ill-advised but completely impossible.

So she tried not to think of it and video-called Trina. Her sister was both deliriously joyful and terribly worried when she picked up.

"Where *are* you? Papa is furious." Her eyes were wide. "I'm scared for you, Vivi."

"I'm okay," she prevaricated. "What about you? You've obviously talked to him. Is he likely to come after you?"

"He doesn't believe this was my decision. He blames

you for all of it and it sounds—I'm not sure what's going on at his office, but things are off the rails and he thinks it's your fault. I'm so sorry, Vivi."

"That doesn't surprise me," Viveka snorted, hiding how scared the news made her. "Are you and Stephanos happy? Was all of this worth it?"

"So happy! I knew he was my soul mate, but oh, Vivi!" Her sister blushed, growing even more radiant, saying in a self-conscious near-whisper, "Being married is even better than I imagined it would be."

Lovemaking. That's what her little sister was really talking about.

Envy, acute and painful, seared through Viveka. She had always felt left out when women traded stories about men and intimacy. Dating for her had mostly been disastrous. Now even her younger sister was ahead of her on that curve. It made Viveka even more insecure in her sexuality than she already was.

They talked a few more minutes and Viveka was wistful when she ended the call. She was glad Trina was living happily-ever-after. At one time, she'd believed in that fairy tale for herself, but had become more pragmatic over the years, first by watching the nightmare that her mother's romance turned into, then challenged by Aunt Hildy for wanting a man to "complete" her.

She hadn't thought of it that way, exactly. Finding a soul mate was a stretch, true, but why shouldn't she want a companion in life? What was the alternative? Live alone and lonely, like Aunt Hildy? Engage in casual hookups like Mikolas had said he preferred?

She was not built for fair-weather frolics.

Her introspection was interrupted by a call from Hildy's doctor. He was impressed that she was able to get her aunt into that particular clinic and wanted to make arrangements to move her the next morning. He assured Viveka she was doing the right thing.

The die was cast. Not long after, the ship docked and Viveka and Mikolas were whisked into a helicopter. It deposited them on top of *his* building, which was an office tower, but he had a penthouse that took up most of an upper floor.

"I have meetings this afternoon," he told her. "A stylist will be here shortly to help you get ready."

Viveka was typically ready to go out within thirty minutes. That included shampooing and drying her hair. She had never in her life started four hours before an appointment, not even when she had fake-married the man who calmly left her passport on a side table like bait and walked out.

Not that this world was so different from living with Grigor, Viveka thought, lifting her baleful gaze from the temptation of her passport to gaze around Mikolas's private domain. Grigor had been a bully, but he'd lived very well. His island mansion had had all the same accoutrements she found in Mikolas's penthouse: a guest room with a full bath, a well-stocked wine fridge and pantry, a pool on a deck overlooking a stunning view.

None of it put her at ease. She was still nervous. Expectation hung over her. Or rather, the question of what Mikolas expected.

And whether she could deliver.

Not sex, she reminded herself, trying to keep her mind off that. She turned to tormenting herself with anxiety over how well she would perform in the social arena. She wasn't shy, but she wasn't particularly outgoing. She wasn't particularly pretty, either, and she had a feeling every other woman at this party would be gorgeous if

Mikolas thought she needed four hours of beautification to bring her up to par.

The stylist's preparation wasn't all shoring up of her looks, however. It was pampering with massage and a mani-pedi, encouragement to doze by the pool while last-minute adjustments were made to her dress, and a final polish on her hair and makeup that gave her more confidence than she expected.

As she eyed herself in the gold cocktail dress, she was floored at how chic she looked. The cowled halter bodice hung low across her modest chest and the snug fabric hugged her hips in a way that flattered her figure without being obvious. The color brought out the lighter strands in her hair and made her skin look like fresh cream.

The stylist had trimmed her mop, then let its natural wave take over, only parting it to the side and adding two little pins so her face was prettily framed while the rest fell away in a shiny waterfall around her shoulders. She applied false eyelashes, but they were just long enough to make her feel extra feminine, not ridiculous.

"I've never known how to make my bottom lip look as wide as the top," Viveka complained as her lips were painted. The bruise Grigor had left there had faded overnight to unnoticeable.

"Why would you want to?" the woman chided her. "You have a very classic look. Like old Hollywood."

Viveka snorted, but she'd take it.

She had to acknowledge she was delighted with the end result, but became shy when she moved into the lounge to find Mikolas waiting for her.

He took her breath, standing at the window with a drink in his hand. He'd paired his suit with a gray shirt and charcoal tie, ever the dark horse. It was all cut to perfection against his frame. His profile was silhouetted against the glow of the Acropolis in the distance. *Zeus*, she thought, and her knees weakened.

He turned his head and even though he was already quite motionless, she sensed time stopping. Maybe they both held their breath. She certainly did, anxious for kind judgment.

Behind her, the stylist left, leaving more tension as the quiet of the apartment settled with the departure of the lift.

Viveka's eyes dampened. She swallowed to ease the dryness in the back of her throat. "I have no idea how to act in this situation," she confessed.

"A date?" he drawled, drawing in a breath as though coming back to life.

"Is that all it is?" Why did it feel so monumental? "I keep thinking that I'm supposed to act like we're involved, but I don't know much about you."

"Don't you?" His cheek ticked and she had the impression he didn't like how much she did know.

"I guess I know you're the kind of man who saves a stranger's life."

That seemed to surprise him.

She searched his enigmatic gaze, asking softly, "Why did you?" Her voice held all of the turbulent emotions he had provoked with the act.

"It was nothing," he dismissed, looking away to set down his glass.

"Please don't say that." But was it realistic to think her life had meant something to him after one glimpse? No. Her heart squeezed. "It wasn't nothing to me."

"I don't know," he admitted tightly. His eyes moved over her like he was looking for clues. "But I wasn't thinking ahead to this. Saving a person's life shouldn't be contingent on repayment. I just reacted."

Unlike his grandfather, who had wanted to know he

was actually getting his grandson before stepping in. *Oh, Mikolas.*

For a moment, the walls between them were gone and the bright, magnetic thing between them tugged. She wanted to move forward and offer comfort. Be whatever he needed her to be.

For one second, he seemed to hover on a tipping point. Then a layer of aloofness fell over him like a cloak.

"I don't think anyone will have trouble believing we're involved when you look at me like that." He smiled, but it was a tad cruel. "If I wasn't finally catching up to someone I've been chasing for a while, I would accept your invitation. But I have other priorities."

She flinched, stunned by the snub.

Fortunately he didn't see it, having turned away to press the call button to bring back the elevator.

She moved on stiff legs to join him, fighting tears of wounded self-worth. Her throat ached. Compassion wasn't a character flaw, she reminded herself. Just because Grigor and Hildy and this *jackass* weren't capable of appreciating what she offered didn't mean she was worthless.

She couldn't help her reaction to him. Maybe if she wasn't such an incurable *virgin*, she'd be able to handle him, she thought furiously, but that's what she was and she hated him for taunting her with it.

She was wallowing so deep in silent offense, she moved automatically, leaving the elevator as the doors opened, barely taking in her surroundings until she heard her worst nightmare say, *"There she is."*

CHAPTER EIGHT

MIKOLAS WAS KICKING himself as the elevator came to a halt.

Viveka had been so beautiful when she had walked into the lounge, his heart had lurched. An unfamiliar light-heartedness had overcome him. It hadn't been the money spent on her appearance. It was the authentic beauty that shone through all the labels and products, the kind that waterfalls and sunsets possessed. You couldn't buy that kind of awe-inspiring magnificence. You couldn't ignore it, either, when it was right in front of you. And when you let yourself appreciate it, it felt almost healing…

He never engaged in rose smelling and sunset gazing. He lived in an armored tank of wealth, emotional distance and superficial relationships. His dates were formalities, a type of foreplay. It wasn't sexism. He invested even less in his dealings with men.

His circle never included people as unguarded as Viveka, with her defensive shyness and yearning for acceptance. Somehow that guilelessness of hers got through his barriers as aggression never would. She'd asked him why he'd saved her life and before he knew it, he was re-living the memory of pleading with everything in him for his grandfather—a stranger at the time—to save *him*.

Erebus hadn't.

Not right away. Not without proof.

Words such as *despair* and *anguish* were not strong enough to describe what came over him when he thought back to it.

She had had an idea what it was, though, without his having to say a word. He had seen more in her eyes than an offer of sex. Empathy, maybe. Whatever it was, it had been something so real, it had scared the hell out of him. He couldn't lie with a woman when his inner psyche was torn open that far. Who knew what else would spill out?

He needed escape and she needed to stay the hell back.

He was so focused on achieving that, he walked out of the elevator not nearly as aware of his surroundings as he should be.

As they came alongside the security desk, he heard, "There she is," and turned to see Grigor lunging at Viveka, nearly pulling her off her feet, filthy vitriol spewing over her scream of alarm.

"—think you can investigate me? I'll show you what murder looks like—"

Reflex took over and Mikolas had broken Grigor's nose before he knew what he was doing.

Grigor fell to the floor, blood leaking between his clutching fingers. Mikolas bent to grab him by the collar, but his security team rushed in from all directions, pressing Mikolas's Neanderthal brain back into its cave.

"Call the police," he bit out, straightening and putting his arm around Viveka. "Make sure you mention his threats against her life."

He escorted Viveka outside to his waiting limo, afraid, genuinely afraid, of what he would do to the man if he stayed.

As her adrenaline rush faded in the safety of the limo, Viveka went from what felt like a screaming pitch of tension to being a spent match, brittle and thin, charred and cold.

It wasn't just Grigor surprising her like that. It was how crazed he'd seemed. If Mikolas hadn't stepped in… But he had and seeing Grigor on the receiving end of the sickening thud of a fist connecting to flesh wasn't as satisfying as she had always imagined it would be.

She *hated* violence.

She figured Mikolas must feel the same, given his past. Those last minutes as they'd come downstairs kept replaying in her mind. She'd been filled with resentment as they'd left the elevator, hotly thinking that if saving a person's life didn't require repayment, why was he forcing her to go to this stupid party? He said she was under his protection, but it was more like she was under his thumb.

But the minute she was threatened, the very second it had happened, he had leaped in to save her. Again.

It was as ground-shaking as the first time.

Especially when the aftermath had him feeling the bones in his repaired hand like he was checking for fractures. His thick silence made her feel sick.

"Mikolas, I'm sorry," Viveka said in a voice that flaked like dry paint.

She was aware of his head swinging around but couldn't look at him.

"You know I only had Trina's interest at heart when I came to Greece, but it was inconsiderate to you. I didn't appreciate the situation I was putting you in with Grigor—"

"That's enough, Viveka."

She jolted, stung by the graveled tone. It made the blood congeal in her veins and she hunched deeper into her seat, turning her gaze to the window.

"That was my fault." Self-recrimination gave his voice

a bitter edge. "We signed papers for the merger today. I made sure he knew why I was squeezing him out. He tried to cheat me."

It was her turn to swing a surprised look at him. He looked like he was barely holding himself in check.

"I wouldn't have discovered it until after I was married to Trina, but your interference gave me a chance to review everything. I wound up getting a lot of concessions beyond our original deal. Things were quite ugly by the end. He was already blaming you so I told him I'd started an investigation. I should have expected something like this. I owe *you* the apology."

She didn't know what to say.

"You helped me by stopping the wedding. Thank you. I hope to hell the investigation puts him in jail," he added tightly.

He was staring at her intently, nostrils flared.

Her mouth trembled. She felt awkward and shy and tried to cover it with a lame attempt at levity. "Between Grigor and Hildy, I've spent most of my life being told I was an albatross of one kind or another. It's refreshing to hear I've had a positive effect for once. I thought for sure you were going to yell at me..." Her voice broke.

She sniffed and tried to catch a tear with a trembling hand before it ruined her makeup.

He swore and before she realized what he was doing, he had her in his lap.

"Did he hurt you? Let me see your arm where he grabbed you," he demanded, his touch incredibly gentle as he lightly explored.

"Don't be sweet to me right now, Mikolas. I'll fall apart."

"You prefer the goon from the lobby?" he growled, making a semihysterical laugh bubble up.

"You're not a goon," she protested, but obeyed the hard arms that closed around her and cuddled into him, numb fingers stealing under the edge of his jacket to warm against his steady heartbeat.

He ran soothing hands over her and let out a breath, tension easing from both of them in small increments.

She was still feeling shaky when they reached the Makricosta Olympus.

"I hate these things," he muttered as he escorted her to the brightly decorated ballroom. "We should have stayed in."

Too late to leave. People were noting their entrance.

"Do you mind if I...?" she asked as she spotted the ladies' room off to the right. She could only imagine how she looked.

A muscle pulsed in his jaw, like he didn't want her out of his sight, but after one dismayed heartbeat he said, "I'll be at the bar."

Reeling under an onslaught of gratitude and confusion and yearning, she hurried to the powder room and moved directly to the mirror to check her makeup. She felt like a disaster, but had only a couple of smudges to dab away.

"Synchórisi," the woman next to her said, gaze down as she fiddled with the straps on her shimmery black dress. Releasing a distinctly British curse she said, "My Greek is nonexistent. Is there any chance you speak English?"

Viveka straightened from the mirror, taking a breath to gather her composure. "I do."

"Oh, you're upset." The woman was a delicate blonde and her smile turned concerned. "I'm sorry. I shouldn't have bothered you."

"No, I'm fine," she dismissed with a wobbly smile. The woman was doing her a favor, not letting her dwell on all the mixed emotions coursing through her. "Not the bad kind of crying."

"Oh, did he do something nice?" she asked with a pleased grin. "Because husbands really ought to, now and again."

"He's not my husband, but…" Viveka thought of Mikolas saving her and thanking her for the wedding debacle. Her heart wobbled again and she had to swallow back a fresh rush of emotion. "He did."

"Good. I'm Clair, by the way." She offered her free hand to shake while her other hand stayed against her chest, the straps of her halter-style bodice dangling over her slender fingers.

"Viveka. Call me Vivi." Eyeing the straps, she guessed, "Wardrobe malfunction?"

"The worst! Is there any chance you have a pin?"

"I don't. Can you tie them?" She circled her finger in the air. "Turn around. Let's see what happened to the catch."

They quickly determined the catch was long gone and they were too short to tie.

"I bet a tiepin would hold it. Give me a minute. I'll ask Mikolas for his," Viveka offered.

"Good idea, but ask my husband," Clair said. "Then I won't have to worry about returning it."

Viveka chuckled. "Let me guess. Your husband is the man in the suit?" She thumbed toward the ballroom filled with a hundred men wearing ties and jackets.

Clair grinned. "Mine's easy to spot. He's the one with a scar here." She touched her cheek, drawing a vertical line. "Also, he's holding my purse. I needed two hands to keep myself together long enough to get in here or I would have texted him to come help me."

"Got it. I'll be right back."

* * *

Mikolas stood with the back of his hand pressed to a scotch on the rocks. So much for behaving mainstream and law-abiding, he thought dourly.

He was watching for Viveka, still worried about her. When she had apologized, he'd been floored, already kicking himself for bringing her downstairs at all. He could be at home making love to her, none of this having happened. Instead, he'd let her be terrorized.

There she was. He tried to catch her eye, but she scanned the room, then made for a small group in the far corner from the band.

Mikolas swore under his breath as she approached his target: Aleksy Dmitriev. The Russian magnate had logistics interests that crossed paths with his own from the Aegean through to the Black Sea. Dmitriev had never once returned Mikolas's calls and it grated. He hated being the petitioner and resented the other man for relegating him to that role.

Mikolas knew why Dmitriev was avoiding him. He was scrupulous about his reputation. He wouldn't risk sullying it by attaching himself to the Petrides name.

While Mikolas knew working with Dmitriev would be another seal of legitimacy for his own organization. That's why he wanted to partner with him.

Dmitriev stared at Viveka like she was from Mars, then handed her his drink. He removed his tiepin, handed it to her, then took back his glass. When she asked him something else, he nodded at a window ledge where a pocketbook sat. Viveka scooped it up and headed back to the ladies' room.

What the *hell*?

Viveka was thankful for the small drama that Clair had provided, but flashed right back to seesaw emotions when she returned to Mikolas's side. He stood out without trying. He wore that look of disinterest that alpha wolves wore with their packs, confident in his superiority so with nothing to prove.

A handful of men in sharp suits had clustered around him. They all wore bored-looking women on their arms.

Mikolas interrupted the conversation when she arrived. He took her hand and made a point of introducing her.

She smiled, but the man who'd been speaking was quick to dismiss her and continue what he was saying. He struck her as the toady type who sucked up to powerful men in hopes of catching scraps. The way the women were held like dogs on a leash was very telling, too.

Viveka let her gaze stray to the other groups, seeing the dynamic was very different in Clair's circle, where she was nodding at whoever was speaking, smiling and fully engaged in the conversation. Her husband was looking their way and she pressed a brief smile onto her mouth.

Nothing.

Mikolas had been right about invisible barriers.

"This must be your new bride if the merger has gone through," one of the other men broke in to say, frowning with confusion as he jumped his gaze between her and Mikolas.

I have a name, Viveka wanted to remind the man, but apparently on this side of the room, she was a "this."

"No," Mikolas replied, offering no further explanation.

Viveka wanted to roll her eyes. It was basic playground etiquette to act friendly if you wanted to be included in the games. That was what he wanted, wasn't it? Was this what he had meant when he had said it was her task to change how he was viewed?

"I stopped the wedding," she blurted. "He was supposed to marry my sister, but…" She cleared her throat as she looked up at Mikolas, laughing inwardly at the ridiculous claim she was about to make. "I fell head over heels. You weren't far behind me, were you?"

Mikolas wore much the same incredulous expression he had when he'd lifted her veil.

"Your sister can't be happy about that," one of the women said, perking up for the first time.

"She's fine with it," Viveka assured with a wave. "She'd be the first to say you should follow your heart, wouldn't she?" she prodded Mikolas, highly entertained with her embellishment on the truth. *Laugh with me*, she entreated.

"Let's dance." His grip on her hand moved to her elbow and he turned her toward the floor. As he took her in his arms seconds later, he said, "I cannot believe you just said that."

"Oh, come on. You said we should appear long-term. Now they think we're in love and by the way, your friends are a pile of sexist jerks."

"I don't have friends," he growled. "Those are people whose names I know."

His touch on her seemed to crackle and spark, making her feel sensitized all over. At the same time, she thought she heard something in his tone that was a warning.

Dancing with him was easy. They moved really well together right out of the gate. She let herself become immersed in the moment, where the music transmitted through them, making them move in unison. He held her in his strong arms and the closeness was deliciously stimulating. Her heart fluttered and she feared she really would tumble into deep feelings for him.

"They should call it heels over head," she said, trying to break the spell. "We're head over heels right now. It means you're upright."

He halted their dance, started to say something, but off to her right, Clair said, "Vivi. Let me introduce you properly. My husband, Aleksy Dmitriev."

Mikolas pulled himself back from a suffocating place where his emotions had knotted up. She'd been joking with all that talk of love, he knew she had, but even having a falsehood put out there to those vultures had made him uncomfortable.

He had been pleased to feel nothing for Trina. He would have introduced her as his wife and the presumption of affection might have been made, but it wouldn't have been true. It certainly wouldn't have been something that could be used to prey on his psyche, not deep down where his soul kept well out of the light.

Viveka was different. Her blasé claim of love between them was an overstatement and he ought to be able to dismiss it. But as much as he wanted to feel nothing toward her, he couldn't. Everything he'd done since meeting her proved to himself that he felt *something*.

He tried to ignore how disarmed that made him feel, concentrating instead on finding himself face-to-face with the man who'd been evading him for two years.

Dmitriev looked seriously peeved, mouth flat and the scar on his face standing out white.

It's the Viveka effect, Mikolas wanted to drawl.

Dmitriev nodded a stiff acknowledgment to Viveka's warm smile.

"Did you think you were being robbed?" Viveka teased him.

"It crossed my mind." Dmitriev lifted a cool gaze to Mikolas. *When I realized she was with you*, he seemed to say.

Mikolas kept a poker face as Viveka finished the introduction, but deep down he waved a flag of triumph over Dmitriev being forced to come to him.

It was only an introduction, he reminded himself. A hook. There was no reeling in this kind of fish without a fight.

"We have to get back to the children," Clair was saying. "But I wanted to thank you again for your help."

"My pleasure. I hope we'll run into each other in future," Viveka said. Mikolas had to give her credit. She was a natural at this role.

"Perhaps you can add us to your donor list," Mikolas said. *I do my homework*, he told Dmitriev with a flick of his gaze. Clair ran a foundation that benefited orphanages across Europe. Mikolas had been waiting for the right opportunity to use this particular door. He had no scruples about walking through it as Viveka's plus one.

"May I?" Clair brightened. "I would love that!"

Mikolas brought out one of his cards and a pen, scrawling Viveka's details on the back, mentally noting he should have some cards of her own printed.

"I'd give you one of mine, but I'm out," Clair said, showing hands that were empty of all but a diamond and platinum wedding band. "I've been talking up my fundraising dinner in Paris all night—oh! Would you happen to be going there at the end of next month? I could put you on that list, too."

"Please do. I'm sure we can make room," Mikolas said smoothly. *We, our, us.* It was a foreign language to him, but surprisingly easy to pick up.

"I'm being shameless, aren't I?" Clair said to her husband, dipping her chin while lifting eyes filled with playful culpability.

The granite in Dmitriev's face eased to what might pass for affection, but he sounded sincere as he contradicted her. "You're passionate. It's one of your many appealing qualities. Don't apologize for it."

He produced one of his own cards and stole the pen Mikolas still held, wordlessly offering both to his wife.

I see what you're doing, Dmitriev said with a level stare at Mikolas while Clair wrote. Dmitriev was of similar height and build to Mikolas. He was probably the only man in the room whom Mikolas would instinctively respect without testing the man first. He emanated the same air of self-governance that Mikolas enjoyed and had more than demonstrated he couldn't be manipulated into doing anything he didn't want to do.

He provoked all of Mikolas's instincts to dominate, which made getting this man's contact details that much more significant.

But even though he wasn't happy to be giving up his direct number, it was clear by Dmitriev's hard look that it was a choice he made consciously and deliberately— for his wife.

Mikolas might have lost a few notches of regard for the man if his hand hadn't still been throbbing from connecting with Grigor's jaw. Which he'd done for Viveka.

It was an uncomfortable moment of realizing it didn't matter how insulated a man believed himself to be. A woman—one for whom he'd gone heels over head—could completely undermine him.

Which was why Mikolas firmed himself against letting Viveka become anything more than the sexual infatuation she was. The only reason he was bent out of shape was because they hadn't had sex yet, he told himself. Once he'd had her, and anticipation was no longer clouding his brain, he'd be fine.

"That was what we came for," he said, after the couple

had departed. He indicated the card Viveka was about to drop into her pocketbook. "We can leave now, too."

Mikolas made a face at the card the doorman handed him on their way in, explaining he was supposed to call the police in the morning to make a statement. They didn't speak until they were in the penthouse.

"I've wanted Dmitriev's private number for a while. You did well tonight," he told her as he moved to pour two glasses at the bar.

"It didn't feel like I did anything," she murmured, quietly glowing under his praise. She yearned for approval more than most people did, having been treated as an annoyance for most of her early years.

"It's easy for you. You don't mind talking to people," he remarked, setting aside the bottle and picking up the glasses to come across and offer hers. "Do you take yours with water?"

"I haven't had ouzo in years," she murmured, trying to hide her reaction to him by inhaling the licorice aroma off the alcohol. "I shouldn't have had it when I did. I was far too young. *Yiamas*."

Mikolas threw most of his back in one go, eyes never leaving hers.

"What, um…?" Oh, this man easily emptied her brain. "You, um, don't like talking to people? You said you hated those sorts of parties."

"I do," he dismissed.

"Why?"

"Many reasons." He shrugged, moving to set aside his glass. "My grandfather had a lot to hide when I first came to live with him. I was too young to be confident in my own opinions and didn't trust anyone with details about myself. As an adult, I'm surrounded by people who are so superficial, crying about ridiculous little trials, I can't summon any interest in whatever it is they're saying."

"Should I be complimented that you talk to me?" she teased.

"I keep trying not to." Even that was delivered with self-deprecation tilting his mouth.

Her heart panged. She longed to know everything about him.

His gaze fixed on her collarbone. He reached out to take her hair back from her shoulder. "You've had one sparkle of glitter here all night," he said, fingertip grazing the spot.

It was a tiny touch, an inconsequential remark, but it devastated her. Her insides trembled and she went very still, her entire being focused on the way he ever so lightly tried to coax the fleck off her skin.

Behind him, the lamps cast amber reflections against the black windows. The pool glowed a ghostly blue on the deck beyond. It made radiance seem to emanate from him, but maybe that was her foolish, dampening eyes.

Painful yearning rose in her. It was familiar, yet held a searing twist. For a long time she had wanted a man in her life. She wanted a confidant, someone she could kiss and touch and sleep beside. She wanted intimacy, physical and emotional.

She had never expected this kind of corporeal desire. She hadn't believed it existed, definitely hadn't known it could overwhelm her like this.

How could she feel so attracted and needy toward a man who was so ambivalent toward her? It was excruciating.

But when he took her glass and set it aside, she didn't resist. She kept holding his gaze as his hands came up to frame her face. And waited.

His gaze lowered to her lips.

They felt like they plumped with anticipation.

She looked at his mouth, not thinking about anything except how much she wanted his kiss. His lips were so beautifully shaped, full, but undeniably masculine. The tip of his tongue wet them, then he lowered his head, came closer.

The first brush of his damp lips against hers made her shudder in release of tension while tightening with anticipation. She gasped in surrender as his hands whispered down to warm her upper arms, then grazed over the fabric of her dress.

Then his mouth opened wider on hers and it was like a straight shot of ouzo, burning down her center and warming her through, making her drunk. Long, dragging kisses made her more and more lethargic by degrees, until he drew back and she realized her hand was at the back of his head, the other curled into the fabric of his shirt beneath his jacket.

He released her long enough to shrug out of his jacket, loosened his tie, then pulled her close again.

Her head felt too heavy for her neck, easily falling into the fingers that combed through her hair and splayed against her scalp. He kissed her again, harder this time, revealing the depth of passion in him. The aggression. It was scary in the way thunder and high winds and landslides were both terrifying and awe-inspiring. She clung to him, moaning in submission. Not just to him, but to her own desire.

They shuffled their feet closer, sealing themselves one against the other, trying to press through clothing and skin so their cells would weave into a single being.

The thrust of his aroused flesh pressed into her stomach and a wrench of conflict went through her. This moment was too perfect. It felt too good to be held like this, to ruin it with humiliating confessions about her defect and entreaties for special treatment. She felt too much toward him, not least gratitude and wonder and a regard that was tied to his compliments and his protection and his hand dragging her to the surface of the water before he'd even known her name.

She ached to share something with him, had since almost the first moment she'd seen him. *Be careful*, she told herself. Sex was powerful. She was already very susceptible to him.

But she couldn't make herself stop touching him. Her hands strayed to feel his shape, tracing him through his pants. It was a bold move for her, but she was entranced. Curious and enthralled. There was a part of her that desperately wanted to know she could please a man, *this* man in particular.

His breath hissed in and his whole body hardened. He gathered his muscles as if he was preparing to dip and lift her against his chest.

She drew back.

His arms twitched in protest, but he let her look at where his erection pressed against the front of his suit pants. He was really aroused. She licked her lips, not superconfident in what she wanted to do, but she wanted to do it.

She unbuckled his belt.

His hands searched under the fall of her hair. His touch ran down her spine, releasing the back of her dress.

As the cool air swirled from her waist around to her belly, her stomach fluttered with nerves. She swallowed, aware of her breasts as her bodice loosened and shifted against her bare nipples. She shivered as his fingertips stroked her bare back. Her hands shook as she pulled his shirt free and clumsily opened his buttons, then spread the edges wide so she could admire his chest.

Pressing her face to his taut skin, she rubbed back and forth and back again, absorbing the feel of him with her brow and lips, drawing in his scent, too moved to smile when he said something in a tight voice and slid his palm under her dress to brand her bottom with his hot palm.

Her mouth opened of its own accord, painting a wet path to his nipple. She explored the shape with her tongue, earned another tight curse, then hit the other one with a draw of her mouth. Foreplay and foreshadowing, she thought with a private smile.

"Bedroom," he growled, bringing his hands out of her dress and setting them on her waist, thumbs against her hip bones as he pressed her back a step.

Dazed at how her own arousal was climbing, Viveka smiled, pleased to see the glitter in his eyes and the flush on his cheeks. It increased her tentative confidence. She placed her hands on his chest and let her gaze stray past him to the armchair, silently urging him toward it.

Mikolas let her have her way out of sheer fascination. He refused to call it weakness, even though he was definitely under a spell of some kind. He had known there was a sensual woman inside Viveka screaming to get out. He hadn't expected this, though.

It wasn't manipulation, either. There were no sly smiles or knowing looks as she slid to her knees between his, kissing his neck, stroking down his front so his abdominals contracted under her tickling fingertips. She was focused and enthralled, timid but genuinely excited. It was erotic to be wanted like this. Beyond exciting.

As she finished opening his pants, his brain shorted

out. He was vaguely aware of lifting his hips so she could better expose him. The sob of want that left her was the kind of siren call that had been the downfall of ancient seamen. He nearly exploded on the spot.

He was thick and aching, so hot he wanted to rip his clothes from his body, but he was transfixed. He gripped the armrest in his aching hand and the back of the chair over his shoulder with the other, trying to hold on to his control.

He shouldn't let her do this, he thought distantly. His discipline was in shreds. But therein lay her power. He couldn't make himself stop her. That was the naked truth.

She took him in hand, her touch light, her pale hands pretty against the dark strain of his flesh. He was so hard he thought he'd break, so aroused he couldn't breathe, and so captivated, he could only hold still and watch through slitted eyes as her head dipped.

He groaned aloud as her hair slid against his exposed skin and her wet mouth took him in, narrowing his world to the tip of his sex. It was the most exquisite sensation, nearly undoing him between one breath and the next. She kept up the tender, lascivious act until he was panting, barely able to speak.

"I can't hold back," he managed to grit out.

Slowly her head lifted, pupils huge as pansies in the dim light, mouth swollen and shiny like he'd been kissing her for hours.

"I don't want you to." Her hot breath teased his wet flesh, tightening all his nerve endings, pulling him to a point that ended where her tongue flicked out and stole what little remained of his willpower.

He gave himself up to her. This was for both of them, he told himself. He would have staying power after this.

He'd make it good for her, as good as this. Nothing could be better, but at least this good—

The universe exploded and he shouted his release to the ceiling.

CHAPTER NINE

VIVEKA HUGGED THE front of her gaping dress to her breasts and could barely meet her own glassy eyes in the mirror. She was flushed and aroused and deeply self-conscious. She couldn't believe what she'd just done, but she had no regrets. She had enjoyed giving Mikolas pleasure. It had been extraordinary.

She had needed that for herself. She wasn't a failure in the bedroom after all. Okay, the lounge, she allowed with a smirk.

Her hand trembled as she removed the pins from her hair, pride quickly giving way to sexual frustration and embarrassment. Even a hint of desolation. If she wasn't such a freak, if she wasn't afraid she'd lose herself completely, they could have found release together.

Being selfless was satisfying in other ways, though. He might be thanking her for breaking up the wedding and saving him a few bucks, but she was deeply grateful for the way he had acknowledged her as worth saving, worth protecting.

The bathroom door that she'd swung almost closed pushed open, making her heart catch.

Mikolas took up a lazy pose that made carnal hunger clench mercilessly in her middle. The flesh that was hot with yearning squeezed and ached.

His open shirt hung off his shoulders, framing the light pattern of hair that ran down from his breastbone. His unfastened pants gaped low across his hips, revealing the narrow line of hair from his navel. His eyelids were heavy, disguising his thoughts, but his voice was gritty enough to make her shiver.

"You're taking too long."

The words were a sensual punch, flushing her with eager heat. At the same time, alarm bells—anxious clangs of performance anxiety—went off within her, cooling her ardor.

"For?" She knew what he meant, but she'd taken care of his need. They were done. Weren't they? If she'd ever had sex before, she wouldn't be so unsure.

"Finishing what you started."

"You did finish. You can't—" Was he growing hard again? It looked like his boxers were straining against the open fly of his pants.

She read. She knew basic biology. She knew he'd climaxed, so how was that happening? Was she really so incapable of gratifying a man that even oral sex failed to do the job?

"You can't… Men don't…again. Can they?" She trailed off, blushing and hating that his first real smile came at the expense of her inexperience.

"I'll last longer this time," he promised drily. "But I don't want to wait. Get your butt in that bed, or I'll have you here, bent over the sink."

Oh, she was never going to be that spontaneous. Ever. And for a first time? While he talked about lasting a *long* time?

"No." She hitched the shoulder of her dress and reached behind herself to close it. "You finished. We're done." Her face was on fire, but inside she was growing cold.

He straightened off the doorjamb. "What?"

"I don't want to have sex." Not entirely true. She longed to understand the mystique behind the act, but his talk of sink-bending only told her how far apart they were in experience. The more she thought about it, the more she went into a state of panic. Not him. Not tonight when she was already an emotional mess.

She struggled to close her zip, then crossed her arms, taking a step backward even though he hadn't moved toward her.

He frowned. "You don't want sex?"

Was he deaf?

"No," she assured him. Her back came up against the towel rail, which was horribly uncomfortable. She waved toward the door he was blocking. "You can go."

He didn't move, only folded his own arms and rocked back on his heels. "Explain this to me. And use small words, because I don't understand what happened between the lounge and here."

"Nothing happened." She couldn't stand that he was making her wallow in her inadequacy. "You...I mean, I *thought* I gave you what you wanted. If you thought—"

He didn't even want her. Not really. He would decide *if* and *when*, she recalled.

Good luck with that, champ. Her body made that decision for everyone involved, no matter what her head said.

Do not cry. Oh, she hated her body right now. Her stupid, dumb body that had made her life go so far sideways she didn't even understand how she was standing here having this awful conversation.

"Can you just go?" She glared at him for making this so hard for her, but her eyes stung. She bet they were red and pathetic looking. If he made her tell him, and he laughed— *"Please?"*

He stayed there one more long moment, searching her gaze, before slowly moving back, taking the door with him, closing it as he left. The click sounded horribly final.

Viveka stepped forward and turned the lock, not because she was afraid he'd come in looking for sex, but afraid he'd come in and catch her crying.

With a wrench of her hand, she started the shower.

Mikolas was sitting in the dark, nursing an ouzo, when he heard Viveka's door open.

He'd closed it himself an hour ago, when he'd gone in to check on her and found her on the guest bed, hair wrapped in a towel, one of his monogramed robes swallowing her in black silk. She'd been fast asleep, her very excellent legs bare to midthigh, a crumpled tissue in her lax grip. Several more had been balled up around her.

Rather than easing his mind, rather than answering any of the million questions crowding his thoughts, the sight had caused the turmoil inside him to expand, spinning in fresh and awful directions. Was he such a bad judge of a woman's needs? Why did he feel as though he'd taken advantage of her? She had pressed him into this very chair. She had opened his pants. She had gone down and told him to let go.

He'd been high as a kite when he had tracked her into her bathroom, certain he'd find her naked and waiting for him. Every red blood cell he possessed had been keening with anticipation.

It hadn't gone that way at all.

She'd felt threatened.

He was a strong, dominant man. He knew that and tried to take his aggressive nature down a notch in the bedroom. He knew what it was like to be brutalized by someone bigger and more powerful. He would never do that to the smaller and weaker.

He kept having flashes of slender, delicate Viveka looking anxious as she noticed he was still hard. He thought about her fear of Grigor. A libido-killing dread had been tying his stomach in knots ever since.

He couldn't bear the idea of her being abused that way. He'd punched Grigor tonight, but he wished he had killed him. There was still time, he kept thinking. He wasn't so far removed from his bloodline that he didn't know how to make a man disappear.

He listened to Viveka's bare feet approach, thinking he couldn't blame her for trying to sneak out on him.

She paused as she arrived at the end of the hall, obviously noticing his shadowed figure. She had changed into pajamas and clipped up her hair. She tucked a stray wisp behind her ear.

"I'm hungry. Do you want toast?" She didn't wait for his response, charging past him through to the kitchen.

He unbent and slowly made his way into the kitchen behind her.

She had turned on the light over the stove and kept her back to him as she filled the kettle at the sink. After she set the switch to Boil, she went to the freezer and found a frozen loaf of sliced bread.

Still keeping her back to him, she broke off four slices and set them in the toaster.

"Viveka."

Her slender back flinched at the sound of his voice.

So did he. The things he was thinking were piercing his heart. He'd been bleeding internally since the likeliest explanation had struck him hours ago. When someone reacted that defensively against sexual contact, the explanation seemed really obvious.

"When you said Grigor abused you…" He wasn't a coward, but he didn't want to speak it. Didn't want to hear it. "Did he…?" His voice failed him.

Viveka really wished he hadn't still been up. In her perfect world, she never would have had to face him again, but as the significance of his broken question struck her, she realized she couldn't avoid telling him.

She buried her face in her hands. "No. That's not it. Not at all."

She *really* didn't want to face him.

But she had to.

Shoulders sagging, she turned and wilted against the cupboards behind her. Her hands stayed against her stinging cheeks.

"Please don't laugh." That's what the one other man she'd told had done. She'd felt so raw it was no wonder she hadn't been able to go all the way with him, either.

She dared a peek at Mikolas. He'd closed a couple of buttons, but his shirt hung loose over his pants. His hair was ruffled, as though his fingers had gone through it a few times. His jaw was shadowed with stubble and he looked tired. Troubled.

"I won't laugh." He hadn't slept, even though it was past two in the morning. For some reason that flipped her heart.

"I wasn't a very happy teenager, obviously," she began. "I did what a lot of disheartened young girls do. I looked for a boy to save me. There was a nice one who didn't have much, but he had a kind heart. I can't say I loved him, not even puppy love, but I liked him. We started seeing each other on the sly, behind Grigor's back. After a while it seemed like the time to, you know, have sex."

The toaster made a few pinging, crackling noises and

the kettle was beginning to hiss. She chewed her lip, fully grown and many years past it, but still chagrined.

"I mean, fourteen is criminally young, I realize that. And not having any really passionate feelings for him... It's not a wonder it didn't work."

"Didn't work," he repeated, like he was testing words he didn't know.

She clenched her eyes shut. "He didn't fit. It hurt too much and I made him stop. Please don't laugh," she rushed to add.

"I'm not laughing." His voice was low and grave. "You're telling me you're a virgin? You never tried again?"

"Oh, I did," she said to the ceiling, insides scraped hollow.

She moved around looking for the tea and butter, trying to escape how acutely humiliating this was.

"My life was a mess for quite a while, though. Grigor found out I'd been seeing the boy and that I'd gone to the police about Mum. He kicked me out and I moved to London. *That* was a culture shock. The weather, the city. Aunt Hildy had all these rules. It wasn't until I finished my A levels and was working that I started dating again. There was a guy from work. He was very smooth. I realize now he was a player, but I was quite taken in."

The toast popped and she buttered it, taking her time, spreading right to the edges.

"He laughed when I told him why I was nervous." She scraped the knife in careful licks across the surface of the toast. "He was so determined to be The One. We fooled around a little, but he was always putting this pressure on me to go all the way. I *wanted* to have sex. It's supposed to be great, right?"

Pressure arrived behind her eyes again. She couldn't look at him, but she listened, waiting for his confirmation that yes, all the sex he'd had with his multitude of lovers had been fantastic.

Silence.

"Finally I said we could try, but it really hurt. He said it was supposed to and didn't want to stop. I lost my temper and threw him out. We haven't spoken since."

"Do you still work with him?"

"No. Old job. Long gone." The toast was buttered before her on two plates, but she couldn't bring herself to turn and see his reaction.

She was all cried out, but familiar, hopeless angst cloaked her. She just wanted to be like most people and have sex and like it.

"Are you laughing?" Her voice was thready and filled with the embarrassed anguish she couldn't disguise.

"Not at all." His voice sounded like he was talking from very far away. "I'm thinking that not in a thousand years would I have guessed that. Nothing you do fits with the way other people behave. It didn't make sense that you would give me pleasure and not want anything for yourself. You respond to me. I couldn't imagine why you didn't want sex."

"I *do* want sex," she said, flailing a frustrated hand. "I just don't want it to *hurt*." She finally turned and set his plate of toast on the island, avoiding his gaze.

The kettle boiled, giving her breathing space as she moved to make the tea. When she sat down, she went around the far end of the island and took the farthest stool from where he stood ignoring the toast and tea she'd made for him.

She couldn't make herself take a bite. Her body was hot and cold, her emotions swinging from hope to despair to worry.

"You're afraid I wouldn't stop if we tried." His voice

was solemn as he promised, "I would, you know. At any point."

A tentative hope moved through her, but she shook her head. "I don't want to be a project." Her spoon clinked lightly as she stirred the sugar into her tea. "I can't face another humiliating attempt. And yes, I've been to a doctor. There's nothing wrong. I'm just…unusually…" She sighed hopelessly. "Can we stop talking about this?"

He only pushed his hands into his pockets. "I wasn't trying to talk you into anything. Not tonight. Unless you want to," he said in a wry mutter, combing distracted fingers through his hair. "I wouldn't say no. You're not a project, Viveka. I want you rather badly."

"Do you?" She scoffed in a strained voice, reminding him, "You said *you* would decide if and when. That *I* was the only one who wanted sex. I can't help the way I react to you, you know. I might have tried with you tonight if I'd thought it would go well, but…"

Tears came into her eyes. It was silly. She was seriously dehydrated from her crying jags earlier. There shouldn't be a drop of moisture left in her.

"I wanted you to like it," she said, heart raw. "I wanted to know I could, you know, *satisfy* a man, but no. I didn't even get that right. You were still hard and—"

He muttered something under his breath and said, "Are you really that oblivious? You *did* satisfy me. You leveled me. Blew my mind. Reset the bar. I don't have words for how good that was." He sounded aggrieved as he waved toward the lounge. "My desire for you is so strong I was aroused all over again just thinking about doing the same to you. *That's* why I was hard again."

If he didn't look so uncomfortable admitting that, she might have disbelieved him.

"When we were on the yacht, you said you thought it

was exciting that I respond to you." Her chest ached as she tried to figure him out. "If the attraction is just as strong for you, why don't you want me to know? Why do you keep—I mean, before we went out tonight, you acted as if you could take it or leave it. It's *not* the same for you, Mikolas. That's why I don't think it would work."

"I never like to be at a disadvantage, Viveka. We had been talking about some difficult things. I needed space."

"But if we're equal in feeling *this* way...? Attracted, I mean, why don't you want me to know that?"

"That's not an advantage, is it?"

His words, that attitude of prevailing without mercy, scraped her down to the bones.

"You'll have to tell me sometime what that's like," she said, dabbing at a crumb and pressing it between her tight lips. "Having the advantage, I mean. Not something I've ever had the pleasure of experiencing. Not something I should want to go to bed with, frankly. So *why do I*?"

He did laugh then, but it was ironic, completely lacking any humor.

"For what it's worth, I feel the same." He walked out, leaving his toast and tea untouched.

Mikolas was trying hard to ignore the way Viveka Brice had turned his life into an amusement park. One minute it was a fun house of distorted mirrors, the next a roller coaster that ratcheted his tension only to throw him down a steep valley and around a corner he hadn't seen.

Home, he kept thinking. It was basic animal instinct. Once he was grounded in his own cave, with the safety of the familiar around him, all the ways that she'd shaken up his world would settle. He would be firmly in control again.

Of course he had to keep his balance in the dizzying teacup of her trim figure appearing in a pair of hip-hugging jeans and a completely asexual T-shirt paired with the doe-eyed wariness that had crushed his chest last night.

He couldn't say he was relieved to hear the details of her sexual misadventures. The idea of her lying naked with other men grated, but at least she hadn't been scarred by the horrifying brutality he'd begun to imagine.

On the other hand, when she had finally opened up, the nakedness in her expression had been difficult to witness. She was tough and brave and earnest and too damned sensitive. Her insecurity had reached into him in a way that antagonism couldn't. The bizarre protectiveness she already inspired in him had flared up, prompting him to assuage her fears, reassure her. He had wound up revealing himself in a way that left him mistrustful and feeling like he'd left a flank unguarded.

Not a comfortable feeling at all.

He hadn't been able to sleep. Much of it had been the ache in his body, craving release in hers. He yearned to *show* her how it could be between them. At the same time, his mind wouldn't stop turning over and over with everything that had happened since she had marched into his life. At what point would she quit pulling the rug out from under him?

"Are you taking me back in time? What is that?" She was looking out the window of the helicopter.

He leaned to see. They were approaching the mansion and the ruins built into the cliff below it.

"That is the tower where you will be imprisoned for the rest of your life." *There* was a solution, he thought.

"Don't quit your day job for comedy."

Her quick rejoinder made humor tug at the corner of his mouth. He was learning she used jokes as a defense, similar to how he was quick to pull rank and impose his control over every situation. The fact she was being cheeky now, when he was in her space, told him she was shoring up her walls against him. That niggled, but wasn't it what he wanted? Distance? Barriers?

"The Venetians built it." He gazed at her clean face so close to his, her naked lips. She smelled like tea and roses and woman. He wanted to eat her alive. "See where the stairs have been worn away by the waves?"

Viveka couldn't take in anything as she felt the warmth off the side of his face and caught the smell of his aftershave. She held herself very still, trying not to react to his closeness, but her lips tingled, longing to graze his jaw and find his mouth. Lock with him in a deep kiss.

"We preserved the ruins as best we could. Given the fortune we spent, we were allowed to build above it."

She forced her gaze to the view, instantly enchanted. What little girl hadn't dreamed of being spirited away to an island castle like in a fairy tale?

The modern mansion at the top of the cliff drew her eye unerringly. The view was never-ending in all directions and the ultracontemporary design was unique and fascinating, sprawling in odd angles that were still perfectly balanced. It was neither imposing nor frivolous. It was solid and sophisticated. Dare she say elegant?

She noticed something on the roof. "Are those solar panels?"

"*Naí.* We also have a field of wind turbines. You can't see them from here. We're planning a tidal generator, too. We only have to finalize the location."

"How ecologically responsible of you." She turned her face and they were practically nose to cheekbone.

He sat back and straightened his cuff.

"I like to be self-sufficient." A tick played at the corner of his mouth.

Under no one's power but his own. She was seeing that pattern very clearly. Should she tell him it made him predictable? she wondered with private humor.

A few minutes later, she followed him into an interior she hadn't expected despite all she'd seen so far of the way he lived. The entrance should have struck her as over the top, with its smooth marble columns and split staircase that went up to a landing overlooking, she was sure, the entire universe.

The design remained spare and masculine, however, the colors subtle and golden in the midday light. Ivory marble and black wrought iron along with accents of Hellenic blue made the place feel much warmer than she expected. As they climbed the stairs, thick fog-gray carpet muffled their steps.

The landing looked to the western horizon.

Viveka paused, experiencing a strange sensation that she was looking back toward a life that was just a blur of memory, no longer hers. Oddly, the idea slid into her heart not like a blade that cut her off from her past, but more like something that caught and anchored her here, tugging her from a sea of turbulence to pin her to this stronghold.

She rubbed her arms at the preternatural shiver that chased up her entire body, catching Mikolas's gaze as he waited for her to follow him up another level.

The uppermost floor was fronted by a lounge that was surrounded by walls of glass shaded by an overhang to keep out the heat. They were at the very top of the world here. That's how it felt. Like she'd arrived at Mount Olympus, where the gods resided.

There was a hot tub on the veranda along with lounge chairs and a small dining area. She stayed inside, glancing around the open-plan space of a breakfast nook, a sitting area with a fireplace and an imposing desk with two flat monitors with a printer on a cabinet behind it, obviously Mikolas's home office.

As she continued exploring, she heard Mikolas speaking, saying her name. She followed to an open door where a uniformed young man came out. He saw her, nodded and introduced himself as Titus, then disappeared toward the stairs.

She peered into the room. It was Trina's boudoir. Had to be. There were fresh flowers, unlit candles beside the bucket of iced champagne, crystal glasses, a peignoir set draped across the foot of the white bed, and a box of chocolates on a side table. The exterior walls were made entirely out of glass and faced east, which pleased her. She liked waking to sun.

Don't love it, she cautioned herself, but it was hard not to be charmed.

"Oh, good grief," she gasped as Mikolas opened a door to what she had assumed was a powder room. It was actually a small warehouse of prêt-à-porter.

"Did you buy all of Paris for her?" She plucked at the cuff of a one-sleeved evening gown in silver-embroidered lavender. The back wall was covered in shoes. "I hate to tell you this, but my foot is a full size bigger than Trina's."

"One of your first tasks will be to go through all of this so the seamstress can alter where necessary. The shoes can be exchanged." He shrugged one shoulder negligently.

The closet was huge, but way too small with both of them in it.

She tried to disguise her self-consciousness by picking up a shoe. When she saw the designer name, she gently rubbed the shoe on her shirt to erase her fingerprint from the patent leather and carefully replaced it.

"Change for lunch with my grandfather. But don't take too long."

"Where are you going?" she asked, poking her head out to watch him cross to a pair of double doors on the other side of her room, not back to the main part of the penthouse.

"My room." He opened one of the double doors as he reached it, revealing what she thought at first was a private sitting room, but that white daybed had a towel rolled up on the foot of it.

Drawn by curiosity, she crossed to follow him into the bathroom. Except it was more like a high-end spa. There was an enormous round tub set in a bow of glass that arched outward so the illusion for the bather was a soak in midair.

"Wow." She slowly spun to take in the extravagance, awestruck when she noted the small forest that grew in a rock garden under a skylight. A path of stones led through it to a shower *area* against the back wall. Nozzles were set into the alcove of tiled walls, ready to spray from every level and direction, including raining from the ceiling.

She clapped her hand over her mouth, laughing.

The masculine side of the room was a double sink and mirror designed along the black-and-white simplistic lines Mikolas seemed to prefer, bracketed by a discreet door to a private toilet stall that also gave access to his bedroom. Her side was a reflection of his, with one sink removed to make way for a makeup bench and a vanity of drawers already filled with unopened cosmetics.

"You live like this," she murmured, closing the drawer.

"So do you. Now."

Temporarily, she reminded herself, but it was still like trying to grasp the expanse of the universe. Too much to comprehend.

A white robe that matched the black ones she'd already worn hung on a hook. She flipped the lapel enough to see the monogram, expecting a T and finding an M. She sputtered out another laugh. He was so predictably possessive!

"Can you be ready in twenty minutes?"

"Of course," she said faintly. "Unless I get lost in the forest on the way back to my room."

My room. Freudian slip. She dropped her gaze to the mosaic in the floor, then walked through her water closet to her room.

It was only as she stood debating a pleated skirt versus a sleeveless floral print dress that the significance of that shared bathroom struck her: he could walk in on her naked. Anytime.

CHAPTER TEN

VIVEKA WASN'T SURE what she expected Mikolas's grandfather to look like. A mafia don from an old American movie? Or like many of the other retired Greek men who sat outside village *kafenions*, maybe wearing a flat cap and a checked shirt, face lined by sun and a hard life in the vineyard or at sea?

Erebus Petrides was the consummate old-world gentleman. He wore a suit as he shared a drink with them before they dined. He had a bushy white mustache and excellent posture despite his stocky weight and the cane he used to walk. He and Mikolas didn't look much alike, but they definitely had the same hammered silver eyes and their voices were two keys of a similar strong, commanding timbre.

Erebus spoke English, but preferred Greek, stretching her to recall a vocabulary she hadn't tested in nine years—something he gently reproached her over. It was a pleasant meal that could have been any "Meet the Parents" occasion as they politely got to know each other. She had to keep reminding herself that the charismatic old man was actually a notorious criminal.

"He seems very nice," she said after Erebus had retired for an afternoon rest.

Mikolas was showing her around the rest of the house.

They'd come out to the pool deck where a cabana was set up like a sheikh's tent off to the side and the Ionian Sea gleamed into the horizon.

Mikolas didn't respond and she glanced up to see his mouth give a cynical twitch.

"No?" she prompted, surprised.

"He wouldn't have saved me if I hadn't proven to be his grandson."

Her heart skipped and veered as she absorbed that none of this would have happened. She wouldn't be here and neither would he. They never would have met. *What would have become of that orphaned boy?*

"Do you wish that your mother had told your father about you?"

"She may have. My father was no saint," he said with disparagement. "And there is no point wishing for anything to be different. Accept what is, Viveka. I learned that long ago."

It wasn't anything she didn't see in a pop philosophy meme on her newsfeed every day, but she always resisted that fatalistic view. She took a few steps away from him as though to distance herself from his pessimism.

"If I accepted what I was given, I would still be listening to Grigor call me ugly and useless." She didn't realize her hands became tight fists, or that he had come up behind her, until his warm grip gently forced her to bend her elbow as he lifted her hand.

He looked at her white knuckles poking like sharp teeth. His thumb stroked along that bumpy line.

"You've reminded me of something. Come." He smoothly inserted his thumb to open her fist and kept her hand as he tugged her into the house.

"Where?"

He only pulled her along through the kitchen and down

the service stairs into a cool room where he turned on the lights to reveal a gym.

Perhaps the original plans had drawn it up as a wine cellar, but it was as much a professional gym as any that pushed memberships every January. Bike, tread, elliptical. Every type of weight equipment, a heavy bag hanging in the corner, skipping ropes dangling from a hook and padded mats on the floor. It was chilly and silent and smelled faintly of leather and air freshener.

"You'll meet me here every morning at six," he told her.

"Pah," she hooted. "Not likely."

"Say that again and I'll make it five."

"You're serious?" She made a face, silently telling him what she thought of that. "For heaven's sake, why? I do cardio most days, but I prefer to work out in the evening."

"I'm going to teach you to throw a punch. This—" he lifted the hand he still held and reshaped it into a fist again "—can do better. And this—" he touched under her chin, lifting her face and letting his thumb tag the spot on her lip where Grigor's mark had been "—won't happen again. Not without your opponent discovering very quickly that he has picked a fight with the wrong woman."

She had been trying to pretend she wasn't vitally aware of her hand in his. Now he was touching her face, looking into her eyes, standing too close.

Somehow she had thought that giving him pleasure would release some of this sexual tension between them. Now everything they'd confessed made it so much worse. The pull was so much *deeper*. He knew things about her. Intensely personal things.

She drew away, breaking all contact, trying to keep a grip on herself as she took in what he was saying.

"You keep surprising me. I thought you were a hardened..." She cut him a glance of apology. "Criminal.

You're actually quite nice, aren't you? Wanting to teach me how to defend myself."

"Everyone who surrounds me is a strength, not a liability. That's all this is."

"Liability." The label winded her, making her look away. It was familiar, but she had hoped there was a growing regard between them. But no. He might be attracted to her sexually, last night might have changed her forever, but she was still that thing he was saddled with.

"Right. Whatever you need me to be, wherever." She fought not to let her smarting show, but from her throat to her navel she burned.

"Do you like feeling helpless?" he demanded.

"No," she choked. This feeling of being at *his* mercy was excruciating.

"Then be here at six prepared to work."

What had he been thinking? Mikolas asked himself the next morning. This was hell.

Viveka showed up in a pair of clinging purple pants that ended below her knees. The spandex was shiny enough to accent every dip and curve of her trim thighs. Her pink T-shirt came off after they'd warmed up with cardio, revealing the unique landscape of her abdomen. Now she wore only a snug blue sports bra that flattened her modest breasts and showed off her creamy shoulders and chest and flat midriff.

He was so distracted by lust, he would get his lights blacked out for sure.

He would deserve it. And he couldn't even make a pass to slake it. He'd told two of his guards who had come in to use the gym that they could stay. They were spotting each other, grunting over the weights, while Mikolas put his hands on Viveka to adjust her stance and coached her through stepping into a punch. She smelled like shampoo and woman sweat. Like they'd been petting each other into acute arousal.

"You're holding back because you're afraid you'll hurt yourself," he told her when she struck his palm. He stopped her to correct her wrist position and traced up the soft skin of her forearm. "Humans have evolved the bone structure in here to withstand the impact of a punch."

"My bones aren't as big as yours," she protested. "I *will* hurt myself in a real fight. Especially if I don't have this." She held up her arm to indicate where he'd wrapped her hands to protect them.

"You might even break your hand," he told her frankly. "But that's better than losing your life, isn't it? I want you on the heavy bag twice a day for half an hour. Get used to how it feels to connect so you won't hesitate when it counts. Learn to use your left with as much power as the right."

Her brow wrinkled with concentration as she went back to jabbing into his palms. She was taking this seriously, at least.

That earnestness worried him, though. It would be just like her to take it to heart that *she* should protect *him*. He'd blurted out that remark about liability last night because he hadn't wanted to admit that her inability to protect herself had been eating at him from the moment he'd seen Grigor throw her around on the deck of a stranger's yacht.

He'd hurt her feelings, of course. She'd made enough mentions of Grigor's disparagement and her aunt's indifference that he understood Viveka had been made to feel like a burden and was very sensitive to it. That heart of hers was so easily bruised!

The more time he spent with her, the more he could

see how utterly wrong they were for each other. He could wind up hurting her quite deeply.

I do want sex. I just don't want it to hurt.

Her jab was off-center, glancing off his palm so she stumbled into him.

"Sorry. I'm getting tired," she said breathlessly.

"I wasn't paying attention," he allowed, helping her find her feet.

Damn it, if he didn't keep his guard up, they were both going to get hurt.

Viveka was still shaking from the most intense workout of her life. Her arms felt like rubber and she needed the seamstress's help to dress as they worked through the gowns in her closet. She would have consigned Mikolas firmly to hell for this morning's punishment, but then his grandfather's physiotherapist arrived on Mikolas's instruction to offer her a massage.

"He said you would need one every day for at least a week."

Viveka had collapsed on the table, groaned with bliss and went without prompting back to the gym that afternoon to spend another half hour on the wretched heavy bag.

"You'll get used to it," Mikolas said without pity at dinner, when she could barely lift her fork.

"Surely that's not necessary, is it?" Erebus admonished Mikolas, once his grandson had explained why Viveka was so done in.

"She wants to learn. Don't you?" Mikolas's tone dared her to contradict him, but he wasn't demanding she agree with him in front of his grandfather. He was insisting on honesty.

"I do," she admitted with a weighted sigh, even though

the very last thing she ever wanted was to engage in a fistfight. She couldn't help wondering if Grigor would have been as quick to hit her if she'd ever hit him back, though. She'd never had the nerve, fearing she'd only make things worse.

Mikolas's treatment of her in the gym, as dispassionate as it had been, had also been heartening. He seemed to have every confidence in her ability to defend herself if she only practiced. That was an incredibly compelling thought. Empowering.

It made her grateful to him all over again. And yes, deep down, it made her want to make him proud. To show him what she was capable of. Show herself.

Of course, the other side of that desire to be plucky and capable was a churning knowledge that she was being a coward when it came to sex. She wanted to be proficient in that arena, too.

The music was on low when they came into the lounge of his penthouse later, the fire glowing and a bottle of wine and glasses waiting. Beyond the windows, stars sparkled in the velvet black sky and moonlight glittered on the sea.

Had he planned this? To seduce her?

Did she want to be seduced?

She sighed a little, not sure what she wanted anymore.

"Sore?" he asked, moving to pour the wine.

"Hmm? Oh, it's not that bad. The massage helped. No, I was just thinking that I'm stuck in a holding pattern."

He lifted his brows with inquiry.

"I thought once Hildy was sorted, I would begin taking my life in hand. Trina was supposed to come live with me. I had some plan that we would rent a flat and take online quizzes, choose a career and register for classes…" She had been looking forward to that, but her sister's life had skewed off from hers and she didn't even have the worry of Hildy any longer. "Instead, my future is a blank page."

On Petrides letterhead, she thought wryly.

"I'll figure it out," she assured herself. "Eventually. I won't be here forever, right?"

That knowledge was the clincher. If it had taken her twenty-three years to find a man who stirred her physically, how long would it take to find another?

She looked over to him.

Whatever was in her face made him set down the bottle, corkscrew angled into the unpopped cork.

"I keep telling myself to give you time." His voice was low and heavy, almost defeated. "But bringing you into my bed is all I can think about. Will you let me? I just want to touch you. Kiss you. Give you what you gave me."

Her belly clenched in anticipation. She couldn't imagine being *that* uninhibited, but she couldn't imagine *not* going to bed with him. She wanted him *so much* and she honestly didn't know how to resist any longer.

Surrender happened with one shaken, "Yes."

He kind of jolted, like he hadn't expected that. Then he came across and took her face in his two hands, covering her lips with his hot, hungry mouth. They kissed like lovers. Like people who had been separated by time and distance and deep misunderstanding. She curled her arms around his neck and he broke away long enough to scoop her up against his chest, then kissed her again as he carried her to his bedroom.

She waited for misgivings and none struck. Her fingers went into his hair as she kissed him back.

He came down on the mattress with her and she opened her eyes only long enough to catch an impression of monochromatic shades lit by the bluish half-moon. The carpet was white, the furniture silver-gray, the bedspread black.

Then Mikolas tucked her beneath him and stroked without hurry from her shoulder, down her rib cage, past her waist and along her hip.

"You can—" she started to say, but he brushed another kiss over her lips, lazy and giving and thorough.

"Don't worry," he murmured and kissed her again. "I just want to touch you." Another soft, sweet, lingering kiss. "I'll stop if you tell me to." Kissing and kissing and kissing.

It was delicious and tender and not the least bit threatening with his heavy hand only making slow, restless circles where her hip met her waist.

She wanted more. She wanted sex. It wasn't like the other times she'd wanted sex. Then it had been something between an obligation and a frustrating goal she was determined to achieve.

This was nothing like that. She wanted *him*. She wanted to share her body with Mikolas, feel him inside her, feel close to him.

Make love to me, she begged him with her lips, and ran her hands over him in a silent message of encouragement. When she rolled and tried to open the zip on her dress, he made a ragged noise and found it for her, dragging it down. He lifted away to draw her sleeve off her arm, exposing her bra. One efficient flick of his fingers and the bra was loose.

With reverence, he eased the strap down her arm, dislodging the cup so her breast thrust round and white, nipple turgid with wanton need.

Insecurity didn't have time to strike. He lowered his head and tongued lightly, cupped with a warm hand, then with another groan of appreciation, opened his mouth in a hot branding, letting her get used to the delicate suction before pulling a little harder.

Her toes curled. She wanted to speak, to tell him this was good, that he wouldn't have to stop, but sensation rocked her, coiling in her abdomen, making her loins weep with need. When his hand stroked to rub her bottom, she dragged at her skirt herself, earning a noise of approval as she drew the ruffled fabric out of the way.

He teased her, tracing patterns on her bare thighs, lifting his head to kiss her again and give her his tongue as he made her wait and wait.

"Mikolas," she gasped.

"This?" He brought his hand to the juncture of her thighs and settled his palm there, letting her get used to the sensation. The intimacy. "I want that, too," he breathed against her mouth.

She bit back a cry of pure joy as the weight of his hand covered her, hot and confident. He rocked slowly, increasing the pressure in increments, inciting her to crook her knee so she was open to his touch. Eyes closed, she let herself bask in this wonderful feeling, tension climbing.

When he lifted his hand, she caught her breath in loss, opening her eyes.

He was watching her while his fingertips traced the edge of her knickers, then began to draw them down her thighs.

The friction of lace against her sensitized skin made her shiver. As the coolness of the room struck her damp, eager flesh, she became starkly aware of how her clothing was askew, her breast exposed, her sex pouted and needy, her body trembling with ridiculously high desire.

For a moment anxiety struck. She wanted to rush past this moment, rush through the hard part, have done with this interminable impasse. She lifted her hips so he could finish skimming them away, but when he came down beside her again, he only combed her hair back from her face.

"I just want to feel you. I'll be gentle," he promised, and kissed her lightly.

Yes, she almost screamed.

Embarrassment ought to be killing her, but arousal was pulsing in her like an electrical current. And when he cradled her against him this way, she felt very safe.

They kissed and his hand covered her again. This time she was naked. The sensation was so acute she jolted under his touch.

"Just feel," he cajoled softly. "Tell me what you like. Is that good?"

He did things then that were gorgeous and honeyed. She knew how her body worked, but she had never felt this turned on. She didn't let herself think, just floated in the deep currents of pleasure he swirled through her.

"Like that?" He kept up the magical play, making tension coil through her so she moaned beneath his kiss, encouraging him. Yes, like that. Exactly like that.

He pressed one finger into her.

She gasped.

"Okay?" he breathed against her cheek.

She clasped him with her inner muscles, loving the sensation even though it felt very snug. She was so aroused, so close, she covered his hand with her own and pressed. She rocked her hips as he made love to her with his hand and shattered into a million pieces, cries muffled by his smothering kiss.

CHAPTER ELEVEN

THEY WERE GOING to kill each other.

Mikolas was fully clothed and if she shaped him through his pants right now, he would explode.

But oh, she was amazing. He licked at her panting lips, wanting to smile at the way she clung to his mouth with her own, but weakly. She was still shivering with the aftershocks of her beautiful, stunning orgasm.

He caressed her very, very gently, coaxing her to remain aroused. He wanted to do that to her again. Taste her. Drown in her.

She made a noise and kissed him back with more response, restless hands picking at his shirt, looking for the buttons.

He broke them open with a couple of yanks, then shrugged it off and discarded it, too hot for clothes. On fire for her.

She pulled her other arm free of her dress and held up her arms for him to come back. Soft curves, velvety skin. He loved the feel of her against his bare chest and biceps. Delicate, but spry. So warm, smelling of rain and tea and the drugging scent of sexual fulfillment.

Her smooth hands traced over his torso and back, making him groan at how good it felt on skin that was taut and sensitized. She tasted like nectarines, he thought, opening his mouth on the swell of her breast. He tongued her nipple, more aggressive than he had been the first time.

She arched for more.

He was going too fast, he cautioned himself, but he wanted to consume her. He wanted her dress out of the way, he wanted her hands everywhere on him—

She arched to strip the garment down.

He slid down the bed as he whisked the dress away, pressing his lips to her quivering belly, blowing softly on the fine hairs of her mound, laughing with delight at finally being here. He was so filled with desire his heart was slamming, pulse reverberating through his entire body.

"Mikolas," she breathed.

Her fingers were in his hair like she was petting a wolf, tugging hard enough to force him to lift his head before he'd barely nuzzled her.

"Make love to me."

A lightning rod of lust went through him. He steeled himself to maintain his control when all he wanted was to push her legs apart and rise over her.

"I am." He was going to make her scream with release.

"I mean really." Her hand moved to cradle his jaw, her touch light against the clenched muscle in his cheek. Entreaty filled her eyes. "Please."

She had come into his life to destroy him in the most subversive yet effective way possible.

He could barely move, but he drew back, coming up on an elbow, trying to hold on to what shreds of gentlemanly conduct he possessed.

"Do you ever do what's expected of you?"

"You don't want to?" The appalled humiliation that crept into her tone scared the hell out of him.

"Of course I *want* to." He spoke too harshly. He was barely hanging on to rational thought over here.

She tensed, wary.

He set his hand on her navel, breathed, tried to find something that passed for civilized behavior, but found only the thief he had once been. His hand stole lower, unable to help himself. His thumb detoured along her cleft, finding her slick and ready. Need pearled into one place that made her gasp raggedly when he found it, circling and teasing.

Her thighs relaxed open. She arched to his touch. "Please," she begged. "I want to know how it feels."

He was only human, not a superhero. He pulled away, hearing her catch back a noise of injury.

Her breath caught in the next instant as she saw he was rising to open his pants. He stripped in jerky, uncoordinated movements, watching her swallow and bite her bottom lip. He made himself take his time retrieving the condom so she had lots of opportunity to change her mind.

"I'll stop if you want me to," he promised as he covered himself, then settled over her. He would. He didn't know how, but he would.

Please don't make me stop.

It would really happen this time. Viveka's nerves sizzled as Mikolas covered her. He was such a big person compared with her. He *loomed.* She skimmed her fingertips over his broad shoulders and was starkly aware of how much space his hips and thighs took up as he settled without hesitation between her own.

She tensed, nervous.

He kissed her in abbreviated catches of her mouth that didn't quite satisfy before he pulled away, then did it again.

She made a noise of impatience and wiggled beneath him. "I want—"

"Me, too," he growled against her mouth. Then he lifted

to trace himself against her folds. "You're sure?" he murmured, looking down to where they touched.

So sure. "Yes," she breathed.

He positioned himself and pressed.

It hurt. So much. She fought her instinctive tension, tried to make herself relax, tried not to resist, but the sting became more and more intense. He seemed huge. Tears came into her eyes. She couldn't hold back a throaty noise of anxiety.

He stilled, shuddering. The sting subsided a little.

"Viveka." His voice was ragged. "That's just the tip—" He hung his head against her shoulder, forehead damp with perspiration, big body shaking.

"Don't stop." She caught her foot behind his thigh and tried to press him forward.

"*Glykia mou*, I don't want to hurt you." He lifted his face and wore a tortured expression.

"That's why it's okay if you do." Her mouth quivered, barely able to form words. It still hurt, but she didn't care. "I trust you. Please don't make me do this with someone else."

He bit out a string of confounded curses, looking into the shadows for a moment. Then he met her gaze and carefully pressed again.

She couldn't help flinching. Tensing. The stretch hurt a lot. He paused again, looked at her with as much frustration as she felt.

"Don't try to be gentle. Just do it," she told him.

He wavered, then made a tight noise of angst, covered her mouth, gathered himself and thrust deep.

She arched at the flash of pain, crying out into his mouth.

They both stayed motionless for a few hissing breaths.

Slowly the pain eased to a tolerable sting. She moved her lips against his and he kissed her gently. Sweetly.

"Do you hate me?" His voice was thick, his brow tense as he set it against hers. His expression was strained.

He didn't move, letting her get used to the feel of a man inside her for the first time. And he held her in such protective arms, her eyes grew wet from the complete opposite of pain: happiness.

She returned his healing kiss with one that was a little more inciting.

"No," she answered, smiling shakily, feeling intensely close to him. She let her arms settle across his back and traced the indent of his spine, enjoying the way he reacted with a shiver.

"Want to stop?" he asked.

"No." Her voice was barely there. Tentatively she moved a little, settling herself more comfortably beneath him. "I'm not sure I want you to move at all," she admitted wryly. "Ever."

His breath released on a jagged chuckle. "You are going to be the death of me."

Very carefully, he shifted so he was angled on his elbow, then he made a gentling noise and touched where they were joined.

"You feel so good," he crooned in Greek, gently soothing and stimulating as he murmured compliments. "I thought nothing could be better than the way you took me apart with your mouth, but this feels incredible. You're so perfect, Viveka. So lovely."

The noise that escaped her then was pure pleasure. He was leading her down the road of stirred desire to real excitement. It felt strange to have him lodged inside her while her arousal intensified. Part of her wanted him to move, but she was still wary of the pain and this felt so good. The way he stretched her accentuated the sensations. She grew taut and deeply aroused. Restless and—

"Oh, Mikolas. Please. Oh—" A powerful climax rocked her. Her sheath clenched and shivered around his hard shape with such power she could hardly breath. Stars imploded behind her eyes and she clung to him, crying out with ecstasy. It was beautiful and selfish and heavenly.

As the spasms faded, he began to pull away. The friction felt good, except sharp. She wasn't sure she could take that in a prolonged way, but then he was gone from her body and she was bereft.

"You didn't, did you?" She reached to find his thick shaft, so hard and hot, obviously unsatisfied.

He folded his hand over hers and pumped into her fist. Two, three times, then he pressed a harsh groan into her shoulder, mouth opening so his teeth sat against her skin, not quite biting while he shuddered and pulsed against her palm.

Shocked, but pleased, she continued to pleasure him until he relaxed and released her. He removed the condom with a practiced twist, then rolled away and sat up to discard it. Before he came back, he dragged the covers down and pulled her with him as he slid under them.

"Why did you do that?" she asked as he molded her to his front, stomach to stomach.

"So we won't be cold while we sleep." He adjusted the edge of the sheet away from her face.

"You know what I mean." She pinched his chest, unable to lie still when it felt so good to rub her naked legs against his and nuzzle his collarbone with her lips.

"Learn to speak plainly when we're in bed," he ordered.

"Or what?" She was giddy, so happy with being his lover she felt like the sun was lodged inside her.

"Or I may not give you what you want."

They were both silent a moment, bodies quieting.

"You did," she said softly, adjusting her head against his shoulder. "Thank you."

He didn't say anything, but his hand moved thoughtfully in her hair.

A frozen spike of insecurity pierced her. "Did *you* like it?"

He snorted. "I have just finessed my way through initiating a particularly delicate virgin. My ego is so enormous right now, it's a wonder you fit in the bed."

Viveka woke to an empty bed, couldn't find Mikolas in the penthouse, realized she was late for the gym and decided she was entitled to a bath. She was climbing out of it, a thick white towel loosely clutched around her middle, when he strolled in wearing his gym shorts and nothing else.

"Lazy," he stated, pausing to give her a long, appreciative look.

"Seriously?" Before that bath, she had ached *everywhere*.

His mouth twitched and he came closer, gaze skimming down her front. "Sore?"

She shrugged a shoulder, instantly so shy she nearly couldn't bear it. The things they'd done!

She blushed, aware that her gaze was coveting the hard planes of his body, and instantly wanted to be close to him. Touch, feel, kiss…more.

She wasn't sure how to issue the invitation across the expanse of the spa-like bathroom, but he wasn't the novice she was. He took the last few laconic steps to reach her, spiky lashes lowering as he stared at her mouth. When his head dipped, she lifted her chin to meet his kiss. Her free hand found his stubbled cheek while her other kept her towel in place.

"Mmm…" she murmured, liking the way he didn't rush, but kissed her slowly and thoroughly.

He drew back and tried taking the towel in his two hands.

She hesitated.

"I only want a peek," he cajoled.

"It's daylight," she argued.

"Exactly."

If she had feared that having sex would weaken her will around him, the fear was justified. She wanted to please him. She wanted to offer her whole self and plead with him to cherish her. Her fingers relaxed under the knowledge she was giving up more than control of a towel.

As he opened it, however, and took a long eyeful of her sucked-in stomach and thrust-out breasts, she saw desire grip him with the same lack of mercy it showed her. He swallowed, body hardening, jaw clenched like he was under some kind of deep stress.

"I was only going to kiss you," he said, lifting lust-filled eyes to hers. "But if you—"

"I do," she assured him.

He let the towel drop and she met him midway, moaning with acquiescence as he pressed her onto the daybed. Her inhibitions about the daylight quickly burned up as his stubble slid down her neck to her breast where he sucked and made her writhe. When he slid even lower, scraping her stomach then her thighs as he knelt on the floor, she threw her arm across her eyes and let him do whatever he wanted.

Because it was what she wanted. Oh, that felt exquisite.

"Don't stop," she pleaded when he lifted his head.

"Can you take me?" he growled, scraping his teeth with mock threat along her inner thigh.

She nodded, little echoes of wariness threatening, but

she couldn't take her eyes off his form as he rose and moved to the mirror over his sink, found a condom and covered himself.

When he came back and stood over her, she stayed exactly as he'd left her, splayed weakly with desire, like some harem girl offered for his pleasure.

His hands flexed like he was struggling against some kind of internal pain.

"Mikolas," she pleaded, holding out her arms.

He made a noise of agony and came down over her, heavy and confident, thighs pressing hers wide as he positioned himself. "I don't want to hurt you." His hand tangled in her hair. "But I want you so damned much. Stop me if it hurts."

"It's okay," she told him, not caring about the burn as she arched, inviting him to press all the way in. It hurt, but his first careful thrusts felt good at the same time. The friction of him moving inside her made the connection that much more intense. She rose to the brink very quickly, climaxing with a sudden gasp, clinging to him, shocked at her reaction.

He shuddered, lips pressed into her neck, and hurried to finish with her, groaning fulfillment against her skin.

She was disappointed when he carefully disengaged and sat up, his back to her.

She started to protest that it was okay, holding him in her didn't hurt anymore, but she was distracted by the marks on his back. They were pocked scars that were visible only because the light was so bright. She'd seen his back on the yacht, but in lamplight she hadn't noticed the scars. They weren't raised, but there were more than a dozen.

"What happened to your back?" she asked, puzzled.

Mikolas rose and walked first to his side of the room,

where he scanned around his sinks, then went across to her vanity, where he found the remote for the shower.

"We should set some ground rules," he said.

"Leave the remote on your side?" she guessed as she rose. She walked past her discarded towel for her white robe, wondering why she bothered when she was thinking of joining him in the shower. She wanted to touch him, to close this distance that had arisen so abruptly between them.

"That," he agreed. "And we'll only be together for a short time. Call me your lover if you want to, but do not expect us to fall in love. Keep your expectations low."

She fell back a step as she tied her robe, giving it a firm yank like the action could tie off the wound he'd just inflicted.

But what did she think they were doing? Like fine weather, they were enjoying each other because they were here. That was all.

"I wasn't fishing for a marriage proposal," she defended.

"So long as we're clear." He aimed the remote and started the shower jets.

Scanning his stiff shoulders, she said, "Is this because I asked about your back? I'm sorry if that was too personal, but I've told you some really personal things about me."

"Talk to me about whatever you want. If I don't want to tell you something, I won't." He spoke with aloof confidence, but his expression faltered briefly, mouth quirking with self-deprecation.

Because he had already shared more than made him comfortable?

"There's nothing wrong with being friends, is there?"

He glanced at her, his expression patient, but resolute.

"You don't have friends," she recalled from the other

night, thinking, *I can see why.* "What's wrong with friendship? Don't you want someone you can confide in? Share jokes with?"

His rebuff was making her feel like a houseguest who had to be tolerated. Surely they were past that! He'd just enjoyed *her* hospitality, hadn't he?

"They're cigar burns," he said abruptly, rattling the remote control onto the space behind the sink. "I have móre on the bottoms of my feet. My captors used to make me scream so my grandfather could hear it over the phone. *There was more than one call.* Is that the sort of confiding you're looking for, Viveka?" he challenged with antagonism.

"Mikolas." Her breath stung like acid against the back of her throat. She unconsciously clutched the robe across her shattered heart.

"That's why I don't want to share more than our bodies. There's nothing else worth sharing."

Mikolas had been hard on Viveka this morning, he knew that. But he'd been the victim of forces greater than himself once before and already felt too powerless around her. The way she had infiltrated his life, the changes he was making for her, were unprecedented.

Earlier that day, he had risen while she slept and spent the morning sparring, trying to work his libido into exhaustion. She had to be sore. He wasn't an animal.

But one glance at her rising from the bath and all his command over himself had evaporated. At one point, he'd been quite sure he was prepared to beg.

Begging was futile. He *knew* that.

But so was thinking he could treat Viveka like every other woman he'd slept with. Many of them had asked about his back. He'd always lied, claiming chicken pox had caused the scars. For some reason, he didn't want to lie to Viveka.

When he had finally blurted out the ugly truth, he'd seen something in her expression that he outwardly rejected, but inwardly craved: agony on his behalf. Sadness for that dark time that had stolen his innocence and left him with even bigger scars that no one would ever see.

Damn it, he was self-aware enough to know he used denial as a coping strategy, but there was no point in raking over the coals of what had been done to him. Nothing would change it. Viveka wanted a jocular companion to share opinions and anecdotes with. He was never going to be that person. There was too much gravity and anger in him.

So he had schooled her on what to expect, and it left him sullen through the rest of the day.

She wasn't much better. In another woman, he would have called her subdued mood passive-aggressive, but he already knew how sensitive Viveka was under all that bravado. His churlish behavior had tamped down her natural cheerfulness. That made him feel even more disgusted with himself.

Then his grandfather asked her to play backgammon and she brightened, disappearing for a couple of hours, coming back to the penthouse only to change for the gym.

Why did that annoy him? He wanted her to be self-sufficient and not look to him to keep her amused. Later that evening, however, when he found her plumping cushions in the lounge, he had to ask, "What are you doing?"

"Tidying up." She carried a teacup and plate to the dumbwaiter and left it there.

"I pay people to do that."

"I carry my weight," she said neutrally.

He pushed his hands into his pockets, watching her

click on a lamp and turn off the overhead light, then lift a houseplant—honest to God, she checked a plant to see if it needed water rather than look at him.

"You're angry with me for what I said this morning."

"I'm not." She sounded truthful and folded her arms defensively, but she finally turned and gave him her attention. "I just never wanted to be in this position again."

The bruised look in her eye made him feel like a heel.

"What position?" he asked warily.

"Being forced on someone who doesn't really want me around." Her tight smile came up, brave, but fatalistic.

"It's not like that," he ground out. "I told you I want you." Admitting it still made him feel like he was being hung by his feet over a ledge.

"Physically," she clarified.

Before the talons of a deeper truth had finished digging into his chest, she looked down, voice so low he almost didn't hear her.

"So do I. That's what worries me," she continued.

"What do you mean?"

She hugged herself, shrugging. Troubled. "Not something worth sharing," she mumbled.

Share, he wanted to demand, but that would be hypocritical. Regret and apology buzzed around him like biting mosquitoes, annoying him.

It had taken him years to come to this point of being completely sure in himself. A few days with this woman, and he was second-guessing everything he was or had or did.

"Can we just go to bed?" Her doe eyes were so vulnerable, it took a moment for him to comprehend what she was saying. He had thought they were fighting.

"Yes," he growled, opening his arms. "Come here."

She pressed into him, her lips touching his throat. He sighed as the turmoil inside him subsided.

Every night, they made love until Viveka didn't even remember falling asleep, but she always woke alone.

Was it personal? she couldn't help wondering. Did Mikolas not see anything in her to like? Or was he simply that removed from the normal needs of humanity that he genuinely didn't want any closer connections? Did he realize his behavior was hurtful? Did he know and not *care*?

Whenever she had dreamed of being in an intimate relationship with a man, it had been intimacy across the board, not this heart-wrenching openness during sex and a deliberate distance outside of it. Was she saying too much? *Asking* too much?

She became hypersensitive to every word she spoke, trying to refrain from getting too personal. The constant weighing and worrying was exhausting.

It was harder when they traveled. At least with his grandfather at the table, the conversation flowed more naturally. As Mikolas dragged her to various events across Europe, she had to find ways to talk to him without putting herself out there too much.

"I might go to the art gallery while you're in meetings this morning. Unless you want to come? I could wait until this afternoon," was a typical, neutral approach. She loved spending time with him, but couldn't say *that*.

"I can make myself available after lunch."

"It's an exhibition of children's art," she clarified. "Is that something you'd want to see?" Now she felt like she was prying. Her belly clenched as she awaited rejection.

He shrugged, indifferent. "Art galleries aren't something I typically do, but if you want to see it, I'll take you."

Which made her feel like she was imposing on his time,

but he was already tapping it into his schedule. Later he paced around the place, not saying much, while she held back asking what he thought. She wanted to tell him about her early aspirations and point to what she liked and ask if he'd ever messed around with finger paints as a child.

She actually found herself speaking more freely to strangers over cocktails than she did with him. He always listened intently, but she didn't know if that was for show or what. If he had interest in her thoughts or ambitions, she kept thinking, he would ask her himself, but he never did.

Tonight she was revealing her old fascination with art history and Greek mythology. It felt good to open up, so she shared a little more than she normally would.

"I actually won an award," she confided with a wrinkle of her nose. "It was just a little thing for a watercolor I painted at school. I was convinced I'd become a world-famous artist," she joked. "I've always wanted to take a degree in art, but there's never been the right time."

It was small talk. They were nice people, owners of a hotel chain whom she'd met more than once.

Deep down, she was congratulating herself on performing well at these events, remembering the names of children and occasionally going on shopping dates. Tonight she had found herself genuinely interested in Adara Makricosta's plans for her hotels. That's how her own career goals had come up. Adara Makricosta was the CEO of a family-owned chain and had asked Viveka about her own work.

Viveka sidestepped the admission she was merely a mistress whose job it was to create this warming trend Mikolas was enjoying among the world's most rich and powerful.

"Why didn't you tell me that before?" Mikolas asked

when Adara and Gideon had moved on. "About wanting to study art," he prompted when she only looked at him blankly.

Viveka's heart lurched and she almost blurted out, *Because you wouldn't care.* She swallowed.

"It's not practical. I thought about taking evening classes around my day job, but I always had Hildy to look after. And I knew once I was in this position, looking to my own future, I would need to devote myself to a proper career, not dabble in something that will never pay the bills."

She ought to be thinking harder about that, not using up all her brain space trying to second-guess the man in front of her.

"You don't have bills now. Sign up for something," he said breezily.

"Where? To what end?" Her throat tightened. "We're constantly on the move and I don't know how long I'll be with you. No. There's no point." It would hurt to see that phoenix of a dream rise up from the ashes only to fly away.

Or was he implying she would be with him for the long term?

She did the unthinkable and searched his expression for some sign that he had feelings for her. That they had a future.

He receded behind a remote mask, horribly quiet for the rest of the night and even while they traveled back to Greece, adding an extra layer of tension to their trip.

Viveka was still smarting over Mikolas's behavior when she woke in his bed the next morning. They were sleeping late after arriving in the wee hours. She stayed motionless, naked in the spoon of his body, not wanting to move and wake him. She often fell asleep in his arms, but she never woke in them. This was a rare moment of closeness.

It was the counterfeit currency that all women—like mother like daughter—too often took in place of real regard.

Because, no matter how distanced she felt from Mikolas during the day, in bed she felt so integral to him it was a type of agony to be anywhere else. When he made love to her, it felt like love. His kisses and caresses were generous, his compliments extravagant. She warmed and tingled just thinking about how good it felt to join with him, but it wasn't just physical pleasure for her. Lying with him, naked and intimate, was emotionally fulfilling.

She was falling for him.

His breathing changed. He hardened against her backside and she bit her lip, heartened by the lazy stroke of his hand and the noise of contentment he made, like he was pleased to wake with her against him.

Such happiness brimmed in her, she couldn't help but wriggle her butt into his hardness, inviting the only affection he seemed to accept, wanting to hold on to this moment of harmony.

His mouth opened on her shoulder and his hand drifted down her belly into the juncture of her thighs. He made a satisfied noise when he found her wet and ready.

She gasped, stimulated by his lazy touch. She stretched her arm to the night table, then handed a condom over her shoulder as she nestled back against him, eager and needy. He adjusted her position and a moment later thrust in, sighing a hot breath against her neck, setting kisses against her nape that were warm and soft. Caring. Surely he cared?

She took him so easily now. It was nothing but pleasure, so much pleasure. She hadn't known her body could be like this: buttery and welcoming. It was almost too good. She was so far ahead of him, having been thinking about this while he slept against her, she soared over the top in moments. She cried out, panting and damp with sweat, overcome and floating, speechless in her orgasmic bliss.

"Greedy," he said in a gritty morning voice, rubbing his mouth against her skin, inhaling and calling her beautiful in Greek. Exquisite. Telling her how much he enjoyed being inside her. How good she made him feel.

He came up on his elbow so he could thrust with more power. His hand went between her legs again, ensuring her pleasure as he moved with more aggression.

She didn't mind his vigor. She was so slick, still so aroused, she reveled in the slap of his hips into her backside, hand knotting in the bottom sheet to brace herself to receive him, making noises close to desperation as she felt a fresh pinnacle hover within reach.

"Don't hold back," he ground out. "Come with me. *Now.*"

He pounded into her, the most unrestrained he'd ever been. She cried out as her excitement peaked. An intense climax rolled through her, leaving her shattered and quaking in ecstasy.

He convulsed with equal strength, arms caging her, hoarse shout hot against her cheek. He jerked as she clenched, continuing to push deep so she was hit by wave after wave of aftershocks while he thrust firmly into her, like he was implanting his essence into her core.

As the sensual storm battered them, he remained pressed over her, crushing her beneath his heavy body. Finally, the crisis began to subside and he exhaled raggedly as he slid flat, his one arm under her neck bending so he could cradle her into his front. They were coated in perspiration. It adhered her back to his front and she could feel his heart still pounding unsteadily against her shoulder blade. Their legs were tangled, their bodies still joined, their breaths slowing to level.

It was the most beautifully imperfect moment of her life. She loved him. Endlessly and completely. But he didn't love her back.

Mikolas had visited hell. Then his grandfather had accepted him and he had returned to the real world, where there were good days and bad days. Now he'd found what looked like heaven and he didn't trust it. Not one little bit.

But he couldn't turn away from it—*from her*—either.

Not without feeling as though he was peeling away his own skin, leaving him raw and vulnerable. He was a molting crab, losing his shell every night and rebuilding it every day.

This morning was the most profound deconstruction yet. He always tried to leave before Viveka woke so he wouldn't start his day impacted by her effect on him, but the sweet way she'd rubbed herself into his groin had undone him. She had gone from a tentative virgin to a sensual goddess capable of stripping him down to nothing but pure sensation.

How could he resist that? How could he not let her press him into service and give himself up to the joy of possessing her. It had been all he could do to hold back so she came with him. Because she owned him. Between the sheets, she completely owned him. Right now, all he wanted in life was to stay in this bed, with her body replete against his, her fingertips drawing light patterns on the back of his hand.

Don't *want*.

He made himself roll away and sit up, to prove himself

master over whatever this thing was that threatened him in a way nothing else could.

She stayed inside him, though. In his body as an intoxicant, and in his head as an unwavering awareness. And because he was so attuned to her, he heard the barely discernible noise she made as he pushed to stand. It was a sniff. A lash. A cat-o'-nine-tails that scored through his thick skin into his soul.

He swung around and saw only the bow of her back, still curled on her side where he'd left her. He dropped his knee into the mattress and caught her shoulder, flattening her so he could see her face.

She gasped in surprise, lifting a hand to quickly try to wipe away the tears that stood in her eyes. Self-conscious agony flashed in her expression before she turned her face to hide it.

His heart fell through the earth.

"I thought you were with me." He spoke through numb lips, horrified with himself. He could have sworn she had been as passionately excited as he was. He had felt her slickness, the ripples of her orgasm. Was he kidding himself with how well he thought he knew her?

"You have to tell me if I'm being too rough," he insisted, his usual command buried in a choke of self-reproach.

"It's not that." Her expression spasmed with dismay. She pushed the back of her wrist across her eye, then brushed his hand off her shoulder so she could roll away and sit up. "I used to be so afraid of sex. Now I like it."

She rubbed her hands up and down her arms, the delicacy of her frame striking like a hammer between his eyes. Her nude body pimpled at the chill as she rose.

"I'm grateful," she claimed, turning to offer him a smile, but her lashes were still matted. "Take a bow. Let me know what I owe you."

Those weren't tears of gratitude.

His heart lurched as he found himself right back in that moment where he had impulsively told her to pursue her interests and she had searched for reassurance that she would be with him for the long haul.

I don't know how long I'll be with you.

It had struck him at that moment that at some point she would leave and he hadn't been able to face it. He skipped past it now, only saying her name.

"Viveka." It hurt his throat. "I told you to keep your expectations low," he reminded, and felt like a coward, especially when her smile died.

She looked at him with betrayal, like he'd smacked her.

"Don't," he bit out.

"Don't what? Don't like it?"

"Don't be hurt." He couldn't bear the idea that he was hurting her. "Don't feel *grateful.*"

She made a choking noise. "Don't tell me what to feel. That is where you control what I feel." She pointed at the rumpled sheets he knelt upon, then tapped her chest and said on a burst of passion, "In here? This is mine. I'll feel whatever the hell I want."

Her blue eyes glowed with angry defiance, but something else ravaged her. Something sweet and powerful and pure that shot like an arrow to pierce his breastbone and sting his heart. He didn't try to put a name to it. He was afraid to, especially when he saw shadows of hopelessness dim her gaze before she looked away.

"I'm not confusing sex with love, if that's what you're worried about." She moved to the chair and pulled on his shirt from the night before, shooting her arms into it and folding the front across her stomach. She was hunched as though bracing for body blows. "My mother made that mistake." Her voice was scuffed and desolate. "I won't. I know the difference."

Why did that make him clench his fist in despair? He ought to be reassured.

He almost told her this wasn't just sex. When he walked into a room with her hand in his, he was so proud it was criminal. When she dropped little tidbits about her life before she met him, he was fascinated. When she looked dejected like that, his armored heart creaked and rose on quivering legs, anxious to show valor in her name.

Instead he stood, saying, "I'll send an email today. To ask how the investigation is coming along. On your mother," he clarified, when she turned a blank look on him.

She snorted, sounding disillusioned as she muttered, "Thanks."

"Your head is not in the game today," Erebus said, dragging Viveka's mind to the *távli* board, where he was placing one of his checkers on top of hers.

Were they at *plakoto* already? Until a few weeks ago, she hadn't played since she and Trina were girls, but the rules and strategies had come back to her very quickly. She sat down with Erebus at least once a day if she was home.

"Jet lag," she murmured, earning a *tsk*.

"We don't lie to each other in this house, *poulaki mou.*"

Viveka was growing fond of the old man. He was very well-read, kept up on world politics and had a wry sense of humor. At the same time, he was interested in *her*. He called her "my little birdie" and always had something nice to say. Today it had been, *"I wish you weren't leaving for Paris. I miss you when you're traveling."*

She'd never had a decent father figure in her life and

knew it was crazy to see this former criminal in that light, but he was also sweetly protective of her. It was endearing.

So she didn't want to offend him by stating that his grandson was tearing her into little pieces.

"I wonder sometimes what Mikolas was like as a child," she prevaricated.

She and Erebus had talked a little about her aunt and he'd shared a few stories from his earliest years. She was deeply curious how such a kind-seeming man could have broken the law and fathered an infamous criminal, but thought it better not to ask.

He nodded thoughtfully, gesturing for her to shake the cup with the dice and take her turn.

She did and set the cup within his reach, but he was staring across the water from their perch outside his private sitting room. In a few weeks it would be too hot to sit out here, but it was balmy and pleasant today. A light breeze moved beneath the awning, carrying his favorite *kantada* folk music with it.

"Pour us an ouzo," he finally said, two papery fingers directing her to the interior of his apartment.

"I'll get in trouble. You're only supposed to have one before dinner."

"I won't tell if you don't," he said, making her smile.

He came in behind her as she filled the small glasses. He took his and canted his head for her to follow him.

She did, slowly pacing with him as he shuffled his cane across his lounge and into his bedroom. There he sat with a heavy sigh into a chair near the window. He picked up the double photo frame on the side table and held it out to her.

She accepted it and took her time studying the black-and-white photo of the young woman on the one side, the boy and girl sitting on a rock at a beach in the other. They were perhaps nine and five.

"Your wife?" she guessed. "And Mikolas's father?"

"Yes. And my daughter. She was… Men always say they want sons, but a daughter is life and light. A way for your wife to live on. Daughters are love in its purest form."

"That's a beautiful thing to say." She wished she knew more about her own father than a few barely recollected facts from her mother. He'd been English and had dropped out of school to work in radio. He'd married her mother because she was pregnant and died from a rare virus that had got into his heart.

She sat on the foot of Erebus's bed, facing him. "Mikolas told me you lost your daughter when she was young. I'm sorry."

He nodded, taking back the frame and looking at it again. "My wife, too. She was beautiful. She looked at me the way you look at Mikolas. I miss that."

Viveka looked into her drink.

"I failed them," Erebus continued grimly. "It was a difficult time in our country's history. Fear of communism, martial law, censorship, persecution. I was young and passionate, courting arrest with my protests. I left to hide on this island, never thinking they would go after my wife."

His cloudy gray eyes couldn't disguise his stricken grief.

"The way my son told me, my daughter was crying, trying to cling to their mother as the military police dragged her away for questioning. They knocked her to the ground. Her ear started bleeding. She never came to. Brain injury, perhaps. I'll never know. My wife died in custody, but not before my son saw her beaten unconscious for trying to go back to our daughter."

Viveka could only cover her mouth, holding back a cry of protest.

"By the time I was reunited with him, my son was twisted beyond repair. I was warped, too. The law? How could I have regard for it? What I did then, bribes, theft, smuggling… None of that sits on my conscience with any great weight. But what my son turned into…"

He cleared his throat and set the photo frame back in its place. His hands shook and he took a long time to speak again.

"My son lost his humanity. The things he did… I couldn't make him stop, couldn't bring him back from that. It was no surprise to me that he was killed so violently. It was the way he lived. When he died I mourned him, but I also mourned what should have been. I was forced to face my many mistakes. The things I had done caused me to outlive my children. I hated the man I had become."

His pain was tangible. Viveka ached for him.

"Into this came a ransom demand. A street rat was claiming to be my grandson. Some of my son's rivals had him."

Her heart clenched. She was listening intently, but was certain she wouldn't be able to bear hearing this.

"You want to know what Mikolas was like as a child? So do I. He came to me as an empty shell. Eyes this big." He made a circle with his finger and thumb. "Thin. Brittle. His hand was crushed, some of his fingernails gone. Three of his teeth gone. He was *broken*." He paused, lined face working to control deep pain, then he admitted, "I think he hoped I would kill him."

She bit her lip, eyes hot and wet, a burn of anguish like a pike spreading from her throat to the pit of her stomach.

"He said that if the blood test hadn't been positive, you

wouldn't have helped him." She couldn't keep the accusation, the blame, out of her voice.

"I honestly can't say what I would have done," Erebus admitted, eyes rheumy. "Looking back from the end of my life, I want to believe my conscience would have demanded I help him regardless, but I wasn't much of a man at the time. They showed me a picture and he looked a little like my son, but..."

His head hung heavy with regret.

"He begged me to believe he was telling the truth, to accept him. I took too long." He took a healthy sip of his ouzo.

She'd forgotten she was holding one herself. She sipped, thinking how forsaken Mikolas must have felt. No wonder he was so impermeable.

"He thinks I want him to redeem the Petrides name, but *I* need redemption. To some extent I have it," Erebus allowed with deep emotion. "I'm proud of all he's accomplished. He's a good man. He told me why he brought you here. He did the right thing."

She suppressed a snort. Mikolas's reasons for keeping her and her reasons for staying were so fraught and complex, she didn't see any way to call them wholly right or wrong.

"He has never recovered his heart, though. All the things he has done? It hasn't been for me. He has built this fortress around himself for good reason. He trusts no one, relies on no one."

"Cares about no one," she murmured despondently.

"Is that what puts that hopeless expression on your face, *poulaki mou*?"

She knocked back her drink, giving a little shiver as the sweet heat spread from her tongue to the tips of her limbs. Shaking back her hair, she braced herself and said, "He'll never love me, will he?"

Erebus didn't bother to hide the sadness in his eyes. Because they didn't lie to each other.

Slowly the glow of hope inside her guttered and doused.

"We should go back to our game," he said.

CHAPTER TWELVE

MIKOLAS GLANCED UP as Viveka came out of the elevator. She never used it unless she was coming from the gym, but today she was dressed in the clothes she'd worn to lunch.

She staggered and he shot to his feet, stepping around his desk to hurry toward her. "Are you all right?"

"Fine." She set a hand on the wall, holding up the other to forestall him. "I just forgot that ouzo sneaks up on you like this."

"You've been *drinking*?"

"With your grandfather. Don't get mad. It was his idea, but I'm going to need a nap before dinner. That's what he was doing when I left him."

"This is what you two get up to over backgammon?" He took her arm, planning to help her to her room.

"Not usually, no." Her hand came to his chest. She didn't move, just stared at her hand on his chest, mouth grave, brow wearing a faint pleat. "We were talking."

That sounded ominous. She glanced up and anguish edged the blue of her irises.

Instinctively, he swallowed. His hand unconsciously tightened on her elbow, but he took a half step back from her. "What were you talking about?"

"He loves you, you know." Her mouth quivered, the corners pulling down. "He wishes you could forgive him."

He flinched, dropping his hand from her arm.

"He understands why you can't. Even if you did reach out to him, I don't think he would forgive himself. It's just…sad. He doesn't know how to reach you and—" She rolled to lean her shoulders against the wall, swallowing. "You won't let anyone in, ever, will you? Is this really all you want, Mikolas? Things? Sex without love?"

He swore silently, lifting his gaze to the ceiling, hands bunching into fists, fighting a wave of helplessness.

"I lied to you," he admitted when he trusted his voice. "That first day we met, I said my grandfather gave me anything I wanted." He lowered his gaze to her searching one. "I didn't want any of those things I asked for."

He had her whole attention.

"It was my test for him." He saw now the gifts had been his grandfather's attempts to earn his trust, but then it had been a game. A deadly, terrifying one. "I asked him for things I didn't care about, to see if he would get them for me. I never told him what I really wanted. I never told anyone."

He looked at his palm, rubbed one of the smooth patches where it had been held against a hot kettle, leaving shiny scar tissue.

"I never tell anyone. Physical torture is inhuman, but psychological torture…" His hand began shaking.

"Mikolas." Her hand came into his. He started to pull away, but his fingers closed over hers involuntarily, holding on, letting her keep him from sinking into the dark memories.

His voice felt like it belonged to someone else. "They would ask me, 'Do you want water?' 'Do you want the bathroom?' 'Do you want us to stop?' Of course I said yes. They never gave me what I wanted."

Her hand squeezed his and her small body came into

the hollow of his front, warm and anxious to soothe, arms going around his stiff frame.

He set his hands on her shoulders, resisting her offer of comfort even though it was all he wanted, ever. He resisted *because* it was what he wanted beyond anything.

"I can't—I'm not trying to hurt him. But if I trust him, if I let him mean too much to me, then what? He's not in a position to be my savior again. He's a weakness to be used against me. I can't leave myself open to that. Can you understand that?"

Her arms around him loosened. For a moment her forehead rested in the center of his chest, then she pressed herself away.

"I do." She took a deep, shaken breath. "I'm going to lie down."

He watched her walk away while two tiny, damp stains on his shirt front stayed cold against his skin.

"Vivi!" Clair exclaimed as she approached with her husband, Aleksy.

Viveka found a real smile for the first time all night. In days, really. Things between her and Mikolas were more poignantly strained than ever. She loved him so much and understood now that he was never going to let himself love her.

"How's the dress?" Viveka teased, rallying out of despondency for her hostess.

"I've taken to carrying a mending kit." Clair ruefully jiggled her pocketbook.

"I've been looking forward to seeing you again," Viveka said sincerely. "I've had a chance to read up on your foundation. I'm floored by all you do! And I have an idea for a fund-raiser that might work for you."

Mikolas watched Viveka brighten for the first time in

days. Her smile caused a pang in his chest that was more of a gong. He wanted to draw that warmth and light of hers against the echoing discord inside him, finally settling it.

"I saw a children's art exhibit when we were in New York. I was impressed by how sophisticated some of it was. It made me think, what if some of your orphans painted pieces for an auction? Here, let me show you." She reached into her purse for her phone, pausing to listen to something Clair was saying about another event they had tried.

Beside him, Aleksy snorted.

Mikolas dragged his gaze off Viveka, lifting a cool brow of inquiry. He had let things progress naturally between the women, not pursuing things on the business front, willing to be patient rather than rush fences and topple his opportunity with the standoffish Russian.

"I find it funny," Aleksy explained. "You went to all this trouble to get my attention, and now you'd rather listen to her than speak to me. I made time in my schedule for you tomorrow morning, if you can tear yourself away…?"

Mikolas bristled at the supercilious look on the other man's face.

Aleksy only lifted his brows, not intimidated by Mikolas's dark glare.

"When we met in Athens, I wondered what the hell you were doing with her. What *she* was doing with *you*. But…" Aleksy's expression grew self-deprecating. "It happens to the best of us, doesn't it?"

Mikolas saw how he had neatly painted himself into a corner. He could dismiss having any regard for Viveka and undo all her good work in getting him this far, or he could suffer the assumption that he had a profound weakness: *her*.

Before he had to act, Viveka said, "Oh, my God," and

looked up from her phone. Her eyes were like dinner plates. "Trina has been trying to reach me. Grigor had a heart attack. He's dead."

Mikolas and Viveka left the party amid expressions of sympathy from Clair and Aleksy.

Viveka murmured a distracted "thank you," but they were words that sat on air, empty of meaning. She was in shock. Numb. She wasn't *glad* Grigor was dead. Her sister was too torn up about the loss when she rang her, expressing regret and sorrow that a better relationship with her father would never manifest. Viveka wouldn't wish any sort of pain on her little sister, but she felt nothing herself.

She didn't even experience guilt when Mikolas surmised that Grigor had been under a lot of stress due to the inquiries Mikolas had ordered. He hadn't had much to report the other day, but ended a fresh call to the investigator as they returned to the hotel.

"The police on the island were starting to talk. They could see that silence looked like incompetence at best, bribery and collusion at worst. Charges were sounding likely for your mother's murder and more. My investigator is preparing a report, but without a proper court case, you'll probably never have the absolute truth on how she died. I'm sorry."

She nodded, accepting that. It was enough to know Grigor had died knowing he hadn't got away with his crimes.

"Trina will need me." It felt like she was stating the obvious, but it was the only concrete thought in her head. "I need to book a flight."

"I've already messaged my pilot. He's doing his pre-flight right now. We'll be in the air as soon as you're ready."

She paused in gathering the things that had been unpacked into drawers for her.

"Didn't I hear Aleksy say something about holding an appointment for you tomorrow?" She looked at the clothes she'd brought to Paris. "Not one thing suitable for a funeral," she murmured. "Would Trina understand if I wore that red gown, do you think?" She pointed across the room to the open closet.

No response from Mikolas.

She turned her head.

He looked like he was trying to drill into her head with his silvery eyes. "I can rebook with Aleksy."

So careful. So watchful. His remark about coming with her penetrated.

"Do you need to talk to Trina?" she asked, trying to think through the pall of details and decisions that would have to be made. "Because she inherits? Does his dying affect the merger?"

Something she couldn't interpret flickered across his expression. "There will be things to discuss, yes, but they can wait until she's dealt with immediate concerns."

"I wonder if he even kept her in his will," she murmured, setting out something comfortable to travel in, then pulling off her earrings. Gathering her hair, she moved to silently request he unlatch the sapphire necklace he'd given her this evening. "Trina told me he blamed me for everything, not her, so I hope he didn't disinherit her. Who else would he leave his wealth to? Charity? Ba-ha-ha. Not."

The necklace slithered away and she fetched the velvet box, handing it to him along with the earrings, then wormed her way out of her gown.

"Trina better be a rich woman, after everything he put her through. It doesn't seem real." She knew she was babbling. She was processing aloud, maybe because she was afraid of what *would* be said if she wasn't already doing the talking. "I've never been able to trust the times when I've thought I was rid of him. Even after I was living with Hildy, things would come up with Trina and I'd realize he was still a specter in my life. I was so sure the wedding was going to be *it*. Snip, snip, snip."

She made little scissors with her fingers, cutting ties to her stepfather, then bounced her butt into the seat of her jeans and zipped. Her push-up bra was overkill, but she pulled a T-shirt over it, not bothering to change into a different one.

"Now it's really here. He's dead. No longer able to wreck my life."

She made herself face him. Face *it*. The truth she had been avoiding.

"I'm finally safe from him."

Which meant Mikolas had no reason to keep her.

Mikolas was a quick study, always had been. He had seen the light of the train coming at him from the end of the tunnel the moment her lips had shaped the words, *He's dead*.

He had watched her pack and change and had listened to her walk herself to the platform and he still wasn't ready when her pale, pale face tilted up to his to say goodbye.

I can rebook with Aleksy. That was as close as he could come to stating that he was willing to continue their affair. He wasn't offering her solace. She wasn't upset beyond concern for her sister. God knew she didn't need *him*. He had deliberately stifled that expectation in her.

She looked down so all he could see of her expression was her pleated brow. "If you could give me some time to work out how to manage things with Aunt Hildy—"

He turned away, instantly pissed off. *So* pissed off. But he was unable to blame anyone but himself. He was the one who had fought letting ties form between them. He'd called what they had chemistry, sexual infatuation, protection.

"We're square," he growled. "Don't worry about it."

"Hardly. I'll get her house on the market as soon as I can—"

"I have what I wanted," he insisted, while a voice in his head asked, *Do you?* "I'm in," he continued doggedly. "None of the contacts I've made can turn their backs on me now."

"Mikolas—" She lowered to the padded bench in front of the vanity, inwardly quailing. *Don't humiliate yourself*, she thought, but stumbled forward like a love-drunk fool. "I care for you." Her voice thickened. "A lot." She had to clear her throat and swallow. Blink. Her fingers were a tangled mess against her knees. "If you would prefer we stay together…just say it. I know that's hard for you, but…" She warily lifted her gaze.

He was a statue, hands fisted in his pockets, immobile. Unmoved.

Her heart sank. "I can't make an assumption. I would feel like I'm still something you took on. I have to be something…" *You want.* Her mouth wouldn't form the words. This was hopeless. She could see it.

Mikolas's fists were so tight he thought his bones would crack. The shell around his heart was brittle as an egg's, threatening to crack.

"It's never going to work between us," he said, speaking as gently as he could, trying so hard not to bruise her. "You want things that I don't. Things I can't give you."

He was trying to be *decent*, but he knew each word was a splash of acid. He felt the blisters forming in his soul. "It's better to end it here."

It happens to the best of us.

What about the worst? What about the ones who pushed it away before they knew what they were refusing?

What about the ones who were afraid because it meant succumbing to something bigger than themselves? Because it meant handing someone, *everyone*, the power to hurt him?

The room seemed to dim and quiet.

She nodded wordlessly, lashes low. Her gorgeous, kissable mouth pursed in melancholy.

And when she was gone, he wondered why, if the threat of Grigor was gone, he was still so worried about her. If he feared so badly that she would hurt him, why was her absence complete agony?

If all he had wanted from her was a damned business contact, why did he blow off his appointment with Aleksy the next morning and sit in a Paris hotel room all day, staring at sapphire jewelry he'd bought because the blue stones matched her eyes, willing his phone to ring?

"You're required to declare funds over ten thousand euros," the male customs agent in London said to Viveka as they entered a room that was like something off a police procedural drama. There was a plain metal table, two chairs, a wastebasket and a camera mounted in the ceiling. If there was a two-way mirror, she couldn't see it, but she felt observed all the same.

And exhausted. The charter from the island after Grigor's funeral had been delayed by weather, forcing her to miss her flight out of Athens. They had rebooked her, but on a crisscross path of whichever flight left soonest in the general direction of London. She hadn't eaten or slept and was positively miserable.

"I forgot I had it," she said flatly.

"You forgot you're carrying twenty-five thousand euros?"

"I was going to put it in the bank in Athens, but I had already missed my connection. I just wanted to get home."

He looked skeptical. "How did you come by this amount of cash?"

"My sister gave it to me. For my aunt."

His brows tilted in a way that said, *Right.*

She sighed. "It's a long story."

"I have time."

She didn't. She felt like she was going to pass out. "Can I use the loo?"

"No." Someone knocked and the agent accepted a file, glancing over the contents before looking at her with more interest. "Tell me about Mikolas Petrides."

"Why?" Her heart tripped just hearing his name. Instantly she was plunged into despair at having broken off with him. When she had left Paris, she had told herself her feelings toward Mikolas were tied up in his protecting her from Grigor, but as the miles between them piled up, she kept thinking of other things: how he'd saved her life. How he'd brought her a life jacket, and said all the right things that night in Athens. How he'd taught her to fight. And make love.

Tears came into her eyes, but now was not the time.

"It looks like you've been traveling with him," the agent said. "That's an infamous family to truck with."

"The money has nothing to do with him!" That was a small lie. Once Viveka had spilled to her sister how she had come to be Mikolas's mistress, Trina had gone straight to her father's safe and emptied it of the cash Grigor had kept there.

Use this for Hildy. She's my aunt, too. I don't want you in his debt.

Viveka had balked, secretly wanting the tie to Mikolas. Trina had accused her of suffering from Stockholm syndrome. Her sister had matured a lot with her marriage and the death of Grigor. She had actually invited Viveka to live with them, but Viveka didn't want to be in that house, on that island, with newlyweds being tested by Trina's reversal of fortunes, since Grigor had indeed left Trina a considerable amount of money. Truth be told, Trina and Stephanos had a lot to work through.

So did Viveka. The two weeks with her sister had been enormously rejuvenating, but now it was time to finally, truly, take the wheel on her own life.

"Look." She sounded as ragged as she felt. "My half sister came into some money through the death of her father. My aunt is in a private facility. It's expensive. My sister was trying to help. That's all."

"Are you sure you didn't steal the money from Petrides? Because your flight path looks like a rabbit trying to outrun a fox."

"He wouldn't care if I did," she muttered, thinking about how generous he'd always been.

The agent's brows went up.

"I'm kidding! Don't involve him." All that work on his part—a lifetime of building himself into the head of a legitimate enterprise—and she was going to tumble it with one stupid quip? *Nice job, Viveka.*

"Tell me about your relationship with him."

"What do you mean?"

"You slept with him?"

"Yes. And no," she rushed on, guessing what he was going to say next. "Not for twenty-five thousand euros."

"Why did you break it off?"

"Reasons."

"Don't be smart, Ms. Brice. I'm your only friend right now. What was the problem? A lover's tiff? And you helped yourself to a little money for a fresh start?"

"There was no tiff." He didn't love her. That was the tiff. He would never love her and *she loved him so much.* "I'm telling you, the money has nothing to do with him. *I* have nothing to do with him. Not anymore."

She was going to cry now, and completely humiliate herself.

Mikolas was standing at the head of a boardroom table when his phone vibrated.

Viveka's picture flashed onto the screen. It was a photo he'd taken stealthily one day when creeping up on her playing backgammon with his grandfather. He'd perfectly caught her expression as she'd made a strong play, excited triumph brightening her face.

"Where's Vivi?" his grandfather had asked when Mikolas returned from Paris without her.

"Gone."

Pappoús had been stunned. Visibly heartbroken, which had concerned Mikolas. He hadn't considered how Viveka's leaving would affect his grandfather.

Pappoús had been devastated for another reason. "Another broken heart on my conscience," he'd said with tears in his eyes.

"It's not your fault." *He* was the one who had forced her to stay with him. He'd seduced her and tried not to lead her on, but she'd been hurt all the same. "She liked you," he tried to mollify. "If anything, you gave her some of what I couldn't."

"No," his grandfather had said with deep emotion. "If I hadn't left you suffering, you would not be so damaged. You would be able to love her as she's meant to be loved."

The words stung, but they weren't meant to be cruel. The truth hurt.

"You have never forgiven me and I wouldn't deserve it if you did," Pappoús went on. "I allowed your father to become a monster. He gave you nothing but a name that put you through hell. That is my fault." His shaking fist struck his chest.

He was so white and anguished, Mikolas tensed, worried his grandfather would put himself into cardiac arrest.

"I wasn't a fit man to take you in, not when you needed someone to heal you," Pappoús declared. "My love came too late and isn't enough. You don't trust it. So you've rejected her. She doesn't deserve that pain and it comes back to me. It's my fault she's suffering."

Mikolas had wanted to argue that what Viveka felt toward him wasn't real love, but if anyone knew how to love, it was her. She loved her sister to the ends of the earth. She experienced every nuance of life at a level that was far deeper than he ever let himself feel.

"She'll find love," Mikolas had growled, and was instantly uncomfortable with the idea of another man holding her at night, making her believe in forever. He hated the invisible man who would make her smile in ways he never had, because she finally felt loved in return.

"Vivi is resilient," his grandfather agreed with poignant pride.

She was very resilient.

When Mikolas had received the final report on Grigor's responsibility for her mother's death, he had been humbled. The report had compiled dozens of reports of assault and other wrongdoings across the island, but it was the unearthed statement made by Viveka that had destroyed him.

How much difference was there between one man pulling his tooth and another bruising a girl's eye? Mikolas had lost his fingernails. Viveka had lost her *mother*. He had been deliberately humiliated, forced to beg for air and water—death even—until his DNA had saved him. She had made her way to a relative who hadn't wanted her and had kept enough of a conscience to care for the woman through a tragic decline.

Viveka would find love because, despite all she had endured, she was *willing* to love.

She wasn't a coward, ducking and weaving, running and hiding, staying in Paris, saying, *It's better that it ends here.*

It wasn't better. It was torment. Deprivation gnawed relentlessly at him.

But the moment her face flashed on his phone, respite arrived.

"I have to take this," Mikolas said to his board, voice and hand trembling. He slid his thumb to answer, dizzy with how just anticipating the sound of her voice eased his suffering. "Yes?"

"I thought I should warn you," she said with remorse. "I've kind of been arrested."

"Arrested." He was aware of everyone stopping their murmuring to stare. Of all the things he might have expected, that was the very last. But that was Viveka. "Are you okay? Where are you? What happened?"

Old instincts flickered, reminding him he was revealing too much, but in this moment he didn't care about himself. He was too concerned for her.

"I'm fine." Her voice was strained. "It's a long story and Trina is trying to find me a lawyer, but they keep bringing up your name. I didn't want to blindside you if it winds up in the papers or something. You've worked so hard to get everything just so. I hate to cast shadows. I'm really sorry, Mikolas."

Only Viveka would call to forewarn him and ask nothing for herself. How in the world had he ever felt so threatened by this woman?

"Where are you?" he repeated with more insistence. "I'll have a lawyer there within the hour."

CHAPTER THIRTEEN

MIKOLAS'S LAWYER LEFT Viveka at Mikolas's London flat, since it was around the corner from his own. She was on her very last nerve and it was two in the morning. She didn't try to get a taxi to her aunt's house. She didn't have the key and would have to ask the neighbor for one tomorrow.

So she prevailed upon Mikolas *again* and didn't bother trying to find bedding for his guest room. She threw a huge pity party for herself in the shower, crying until she couldn't stand, then she folded Mikolas's black robe into a firm hug around her and crawled into his bed with a box of tissues that she dabbed against her leaking eyes.

Sleep was her blessed escape from feeling like she'd only alienated him further with this stupid questioning. The customs agents were hanging on to the money for forty-eight hours, because they could, but the lawyer seemed to think they'd give it up after that. She really didn't care, she was just so exhausted and dejected and she missed Mikolas so bad…

A weight came onto the mattress beside her and a warm hand cupped the side of her neck. The lamp came on as a man's voice said, "Viveka."

She jerked awake, sitting up in shock.

"Shh, it's okay," he soothed. "It's just me. I was trying not to scare you."

She clutched her hand across her heart. "What are you doing here?"

His image impacted her. Not just his natural sex appeal in a rumpled shirt and open collar. Not just his stubbled cheeks and bruised eyes. There was such tenderness in his gaze, her fragile composure threatened to crumple.

"Your lawyer said you were in Barcelona." She had protested against Mikolas sending the lawyer, insisting she was just informing him as a courtesy, but he'd got most of the story out of her before her time on the telephone had run out.

"I was." His hooded lids lowered to disguise what he was thinking and his tongue touched his lip. "And I'm sorry to wake you, but I didn't want to scare you if I crawled in beside you."

She followed his gaze to the crushed tissues littering the bed and hated herself for being so obvious. "I was being lazy about making up the other bed. I'll go—"

"No. We need to talk. I don't want to wait." He tucked her hair back from her cheek, behind her ear. "Vivi."

"Why did you just call me that?" She searched his gaze, her brow pulled into a wrinkle of uncertainty, her pretty bottom lip pinched by her teeth.

"Because I want to. I have wanted to. For a long time." It wasn't nearly so unsettling to admit that as he'd feared. He had expected letting her into his heart would be terrifying. Instead, it was like coming home. "Everyone else does."

A tentative hope lit her expression. "Since when do you want to be like everyone else?"

He acknowledged that with a flick of his brow, but the tiny flame in his chest grew bigger and warmer.

"Since when do I tell you or anyone what I want? Is

that what you're really wondering?" He wanted so badly to hold her. Gather all that healing warmth she radiated against him and close up the final gaps in his soul. He made himself give her what she needed first. "I want *you*, Vivi. Not just for sex, but for things I can't even articulate. That scares me to say, but I want you to know it."

She sucked in a breath and covered her mouth with both hands.

This can't be real, Viveka thought, blinking her gritty eyes. She pinched herself and he let out a husk of a laugh, immediately trying to erase the sting with a gentle rub of his thumb.

His hand stayed on her arm. His gaze lifted to her face while a deeply tender glow in his eyes went all the way through her to her soul.

"I was terrified that if I let myself care for you, someone would use that against me. So what did I do? I pushed you away and inflicted the pain on myself. I was right to fear how much it would hurt if you were out of my reach. It's unbearable."

"Oh, Mikolas." Her mouth trembled. "You inflicted it on both of us. I want to be with you. If you want me, I'm right here."

He gathered her up, unable to help himself. For a long time he held her, just absorbing the beauty of having her against him. He was aware of a tickling trickle on his cheek and dipped his head to dry his cheek against her hair.

"Thank you for saying you want me," she said. Her slender arms tightened until she pressed the breath from his lungs. "It's enough, you know." She lifted her red eyes to regard him. "I won't ask you to say you love me. But I should have said it myself before I left Paris. I've been sorry that I didn't. I was trying to protect myself from being more hurt than I was. It didn't work," she said ruefully. "I love you so much."

"You're too generous." He cupped her cheek, wiping away her tear track with the pad of his thumb, humbled. "I want your love, Vivi. I will pay any price for that. Don't let me be a coward. Make me give you what you need. Make me say it and mean it."

"You're not a coward." Fresh tears of empathy welled in her eyes, seeping into all those cracks and fissures around his heart, widening them so there was more room for her to come in.

"I was afraid to tell you I was coming," he admitted. "I was afraid you wouldn't be here if you knew. That you wouldn't let me try to convince you to stay with me."

Viveka's heart was pattering so fast she could hardly breathe. "You only have to ask," she reminded.

"Ask." Mikolas smoothed her hair back from her face, gazing at her, humbly offering his heart as a flawed human being. "I can't insult you by asking you to *stay* with me. I must ask you the big question. Will you be my wife?"

Viveka's heart staggered and lurched. "Are you serious?"

"Of course I'm serious!" He was offended, but wound up chuckling. "I will have the right woman under the veil this time, too. Actually," he added with a light kiss on her nose, "I did the first time. I just didn't know it yet."

Tears of happiness filled her eyes. She threw her arms around his neck, needing to kiss him then. To hold him and *love* him. "Yes. Of course I'll marry you!"

Their kiss was a poignant, tender reunion, making all of her ache. The physical sparks between them were stronger than ever, but the moment was so much more than that, imbued with trust and openness. It was expansive and scary and uncharted.

Beautiful.

"I want to make love to you," he said, dragging his mouth to her neck. "*Love*, Vivi. I want to wake next to you and make the best of every day we are given together."

"Me, too," she assured him with a catch of joy in her voice. "I love you."

EPILOGUE

"Papa, I'm cold."

Viveka heard the words from her studio. She was in the middle of a still life of Callia's toys for the advanced painting class she'd been accepted into. Three years of sketching and pastels, oils and watercolors, and she was starting to think she wasn't half bad. Her husband was always quick to praise, of course, but he was shamelessly biased.

She wiped the paint off her fingers before she picked up the small pink jumper her daughter had left there on the floor. When she came into the lounge, however, she saw that it was superfluous. Mikolas was already turning from his desk to scoop their three-year-old into his lap.

Callia stood on his thigh to curl her arms around his neck before bending her knees and snuggling into his chest, light brown curls tucked trustingly against his shoulder. "I love you," she told him in her high, doll-like voice.

"I love you, too," Mikolas said with the deep timbre of sincerity that absolutely undid Viveka every time she heard it.

"I love Leo, too," she said in a poignant little tone, mentioning her cousin, Trina's newborn son. She had cried when they'd had to come home. She looked up at Mikolas. "Do you love Leo?"

"He spit up on my new shirt," Mikolas reminded drily, then magnanimously added, "But yes, I do."

Callia giggled, then began turning it into a game. "Do you love Theítsa Trina?"

"I've grown very fond of her, yes."

"Do you love Theíos Stephanos?"

"I consider him a good friend."

"Did you love Pappoús?" She pointed at the photo on his desk.

"I did love him, very much."

Callia didn't remember her great-grandfather, but he had held her swaddled form, saying to Viveka, *She has your eyes*, and proclaiming Mikolas to be a very lucky man.

Mikolas had agreed wholeheartedly.

Losing Erebus had been hard for him. For both of them, really. Fortunately, they'd had a newborn to distract them. Falling pregnant had been a complete surprise to both of them, but the shock had quickly turned to excitement and they were so enamored with family life, they were talking of expanding it even more.

"Do you love Mama?" Callia asked.

Mikolas's head came up and he looked across at Viveka, telling her he'd been aware of her the whole time. His love for her shone like a beacon across the space between them.

"My love for your mother is the strongest thing in me."

* * * * *

LET'S TALK
Romance

For exclusive extracts, competitions
and special offers, find us online:

f facebook.com/millsandboon
🐦 @MillsandBoon
⭘ @MillsandBoonUK

Get in touch on 01413 063232

For all the latest titles coming soon, visit
millsandboon.co.uk/nextmonth

MILLS & BOON

THE HEART OF ROMANCE

A ROMANCE FOR EVERY READER

MODERN

Prepare to be swept off your feet by sophisticated, sexy and seductive heroes, in some of the world's most glamourous and romantic locations, where power and passion collide.

HISTORICAL

Escape with historical heroes from time gone by. Whether your passion is for wicked Regency Rakes, muscled Vikings or rugged Highlanders, awaken the romance of the past.

MEDICAL

Set your pulse racing with dedicated, delectable doctors in the high-pressure world of medicine, where emotions run high and passion, comfort and love are the best medicine.

True Love

Celebrate true love with tender stories of heartfelt romance, from the rush of falling in love to the joy a new baby can bring, and a focus on the emotional heart of a relationship.

Desire

Indulge in secrets and scandal, intense drama and plenty of sizzling hot action with powerful and passionate heroes who have it all: wealth, status, good looks…everything but the right woman.

HEROES

Experience all the excitement of a gripping thriller, with an intense romance at its heart. Resourceful, true-to-life women and strong, fearless men face danger and desire - a killer combination!

To see which titles are coming soon, please visit

millsandboon.co.uk/nextmonth

JOIN US ON SOCIAL MEDIA!

Stay up to date with our latest releases, author news and gossip, special offers and discounts, and all the behind-the-scenes action from Mills & Boon...

 millsandboon

 millsandboonuk

 millsandboon

It might just be true love...